THE MASTER
OF THE HOUSE

Radcliffe Hall

THE MASTER OF THE HOUSE

'. . . for ye know not when the master of the house cometh, at even, or at midnight, or at cockcrowing, or in the morning. . . .'

The Falcon Press

First published in 1932
by Jonathan Cape Limited

This edition published in 1952
by the Falcon Press (London) Limited
6 & 7 Crown Passage, Pall Mall, London, S.W.1

Printed in Great Britain
by Willmer Bros. & Co. Limited
Birkenhead

403679-4

TO
OUR THREE SELVES

AUTHOR'S FOREWORD

For the satisfaction of those readers who may wish for guidance as to the more generally accepted pronunciation of some of the names and sentences in the Provençal language that occur throughout this book, a brief pronouncing glossary is appended.

Some readers may even be sufficiently interested to care to know that the language in question is no humble dialect but is the ancient Langue d'Oc of the troubadours, the language spoken in the twelfth and thirteenth centuries not only throughout France from Bordeaux to the Alps and from Auvergne to the Mediterranean, but also in England at the court of King Richard the Lion Heart, while tradition avers that Dante hesitated long between the beauties of Provençal and of Tuscan before deciding to express himself in the latter language.

Had he decided otherwise it is certain that the Provençal tongue would have been spared those centuries of eclipse during which, owing to its gradually enforced subjection, in all official concerns, to the French idiom, it found its only home in the hearts and on the lips of the peasants, from which neither time nor authority ever contrived to evict it.

It was there that its long-despised beauties at length attracted the attention, in the middle of the nineteenth century, of Frédéric Mistral and the other patriot poets of the Félibrige, and thus to poet and peasant alike is due the fact that to-day the youth of Provence can study its native language, with all its variants, survivals and still debatable alternatives, in more than twenty-five colleges and schools of the South of France.

It can also be studied in the markets, at the street corners, in the village shops, in the lowly homes and in the vineyards of that pleasant land.

PRONOUNCING GLOSSARY

All the vowels are pronounced approximately as in French.

Ai! las	A-i-lasse
Anas vous en au tron de Diéune	Anasse vous enne a-ou tronne de Diéoune
Anfos	Anne-fosse
Aurano	A-ourano
Baumo de la Masco Taven	Ba-ou-mo de la Masco Tavenne
Bèu Diéu	Bé-ou Dié-ou
Bono Maire de Diéu	Bono Ma-i-ré de Dié-ou
Bono nue	Bono noué
Cafourno de la Chaucho Vièjo	Cafourno de la Tcha-oucho Viéyo
Eusèbe	E-ou-sé-bé
Enfantounet	Enne-fanne-tounette
Goundran	Gounne-dranne
Gourgarèu Infernau	Gourga-réou Inne-ferna-ou
Home bosa	Homé bosa
Jan	Dzanne
Jóusè	Dzo-ou-zé
Lou Corredou de l'Esperit Fantasti	Lou Corrédou de l'Espéritte Fanne-tasti
Lou vin es fa pèr béure	Lou vinne ez fa per bé-ou-ré
Oulo di Set Ca⁺	Oulo di Sette Catte
Pas de l'Agneu Negre	Passe de l'Agné-ou Nègré
Paure pichounet	Pa-ou-ré pichounette
Pecaire	Pé-ca-iré
Ravous	Ravousse
Recatadou di Rato-Penado	Ré-ca-ta-dou di Rato-Pénado
Roustan	Roustanne
Santo Ano d'At	Sanne-to Ano d'Atte
Santouno	Sanne-touno
Sarnipabiéune	Sarnipabiéoune
Tafort	Taforte
Zóu	Zo-ou

CHAPTER ONE

I

In a quiet curve of the coast of Provence, on a stretch of
that coast which before the war was seldom if ever visited
by strangers, lies the small seaport town of Saint-Loup-
sur-mer, cleansed by strong winds and purified by
sunshine. Its Patron—if one may credit report—was a
warrior-bishop of no mean attainments, since of him it is
told that he checked the advance of Attila, Mighty Scourge
of the Lord, though by what precise method remains somewhat uncertain. But his memory is mellowed by gentler
legends even as the years have mellowed his statues, so that
of him it is also told that he felt great concern for the sorrows
of women, and a great tenderness towards newborn things,
having once restored its life to a fledgling. And since this
bird was a nightingale it would come with the darkness to
sing in his garden: 'Praise God in His Golden Saints,' it
would sing, as everyone knew very well at the time—that
is to say, in the year 400, when Saint Loup had not yet
been privileged to hear the harps and the angelic songs of
heaven.

His town has a harbour with numerous vessels and many
simple activities; a fine view from such windows as look over
the quay and thus out beyond to a stretch of blue water, and
a wall of dark peaks from such as look sideways or backward towards the long range of the Maures, Saint Loup
being partly encircled by mountains. There is also the
church with its open belfry in which one may see the chime
of bells swinging; the old fish-market renowned for fine
langoustes, and three cafés frequented by fishermen, sailors,
and sometimes by artists with their wives and their models.
The streets, which are narrow and tortuous, are but ill
adapted for the passage of motors; moreover in summer
their heat is relentless, while in winter they are swept

9

and re-swept by the mistral. Yet innumerable fruit trees surround the town, and these in the midst of plentiful vineyards.

On a day of insistent fertility towards the end of a perfect April, when the vines were beginning to extend their pink shoots, and the small peach trees to grow restless with sap, and the bountiful soil that will make men lazy was stirred by a constant thrusting and growing, and the very earth-worms under the soil must curl and uncurl for the joy of living—on such a day, Mirèio, the gaunt yellow bitch, brought forth her large litter of lusty puppies in the sawdust and shavings of the carpenter's shop belonging to Jóusè Bénédit—in great anguish and joy she brought forth her puppies. While above, in a bedroom under the eaves, Marie Bénédit cried out again and again, so that Jóusè, her husband, must cover his ears, for he could not endure those sounds of her travail. Marie Bénédit cried out, yet not solely in pain, for hers was the purposeful suffering of women; and this she well knew, so that while she protested her brown peasant body strove bravely in labour and her cries and her wails held a note of triumph which partook of the age-old cry of creation.

Towards dusk Marie Bénédit gave birth to a son; and after the midwife had cleansed his limbs and swathed him in flannel she took him to his mother, while Jóusè stood gaping at this sacrament of life which he had raised up through the seed of his loins—too confounded for speech he must just stand gaping. And below in the darkening carpenter's shop Mirèio, the bitch, gave her teats to her young, rolling side-ways that they might come at her belly.

2

Christophe Marie Bénédit began squealing loudly at the very onset of his baptismal service, so that Monsieur le Curé had some ado to anoint his breast with the Holy Chrism, and even more to place salt on his tongue in accordance with the ritual of Mother Church and the time-honoured Christian custom. But when drops of cold water were splashed on his head then he lost every vestige of self-control and beat with his heels on his godmother's stomach. In addition to being his sponsor before God, she was also his aunt though he did not know it.

Madame Roustan frowned and gripped him more firmly as she watched this momentous struggle with Satan. 'It is clear that the devil is excessively angry,' she whispered to Goundran, the child's godfather, 'he is blistered, no doubt, by the Holy Oil and scourged by our good priest's exorcisms!'

But Goundran was young and a fisherman; he had known far worse struggles than this in foul weather, so that while Madame Roustan continued to frown at their godson, he smiled at the turbulent infant—when he smiled his large teeth gleamed startlingly white in a face that was tanned to the colour of copper.

Arm in arm near the font stood the earthly parents: Jóusè, a mighty and comely man in spite of the fact that he was ageing. His head was covered with thick, small curls, and his plentiful beard was also curly. The hair of his head and his beard was red-gold, but touched here and there with streaks of grey, for at this time Jóusè was nearing fifty. Marie, a woman of twenty-nine, was as brown as the soil and as patiently faithful. Her eyes were the eyes of the beasts of the field who eat, sleep, and beget their kind without question. But unlike these, Marie would seldom rest; for ever finding some new task to do she must busy herself with perpetual housework. And wiry she was and uncommonly strong when it came to the moving of chests and cupboards; so that Jóusè would laugh and would say to tease her: 'You will surely be able to carry my coffin!' Then Marie would sign herself with the cross—it was always foolhardy to jest about Death, one could never be certain that jests would not bring him.

For five years these two had been man and wife, but Marie had often felt heavy in spirit, oppressed by the thought of her empty womb. For five years she had earnestly prayed to Saint Loup who was known to be sympathetic to women. And at last that kind Patron had answered her prayers, giving her not only a child but a son wherewith to rejoice the heart of her husband. So now here they stood arm in arm near the font, both deeply moved by their simple faith in the goodness of God and His Golden Saints; and deeply

11

moved to behold their own flesh and blood in so small yet so perfect a being. Indeed Marie's patient brown eyes overflowed, and Jóusè must lend her his big bandana, himself scarcely able to keep from weeping.

The ancient ritual drew to its close, and Christophe was anointed as a king before God, as a priest, and finally as a prophet. As a king with dominion over his passions, as a priest who must offer himself to the Lord as a living sacrifice of sweet odour, as a prophet who must proclaim through his life the rewards that await the righteous in heaven. Then the Curé handed a lighted candle to Goundran who held it with scrupulous care—for Christophe's pink fists were as yet too weak to grasp this symbolic light of his faith, so that Goundran the fisher must grasp it for him. And after the priest had given them his blessing Madame Roustan wrapped a new, white woolly shawl about Christophe's now new and sinless body; and Goundran solemnly blew out his candle; and Jóusè solemnly blew his nose on the damp handkerchief handed back by Marie. The townsfolk who had come to see the event turned and left the old church with much whispering and smiling; while the little party chiefly concerned prepared to go back to the Bénédit's house with their friends, there to celebrate the occasion.

3

The small parlour was crowded to overflowing, for not everyone opened so much good wine solely in honour of an infant Christian; indeed many baptisms went unnoticed. But as Jóusè had said: it was not every man who could sire so fine and healthy a son when he himself was approaching fifty; and so there was plenty to eat and drink, the wine gleaming as golden as Jóusè's beard and as red as his cheeks, in its generous glasses.

Madame Roustan—as a mother-in-God who had witnessed so robust and valiant a fight with the devil—Madame Roustan drank a tumbler of Camp Romain rouge which flushed her plump face and set her perspiring; after which she must glance from the corner of an eye at Goundran, her fellow parent-in-God, for she was a widow but not past mating. Despite her encroaching flesh she looked young, and like Jóusè her brother, had a clear, fair complexion.

Germaine Roustan had been deprived of her man, a linen-draper, by one of those strokes that occasionally come in the wake of great heat—he had died in rather less than an hour, having been smitten down while measuring ribbon. And now here she was with a posthumous son of four months old, but alas, with no husband; with a drapery shop, but alas, with no male to assist her in keeping the business together; with a healthful and willing body enough, but alas, with small prospect of future breeding. And so, after that tumbler of Camp Romain rouge, it was natural perhaps that her thoughts should be turned away from the dead and towards the living. But Goundran was a lover and lord of the sea, and appeared to be little attracted by women.

Jóusè drank, laughing many times as he did so. He laughed in pure joy at his fine situation; and his mighty fist came down on the table while his mighty voice pressed hospitality, urging his guests to fill up their glasses:

'Hoi, tafort! Have courage my friends!' he roared in the Provençal tongue which they dearly loved speaking, 'Hoi, tafort! Lou vin es fa pèr béure!' And undoubtedly this wine seemed made to be drunk, for, cheap though it was in that land of plenty, it possessed no mean flavour to tickle the palate.

Then Goundran lifted his glass to the child who lay quietly asleep on the knees of his mother: 'May you live many years and prosper, little godson; and may you become a good fisherman, for the sea is the finest thing in creation.'

Jóusè grinned: 'May he learn to work in my shop; may he learn to make comfortable chairs and strong tables.'

'May he prosper,' they all murmured fervently, while Christophe, worn out, still continued to sleep, completely indifferent, it seemed, to his future.

But now Eusèbe, the sandal-maker, who plied his trade just across the street in a house that at one time had been a convent, Eusèbe, not content with so seemly a toast, must dip a gnarled finger into his wine and dab a red splotch on the infant's forehead:

'May he love the good fruits of the earth,' he exclaimed, 'and the juice that comes from the fruits of the earth; these are surely the things that all men should love, and not the netting of cold little fishes and the hammering of wood to make chairs and tables.'

'Sant Jan l'ami de Diéu,' muttered Madame Roustan, 'what is this he has done? It cannot be Christian. . . .'

Marie said quietly: 'You are drunk, Eusèbe,' and she wiped the red mark away with her hand, but her peaceful brown face had turned very pale, for she was a peasant and superstitious.

It was true that Eusèbe was exceedingly drunk on this, as on many a previous occasion; that his heathenish ways and intemperate habits had caused a great scandal throughout the parish. It was also true that he cared not a jot, so callous was he towards God and his neighbour. He looked old and yet nobody quite knew his age, for the south which brings early maturity will occasionally bring an early decline, and thus it is unwise to judge by appearance. Eusèbe's tanned face was a network of lines, and the eyes in that face did not match any more, which gave him a disconcerting expression —he was blind of an eye and that eye was blue-white, while its fellow had remained of a most fiery blackness. A small man, he was often still further dwarfed by wearing an unusually long leather apron. His habits were not only eccentric but uncleanly; in the summer he might sometimes go down to bathe, for the rest he appeared to wash very little. Just now his hands were heavily stained by hides, boot polish and cobbler's wax—he had not even troubled to cleanse his hands; it was all of a piece with his general disorder. But then neither had he troubled to cleanse his feet, which showed scarred and neglected in his dusty sandals.

This making of sandals had been taught him, it was said, by an artist who had stayed for a while in the town, but whom no one had ever again seen or heard of. And now many of the peasants as well as the townsfolk had discarded the wearing of boots and shoes in favour of what Madame Roustan declared to be clearly a pagan snare of the devil. For Eusèbe's sandals were both durable and cheap, and were made from a pliant and excellent leather, so that they clung to the instep and heel without galling or causing the slightest restriction. He could make two patterns, the Pompeian and the Spartan, the former requiring the minutest adjustment, since no buckles or fastenings must mar the line which was of an extreme simplicity, yet tricky enough when it came to the fitting. These sandals paid less well than boots and shoes, but Eusèbe never seemed short of money.

His dead wife had owned vineyards beyond the town, and these he very knowingly tended. He possessed an uncanny intuition about vines so that many a farmer would come to consult him. It was said that Eusèbe could squeeze gold from the soil, and certain it was that his excellent grapes always clustered more richly than other people's. But did he give so much as a sou to the Curé? He did not, the unregenerate old sinner. And did he attend Holy Mass on Sundays? He did not; on Sundays he walked in his vineyards—small wonder that such behaviour caused scandal. And again, he lived by himself above his shop and would let no one in to attend to the housework. His rooms went unswept and his bed unmade except when a species of frenzy would seize him; then, grasping a broom he would sweep and sweep as though the devil were hard at his heels, after which he would drag off his old feather bed and hang it to air from an upper window. This decayed feather bed was a local disgrace, while as for the dirt . . . people all but choked with the thick clouds of dust if they chanced to be passing. A granddaughter, his sole surviving relation, was being brought up by the sisters at Arles—a town that he proudly claimed as his birthplace. She was three years old but she never came home, which the Curé considered was all to her advantage.

Of course Bacchus alone had attracted Eusèbe to the christening feast on this hot afternoon; still, he need not have become so exceedingly drunk, nor splashed quite so much wine on the clean table linen: 'Boudiéu,' he was gurgling, now deep in his cups, 'Boudiéu, what a balm to the stomach is good wine; surely a most proper balm to the stomach . . .'. And he tipped his chair backward, upsetting his glass; indeed Goundran's quick hand alone saved him from falling.

Christophe woke up and started to cry. Unfastening her bodice, Marie gave him her breast which he clutched at blindly, beginning to suck, and making small, animal sounds in the process.

The heat of the room grew intolerable, for the sun took quite a long time about setting, and the air was heavy with the fumes of wine, with the fumes of tobacco and sweating bodies. The sweat trickled down Jóusè's beaming face and clung like dew to the hair on his chest which showed wiry and red where his shirt fell open. Tongues were loosened; everyone talked at once. The men had begun to discard their coats, sighing and spitting with relief in the process. Jóusè, whose clothes felt increasingly tight, unfastened the top button of his linen trousers. They had more than done justice to the excellent fare, eating their fill of the aïoli, that mysterious and well nigh sacred dish compounded of garlic pods, yolk of egg, olive oil, pepper and vinegar; of potatoes boiled (skins and all) in salt water together with artichokes, carrots, french beans, cauliflower, cod fish, coal fish and snails, to say nothing of other delectable things very dearly beloved of the Provençal stomach. They had passed from the honest Camp Romain rouge to a soft boiled wine, insidious and heady; this they drank with the little festal cakes which were so honey-sweet that they made the teeth ache. And now everyone talked about nothing at all, but loudly, so that Marie glanced down at her child who, himself replete, had once more dropped asleep. Swaying gently she rocked him as he lay in her arms, grown fearful lest the boisterous laughter should wake him. But Christophe slept on with one very small foot dangling limply in a pink woollen sock with a tassel. A faint dribble of milk that remained on his chin testified to his eager and greedy sucking.

Jóusè thought: 'I have waited long for this day when I should possess a son of my own. Hoi, it is splendid to be a father.'

And Marie was thinking: 'So helpless he is, and so treasured; it is sweet to become a mother.'

From the kitchen came a long-drawn, disconsolate sound, as of something inarticulate, weeping: 'Ai! las . . .' murmured Marie, 'Mirèio complains; only yesterday have we drowned her eight puppies.'

A neighbour started to sing an old song:

'Chatouno, chatouno, I will be as the Mistral;
And who may hope to resist his might?
Not you, not you, not you, chatouno!'

Jóusè wagged his large curly head to the rhythm.

Presently Goundran got up to go: 'I have promised to meet a man at the port about some new tackle—I am late already.'

'And I must return to my little Jan who by now will be hungry,' smiled Madame Roustan; and her smile was less for the little Jan than for him whom she hoped to make his step-father. 'Come,' she coaxed, 'we will keep each other company since both of us are bound for the port; and when you have finished discussing your affairs you shall come in and give me a few words of advice as to how I must deal with my dishonest landlord. He refuses to make good those broken gutters. Houi, a woman without her own man is surely the prey of all other men; yes, yes, so it is . . . but you I will trust, you shall tell me how I must deal with my landlord.'

Goundran sighed largely and ruffled his hair, as he turned to follow her out of the parlour.

Then one after another the guests departed, until finally only Eusèbe remained, half asleep in front of an empty bottle.

Jóusè shook him: 'Get up! Rouse yourself you old sot, and cease from slobbering over your shirt. In another moment you will sink to the floor, and then it is I who must carry you home—gramaci, and that in God's good daylight! Do you hear me? I insist that you rouse yourself.' And he tugged at Eusèbe's ear none too gently.

'Zóu . . .' muttered Eusèbe. And then: 'Bono-nue . . . but first I must finish this wine of God.'

'Not at all; you will go at once,' Jóusè told him as he hauled the toper on to his feet, 'you will go at once. Allons, I will support you.' And slipping an arm round Eusèbe's waist, he managed to drag him out of the house and across the street to his own little shop where he left him squatting among his sandals.

Presently Jóusè returned to the parlour, and he stood gazing down at his wife and child: 'Nosto-Damo-d'Amour!' he exclaimed blissfully, 'Did ever a man know such joy as mine? Did ever a man have so fine a son, or so gentle a wife, or so prosperous a business, or so many good friends? God has surely been kind.'

Looking up with a smile Marie met his rough kiss; then they kissed yet again in complete contentment.

But beyond in the kitchen, Mirèio, the bitch, paced miserably, always seeking her puppies. And her teats hung heavy and painful with milk so that they dragged at the skin of her sides, revealing her massive ribs in their gauntness. And she gave forth a long-drawn, disconsolate sound as of something inarticulate, weeping.

CHAPTER TWO

I

Jóusè's workshop was a long, low vault of a place dependent for light upon its arched entrance. A small door at the back led into the house, but the entrance gave direct on to the street, and here Jóusè would work half in and half out whenever his job permitted of this, for he dearly loved the fresh air and the sunshine. Spitting upon the rough palms of his hands he would pause to exchange the time of day or some crude but harmless joke with a neighbour, and as likely as not, from across the street, Eusèbe would start to make jokes of his own which, it must be admitted, were seldom quite harmless.

Jóusè had an apprentice, one Anfos by name, a youth of seventeen who was simple-minded. He was tall and robust and his lips and cheeks were already well covered with straggling black hair, for Anfos was too childish to handle a razor. His brown eyes were like those of Mirèio, the bitch, apologetic and slightly bewildered. In body a man for more than three years, his mind still dwelt in the pastures of childhood, but at times this mind of his realized vaguely that all was not well any more with those pastures, that something wider might stretch just beyond, and then his brown eyes would look slightly bewildered.

Anfos was a distant cousin of Marie's whom Jóusè had taken on out of pity a few weeks after Christophe's birth; and this he had done to please his wife, feeling that he could refuse her nothing. Marie had begged him to go into the mountains and bring home the poor orphan of whom the priest wrote with so much compassionate affection.

'He is not really mad,' the good priest had written, 'he is rather one of those who have never strayed from the path of childish innocence; and what did our dear Lord Jesus say? "Except ye become as little children." Therefore now that both his parents are dead I must write to you, dear Madame Bénédit, for you it was whom his mother spoke of as perhaps being willing to befriend her son, and this she did, Madame, when she lay dying. . . .'

So Marie had sent Jóusè off to the mountains—a long, tedious journey right up into the Maures, on a spur of which rested the little village where Anfos had lived in great poverty all the days of his short and harmless existence. And since Jóusè's last apprentice had but lately left him to find more lucrative employment at Arles, Marie had begged him to train this youth whom the priest had assured her was not really mad but rather one of those little ones who were always welcome in the Kingdom of Heaven. Jóusè had shaken his curly head and had nibbled the tip of his beard in misgiving.

'And what if he saw off his finger or his thumb? Can I let a poor half-wit play with sharp tools? Would it not be better to enquire of our Curé where we could put the boy to be cared for?'

But Marie had set her mild lips quite firmly: 'That no. His mother was my cousin and my friend, and although I had not seen her for years, I cannot forget that we were girls together. Moreover I am sure that Saint Loup desires us to make a home for this unhappy creature.'

Then Jóusè had known that words would be vain, for gentle though Marie undoubtedly was, she could be as firm as the peak of La Sauvette when she felt that she had good Saint Loup behind her.

'Acò s'acò,' Jóusè had sighed resignedly, and had set out in no very sanguine humour, for what man who has just bred a fine little son would wish to adopt a large, hulking half-wit? Then again there was none too much room in the house, so that Jóusè would have to give up the attic in which he had hoarded certain odds and ends of carving by which he set immense store, since most of them had come out of ancient buildings. But when he had seen the afflicted Anfos and had realized his great desolation as he wandered about the empty hovel, Jóusè had taken the youth by the hand.

'Will you not come home to us now?' he had asked him.

Anfos had said nothing, but when Jóusè had turned to the door he had followed like a dog at his heels. Thus in silence

20

they had journeyed for the best part of a day, and still in silence they had reached Saint Loup at the Vesper hour on a summer evening.

2

As though virtue were being its own reward, Jóusè soon found to his great amazement that he had obtained an excellent apprentice, for this Anfos was remarkably deft with his hands, and strangely enough with his mind as well when it came to the technical details of his trade, all of which must be taught to him by Jóusè. Jóusè's work had become a kind of compound of carpentry-joinery and cabinet-making; indeed whenever wood had to be cut or fashioned for no matter what local purpose, there was Jóusè ready to cut or to fashion. A most handy man, he could build you a shed or a house for that matter, and then he could make nearly all those things you required for your house; chairs and tables that you might bequeath to your children, strong cupboards and chests, and fine massive beds; beds worthy to share the secrets of mating and the strange, unfathomable mystery of birth, aye, and the infinite mystery of death, for a steadfast and trusted and honourable bed can be as a friend when it comest o dying.

Jóusè had once been as far north as Lisieux, and there he had seen the old timbered houses decaying in their narrow forgotten byways. And something had smitten him as he gazed: 'It was as though a hand were squeezing my bowels!' That was how he had afterwards described it to Marie. For the past which is always waiting to pounce and drag us down into the deep reservoir that is timeless, the bottomless well of existence, the past had laid hold on this man's slow mind, so that he, who was unimaginative in all else, had been fired by the beauty of his craft as set forth in the toil of those long-dead craftsmen. This had happened a good many years ago, since when Jóusè had regretfully been forced to admit that a man must try to conform to his age, and moreover that the timbered dwellings of the north were unsuitable to the southern climate. All the same this experience had influenced his work, so that he laboured with meticulous care and inclined to an honest solidity in the things that he made, as though indeed he were fashioning them for a future generation.

The collection of odds and ends of old carving which had had to give place to Anfos in the attic, was now stored away in a corner of the workshop, and quite often Jóusè would show it to the youth, and would try to expound why the chaste designs seemed to him to attain to all dignity and beauty.

'Look,' he would say, 'the quiet, lovely curve...' and then he would stop, at a loss for words, stroking the undulating surface of the oak as though the old wood could draw comfort from his fingers.

Anfos would murmur: 'Bèu Diéu' very softly and perhaps a great many times, for he often evoked a beautiful God when his heart and his struggling childish mind were stirred by pleasure or admiration. So while Jóusè fondled the venerable oak, Anfos would murmur: 'Bèu Diéu.'

Jóusè had much to teach his apprentice, and he found that he took a real pleasure in this teaching. The young man who had left him to go to Arles had been a very ungracious fellow, full of sullen and envious discontents, so that Jóusè turned with relief to Anfos who listened like a good and intelligent child, despite the fact that they called him half-witted. And although he could not be trusted with a razor, perhaps because this concerned him alone, he could always be trusted with the tools of his craft which concerned the great, sweet-smelling blocks of timber.

Many implements are used in the working of wood, and the ways of all these must be studied with care, for some are uncertain in their dispositions. Thus Anfos must study the holding tools, the stalwart oak bench with its heavy vices, the holdfasts, the endless family of cramps, and last but not least, the versatile pincers. The paring and shaving tools he must learn, and the angle at which it is best to work a chisel, the balance of forces in using the knife, the capacities of planes, gouges and the rest—all deadly weapons unless wielded with skill, with the calm and purposeful skill of the creator. Yes, and then he must learn how to purchase a saw; how to test it by laying hold of the handle which should fit the hand as neatly as a glove, and moreover be fashioned of well-seasoned wood lest it shrink and loosen the blade by so doing. He must learn that a thick blade is often a weak blade, that thin steel is the best when it comes to sawing; that the truest blades have a clear, bell-like ring when craftily struck with the ball of the finger. And then he must learn how to press his knee on the plank and how to begin the cut with the sharp, eager teeth so near his thumb that just for a moment they made him feel frightened. And finally, having learnt all these things and others too numerous to be recorded, he must learn from Jóusè the romance of the adze that had shaped the stout beams of the Middle Ages. The romance of the hammer Jóusè also taught him, telling of how that most ancient of tools had used to be fashioned by the water from stone, long ago, before history was first recorded.

This knowledge the good Jóusè had gleaned through a book soon after that memorable visit to Lisieux; and this battered old book which he had picked up at a rag-and-bone shop not far from the quay, was the only volume he had opened in years—always, of course, excepting his Missal—for reading had never come easily to Jóusè. But now it was pleasant to show off his learning to his new apprentice who would listen for hours, and whose brown, dog-like eyes would follow him about with gratitude mingled with deep respect. Indeed Jóusè had taken to saying to his wife: 'I begin to doubt whether your cousin is half-witted.'

So the summer days passed happily enough while Christophe grew strong at his mother's breast, and Anfos grew wise despite his weak mind, and Jóusè grew more and more contented and in consequence always a trifle stouter. That summer too, Mirèio seemed well content, for she had attached herself to the baby, finding, no doubt, that the difference was slight between this small, hairless human thing and one of her own robust hairy puppies.

3

Marie became fond of her husband's apprentice, not only for his mother's sake but for his own. There was something so solemn and so gentle about him, and his innocent brown eyes were so queerly appealing, gazing at her out of his bearded face, that Marie would trust him to play with her son and would let him take Christophe into the workshop should she herself chance to be extra busy.

Christophe was a healthy and commonplace baby, subject to his good days but also to his bad, like thousands of other babies. On his good days he smiled and made friends with the world, digested his food and gave everyone pleasure. On his bad days he howled incessantly and occasionally made himself sick in the process, so that Joúsè must leave his work at the bench and take a large hand in quieting his offspring.

'Hòu!' he would shout, 'What are all these tears? One would think you were the penitent Marie Madeleine instead of a recently baptised infant with all its original sin washed away. Hòu! But six months have you been in this world yet already you make such a terrible commotion!'

And his deep, booming voice would astonish Christophe so completely that he must perforce stop howling. Then Joúsè would solemnly return to his work, and the grating, relentless sound of the saw, or the silky, furtive sound of the plane would reach Marie as she bustled about in the kitchen.

It was curious to watch Anfos with the child, quite merry he could be, and yet there were times when he seemed almost reverential. He had a way of dropping on to his knees and offering the baby small, simple presents. Thus one morning he carved a bird out of wood—for Anfos had a natural aptitude for carving—and this done he whistled the soft double note wherewith he had used to attract the wild birds when he lived in that village high up in the mountains. And he moved his carved bird about and about, and made it pretend to be bowing to Christophe. Then Christophe grabbed it and sucked its head, and kicked his plump legs till his socks came off and he finally fell back and sprawled in the shavings. After this Anfos also sprawled on the floor, overcome for the moment by his own childish instincts; and he made little hillocks of golden sawdust so that Christophe might slap at them with his hands and crow with delight when the hillocks were scattered; and they both uttered young, embryonic sounds—which apparently both of them understood—until Anfos got once more on to his knees and knelt gazing earnestly down at Christophe.

Jóusè said quietly: 'To live one must eat, and to eat one must work.' So Anfos stumbled up and returned to the table leg he was making.

Christophe watched him out of pale blue-grey orbs which were so wide apart that they made Jóusè laugh, for they gave to the rounded, infantile face an absurdly candid and wise expression. Christophe watched him, but Anfos was intent on his job and was therefore no longer of very great interest; of less interest indeed than the sawdust and chips which, failing all else, could at least be eaten.

'Marie!' bawled Jóusè, 'Marie, come quick! Our child is no longer content with your milk and endeavours to nourish himself upon wood!' Then Marie came running in from the kitchen, wiping the soap from her hands on her apron.

'Santo Ano d'At!' she exclaimed very loudly, for she always invoked this saint when annoyed. 'Santo Ano d'At! Are you also a child that you cannot keep one small baby in order but must stand there grinning while he kills himself by swallowing God knows how many sharp splinters? Pichounet, come here!' And picking up Christophe she proceeded to grope in his mouth with her thumb which he tried to spit out, disliking its taste, because it was salt and decidedly soapy.

Marie scolded: 'Not an hour can I trust you, it seems, and yet well do you know I have much to do, for on Monday I always scrub out the kitchen; there is also the washing which I must iron; there are also your socks and not one with a heel—I cannot imagine what you do to your heels, ai, there are holes the size of duck's eggs. Santo Ano d'At! Here are two hulking men yet neither can lift a child from the floor. I had better have left him in the charge of Mirèio.'

And because she was so seldom angry with them, Jóusè and Anfos were at first nonplussed; then each in his own way felt rather alarmed.

Jóusè stammered: 'It comes of his being very small yet terribly active—a wood-louse crawls slower. A wood-louse I can catch. . . .'

But here Marie broke in: 'He has not crawled an inch; he sits under your nose with his mouth full of shavings and you find it amusing. As for Anfos, he pretends to be fond of the child yet does nothing at all when he sees him in danger!'

25

And these things she said, not from hardness of heart but because she had really been badly frightened.

Poor Anfos made a queer rough sound in his throat as he tried to swallow the lump that had risen—his brain was groping for suitable words, and the more it groped the more it felt muddled. Meanwhile Christophe had begun to howl dismally, vaguely sensing some kind of domestic upheaval.

Marie soothed him, stroking his straight red hair, the hair that was so much redder than his father's; the hair that would always refuse to curl, try though she might to coax it round her finger: 'Enfantounet, do not cry, do not cry, paure pichounet. There, there, all goes well and you are not hurt—though that is no thanks to your foolish father.'

'Bigre! I am foolish indeed,' murmured Jóusè. Then he wheedled: 'Marioun, do not scold any more. Listen, Marioun, I am but a man, and all men are foolish by comparison with women, especially when they must look after babies!'

She nodded slowly, but now she was smiling. And because he had called her Marioun—which might mean that she was exceedingly small, or again, that she was exceedingly old, but which always meant that her husband loved her—because he had called her Marioun, she must suddenly stroke his thick, ageing back to which the coarse shirt clung closely with sweat, for the autumn days were as hot as the summer. And then she must turn kind eyes upon Anfos.

'Do not be late for dinner'; she warned them, 'Goundran has just brought us some magnificent fish with which I am making the bouillabaisse blanche.' For she knew that her Jóusè liked good things to eat, setting great store by the lusts of the stomach.

26

CHAPTER THREE

I

THE following March Marie Bénédit was once again brought to bed of child, and Christophe was sent to stay for a week with his aunt Germaine Roustan down at the harbour. Madame Roustan could not very well refuse to take him, although at the moment her hands were full, what with Jan who was angrily cutting his teeth and causing a great deal of trouble in the process, and Goundran who was showing himself much averse from her carefully schemed matrimonial projects, and the landlord who was threatening a procès légal on account of those hotly disputed gutters, and the traveller from Toulon who had brought the wrong samples. Yes, one way and another her hands were quite full, and now in addition she was saddled with Christophe.

It was spring and much mating was afloat in the air, so that foolish fancies assailed Madame Roustan, and she wished to go forth and walk on the hills, picking myrtle for love, for the love of Goundran; and she wished to sail the seas in a boat, in a fisherman's boat, and that fisherman Goundran; and she wished to lie close to a man in her bed, a strong, comely man, and that man Goundran. These and similar things she much wished to do, one and all of which were connected with Goundran. And since, instead, she must stay in the shop and observe whenever she glanced in the mirror that although the spring might be eternally young, she was not, that indeed at her time of life unruly emotions were apt to be ageing; and since such reflections are very distressing even to the least conceited of women, Madame Roustan was feeling decidedly cross, for love unrequited is bad for the temper. Then, as if to augment her sense of irritation, as she left the Bénédit's house with

Christophe she perceived Eusèbe standing at his door, and he looking as knowing as any old monkey.

'Santouno!' exclaimed Eusèbe, spitting, the while he evoked all the female saints, 'Santouno! How sprightly and gay you appear; one would think, Madame, that you tripped to your wedding. But who was it who said: "It is easier far to net conger-eels than a wily fisher"!' For Eusèbe could be very spiteful at times, and moreover he greatly disliked Madame Roustan.

Madame Roustan shrugged her shoulders and would have passed on, but Eusèbe now pretended to play with the baby: 'Ho, hoi!' he cried loudly; and again, 'Ho, hoi!' wagging his head and clapping his hands, until Christophe, lacking all tact, responded.

Eusèbe's breath smelt of alcohol, and his eye was blacker than usual with mischief: 'Do not hurry away from a lonely old man; come in and have a small cognac,' he suggested.

Madame Roustan looked shocked: 'And to think,' she said sternly, 'that this place where you stand was once holy ground; to think that your shop was once part of a convent!'

'That is so,' he nodded, winking at Christophe, 'and when I was a lad the good sisters still lived here. Ah, yes, and I had a great ambition—when one is young one is drawn to religion.'

'And what was this great ambition of yours?' enquired Madame Roustan, very unwisely.

Then Eusèbe chuckled: 'It was this, Madame; I much longed to sleep with one of the sisters. Houi, and now I live in their house, but what is the shell without the kernel?'

Madame Roustan clasped Christophe to her outraged breast: 'Ah, mais non,' she protested, 'the man goes too far; his conversation has ceased to be decent.'

Eusèbe watched her as she hurried away, and his eye became composite in expression; angry, amused and lascivious it looked, which was very much what its owner was feeling. 'That widow,' he muttered, 'is as full of bad sap as a wicked old ivy about to strangle. I have very great fears for the unhappy Goundran, yes, in spite of that saying about the fisher.' And shaking his head he retired into his shop, there to ease those same fears by recourse to the bottle.

Christophe's visit to Jan Roustan and his parent was the first really intimate meeting of these cousins. They had met several times before, it is true, but only at a distance, from the laps of their mothers.

When Madame Roustan returned to her house, still outraged by Eusèbe's coarse conversation, she carried Christophe upstairs to her bedroom where Jan had been left in the charge of a girl from the country, engaged to assist by Jóusè.

Jan was a year and four months old; a dark-skinned, aggressive and hot-tempered baby. He was squirming like Eusèbe's proverbial eels, for he deeply resented the liberties that rough peasant hands were taking with him—but unlike those proverbial eels he was screaming.

'Rampau de Diéu!' cried Madame Roustan, plumping Christophe on to his feet, 'Rampau de Diéu! It must be a pin. He will never endure the prick of a pin—that he will not support for so much as an instant!' Sitting down she took her son on to her lap and began with all possible speed to undress him.

Christophe gazed at his cousin with pale, intent eyes in which there was more than a little interest. Then—as if he himself had never been known to scream, whatever the provocation—he suddenly smiled a broad, placid smile, and staggering across the bedroom to Jan, he touched him with a doubtful and experimental finger. As though by a miracle Jan stopped screaming.

The girl from the country gaped in surprise: 'He has howled without ceasing ever since you left him, yet now he is quiet and friendly again. Can it be because he has seen his cousin? Ah, Diéu, but this Christophe has the look of an angel!' she babbled to the worried and preoccupied mother.

'I cannot find so much as the trace of a pin; perhaps he has wind in the stomach,' sighed Madame Roustan. And handing her offspring back to the girl, she went down to the shop to attend to business.

But if Christophe had appeared to be as an angel, then his subsequent behaviour was a fall from grace, for he also resented the girl's clumsy hands and was soon at some pains to express his resentment. From her post behind the well-worn counter Madame Roustan would hear sounds of squealing and wailing. First one, then the other baby would begin, and after a while there might be a duet, partly owing to colic but partly to temper. Moreover, since the cousins had now learnt to walk, they found plenty of ways of tormenting their elders; so the girl from the country must quite often weep—not infrequently all three of them would be weeping.

Madame Roustan was soon to be further distracted by the sudden appearance of Mirèio one morning. There she stood with her muzzle pressed close to the door, making loud, blowing noises that were very unnerving. The moment the shop door was opened she shot in and proceeded to put her front paws on the counter. Now Mirèio was a very large bitch indeed, and she fixed Madame Roustan with a pair of brown eyes that were somehow no longer apologetic.

'Va t'en! Mais, va t'en!' Madame Roustan commanded in a voice which she tried hard to keep from trembling.

Whereupon Mirèio displayed her fangs—although this she did simply because she must smile, for as every stray cur in Saint Loup was aware, Madame Roustan could never support words with deeds, being terrified of the whole canine species. But after a moment the smile died away and Mirèio settled doggedly down to business; and her business consisted of ransacking the shop, then the scullery and kitchen in search of Christophe, which she did with remarkable thoroughness, upsetting a new can of oil in the process. But since Christophe was seemingly being concealed, and the door at the foot of the stairs had been closed, it very soon roused Mirèio's suspicions; quite naturally, therefore, she used her strong claws with devastating results to the paintwork.

'Ai! las, ai! las,' Madame Roustan kept wailing, for already she must mend every gutter on the house, and that door had but recently been repainted. 'Ai! las, that my poor Geoffroi should have died; he would never have allowed me to be so put upon. How helpless is the woman who has lost her husband!' And she actually started to wring her plump hands while her eyes filled with large, childish tears of self-pity.

Then Mirèio sat down rather suddenly, and, stretching her thin neck over her shoulder, she proceeded to hunt for the greedy ticks that sucked so much life-blood out of her body.   ·

At this moment who should stroll in but Goundran; he had come to buy needles, cottons, and buttons wherewith he himself would repair his clothes, and this far more neatly than many a woman. At the sight of him Madame Roustan burst into sobs, so relieved was she by his timely arrival; and she pointed to the hopelessly blemished door and then to Mirèio, still intent on her hunting.

'But why has the dirty beast come here?' she sobbed, 'Not only has she upset my new can of oil and ruined my beautifully painted door, but now she must start disengaging her ticks—she has surely more ticks on that carcase of hers than any stray dog this side of Lyon.'

Goundran said: 'I think she has come for the child—it is strange when one sees a dumb creature so devoted. As for her ticks, I blame those who own her. Jóusè should get some paste from the vet.' And he gazed at Mirèio with his bright blue eyes in which there was always a look of the sea, and just now a flicker of real understanding. 'Come,' he urged, stroking the beast's tawny head, 'come Mirèio, you need have no anxiety for Christophe.' Then he led her gently to the door of the shop, and when Goundran said: 'Va t'en!' Mirèio obeyed him.

By now Madame Roustan was drying her tears, the while her heart began beating more quickly, for Goundran was a lovely man in her sight. But she thought: 'All these men of the sea are so strange. How strange was the way that he spoke to that bitch—it was almost as though he considered her human. Paste from the vet he would have Jóusè buy. Tè! And what next would he have him do? He must think the poor Jóusè has plenty of money!' Then she went to a drawer for the needles and threads, and finally got out a large box of buttons.

Goundran made his selection very slowly and gravely, for when a fisherman mends his own clothes—however expert he may have become—he must always be careful in regard to those things that large and rope-hardened fingers will handle. Thus the needles he chose had conspicuous eyes, while the cottons were stout and unlikely to break as some cottons will do on the least provocation. His buttons also he would have very strong; good, hefty bone buttons guaranteed not to split—Madame Roustan ordered them specially for him. And such purchases he invariably carried away in his pocket to a house lower down on the quay, the house where he had boarded since the death of his parents. It belonged to a woman of so venerable an age that, according to fable, she was nearly a hundred.

Madame Roustan did up his small parcel with care, but her heart was angry and suspicious within her, for this woman had recently sent for a niece, on the pretext of failing activity and eyesight. It is true that this niece was only a child, a thin, quiet little girl still pale from the city, but as Madame Roustan was wont to remark, and with obvious truth: 'All cats were once kittens.' So now while she did up his parcel with care, her heart was angry and suspicious within her.

She said—and it was extremely foolish, but then love is apt to make the tongue tactless—she said: 'All this buying of womanish things! If I were a handsome young fellow like you, I would soon get a wife who would do my mending.' Then she looked a great deal which she did not say, so that Goundran shuffled about with his feet and nervously held out his hand for the parcel.

And now Madame Roustan must laugh none too kindly: 'Tè, but perhaps you have a wife in your eye; though surely the little Elise is too young—she is fitter to play with dolls than to bear children. However, as my grandmother used to say: "All cats were once kittens," and Elise will grow up; no doubt it is only a question of waiting. Ah, but that old aunt of hers is crafty, although I am told that she pretends to be blind and deaf and unable to move her body. It may soon be a case of the catcher caught, for undoubtedly she wishes to marry her niece to a man who has purchased his own fishing vessel. . . .'

She paused, feeling more than a little breathless, while he stared at her out of his bright blue eyes as though he were lacking in comprehension. And this was what made him so hard to woo, this vague, rather stupid look that he had whenever she tried to talk about women.

32

'Madame, you mistake'; he said patiently, 'the little Elise, as you say, is a child. Moreover it is true that old Mathilde goes blind; I was speaking only this morning with the doctor. I have much to consider now that I have bought my boat, and hardly a centime left in the bank. No, madame, I am not contemplating this marriage—or any other marriage, if it comes to that. I find myself well enough as I am, and surely a man should not marry a wife merely because she will do his mending?'

'Ah, how like him,' she thought, 'to have seized upon the words which must make me appear to be lacking in feeling.' But aloud she said: 'Go your ways, my good Goundran, only when you are caught do not come to my shop and complain that your dinner is badly prepared, that your house is ill kept and your socks ill darned because you have married a chit from the city. Do not complain, for you will have been warned. I have long thought that old Mathilde is a witch, and witches are said to give men love-potions!'

Then Goundran laughed: 'Ah, madame, if you knew her—old she is, but so kind and so full of wisdom. If Mathilde is a witch, as you wish me to believe, then you and I will meet witches in heaven. Yes, and possibly the devil will be there to let them in, standing at the gate side by side with Saint Peter.' And still laughing he turned and went out of the shop.

'He is stubborn, that Goundran,' sighed Madame Roustan.

3

Three nights later Madame Roustan, feeling thoroughly tired, decided to go to her bed rather early. The weather was hot for the time of year and her small sitting-room seemed unpleasantly airless; added to which a high, clarion note had just announced the first spiteful mosquito.

Madame Roustan both liked and admired her bedroom with its shiny mock-mahogany suite purchased by her late husband in Toulon; with its salmon-pink neatly distempered walls, and its double bed made of the best lacquered brass, from the arms of which depended pink curtains; with its crucifix hanging above the bed in a species of very ornate

33   B

glazed coffin; with its piety books on their little gilt shelf, and its prie-dieu at which she now so seldom knelt, the moths having eaten away its cushion. All these furnishings seemed to her very select—she felt that they set her apart from her neighbours.

In a stout and fairly capacious cot made by Joúsè and considered by Madame Roustan to be the one blemish upon the apartment, lay the infant cousins, Christophe and Jan. To Madame Roustan's enormous relief as she tiptoed about, they were placidly sleeping. Every night since her godson's unwelcome advent her much-needed rest had been ruthlessly broken—either by Christophe who ground his gums, then woke up in a consequent sweat of anguish, or by Jan, who, preferring his cot to himself, was not always polite to the new arrival. But now—praise be to God and the Holy Flower—they seemed peaceful enough and were actually sleeping. Madame Roustan smothered a noisy yawn, and after a while she started to undress, having carefully closed and bolted the shutters.

Divesting herself of her skirt and blouse she stood forth in a short cotton petticoat and black stays, the latter supporting her breasts at a lofty and somewhat aggressive angle. Her fat legs ended disconcertingly in a pair of very tight high-heeled shoes which cut into the flesh of her insteps and ankles. She was above all a creature of routine, as methodical in personal habits as in business. For years she had dressed and undressed by rote and at this stage she always let down her hair, so that now she withdrew the discoloured bronze hairpins; after which she scraped her scalp with the comb and proceeded to brush out the consequent dandruff. Having made a firm plait—for her hair was still thick—she untied the strings of her coarse undergarments, and these neatly disposed of on a neighbouring chair, she heaved a deep sigh of anticipation, for the moment of release had arrived at last; she had longed for this moment intensely all the evening. Madame Roustan released herself from her stays, and the heavy white flesh billowed out unrebuked as her figure resumed its natural proportions; and the breath passed freely through her long-suffering lungs, since her belly had ceased to be one with her bosom. But not all the flea-bitten tick-pestered dogs who rubbed against walls or

34

sat scratching at corners, not all that mangy and bastard crew could have itched more consumedly than did Madame Roustan. Slipping a hand beneath her chemise, she scratched with a kind of agonized rapture.

It was while she was scratching the small of her back that she suddenly heard a surreptitious noise as of someone lurking under the bed. Panic-stricken she stood, and her fingers stiffened. As she listened came the sound of a body that moved, that appeared to be quietly turning over; and deep breathing she heard, then a long-drawn sigh, then something not very unlike a yawn; and all this from beneath her respectable bed where she kept the cardboard box of the hat in which she was wont to attend Mass on Sundays. Madame Roustan was a timid woman by nature and had long lived in nightly terror of thieves—that was why, no matter how stifling the weather, she invariably closed and bolted her shutters. But now, though the shutters were bolted as usual, there could be little doubt that a thief had entered; and she standing stripped all but down to the skin, which would place many women at a grave disadvantage. Madame Roustan felt that God was not kind, for she bitterly regretted her discarded stays which had now assumed the importance of armour. All the same she ran over a long list of saints, for God alone through His saints could help her.

'O Santi Mario,' she prayed desperately, feeling that there must be safety in numbers, since three Holy Marys would surely be stronger than one when it came to smiting an assassin: 'O Mary the mother of James and John; O Mary the sister of the blessèd Virgin, O Mary Magdalene come to my aid. I beseech you to preserve my life and my virtue!'

Now whether the Holy Three heard her prayer, or whether Madame Roustan's feminine nerves were not really so weak as she often imagined, is a question which must perforce go unanswered. But the fact remains that snatching up a shawl for propriety's sake, she peered under the bed, where she found what was almost worse than a man—a watchful, determined and aggressive Mirèio.

Mirèio eyed Madame Roustan's fat calves with an interest that quite plainly bespoke her intentions; and as Madame Roustan straightened her back, Mirèio straightened her back, growling darkly. It was clear that the creature intended to remain precisely where she was, on guard near Christophe.

Then Madame Roustan flung herself into her clothes, caring not a fig if she woke both the babies; indeed all but forgetting her erstwhile fears in a sudden uprush of Meridional temper. Hiking the protesting Jan from his cot, she dumped him in the sitting-room behind the shop, where she locked him for safety during her absence—Christophe, she decided, it was wiser to leave where he was, in view of his watchful guardian. Breathless and perspiring with anger and heat, she made her way round to the Bénédit's house where she knocked with such vigour that the curious Eusèbe must get up and thrust his head out of the window.

'Póu!' he remarked with enormous disdain, 'It would seem that the widow prowls the tiles; out at this hour alone on the streets. But what does she want with the Bénédits? Does she think that Goundran now boards with her brother?'

Jóusè, who had run to the door in his night-shirt, stood blinking at his sister in sleepy amazement: 'Eh bien—has the devil come to Saint Loup and stolen the church bells to melt them in hell? Or is it that we have a new Prussian invasion? But whatever it is, need you break down the house when my wife was confined only yesterday morning?' Then a sudden great fear came into his eyes: 'Do not tell me that all is not well with Christophe. . . ?'

'Christophe,' she told him, 'is very well indeed. At this moment he is being guarded by your bitch. But my little Jan I have had to lock up—as for myself, I have been in great peril. I have left the beast crouching under my bed. She growled like a fiend when she saw my bare legs, in another moment she would have attacked me. Had the Holy Marys not inspired me with the courage to get into my clothes and then rush from the house, I scarcely dare contemplate what might have happened. I insist that you accompany me home on the instant!'

Jóusè was a placid man as a rule, but his nerves at the moment were badly on edge, for Marie had been through a dangerous confinement. Thus the element of fear may have been to blame for the sudden and unexpected fury with which he now turned and upbraided his sister.

'Imbecile!' he bellowed, 'You come to my home and make a noise likely to wake up the dead when my wife, who has suffered the tortures of the damned, has only just managed to get off to sleep; yes, and you wake up our ailing baby. Could you not have come and told me discreetly? Ah, and you save your Jan but leave Christophe. Who can say that Mirèio has not got the rage? Yet you leave my son alone with her in the room! Did you bring Christophe with you as you should have done? Ah, no, for you only think of saving your skin, and the dirty skin of your miserable Jan. Diéu, what a woman I have for a sister!'

He paused, ransacking his brain for fresh insults, but before he had found them his sister was ready.

'I would rather a mad dog than you'; she told him, 'a nice scandal you make rousing up the whole street—already Eusèbe hangs out of his window! It is not I who wake up your wife and baby, but you with all this indecent shouting. And if Marie has borne you a sickly child it is surely your doing who are no longer young and are probably past the time for strong breeding. As for Mirèio, is it my fault that you keep a savage and verminous bitch who threatens to kill me in my own bedroom? As for Christophe, had I lifted him out of the cot Mirèio would surely have torn my throat. It is you and not I who shall deal with Mirèio!'

Then Jóusè dragged hard at his beard and swore, and his oaths embraced the whole calendar of saints, not even excepting the three Holy Marys. And he lost his thread and swore by his sister; then he lost it again and swore by his bitch; then he found it and swore by the sword of Saint Loup—the sword that had vanquished the hordes of the heathen. Indeed, so bewildered did Jóusè become—for his anger had gone to his head like liquor—that in the end it was hard to decide who, or what, had roused up this access of fury.

'Malan de Diéu,' he swore finally, 'it is time that I go and punish the beast—who knows but that it is time I killed her! And you also I would very much like to thrash. Diéu, there is little to choose between you!' Slipping into a dusty old overcoat which he took from a peg just inside the doorway, he went round to the yard and fetched a strong chain, and a stick wherewith he would beat Mirèio. Then he turned to his sister: 'Come, let us go quickly!'

When they finally reached Madame Roustan's house, Jóusè rushed to the bedroom in search of his son. Christophe lay sprawled in the cot sound asleep. 'Now may Jesus and His Mother be thanked,' whispered Jóusè. Then he dragged the bitch from under the bed, who, knowing her master, came unprotesting; and when he had got her outside on the road he twisted her collar and started to beat her. And the stick crashed ruthlessly down on her bones, for her flesh was scanty through long under-feeding.

But Mirèio endured with never a cry, for hers was a dumbly courageous nature, and moreover she well knew that she would endure even death, if need be, for the sake of Christophe. And so while the stick crashed down on her bones, there leapt up in her poor and much battered body, a thing very nearly akin to God, a gleam of the selfless love of the spirit—for who may presume to qualify love which is one with the God who is one with His creatures?

Presently, Jóusè's wrath being spent, he must throw away the stick, for he felt deeply shamed by his own unexpected brutality, and the stick which was bloody would have been a reminder. Very slowly the two of them turned towards home, he with bent head and she limping a little; while the moon which had risen up over the bay, touched a trickle of blood on Mirèio's gaunt side, so that Jóusè must look in another direction. All the same, he determined to chain the bitch closely, for his mind could not hold very many emotions, and now it was once again full of his wife who lay feverish and ill with a sickly baby. On no account therefore must she be disturbed, and so he determined to chain the bitch closely.

CHAPTER FOUR

I

WHEN Marie was once more up and about, which was not until nearly three weeks later, Jóusè walked slowly to his sister's house; he was feeling awkward and embarrassed. Two tasks were confronting him on this occasion—the one pleasant, the other humiliating: he was going to carry his little son home, but before doing so he must apologize to Germaine for his own inexcusable temper.

He had had to leave Christophe with Madame Roustan much longer than he and his wife had intended, and this because Marie had been very ill. Only with considerable difficulty had they saved her life and that of the baby. So determined had this second child seemed to be to return to that haven from which they had called him, that the Curé had been sent for during the night in order that the small and complaining soul might display the badge of a Christian to Saint Peter—a hasty and melancholy baptism indeed, neither patronized by friends nor followed by feasting.

Madame Roustan was in her sitting-room when Jóusè arrived looking rather sheepish. These two had not met since their noisy quarrel, all communications having been written with great brevity and exchanged through Anfos.

'Ah,' Madame Roustan snapped, 'so it is you!' which did not strike Jóusè as a hopeful beginning.

'I have called for Christophe, my sister . . .' he mumbled, combing his curly beard with his fingers.

'He still lives!' she remarked satirically; after which there was silence for more than a minute.

Then Jóusè grasped the bull by the horns: 'I am truly sorry for all that has happened. I admit that I found myself in a rage . . . I was terribly anxious about my poor wife . . .

Eh bien, there it is, I apologize, and more than that no brother can do; so now I hope we are friends again, Germaine.' And he clumsily bent down and kissed her on both cheeks, for a family feud was not to be thought of.

Madame Roustan accepted this embrace with coldness; nevertheless she enquired about Marie and would have the latest details of the child, for she had a vast curiosity in regard to all matrimonial matters. Jóusè told her as well as he could, which was not very well it must be admitted, and after she had heard him out to the end, she announced her intention of paying them a visit.

'No doubt had I been in charge,' she said sternly, 'all these complications would never have happened.' So Jóusè knew that the breach was now healed, for which he was more than a little thankful.

But one other thing, and the hardest of all, he must say to his sister before he left her: 'Germaine . . .' he began, 'I will ask a favour. It is something which I beg that you will not tell Marie. It concerns Mirèio whom I beat that night . . . I do not want Marie to know what I did—she is still in a state when it might upset her.'

Madame Roustan bridled: 'Must you then spare the bitch but allow your own sister to be torn to pieces?'

'No, no,' he said hastily, 'not that, of course. But . . . well, I do beg that you will say nothing. I am far from a violent man as a rule, and although Marie feels no affection for the bitch, I would rather she did not hear of the beating.' And in this he was wise, for if Marie had known she would surely have been very deeply grieved, though much less for Mirèio than for her husband.

'If you do not wish me to speak of my peril, I suppose that I must try not to do so,' frowned his sister, 'though when one has returned from the jaws of death, one may well not remember to hold one's tongue.' And with this Jóusè had perforce to be contented.

But presently Christophe was in his arms and his heart was rejoicing at his son's firm body, rejoicing at the healthful vigour of this child whom he had fathered when nearing fifty, so that just for the moment he was vastly content, forgetting the ailing and premature baby.

'Ho, Christophe, enfantounet! Ho, here is your father!

40

That is grand, little fist of iron, pull my beard—if you pull hard enough you may make it uncurl. That is splendid, I would have you kick with your legs, for only by kicking will the small legs grow stronger. Hóu, but they are mighty already, these legs. And what arms for the son of a carpenter; it is you who shall carry the heaviest timber! Hóu, but some day you shall carry a tree! Laugh, enfantounet! See, Germaine, how he laughs . . . And now we must go, for his mother waits; but first he would say farewell to his cousin.'

So Madame Roustan fetched her own son—that dark-skinned, aggressive and hot-tempered baby. And the cousins grabbed at each other and smiled; then they suddenly stared at each other very gravely.

'Jan is also a fine little fellow,' said Jóusè, wishing to make up for that turbulent night.

'Mais oui,' sighed his sister, 'yet how sad is the child who having a mother has lost his father!'

'Ah, but there is surely time,' Jóusè consoled her. 'If he loses one father you should give him another, and that you must make up your mind to do.' For he felt so happy with Christophe in his arms, that he very much wished all the world to be happy. But when she flushed darkly and did not reply, he grew awkward again, remembering Goundran. 'Oh, well,' he temporized tactlessly, 'some women are glad to be rid of their men, and after all you will have a good son . . . Who knows but that sons are better than husbands?'

'Pecaire!' he thought, 'I anger her again—yet to-day I have wished to be kind to Germaine.' Then feeling that words were treacherous things, he kissed Madame Roustan once more and departed.

2

Le tout petit Loup, as they called the new infant, firstly because this baptismal name must surely attract the good Saint's attention, and secondly because he was indeed very small—much smaller, they felt, than were most other infants—le tout petit Loup suffered greatly from his stomach which was weak, from his skin which broke out in rashes, from his rickety limbs which ached badly at times, and from quite a number of other discomforts, since from birth he had been an unhealthy baby. Le tout petit Loup very seldom laughed, though he wept and made other disconsolate noises, so that Marie augmented her daily prayers to the warrior-bishop who had loved helpless things; she even reminded him of the bird that had lived, through his mercy, to sing in his garden.

There were now two children to clothe and to feed, so Jóusè must keep his account-book more neatly, and must send in his bills as they became due, in the hope that he would receive prompt payment; for the doctor and the chemist had also to live if Loup were not to slip out of existence. Sometimes Jóusè would catch himself wondering how a thing so minute could absorb so much money, whereupon he would feel very penitent and would make a rough effort to fondle the baby.

Marie would push away his great hand, not unkindly, indeed often smiling a little, but: 'Take care,' she would warn, 'he is fretful to-day, and your hand is so rough that it may torment him.' And then she herself would fondle the hand as though it might possibly be feeling offended.

As the months went by it became apparent that Loup took but little interest in Christophe and that Christophe took but little interest in Loup. Sometimes Jóusè would hold them both on his knees, tickling first one child then the other in an effort to make them more affable and friendly, but without much success:

'It is queer,' he would muse, 'one would think that my children were strangers in blood.' And then he would give Christophe a mighty hug, but Loup he would hand gravely back to his mother.

Le tout petit Loup was afraid of Mirèio and he screamed whenever the bitch went near him. Jóusè would cuff her severely at times and would shut her up in a shed in the yard, for this fear of Mirèio who was always so gentle with the babies, shamed not only his pride but his manhood.

'It seems that I no longer sire courage,' he would mutter, and then he would let his eyes rest upon Christophe, seeking in him to find consolation.

Anfos was kind to the ailing baby, for he was a kindly and good-natured fellow; but his love once given would never be shared—like Mirèio, he adored only one human being.

Christophe they adored and Christophe alone, these two simple-minded and primitive creatures.

And so it happened that le tout petit Loup must root deeply in the anxious heart of his mother. He who was ailing and weak in all else was yet lusty when it came to his need of Marie; and she feeling this need as he lay at her breast or whimpered because his small limbs were aching—she feeling this urgent and ruthless need, rallied all her maternal strength to meet it. If Christophe was the apple of his mother's eye, le tout petit Loup was the fruit of her compassion. And because of the care which she lavished upon him, a care that was selfless and wellnigh unceasing, he actually lived, le tout petit Loup, and became almost reconciled to existence. Strong, as Christophe was strong, he would never be, but one morning the doctor was more reassuring:

'Give him time and his troubles should pass away. He will not grow so fast as your other son, still, I think we shall see him grow into a man.'

'May the Golden Saints be blessed!' exclaimed Marie. And that same afternoon she went to the church where she lighted many candles for the ailing child, and left them to plead at the shrine of his Patron.

3

The spring had given place to the summer which, in its turn, had given place to the autumn; then had come the winter with its turbulent mistral, to be followed by spring, and yet once more by summer. Christophe and his cousin Jan grew apace, both in stature and in their marked mutual affection. At two years old they would cry for each other, resenting, it seemed, their enforced separation. Indeed they were tiresome enough at times, and inclined to wear on the nerves of their parents.

There was little to mark the passing of the days during that semi-tropical weather when the heat hung in motionless mist on the hills, creeping vineyard by vineyard up to the mountains. Marie, though less vigorous since the birth of Loup, was able to take up her old busy existence; Jóusè and Anfos worked in the shop; Christophe crawled in the shavings or slept in the sunshine; Mirèio eternally hunted her ticks, and Eusèbe squatted among his sandals. While down at the port Goundran painted his boat a bright green that matched certain moods of the sea; and a band of deep blue his boat must have also—deep blue and bright green for the sea in a mistral.

The port smelt of tar, fishing tackle and wine as the sun beat down in his full August glory, making the tar turn sticky on the planks, and the scales that still clung to the fishermen's nets gleam softly like strange, opalescent jewels, and the dregs that still lurked in the empty wine casks reek with a queer, very ancient reek which stirred thoughts of the Godless god that was Bacchus. For now in this tranquil, propitious weather, there had come the tartanes with their broad lateen sails, bringing the casks to be filled with wine— the casks which a man could roll with such ease when empty, but which when their round bellies were full needed two men or more to attend to the rolling. Once loaded the tartanes would sail down the coast, their decks darkly stained, their hulls low to water; while some, greatly daring, might put out to sea and steer for the shores of Africa where the Provençal wines found an excellent market. The crews of the tartanes, when they came ashore, would be treated to drinks, and this fairly often, for these were adventurous fellows who, when drunk, could be trusted to tell many full-blooded yarns, most of which would be closely connected with women. They could also tell of a wind far more deadly than that which came from the desert of La Crau, so well known to all those who lived in Saint Loup that its advent had ceased to be of much interest. And a sun they could tell of—if they spoke God's truth—that would turn the sunshine of Saint Loup into moonlight.

To the port would come the old toper Eusèbe sniffing the air with distended nostrils, and as likely as not neglecting his work while some client must wait for a new pair of sandals. Eusèbe's one eye would ogle the girls who, bare-headed and comely, went about their own business: 'Tè,' he would grunt, 'a good figure she has—when she is older she should have a fine bosom.' And other very personal things he would say to himself, or to anyone else who would listen.

When the large southern moon swung up over the sea,

she might find Eusèbe sitting in a café. The Café de la Tarasque was the one he preferred because there he believed that he drank the best wine, since much of it came from his own prized vineyards; there also the fishermen danced with their sweethearts and would sometimes make love in conspicuous corners. But Eusèbe must guard his roving black eye, for tempers were short while knives could be long on those hot summer nights when the blood throbbed hard, and the little violinist with the hump on his back stirred more than the air by his shrill, teasing music. Eusèbe must think of his long-dead wife until he had transformed her into a houri; and the deeper he drank of the juice of the grape, the more scandalous became his unseemly visions. It was certainly as well that he always forgot them the next morning, since who knows what he might have told Madame Roustan—or even the Curé, for that matter!

The men from the tartanes would jostle his table and make fun of the eye that he could not see with: 'Oh, le vieux bougre, he has a stone eye!' And perhaps one of them would thrust his girl forward on Eusèbe's blind side: 'Behold!' he might say amid roars of appreciation and laughter. But Eusèbe by this time would be lost in his dreams, which had wafted him far away from la Tarasque and Saint Loup to the paradise of Mahomet.

Sometimes Madame Roustan would come in and drink coffee, for although she was always berating the place, there was just a vague chance that she might glimpse Goundran. But Goundran seldom went to cafés these days, for now it was needful that he should save money—fishing vessels cost a good deal to run when a man is responsible for his own tackle—so after a while Madame Roustan would go home very angry indeed with the little Elise and her aunt, whom she blamed for her wasted evening.

Joúsè might wander along from the town to get a breath of salt air at the harbour; he might even stop for a glass of beer and a small cigarette with the patronne of la Tarasque. She was stout, beetle-browed, and courageous in brawls; indeed she had once seized a drunken sailor by the hair and had dragged him into the street, whereupon he had burst into tears on her bosom. When the fun ran so high that it ended in tempers—for these people were but little removed from children—the patronne would thump her fist on the desk, and would threaten to close the bar for the night, which quite often reduced the chaos to order. Mère Mélanie, they called her, though why God only knew, for in wedlock she had proved herself stubbornly sterile. And now that her husband had been drowned at sea, it was said that she lived with the little violinist—the little violinist with the hump on his back who drew such shrill, teasing tunes from his fiddle. It was also said that she beat him when he drank, and conversely, that he beat her hard every night before they retired to their unhallowed couch; but since neither of the pair ever turned black and blue it was not at all easy to prove these assertions. Moreover Mère Mélanie was piously inclined and made many novenas—this at least was a fact. She also gave largely of her profits to the Church, which was strange in view of the little violinist. Anyhow, she seemed well content with her God, with herself, with her business, and with most of her clients.

Jóusè never stayed overlong at la Tarasque, for Marie could now seldom leave the babies, and Jóusè could not very well leave his wife—there was so much to be done for le tout petit Loup whose temperature still went up in the evenings. Anfos never went to the Café at all, being far too timid, since he was half-witted; while Mirèio might not go because of a feud which she had with the patronne's chienne de chasse—a base-born, red-pelted amazon with a lust for war and a devilish temper.

Nor can it be denied that the mayor of Saint Loup, the Curé, and indeed not a few of the townsfolk, had cast disapproving glances at the Café de la Tarasque, for the noise would continue throughout the night and well into the early hours of the morning. Why, on one particularly shameful occasion, it had not subsided by six o'clock when the Curé was ringing the bell for Mass and the faithful were on their way to Communion.

And yet . . . when the moon was abnormally large and the water beneath her seemed cut out of silver, while the purposeful masts of the anchored ships thrust up through her beams with relentless vigour; when the port and starboard lights shifted and glowed like the eyes of so many fabulous dragons; when the midnight heat grew articulate

46

by reason of a deeply significant silence holding in it those reeking odours of wine, and those thoughts of the Godless god that was Bacchus; when the girls could not sleep on their virginal beds, and the youths could not sleep for their thoughts of virgins, and the men coming back to dry land from the sea with their hard-gotten cash, burned to spend it on women. . . . When all these things merged and were liquefied, producing a bitter-sweet and most heady potion, then the Café de la Tarasque seemed a pretty fine place to those who were leniently disposed towards themselves, and also towards human nature in general. And if tempers were short while knives could be long; and if Eusèbe took liberties with a virtuous wife who had gone to Heaven; and if Mère Mélanie gave to her Church rather less than she gave to her hump-backed violinist; if all this was the very deplorable truth—and alas, there is little room left for doubting—then it must be remembered that the town of Saint Loup was, and is, in a curve of the coast of Provence, so that those who would judge the south by the north might profitably ask good Saint Loup himself to develop their wisdom and understanding.

CHAPTER FIVE

I

Antoine Martel, Curé of Saint Loup, sat at his shabby mahogany desk with his pen in his hand, but his pen was idle. He should have been writing his weekly sermon, but instead he was staring across at the window through which he could glimpse an old orange tree which was now in full bloom in his little garden. The Curé Martel did not care much for trees, being, on the whole, indifferent to nature, and so while he stared across at the window, he perceived and yet did not perceive the blossoms.

The room was humble except for its books which covered the walls from floor to ceiling. Above a tubular iron stove hung a cheap crucifix, while upon the desk stood a garish statue of the Madonna. An arm-chair, well worn and sagging in the seat, together with one or two rush-bottom chairs completed the furnishing of the apartment.

The Curé was a man of fifty-nine, tall, untidy, and of an exceeding thinness. He possessed the slightly prominent eyes which so frequently characterize the religious. His mouth, which had once been handsome but weak, was austere from long years of physical repression, his teeth were discoloured and somewhat decayed and his chin appeared dirty because it was unshaven. For the rest, his hair was prematurely white and his high, massive brow was that of a scholar.

The Curé Martel had been born in Paris, and there he had lived during all his childhood, and there he had made his clerical studies. There also he had passed through the most vital days, the most poignant days of his budding manhood, when desiring to serve—first God, then the flesh, but finally God, he had thrust away all thoughts of a home and a wife and children. But as sometimes happens, an old

48

Battlefield upon which men have bled and striven and suffered will hold for them a certain romance, and so it was with the Curé and Paris; he could seldom remember the city without feeling regret for those days of his youthful warfare.

He would never have chosen to work for the Lord in a small seaport town on the coast of Provence; indeed, when he thought of the matter at all, he would find himself wondering how he had got there. Had it been his desire for solitude at a time when he was spiritually and physically exhausted? Or had some unknown ill-wisher in the Church contrived to get him sent into exile? Or had it been the purpose of Almighty God, which could only be seen as through a glass darkly? If the Curé found himself unable to decide, it was because he invariably left an important factor out of his reckoning; he forgot that he was above all else a student, and that those who dwell too much in the realms of thought are sometimes but poorly equipped for action. Thus, despite the more valiant days of his youth; his war with the flesh and his ultimate triumph; his brilliant career at the seminary; his good birth, and his then distinguished appearance, Mother Church—who had gained a sound knowledge of men in the bitter but useful school of disillusion—had quietly packed him off to Saint Loup, where he had now been for close on thirty years, and where he seemed likely enough to remain until he presented himself to Saint Peter.

A good man, a kind man in his own dusty way, he was yet never quite at ease with his flock—with those people who lived in perpetual sunshine. Nor was he quite at ease with their land, so ardently productive, so persistently pagan. The ample hills leaning back to the mountains; the valleys splashed with the live green of vineyards; the sweet yet virile smell of wild shrubs, which crept even into the town on spring evenings; the tideless but often treacherous sea of so vast and so incredible a blueness, these things would disturb him strangely at times, in spite of his habitual indifference to nature, so that he would feel a little afraid and more than a little homesick for Paris. And then there was the language. This was also disturbing, for it seemed to be one with the sun-drenched landscape. Like the scent of the maquis it was virile yet sweet, the old singing tongue of the

49 c

troubadour poets; having in its words many sounds of love, many sounds of desire, many sounds as of sighing, as of weeping, as of laughing—aye, and deep notes of war wherewith to contrast its persuasive sweetness. His stiff northern tongue could not compass this speech, and so it invariably made him uneasy. And then there was the primitive faith of the people, which to him appeared riddled with superstition; nay worse, it appeared to partake of those things which belonged to an age that was frankly unchristian. Bèu Diéu might apply to his God, it was true, but it equally might apply to Apollo; nor did he consider Nosto-Damo-d'Amour a suitable way of addressing the Virgin. Truth to tell, the Curé disliked the south, mistrusting its religion quite as much as its sunshine.

And yet the south was getting him under, for to those who are born and reared in the north, the south may become an insidious poison; moreover the Curé was predisposed to the virus by very reason of his nature. Thus year by year he was growing less vital and less wishful to take an active interest in events which transpired in the outer world, or indeed within his own limited parish.

It had not always been so with the Curé. When he had first arrived at Saint Loup he had had quite a crop of political opinions. The Royalist intrigue of Marshal Mac-Mahon had found in him an ardent supporter. And again, when in 1886 Boulanger spread his Chauvinistic doctrines, the Curé had preached Chauvinism from his pulpit—for this man was a fanatical patriot despite his retiring disposition. But try as he might, he had never succeeded in rousing the members of his little flock to more than a fleeting enthusiasm. Whatever the temper of adjacent coast-towns, the inhabitants of the town of Saint Loup seemed to lack the political disposition. They remained indifferent to governments so long as there was no undue taxation which affected their particular industries, the chief of which were vine growing and fishing. For they argued that the sun shone impartially on the just as on the unjust politician; that the vines grew ripe and gave forth their grapes, which in turn found their profitable way to the presses; that the wine was good, cheap, and near at hand, and that so, for the matter of that, were the fishes; and that since everybody was well content, governmental disputes were none of their business. Thus, reluctantly—very reluctantly at first—the Curé had abandoned political opinions, for what was the good of provocative speech when nobody troubled to contradict you? As time went on he lived only for his books, caring less and less about his personal appearance, allowing his once strong teeth to decay rather than exert himself to go to the dentist; spilling his onion soup down his soutane and not always troubling to wash off the stains, any more than he troubled to shave every morning; while his mind, except when focused on the page of some obscure but erudite volume, sank into a sun-doped lethargy from which nothing seemed significant enough to wake it.

Yet now, on this Saturday afternoon when the Curé sat staring out of the window, his mind was actually very wide awake, for his thoughts were engrossed by a human affection. Every Sunday, in the parish church before Vespers, the Curé must give religious instruction to the children who attended the secular school, where most things were taught except religion. It was while he had been taking this particular class that he had first noticed Jan and Christophe —two neat little boys of six years old, very shiny and clean because it was Sunday. The Curé had baptized them both, it is true, but then he baptized so many babies in the fruitful town of Saint-Loup-sur-mer that he quite lost count once they ceased to be infants. But for some strange reason he had looked at these boys intently, with a sudden awakening of interest. That evening he had found himself thinking about them, and smiling a little as he remembered Christophe's eager and over-sanguine reply to a question regarding the Day of Judgment: 'And what will our Lord say to sinners,' he had asked him, 'to those sinful and very unhappy creatures who are weeping outside the gates of Heaven?' 'Come unto Me,' Christophe had answered. But his friend had looked both shamed and aghast: 'That is wrong—that is terribly wrong!' he had whispered. So the Curé had given Jan a book which explained to the young the Christian religion; and another book he had given to Christophe, which explained to the young the beliefs of the Church concerning the wicked and Life Everlasting; after which he had asked the children their names, and had written them neatly on each paper cover. This had happened more than a year ago, so that now his pupils were over seven.

Jóusè and Marie were humble people; very grateful and flattered when they found that the Curé was showing an interest in their elder son, and had even put himself to the trouble of enquiring whether le tout petit Loup might accompany his brother to the Sunday classes. Le tout petit Loup was still rather fragile and was not at all well disposed towards religion, being fretful or impish when saying his prayers, and this despite his illustrious patron. However, he was now made to wash his small hands, and to clean his small nails—which were shockingly bitten—and to blow his small nose with a decent care, and to walk without trying to hop like a frog as he went to the church with Christophe on Sundays. For Marie would have her sons well-grounded in their faith—in such matters she could be conscientious to sternness.

The Curé did not much like le tout petit Loup who fidgeted and shuffled his feet without ceasing, and who made himself sticky with the sucre de pomme which was always slyly concealed on his person. Moreover, if le tout petit Loup looked annoyed, as he frequently did when the Curé asked him questions, Christophe had a habit of producing toys—little figures of beasts and birds carved by Anfos; and unless the subject should chance to be the ark, these toys would be quite out of place in the lesson. However, they would cheer up le tout petit Loup, and when Christophe was remonstrated with by the Curé, he would always reply in much the same vein: 'I have brought them in order to stop him crying.' So the Curé must make the best of the thing by reminding his pupils of the Creation. But once he had said: 'And God created great whales,' which had so much excited le tout petit Loup that instead of allowing the matter to drop he had promptly demanded to be told all about them. No, the Curé did not like this wisp of a creature whom he had baptized in the middle of the night lest his soul should decide to set out for limbo.

It was Jan who had quickly become his favourite, and for whom he now felt that deep human affection—the rather pathetic affection of a man who must love a child, himself being childless. And although he took an interest in Christophe, perhaps because it was hard to divide them—for these cousins were very seldom apart—it was Jan who had stirred an old fire of ambition which the Curé had fancied must long be extinguished; only now this ambition was centred in Jan, who his mother had decided should enter the priesthood.

Oh, but she was hard to endure, Madame Roustan, for ever tormenting the Curé with her questions, for ever wanting to know this or that in regard to the clerical education; for ever pumping the unhappy man about his influential relations.

'Madame, I see none of them'; he might say, 'I assure you they have quite forgotten my existence.'

But Madame Roustan, who learnt many things, had learnt among others that his cousin was a bishop, and could thus be extremely useful to Jan when he, in his turn, should become a Curé, so that now she haunted the presbytery on the slenderest pretext in and out of season. Moreover, she was one of those penitents who enjoyed a long and detailed confession, keeping the Curé shut up in his box with his ear to the grille while her most deadly sins would boil down to gossip or over-eating—even Goundran had ceased to provide a relief, for now she had given up all hope of mating. The Curé had tried many grades of penance, from five Our Fathers and five Hail Marys to the rosary, told from first to last bead, three times in front of Saint Loup's privileged altar. But neither bruised knees, nor the privileged altar, nor the sorely tried saint who must stand above it, seemed able to damp Madame Roustan's desire to talk over herself when she went to confession, more especially these days when, thanks to her son, she felt that she had every right to attention.

The Curé had never suffered bores gladly, indeed even after the years at Saint Loup had sucked the vitality out of his spirit, he still preferred a good honest sinner; for although such an one might slide down into Hell, he might, given a helpful push, slip into Heaven. Yet Madame Roustan he tolerated with a patience which sprang from that great affection which he had conceived for this woman's son, and from his hopes of the boy's brilliant future. For young though Jan was, and over-impetuous—being a child of a proud and high temper—he already seemed greatly drawn to the Church, and would speak of the time when he should enter the priesthood as though his career were a foregone conclusion.

'When I shall become a priest . . .' he would say; and then he would start to talk of the heathen, and of how he would go in a ship like Saint Paul and perhaps get shipwrecked, or thrown into gaol; for he read very well considering his age and Saint Paul had stirred his imagination. The Curé was no fool, and he realized that the Saint had but ousted Robinson Crusoe, and that all this fine talk about shipwrecks and gaols sprang in part from a youthful desire for adventure. Yet he thought that he discerned, deep down in this child, that subtle but unmistakable urge which compels certain men to serve only the Spirit. The Curé was pondering these things now, at a time when he should have been writing his sermon.

Presently he started to compare Jan with Christophe—in nearly every respect they seemed to differ. Jan was dark and wiry, having aquiline features, black eyes, and quick, rather impulsive movements. Christophe was a red-haired little boy who moved with a certain deliberation, and whose features might one day grow to be rugged. There was nothing remarkable about him save his eyes—the pale eyes that were set so far apart that his father had laughed when he was a baby. But now there were times when the expression of those eyes would suddenly rivet the Curé's attention; for into them there would creep a great wisdom, together with a great and most comprehending kindness. The Curé would feel a little nonplussed at seeing so strange a thing in a boy who appeared to be much as were other children. For despite his rather deliberate movements, his queer eyes, and a slow and thoughtful way which he not infrequently had of speaking, Christophe was by no means an exemplary child, indeed he was more in than out of mischief. He and Jan made a practice of combining forces, as, for instance, when they vivisected the watch left to Jóusè by his maternal grandfather; and again, when, having learnt of the existence of snow, they ripped open Marie's best feather pillows. And the worst of it was that le tout petit Loup must insist upon trying to emulate them, which would always end in

54

much the same manner—le tout petit Loup would have a pain in his stomach; for whenever he got excited or tired, he invariably suffered from indigestion.

The Curé's thoughts continued to run on, now amused and now tinged with an inevitable sadness, for this very faith which he centred in Jan did but show him more clearly his own complete failure. All that this boy would become he might have been had he only chosen the path of the fighter. As a priest he had made scarcely any impression, as a student he was almost equally useless for his wisdom was sterile; he could not create and thus pass on the bright torch of knowledge. If he died not a soul in his parish would mourn him except perhaps the ambitious Madame Roustan, for Jan was as yet very young to feel grief for an ageing man who had been his teacher. His depression deepened; it became like a mist that was blurring his mental and spiritual vision, and he dreaded these moods of despondency which of late had begun to obsess him so often; for these moods were always allied with fear—the fear of one day becoming too lonely.

Then—and who can explain the workings of the mind, or fathom the depths from which thoughts assail us?—he suddenly remembered Christophe's eyes in which there was so much wisdom and kindness.

'Why am I thinking about Christophe's eyes? I am growing childish,' he told himself sternly.

But now he seemed unable to avoid those eyes: wherever he looked he fancied that he saw them, and when he covered his face with his hands they were there, still seen by some inward vision. He got up and began to pace the room, for he felt an irresistible restlessness which was less of the body than of the spirit. Pausing in front of his crucifix he stared at the clumsily moulded Christ—so grotesque, so lacking in dignity, a machine-made thing devoid of all feeling. And because he perceived its unworthiness, he was filled with a sense of deep shame and pity.

Then he spoke to his Lord: 'Once they fashioned You gently from the wood upon which You purchased our salvation; very gravely and gently they worked with their hands, lest they err in depicting Your sacred body; or they carved You from flawless ivory; or they moulded You out of the purest gold, which to them seemed too base and impure a metal. But this is a callous and idle age in which I have surely been the most callous. And idle I have been, sitting down in the sun, neglecting Your work and forgetting Your mission, content to consider myself a wise man because of my books, whereas I know nothing. But listen; I may yet come to serve You well by helping another to go forth and serve You. In him You shall find all that You have missed in me, Your unfaithful priest and servant. He is young, very young, but already he is brave, and of him I will make a courageous Christian. and his name is . . . his name is . . .' He suddenly faltered, pressing his hand to his aching forehead in bewilderment, for he could not speak the name. 'Lord, I am grown very stupid,' he muttered.

CHAPTER SIX

1

SAINT LOUP with its inexhaustible sunshine, its port, its wooded hills, and its beach with the safe and very excellent bathing, was a happy and pleasant place for children. Their school over, Christophe and Jan would set forth side by side on a voyage of discovery, since now that they possessed strong and active legs they were finding the world a constant adventure.

And true it was that those sun-warmed hillsides teemed with a host of exciting creatures, for there the large ants filed into their castles, or marched out upon gravely contrived expeditions; and there the lizards streaked through the rocks; and there the slow-moving, knightly beetles displayed the bronze and green of their armour. But there also, the couleuvres—those innocuous snakes which are yet of such disconcerting proportions—were for ever giving themselves away by their rustlings and wrigglings and lengthy uncoilings; or, worse still, by heaving across the paths—the couleuvres are most unintelligent reptiles.

Despite their deep and enduring affection, the cousins would not infrequently quarrel, for Jan always wanted to take the lead and when opposed he would lose his temper; but their bitterest source of disagreement, at this time, undoubtedly lay in the couleuvres. Jan possessed a boy's hot instinct to kill, that primitive and incomprehensible instinct which occasionally springs from a great joy of living, he was always hitting at the snakes with a stick, and as often as not he would leave them sore stricken. But Christophe would try to snatch the stick from him, for he could not endure to see dumb creatures suffer; then a struggle would ensue, perhaps even a fight, both the children being extremely tenacious.

Yet Christophe would sometimes try to reason with

Jan: 'They have never harmed us—why must you torment them?'

Jan would usually answer in much the same words: 'All serpents are wicked and belong to the devil. A serpent tempted Adam and Eve; the Curé has taught us that from the Bible.'

So Christophe must tell his cousin about pain, which he seemed to divine as by intuition, while Jan listened without understanding his words, unable as yet to envisage suffering. But one evening as Jan struck hard at a couleuvre which his sharp young ears had detected in a thicket, Christophe suddenly flinched and sprang away:

'Stop, stop!' he screamed, 'You are hurting my shoulders. . . .'

Jan ran to him: 'How have I hurt you—but how? You know very well that I have not touched you! Christophe, tell me quickly what I have done? I would never, never hit you with a stick . . .' and he looked as though he were going to cry, 'tell me how I have hurt you, Christophe,' he pleaded.

Very slowly Christophe pulled off his jersey, and there on his back was a long, red weal. Jan stared at it, terrified and amazed—then, even while he stood staring, it faded. The rest of that walk was very silent; indeed there was little enough to say, since the thing transcended their comprehension; but Jan kept a tight hold of Christophe's hand, as though suddenly fearful that he might lose him. Thus they passed through the thicket and out beyond, their eyes puzzled, their hearts full of an undefined dread, their childish faces pale in the twilight. Yet when they at last returned to their homes, neither of the boys spoke of what had occurred—for some inexplicable reason they were silent.

After this Jan left the couleuvres in peace, turning firmly aside from the frequent temptation of their innocent but foolhardy coils, though he still remained secretly of the opinion that the couleuvres, like all the rest of their kind, were sinful, being closely allied to Satan.

2

Le tout petit Loup was growing more and more aggressive, making up by the surprising strength of his will for what he lacked of strength in his body. He was now never willing to be left out of things, but must always be taken upon every excursion. Thus if Christophe and Jan went down to the beach and paddled, as they did on half holidays, le tout petit Loup would also paddle although he was forbidden to go near the water. If they went to the port to meet certain school-friends who had recently made up their minds to be pirates, le tout petit Loup would join in the mêlée and would usually get himself hurt in the process. If they went for a walk on the neighbouring hills, le tout petit Loup must make one of the party although he would quickly begin to wilt, and would end by getting a pain in his stomach.

'I have a hot ache in my middle,' he would say; then as likely as not would squat down in the dust if nothing more propitious chanced to be handy.

Jan would grumble: 'It all comes of your being such a baby. You spoil everything, why cannot you stay with your mother?'

But at this le tout petit Loup would grow enraged: 'I am nearly as old as you are,' he would splutter, 'and moreover it is only that I *hate* this walk which is stupid—that is why I have an ache in my middle.' After which he might suddenly burst into tears, half of anger but certainly half of exhaustion.

Then Christophe would heave a large, tolerant sigh, for although he and Loup had nothing in common he was usually patient with this ailing brother: 'If you will now try to walk on and stop crying, you shall have a fine present,' he might start to bribe, 'perhaps even my wooden bear made by Anfos.'

But one day le tout petit Loup replied promptly: 'I will cry and will have your wooden bear also.' For he had the acquisitive instinct of the weak, who in sheer self-defence must take all and give nothing.

Christophe laughed: 'Very well, but then you must cry a long time—you must cry until we get home!'

Whereupon le tout petit Loup ceased to cry: 'I will nevertheless have your bear,' he mumbled.

Dear God, but he was a contrary child with his face and his eyes of a sick marmoset, with his rickety limbs and his stubborn temper. His scant brown hair stuck out in a wisp for the reason that it could not be properly trimmed, so loudly would he yell at the touch of the scissors; while his clothes always looked disturbingly loose, so thin was the body that he had to put in them. Marie spoilt him because he still remained fragile, because as an infant she had so nearly lost him, and because she had named him after Saint Loup. None of which were entirely adequate reasons for condoning her younger son's endless whims, but then as she sometimes remarked to her husband: 'You are only his father, whereas I am his mother.' And since there was no gainsaying this fact, Jóusè must shake his large head and fall silent. He and Anfos would stolidly go on with their work while le tout petit Loup stamped and howled in fury because he was forbidden to play with the saw or indulge in some equally dangerous pastime. And each might be thinking as he bent to his task: 'I have Christophe, therefore what does anything matter?' At least this might very well be Jóusè's thought—poor Anfos could not always think quite so clearly.

And yet despite his innumerable faults, le tout petit Loup was rather pathetic, so hard did he strive after physical strength, so much did he wish to be strong like his brother. And his will to battle a weak way through life, his instinctive fear of getting pushed under, would suddenly impress Christophe's youthful mind so that he had moments of real understanding. When this happened he would play with le tout petit Loup, being careful to allow him to do all the winning, being careful to appear very greatly annoyed at le tout petit Loup's repeated triumphs. And sometimes this succeeded but sometimes it did not, for le tout petit Loup had the brain of a gimlet, and if he suspected the subterfuge he would cry and work himself into a fever. Then Marie might turn to her elder son and start rebuking him almost sharply; but he would not resent it, because on the whole he was little given to feeling resentment, and because when he looked at her anxious face there would come one of those moments of understanding.

3

Next to Jan, Christophe loved Mirèio, the bitch, who followed him about like a gaunt, limping shadow. She was ageing, and now at the times of great heat she would get many sores on her poor troubled body, and no one at-tempted to cure these sores, which greatly distressed and bewildered Christophe. He would watch her with an anxious and pitiful concern as she turned her head stiffly, trying to lick them; and then he would touch his father's arm:

'Look, she is very unhappy,' he would say, and would wait for some reassuring answer.

Jóusè might wipe the sweat from his brow and grunt, because his own back was aching: 'Do not worry me now—run away, little son. I must hurry myself and finish this cupboard.' For although a good man and kind on the whole, he had two young children dependent upon him and money was not always easy to come by—there was certainly none to spare for Mirèio.

Then Christophe would wander across to Anfos:

'Look,' he would say, 'she is very unhappy.'

But Anfos might not even glance at the bitch, for what could he do who himself was half child? 'I will make you a horse upon wheels,' he had promised one morning, by way of consolation.

Finally Christophe would seek out his mother where she bent above her stove in the kitchen: 'Mirèio is very un-happy,' he would say, 'she has places that bleed all over her skin. Cannot you give me some ointment for her, the sort that you put on my knees when I scrape them?'

But Marie would sigh and would shake her head: 'Enfantounet, the chemist has still to be paid. Poor Mirèio, ai! las, is no longer young, and when we are old we must frequently suffer.' And then she would go on stirring the soup, or whatever it was that she chanced to be making.

At last Christophe spoke to the Curé one Sunday after the usual religious instruction: 'Mon père, our Mirèio is grow-ing old and so she has many sores on her body—she tries hard to lick them but her tongue seems too short. I would like you to tell me, please, how I can heal them.'

The Curé nodded: 'Most dogs in these parts get sores on their bodies sooner or later, the poor beasts . . . I fear there is nothing to be done. Here is your book, and I hope by next Sunday that you will have learnt your catechism.'

But Christophe persisted: 'I think she feels pain. Sometimes I can hear her crying all night, and I do not like to hear Mirèio crying.'

'Yet she probably suffers much less than you think, animals cannot feel pain as we do.' And the Curé started to turn away, for by now his spiritual restlessness was passing. He had asked that Anfos should carve him a Christ in fine wood to be nailed to an ebony cross, and when this was completed it would hang in his study, a more worthy presentment no doubt than the last—but the Curé's spiritual restlessness was passing.

Christophe eyed him very gravely for a moment, and when next he spoke his words puzzled his teacher: 'I know there is something I could do with my hands that would help her . . . It is something I could do with my hands . . . only . . . I cannot think the thought.'

'What thought?' the Curé enquired, looking round.

But now it was Christophe's turn to be puzzled: 'That I cannot tell you . . .' he answered dully.

When they had finally left the church, Jan frowned at his cousin and started to reproach him: 'You ought not to have troubled Monsieur le Curé with those stupid questions about Mirèio. He will think you an imbecile if you continue to make all this fuss about an old dog which when it is dead cannot go to heaven. And what did you mean about your hands? It sounded so silly. . . .'

Christophe said nothing.

CHAPTER SEVEN

I

DURING that summer two events occurred which made a deep impression upon Christophe—he became a more intimate friend of the sea, and he went to visit Goundran's landlady.

Goundran was very proud of his godson and would have him a skilful and fearless swimmer, so one glorious day he towed him well out of his depth while Christophe hung on to a life-buoy.

Then: 'Let go, my fine fish and begin to swim!'

And Christophe, nothing daunted, kicked about with his legs and paddled with his hands as though he were a puppy. After this Goundran gave him a lesson most evenings, unless he should happen to be away fishing.

Perhaps few things are more satisfying than a child's first experience of conquering the water—although conquering is not quite the right word, for once understood and thus no longer feared, the water can be uncommonly friendly, as indeed the sea was to its new disciple. There it lay in the sunshine, so smiling and so gentle that the fishermen all but forgot the mistral, and so buoyant that Christophe bobbed about like a cork and had some ado to keep his head down for a moment, and this though he very soon wished to imitate Goundran and swim under water. For Christophe was one of those fortunate people whom the sea adopts at their first real contact, and now he could think about little else, and must always be urging Jan to prove for himself how extremely simple a thing was swimming:

'You have only to move your arms and legs, et voilà, it is done! Come in deeper and try. If you learn we can then swim together,' he kept urging.

But Jan, who was quite a courageous child upon land,

had not been adopted by the sea, and this being so he instinctively feared it. Sulky, because at a disadvantage, he would paddle while Christophe swam near-by to tease him; and, it must be admitted, while Christophe showed off with a very great deal of splashing and spluttering:

'Jan, look—this is how one swims on one's back!' Or: 'Now I will show how I do the crawl!' And then he would proceed to lash with his toes and to claw with his hands which, although it looked fine, would not get him very much nearer to Goundran.

Then Goundran would laugh: 'Too much fuss, too much noise. You are almost as bad as a motor-engine!'

So Christophe would subside into less flashy breast strokes, and would thereby succeed in making fair progress.

'Is it you,' he shouted to Jan one evening, 'is it you who talk of going in a boat like Saint Paul? Póu! What would happen if the boat turned over?' For he sometimes grew rather tired of hearing about all the fine things that his cousin would achieve when he should set forth to convert the heathen.

Jan hesitated, then he shouted back crossly: 'Having faith, I would naturally walk on the water!'

'So you think yourself finer than Saint Peter!' mocked Christophe, turning a couple of somersaults.

'It might well be safer to swim,' smiled Goundran.

But Jan would not be persuaded, and so in the end they left him alone to his sulks and his paddling; for dearly as Christophe loved his friend, he had now conceived a great love for the sea and must always be courting this splendid new friendship which Jan was too stubborn and too fearful to share, so that all he could do was to sulk and grow jealous.

2

One night Goundran took Christophe out fishing with him, but this was not at all a success, for Christophe began to pity the fishes as they knocked off their scales with their gasping and plunging, so Goundran must stun as many as he could by beating their heads on the side of his boot—a proceeding which did not bring much consolation.

Goundran grumbled: 'Do not be so foolish, little godson —they feel nothing at all for they are cold-blooded. Segnour Diéu, one would think you were Saint Anthony who, when he by accident caught a fish must immediately throw it back into the water! It is well to be seen that he was a saint and so was not forced to gain his own living!' For Goundran rather pitied the creatures himself, which made him feel irritable with Christophe.

The lad who helped Goundran to sail his boat was a clumsy fellow who had no imagination. He trod hard upon one unfortunate victim, slipped and trod on several more in the slipping; then he cursed and kicked them out of the way.

'Imbecile! Do not bruise their flesh! shouted Goundran.

Christophe watched the proceedings in miserable silence, and observing the anxious look on his face, Goundran paused in his labours and tried to cheer him:

'Listen, enfantounet, what about Jesus who caused the miraculous draught of fishes?' For the child was obviously very near tears.

'I do not believe that He did it,' said Christophe.

Now Goundran, as an earnest parent-in-God, should by rights have rebuked this doubting of the Scriptures, but something in Christophe's bewildered eyes made him sorry for the boy, and so he was silent.

He thought: 'He is only as yet very small . . . I am certain our Lord will not feel offended.' Then he thumped a whiting very hard on the boards in a crude but well-meant endeavour to stun it.

No, assuredly the fishing was not a success, and Goundran regretted having brought his godson.

* * *

The next day Christophe could not eat his bouillabaisse, although Marie had prepared it with unusual care because he and his father so particularly liked it.

'Are you not well, paure pichounet?' she enquired of her elder son anxiously. 'It is strange to see you refuse your dinner—I think I had better give you a purge, for doubtless you felt a little bit sea-sick when Goundran insisted on taking you fishing.'

E

Christophe said nothing, and that night he drank his purge, preferring to swallow the noxious potion rather than to tell the real cause of his trouble, for he felt very doubtful of his mother's understanding. And after a while the trouble passed away, so that he could once more enjoy bouillabaisse, since at seven years old but few troubles are lasting. But he never went fishing with Goundran again, nor did Goundran attempt to urge him to do so.

3

Mathilde who, if rumour had been correct, must long ago have gone to her grave, was actually in her ninetieth year when she asked abruptly one day to see Christophe.

'Bring me the Bénédit's elder son,' she demanded, 'I would know him before I die—and do not be too long about it, either.'

Goundran glanced at Elise who was soon to be twenty, and in whose good judgment he placed much reliance: 'But why does she want to know Christophe?' he whispered, 'She has never until now shown the slightest interest. . . .'

Elise shook her head: 'It seems to me strange—yet I do not think that we ought to oppose her.'

And Goundran agreed, for although it did seem strange, he greatly respected his landlady's wisdom.

Wise she most certainly was, the old Mathilde; she could often divine the secrets of the weather, so that many a sailor-man asked her advice, especially those who sailed in the tartanes. Then again, she undoubtedly possessed second sight and could sometimes see clearly into the future, discerning many things which would make her feel sad, and others which would make her feel very happy. And although Madame Roustan thought her a witch—a belief which was shared by quite a few people—there were those who declared her to be a saint, testifying that Mathilde had the gift of healing. Goundran thought her neither a witch nor a saint, but merely a wise and kindly old woman.

Many years ago she had come to Saint Loup as a bride from her village in Normandy, where, of course, there are many miraculous shrines, and where people have even been known to see fairies. In those days she had been full-bosomed and tall, a fine girl, although no one was left to remember—for Mathilde by living so unconscionably long, had survived all the friends of her own generation. Her husband, a saddler, had been dead for years; while her only brother who had made a late marriage—becoming the father of but one child, Elise—had lost his wife and had then died also. Thus there was no one left to recall just how Mathilde had looked at her wedding, or how she had looked when she had come to Saint Loup as the youthful bride of a prosperous saddler.

For some reason she had never returned to the North, and when Goundran had asked her about this one morning: 'Tante Mathilde, tell me why you have stayed on here.'

Mathilde had replied: 'Because I am waiting.'

And when he had persisted: 'But for what do you wait?' Mathilde, as was sometimes her way, had not answered.

Well, and so now she wished to know Christophe, and Elise did not think it wise to oppose her; nor could Goundran see any reason to refuse:

'I will certainly bring the boy to you,' he promised.

4

Three days later Christophe stood holding Goundran's hand and staring wide-eyed at the oldest person that he had yet seen in his short existence—a person who appeared so incredibly ancient that he thought she must be the statue of Saint Loup come to life, and he suddenly felt rather frightened. For the statue of Saint Loup, which still stands in the church and is carved out of wood, has time-blurred features, so that it really does resemble Mathilde as she looked when she was well over eighty, since all that is old has a strange resemblance.

Mathilde was sitting in a small wheel-chair, for her limbs had become intolerably feeble; while her eyes were even less bright than the saint's, being heavily filmed by approaching blindness. Her olive skin, grown darker with age, had mellowed as had the venerable oak which Jóusè collected and set such great store by; like it, too, her face was very much worn, having many deep ruts and undulations. But even as oak remains polished and clean—a symbol of courageous and seemly endurance—so the old Mathilde remained polished and clean, especially about the region of the cheek bones, and her peasant cap was whiter than snow, as was also her neat little muslin apron. Nor was her parlour any less spotless, for Elise had become an excellent house-wife, and being deeply attached to her aunt she worked all the harder because of those eyes that were heavily filmed by approaching blindness.

'It is what tante Mathilde can no longer see that I strive to make shine,' she had once told Goundran.

And now Goundran said, pushing Christophe forward: 'Here is the Bénédit's elder son; I have brought him to you, ma tante, as I promised.'

Mathilde turned herself in the child's direction: 'Come to me, little Christophe,' she called very gently.

But her voice sounded muted and far away as is sometimes the case with the voices of old people. And because it fell strangely upon his ears, which being so youthful were unaccustomed, Christophe looked round in search of Goundran, for now once again he was feeling rather frightened.

Then Mathilde held out a thin, questioning hand: 'Where are you, Christophe? I am nearly blind, so unless you will come I shall never find you.'

He answered: 'I am coming'; and he went to her side, forgetting his fear through compassion for her blindness.

She peered into his face, then she touched his cropped head, and her hand felt cold as though it were lifeless: 'Very little you are . . . very little and young to begin such a journey as yours,' she murmured. 'But when you are come to the end of the journey remember me, Christophe Bénédit. . . .'

He gazed at her not understanding her words, and being too shy to answer, he nodded.

When she stopped speaking the room grew very still; neither Elise nor Goundran moved—for some reason they were loath to break that stillness. Once only did Goundran glance across at the girl with a slightly anxious look of enquiry. Then an unexpected and disturbing thing hap-pened; two large tears welled up in Mathilde's dim eyes and, overflowing, splashed on to her apron.

Seeing this, Elise went quickly to her chair: 'Why are you weeping?' she asked her kindly.

And Goundran called Christophe: 'Enfantounet, come here!' For he thought that their visit had proved too tiring. 'She is old, very old,' he explained in a low voice, 'and sometimes the old may resemble young children, so that they cry when they are fatigued. Now stand still for a little until she is rested.'

But Mathilde said slowly: 'I am weeping for joy . . . there is so little difference between joy and sorrow; like everything else they are intertwined . . . the bright light that brings with it the deepest shadow . . . there is so little difference, yet I cannot explain. . . .'

'Do not worry yourself any more,' Goundran soothed her, 'And now I think that Elise shall fetch wine and cakes, for I seem to remember that Christophe is as fond of sweet things as his greedy godfather!'

So Elise went and fetched two dishes of cakes—pink and white heart-shaped cakes of her own special baking. And a bottle of wine she set upon the table, then proceeded to pour out the wine for Goundran; and when she had done this she handed him the glass together with a small, pink, sugary heart—very beautifully iced, very skilfully fashioned.

'Let us drink to our Christophe here,' he said smiling. 'I drank to him at his baptismal feast—yes, I drank to his becoming a fisherman—and now he would like me to throw back all my fishes. Is that not so, little foolish one? Perhaps you believe that the fishes are Christians!'

But Christophe was feeling pleasantly hungry, and the pink and white hearts were very alluring, so that while he had not forgotten the fishes he was frankly engrossed by the needs of his stomach. He helped himself to a cake, then a second, then a third, for they seemed to melt in his mouth and be no more there when he wanted to taste them; and because the icing was both sticky and soft he quite unashamedly licked his fingers. Presently Elise made him sit on her lap where he felt very restless and rather embarrassed, for she would keep breathing against his neck, and her breath was not only hot but it tickled. However, he endured it patiently, for he was a patient child by nature. Then Elise began dodging first this way then that as she tried to see

Goundran over his shoulder, and once she pressed his head down on her breast in order to get it out of the way. . . .

'If only she would let me stand up!' thought Christophe.

Yet he liked Elise who was friendly and young, and whose cheeks were as pink and white as the hearts of which by now he had eaten a great many. She had hair so blonde that it reminded him of moonlight, and small even teeth which he thought very pretty, and whenever she spoke to Goundran she smiled—although perched on her knee Christophe could not see this—and whenever Goundran spoke to her she blushed, and her arm would suddenly tighten round Christophe.

He was speaking to her now: 'It is pleasant to see you with a child on your lap; but, my little Elise, it is time that you had a son of your own, it is time that we found you a suitable husband. Indeed I have just the right fellow in my mind—a captain he is, although still quite young—he comes from Marseille and his name is Bertrand. In any case I shall bring him along so that you and your aunt may look him over. At your wedding I, of course, will be the best man; and if I am lucky and catch many fish I will surely provide you with excellent wine. Ah, yes, it is time that we thought of your wedding.' For Goundran was a lover and lord of the sea, and appeared to be little attracted by women.

Elise allowed Christophe to stand up at last; then she sighed as she looked at the heart-shaped cakes which she had so skilfully fashioned that morning. And Christophe was puzzled when he heard her deep sigh, wondering if Elise were still feeling hungry, for at times he was very much a child, quite untroubled by flashes of understanding.

He said politely: 'Will you eat another cake?' and he passed her the plate feeling suddenly hopeful. Nor was he to be disappointed in his hope, for although Elise shook her head rather sadly, she urged him to finish the rest of the hearts, which he did to the great amusement of Goundran.

'You will surely be terribly sick,' Goundran warned him, 'but what matter? Elise's sweetmeats are well worth it.' Then he turned to the girl with his innocent smile: 'You become a most excellent cook,' he told her.

Away in her corner the old Mathilde slept, and her head now drooped limply on to her bosom: 'La pauvre,' sighed

Elise, 'she grows terribly old, that is why she wept as she did over Christophe; her mind wanders at times, it was doubtless that—or perhaps she feels sad when a child is near, because she herself never had any children.'

*   *   *

On the way home Christophe gravely remarked: 'When I have come to the end of my journey I am going to think hard about tante Mathilde, and this I shall do because it will please her, and because she so much resembles Saint Loup in our church—except that she wears a cap instead of a pointed hat on her head . . .' Then he suddenly caught hold of Goundran's sleeve: 'But what did she mean about a journey?'

Goundran looked vague: 'Who knows? Who can say? She is nearly ninety and at her age one dreams, which I do not doubt is God's merciful kindness.'

CHAPTER EIGHT

I

IF Mathilde had expressed an unexpected desire to know the Bénédit's elder son, something happened during the autumn which was, in a way, quite as unexpected—Eusèbe, of all people, made friendly advances not only to Christophe but to his brother.

Hitherto, if a child had peered into his workshop, fascinated by the large, tempting strips of leather, Eusèbe had looked up with a furious eye: 'Sarnipabiéune! Be off!' he had shouted, and other very inhospitable things; from which it had been gathered that he did not like children.

Yet when Christophe and Loup had stood gaping one morning, yes, and actually fingering his precious leather, Eusèbe had wagged his head at them and grinned: 'Eh bien? Why not come right inside and look closer?' Nothing loath, they had taken him at his word, and when next they had visited the shop Jan had joined them.

Joúsè thought that the welcome accorded his offspring was a trap very skilfully laid to catch Jan, and this in order to anger his mother. For now more than ever did Madame Roustan disapprove of the unregenerate Eusèbe, and now more than ever did Eusèbe despise and detest the self-righteous Madame Roustan—indeed, he could never open his mouth in her presence these days without trying to shock her.

Joúsè confided his suspicion to his wife: 'Hóu, the old fox, he is certainly crafty! Where our Christophe goes there his cousin will go, and Germaine is consuming herself with fury. "Is it proper," she comes here and says to me, "is it proper that my son who will be a priest should associate with that spawn of the devil?" And I answer: "Mais oui, it is excellent practice; what are priests for but to combat the devil?" Then she grows still more angry, and accuses us of

72

neglecting the spiritual welfare of our children. Ehèi, I permit her to say many things, for a man cannot quarrel with his own flesh and blood, and in any case what does her foolishness matter?'

But Marie was not quite so easy in her mind, for she also had been visited by Madame Roustan: 'It must be admitted,' she said doubtfully, 'that Eusèbe is more often drunk than sober—I would rather that our sons kept out of his shop. . . .'

'Yet I do not think he will harm them,' smiled Jóusè.

However, it soon became only too apparent that whether Eusèbe would harm them or not, he possessed an irresistible fascination, especially for le tout petit Loup to whom he presented odds and ends of hide, rusty buckles, boot buttons, and similar rubbish. In vain did Marie try to persuade her sons that Eusèbe was both hideous and dirty; in vain did Madame Roustan protest that unless Jan kept away from the man, she would feel it her duty to speak to the Curé. It was all of not the slightest avail, so great was Eusèbe's charm for the children. And the most disconcerting part of it was this: Eusèbe now developed an imagination, evolving all sorts of amusing schemes wherewith to add glamour to the children's visits. Thus one fine and salubrious autumn evening, he tempted the three of them away from the beach—although Christophe had fully intended to bathe—by describing the grapes in his dead wife's vineyards.

'Let us go and have a look,' he remarked craftily, 'and when we have looked long enough we might eat them!'

So off they all went with never so much as a word to Marie or Madame Roustan; le tout petit Loup stepping out like a man and not once complaining of pain in his stomach, while Jan and Christophe skipped about like young goats or ran races in order to feel the more hungry.

The vineyards were a sight to rejoice sore eyes—at least this was true of Eusèbe's vineyards, for his vines were so heavily fructified that they bowed themselves down to the earth with their burden. In and out of the narrow green paths the four wandered, while Eusèbe told the story of Bacchus who had loved such clusters of opulent fruit, and had taken them under his special protection.

'There were ladies who brought him his wine,' said Eusèbe; 'they were not at all like the ladies we know—

73

although many of these are certainly pretty—but the ladies who brought Bacchus his marvellous wine were called nymphs because they were more than human; and so beautiful they were that people went blind if by accident they should happen to see them. Yes, nymphs they were called, and they much liked sweet things, so that those who were wise always left them honey.'

'But where did they leave it?' demanded Loup, who in spite of his weak digestion was greedy.

'Sometimes under the vines, sometimes under a tree—or perhaps they would set it upon a flat rock and then turn their backs quickly,' Eusèbe told him.

Then he went on to say that a long time ago many gods had been served in the land of Provence, and that even yet one might find a few stones which had once formed a part of some vast white temple; and that in the town of his birth, which was Arles, there were ruins to remind one of the great pagan builders—an arena so large that its generous girth could encompass twenty-six thousand people. And he muttered, as though he were thinking aloud: 'Those were surely magnificent days to live in!'

The children listened wide-eyed and enthralled; and after awhile he cut bunches of grapes, being careful to select only such as were sweet—for not all the wine-grapes are sweet when eaten. And these they carried up to a farm which they learned belonged to Eusèbe also; and the farmer's wife brought them milk and rough bread—the honest rough bread that is baked by the peasants. Then they feasted while Eusèbe drank two tumblers of wine, but no more, since he wished to arrive home sober.

Naturally Marie was extremely anxious and naturally Madame Roustan was angry, for the new moon had risen above the hills before the children returned to their parents. Nor were matters improved by le tout petit Loup who announced at supper as he sipped his vin coupé, that both he and his name had been changed by the nymphs, so that now he was no longer Loup but Bacchus.

2

This story of Bacchus and his honey-loving nymphs was only the beginning of many other stories which, although they were less educational perhaps, were quite frequently very much more exciting. Eusèbe knew a host of Provençal legends, most of which the children would find hair-raising —especially when they were told at dusk in the dim little shop with its arched stone ceiling. Squatting on the floor among clippings of hide, with his three small guests gathered breathlessly round him, Eusèbe would tell of that terrible lair the Recatadou di Rato-Penado, wherein there lurked monstrous armies of bats who, when thirsty, consumed human blood by the gallon. There was also the Baumo de la Masco Taven, the abode of a yellow-eyed sorceress whose spells were particularly unpleasant. And an imp there was who stuck pins in your pillow—points upward of course —and who lived by himself in a place with a very high-sounding name: Lou Corredou de l'Esperit Fantasti! But what about the haunt of the grisly nightmare, the horrid Cafourno de la Chaucho Vièjo? This indeed was a spot it were best to avoid, lest the nightmare leap out and start to pursue you; nor must you mention its name after dark, lest the nightmare come in at your bedroom window! And then there was the Pas de l'Agneu Negre, that hoof print of the little black lamb of Satan—it was not a great distance from the Oulo di Set Cat where the seven unholy felines made merry. If you should chance to be off your guard, you might find yourself drowning in the Gourgarèu Infernau, which, Eusèbe explained, was an aqueduct of hell, and so placed that it constantly trapped pious Christians.

Eusèbe's blue-white eye that was blind, would appear to gleam luminously through the shadows, as though it were possessed of latent sight, seeing much that was hidden away from its fellow; while his voice, which vibrated all over the room, would seem to call forth an uncanny echo.

'Hèi!' he would exclaim, 'There are wonderful things to be found everywhere in our land of Provence!'

Then Christophe would move a little nearer to Jan, and Jan would move a little nearer to Christophe, and Loup would move a little nearer to them both, so that in the end they would be huddled together; while the autumn dusk would abruptly give place to uncompromising southern nightfall. Eusèbe would light his malodorous lamp which but served to accentuate the black shadows; after which the

75

children must get up and go home, for the lamp always meant the end of the stories.

Once out in the street Jan would talk very bravely: 'I do not believe in the Rato-Penado; and I do not believe in that sorceress, or in anything else Eusèbe has told us. And if I did believe I should not be afraid—I would merely sprinkle much holy water!' Yes, but then he might add: 'Christophe, come back with me—let us do our lessons together this evening. . . .' For in spite of his faith the long street to the port would seem uncommonly dark and lonely.

Sometimes Christophe would go with him, but at other times he would lack the courage for his own return journey. Yet they always begged for more legends and more, so thrilling a story-teller was Eusèbe.

3

Marie very soon learnt about what was happening—indeed she could not well do otherwise, for le tout petit Loup would now wake up screaming. But when she forbade him to go near Eusèbe—and for her she spoke with comparative sternness—le tout petit Loup made a terrible scene, stamping his foot and protesting loudly.

'Je veux, je veux, je *veux*!' he protested, and such tempers always upset his digestion.

Jóusè, who had much work on hand at the moment, shrugged his shoulders and appeared to be utterly helpless. And when Marie turned to his sister for help:

'This is entirely your own faults,' snapped Madame Roustan, 'I warned you not to let your sons know the old drunkard. Jan would never have known him had it not been for you—I consider that he has been led astray by Christophe!' After which she flounced out of the Bénédit's house and went off to make her complaints to the Curé.

The Curé, very bored, and greatly annoyed at being disturbed in the middle of his reading, promised vaguely to speak to Eusèbe himself, but once back with his books forgot all about it. He was not in the least uneasy for Jan, who could never, he felt sure, be harmed by such nonsense.

So Marie must do her unaided best by telling her children kindlier stories, and these she would tell them on Sunday evenings after they had all returned from Benediction. She would tell how the tear of the Magdalene was placed in a golden cup by the angels—and she bruised in spirit because of her sins, and because of her penitence bruised in body. And of how those same angels being filled with compassion, would gather her into their merciful arms and bear her away over valleys and hills to a place of infinite peace and refreshment. And of how there would come many flocks of wild birds to be blessed by the sainted penitent sinner, who continued to weep so persistently that her tears formed a spring of miraculous water. And then Marie would tell of that wonderful voyage which the Holy Ones made on their way to Provence—they had come in a sailless and rudderless ship, guided always by God's inscrutable wisdom. The three Holy Marys-of-the-sea had come, and Maximus who promptly converted Aix, and Lazarus who converted Marseille, and the pitiful Joseph of Arimathea who had felt such concern for his Saviour's body. Aye, and many others had arrived in that vessel to raise Christ's cross on the soil of the pagan. Then one evening she remembered that those saints had brought with them a devoted female slave, by name Sara, and that Sara had not been white-skinned but black:

'Which shows you, my children,' said Marie gravely, that we are all equal in the sight of heaven, for that faithful black slave is now also sainted.'

But at this le tout petit Loup clapped his hands: 'And Saint Sara had a lamb,' he broke in with animation, 'and its coat was quite black to match her skin!'

'No,' said Christophe, 'you are thinking of the little black lamb that Eusèbe told us belonged to Satan!'

There ensued a somewhat heated discussion, for Loup maintained that their mother had just said that heaven took no account of colour; and so cross did he become that he pinched Christophe hard.

'Ow! Do not do that, it hurts!' squealed Christophe.

Marie searched her brain quickly in an effort to provide le tout petit Loup with a counter-attraction, and she told them about quite another lamb, from whose fleece had been woven a cloak for Saint Francis. But she also told of the contrite wolf, that having merited death as a slayer, had nevertheless been spared by the saint who had preached it a very wonderful sermon, explaining God's merciful fatherly love and kindness towards all His lesser creatures.

'So,' said Marie, the 'wolf became as faithful as a dog, and he followed Saint Francis about like Mirèio.'

She paused, and stared at her elder son in bewilderment, for Christophe was weeping.

'Ai, ai,' he wept, 'why is Saint Francis not here. . .I want him to come back and heal Mirèio . . . I want him to tell her all about God! Why have none of you told her about God's love?'

'Bèlli Santo d'or!' exclaimed Marie, much distressed, 'Such things cannot happen every day, my little Christophe!'

He gazed at her out of tearful eyes, while into his childish and groping mind there gradually crept a miserable conviction: 'She will never feel about poor Mirèio as Saint Francis felt about that wolf . . . but why?' For he could not understand how it came that his mother who praised the saint for his acts of mercy, made no effort to ease Mirèio's suffering. No one else did, either, as Christophe well knew, but his mother seemed different—so tender, so gentle, so anxious to tell them about Saint Francis. . . .

Then: 'Such things cannot happen every day,' she repeated; as though that were a good and sufficient explanation.

Yet Christophe was neither convinced nor consoled; and seeing her son continue to weep, Marie took him quietly on to her lap and rocked him as though he were once more a baby.

4

After this, for quite a number of weeks, Marie told only fairy tales to the children. Then one Sunday when Jan came back with them from church, he started to beg for the legends of the saints, in particular of those who had suffered as martyrs. But Marie did not wish her Loup to have nightmares so she would not discuss Saint Laurence's gridiron, nor Saint John's boiling oil, nor Saint Vitus's cauldron, nor even Saint Denis's strange behaviour.

'Let us speak of more pleasant things,' she remarked, glancing rather apprehensively at Loup, 'Supposing I tell you about Christophe's Patron?' For although this good saint was indeed martyrized, that fact does not enter into his legend.

'Saint Christophe was a ferryman,' she began.

But Loup interruped: 'Like the man at the port—the one whose face is all covered with pimples?'

'Yes—only Saint Christophe had a clear, healthy skin.'

'How can one be certain?' persisted Loup.

'Because saints never do have pimples,' said Jan firmly.

Marie began all over again: 'Saint Christophe was a ferryman and one stormy evening, just as he was going to sit down by his fire and was saying to himself: "Diéu, que ventaras!" —for the mistral was blowing unbelievably hard—he suddenly heard someone calling his name:

' "Christophe! Christophe!" someone was calling.

'Saint Christophe did not want to leave his warm hut: "Santouno," he sighed as he thought of the ferry, "Santouno, who can wish to cross on such a night? Ai! las . . ." and he sadly lighted his lantern. By the brink of the river he perceived a little boy who was not much bigger than le tout petit Loup—indeed he was just about the same size: "Can it have been your small voice?" Christophe asked him.

'And the child said: "Yes, for although I am small and the river is in flood I must none the less cross it. Christophe, I have very much work to do, and therefore I beg you to carry me over."

'Good Saint Christophe could scarcely believe his ears: "But you ought to be tucked up in bed," he protested; "tè, what can your parents be thinking about?"

'The child answered: "It was my Father who sent me."

' "And who may your father be?" asked the saint.

' "My Father is also your Father, Christophe."

'Now the poor little boy was a total stranger, so the saint thought that he was probably sleepy, for when children are sleepy they will grow confused: "Pichounet, you are making a mistake," he said kindly. But at this the child gave so profound a sigh that Saint Christophe lifted him on to his shoulder.

'Mes enfants, you have heard that the river was dangerous; all the same, just at first they got on very nicely, for Christophe was a strong and courageous man, and he knew what

79

he had to expect from the mistral. But after awhile he was greatly alarmed to find that the water was growing much deeper—so deep that the flood came up to his chest, and he said to himself: "Without doubt we are drowning!" Yes, and not only this, but that very small being—he was really no bigger than le tout petit Loup—became so heavy that the saint groaned aloud; never, never before had he borne such a burden; and with each step he took the burden grew worse:

' "Bono Maire de Diéu! What has happened?" groaned Christophe.

'Then just when he felt that he could not endure it, that not one tiny drop of strength was left to him, he found himself struggling up the far bank and finally standing quite safe in a meadow: "May the Holy Sailors be praised!" gasped the saint as he lifted that terrible weight from his shoulder.

'He did not know what he expected to see, but all that he saw was the same little boy who had asked to be carried across the ferry, and in his amazement Saint Christophe exclaimed: "You should weigh scarcely anything, enfantounet! How comes it that I bore so fearful a load?"

' "You have borne all the sorrows of the world," the child answered. Then suddenly there was no child any more, and our Lord was standing before Saint Christophe. . . .'

As Marie stopped speaking her eyes filled with tears, for she loved this simple and beautiful legend. And she looked at her son who was named for the saint with an uprush of pride and great tenderness:

'My Christophe, come here to me,' she murmured.

He went, and stood leaning against her arm, while the other two children sat on in silence.

Then Jóusè and Anfos came lumbering in—they were both feeling hungry and wanting their suppers. Jóusè said: 'My poor stomach is as empty as a drum; it is getting terribly late, Marioun!' So Marie pushed Christophe gently away, and went off to fetch food and wine from the kitchen.

5

Christophe had been deeply impressed by the legend, and so for the matter of that had Jan, yet it led them both into very grave mischief. Into mischief so enormous that Madame Roustan could but put the whole affair down to the devil.

As she afterwards said: 'He was listening no doubt, and he always grows spiteful when the dear saints are mentioned.'

In any case, it certainly appeared largely to be due to Jan's pious leanings. He was much addicted to religious games in which he invariably wished to play the hero; thus Christophe must be Isaac to Jan's Abraham; or Goliath to Jan's somewhat boastful David; or a very bored lion that of course must not bite, to Jan's complacent and self-righteous Daniel, so that many a game would begin with a dispute and, as likely as not, would end with a quarrel. But on the occasion of the escapade in which Madame Roustan detected Satan, Christophe had for once got the upper hand, and he would not relinquish his rights without a struggle.

He and Jan together with le tout petit Loup, had gone down to the beach, Christophe meaning to bathe in spite of a rough sea owing to the mistral. But just as he was about to plunge in, Jan had one of his sudden inspirations.

'I have thought of a marvellous game,' he announced; 'I will be Saint Christophe and Loup shall be our Lord. I will paddle and he shall sit on my shoulder!'

Christophe frowned: 'Ça, non! That I will not allow. Why should you always grab all the fun?' he asked hotly. 'To-day, if you please, I will be my own name, and Loup shall come and sit on *my* shoulder!' And so fierce did he look in this sudden revolt, with his close-cropped red pate, and his fist doubled up in angry defence of his baptismal privilege, that Jan unexpectedly gave way:

'Eh bien—if you wish you shall be Saint Christophe; but afterwards I shall be John the Baptist!' And he marched off in search of le tout petit Loup who, standing a little apart, had been listening.

However, they had reckoned without their host, for in spite of his will to emulate them, le tout petit Loup now stiffened his legs and dug his toes into the sand quite firmly. He mistrusted the truculent look of the sea combined with his brother's inadequate proportions, and when Jan tried to lift him he squealed like a pig, then pinched with his skinny vindictive fingers.

'What is wrong?' enquired Jan, 'You should feel very proud; are we not permitting you to be our Lord? Stop pinching at once, and do as I tell you. You are always wanting to take part in our games, very well, you are going to take part in this one!'

Then le tout petit Loup asserted himself: 'I will *not* be our Lord,' he announced with decision; 'I wish to remain le tout petit Loup, and moreover I wish to remain on the beach—I have got a hot ache in my middle,' he concluded.

Now the only excuse to be offered for Christophe is that he had played second fiddle so long that he naturally clung to his present advantage, and yet Jan would be far too heavy to carry . . .

'Catch hold of him,' he ordered; 'allon, vite, vite!' and before le tout petit Loup could say 'knife,' he was being hiked into his perilous position.

His weak arms went desperately round Christophe's neck and his legs round his waist; he was terribly frightened. And this Christophe well knew, yet he straightened his back and proceeded to wade grandly into the water.

'Do not be afraid, you are quite safe,' he bragged, 'Can you not feel the great strength of my muscles?'

Jan followed them in, but not very far, although he was now intensely excited—so excited that he had forgotten to sulk, and must spur Christophe on to yet greater prowess.

'You are only just up to your knees,' he shouted, 'whereas the saint was right up to his chest—however, perhaps you have not got his courage!'

Le tout petit Loup said nothing at all, for by now he was smitten dumb with terror. Had he only screamed all might yet have been well, but Christophe was reassured by his silence.

'I am fighting the flood; I am brave, I am strong; it is fine that the sea is so rough!' he told him. Then, scowling at Jan: 'If you think me a coward I will show you!' and he quickly waded in deeper.

At that moment a wave slapped le tout petit Loup, and before he had recovered his breath, came another. The next second Christophe was out of his depth and found himself swimming about rather wildly.

'Loup—Loup!' he spluttered, 'Hang on to me, Loup. It is really all right . . .' But Loup did not answer.

It was only by the merest chance that Goundran happened to be strolling along the beach at an hour when the shore was completely deserted, and that hearing Jan's ear-splitting yells for help, he realized in a flash what had happened. Plunging in he dragged out le tout petit Loup, who although he was certainly not unconscious, proceeded to be very terribly sick, having managed to swallow a lot of salt water; however, he was left to fend for himself while Goundran turned his attention to Christophe. He found him swimming against the current, distractedly trying to find his brother, and so dazed and spent that he did not realize that Loup had already been carried to safety.

'Here, catch hold of my hand. I am still in my depth and can tow you along—look sharp!' ordered Goundran.

*   *   *

A nice party it was, and no mistake, that arrived all dripping at the Bénédit's house; for even Jan was wet to the skin, having braved the sea to above his waist in his anguish at the thought that Christophe was drowning. Goundran was carrying le tout petit Loup who by now was able to wail quite loudly; and after him walked the culprits side by side, both extremely abashed, down-hearted and silent.

'Ma Santo-Vierge! What has happened?' cried Marie, 'Ai! las, mon tout petit Loup—he is dead!' And she promptly burst into heart-broken tears.

'The dead do not wail as he wails,' consoled Goundran.

Then out of the shop dashed Jóusè and Anfos, to be followed by Mirèio who was barking hoarsely. And Mirèio leapt up and licked Christophe's face, while Anfos said:

'God be praised, little master . . .Oh, may God be praised that I see you are safe!'

But Jóusè looked sternly at the two older boys, the while he begged Goundran for an explanation.

So Goundran began to explain the misfortune; but now there came running up Madame Roustan, who was grown so stout that she panted for breath and was forced to cling to the arm of her brother. Then she wished to be informed who had tried to drown Jan, and why Jóusè was so criminally weak with his children.

Eusèbe scuttled across to the group, clutching in one hand an unfinished sandal: 'En voilà une jolie affaire!' he remarked. And turning to Madame Roustan with a bow: 'Your dear son was safer, it would seem, in my vineyards.'

'Do not speak to me, shameless old man,' she gasped, 'I suspect that this misery is largely your doing!'

After this they all started to talk at once, while Mirèio still barked, and le tout petit Loup began to wail even more dolefully, because of the cramp that was twisting his entrails. So at last Marie carried him upstairs to bed and Jóusè bethought himself of the doctor.

6

Le tout petit Loup was ill for a month; he was suffering from shock and acute gastritis. The doctor informed them that a dangerous chill had promptly attacked his delicate stomach. Jan developed a furious cold in the head to the great indignation of his anxious parent, while Goundran and Christophe got off scot free—this in spite of drenched clothes and a biting mistral.

But Christophe was very severely punished by his usually easy-going father. Every day of that month, when he got home from school, he was sent to bed in his tiny attic; and there he must lie supperless and alone contemplating his serious misdemeanour. Neither Anfos nor Mirèio might pay him a visit during those dreary hours of his penance; and when Jóusè caught Anfos emerging from the larder with a plateful of titbits for the hungry sinner, he administered a workmanlike box on the ear, for Jóusè's temper was decidedly short, since in punishing Christophe he was punishing Jóusè.

All the same, Anfos managed to sneak out at night and to stand under Christophe's small dormer-window. And sometimes he would whistle the soft double note wherewith he had used to attract the wild birds when he lived in that village high up in the mountains; then Christophe would turn over in his sleep and smile. But if Jóusè should hear he would grumble to his wife:

'Pecaire, your cousin is indeed half-witted!'

CHAPTER NINE

I

THE following summer Jóusè said to Christophe:
'It is time that you started to learn your trade,
for although you are only eight years old, early
training makes the hands grow strong and supple.
I think that I will teach you in the evenings,
my son, after you have finished your school preparation;
and sometimes you must work on half-holidays also, as I
had to do when I was your age and must very often assist
my father.'

So Christophe began his youthful career by acquiring a
knowledge of the ways of tools, even as Anfos had done
before him.

He did not resent this additional work, indeed it seemed
to him right enough, for many another boy at the school
must contribute his share towards helping his parents, and
moreover he rather enjoyed the small tasks with which he
would now find himself entrusted. At eight years old he was
tall for his age and gave promise of very great physical
strength, so that he could hammer away with a will, and
could presently use even a light saw, driving it strongly
through the planks with an accuracy which surprised
his father.

'Segnour Diéu!' Jóusè would exclaim, delighted. 'But
this is excellent, pichounet—one would think that you had
long been accustomed to the job!'

Then Christophe would flush with pride and pleasure.

And indeed he did show a great aptitude for all that pertained to his father's trade, an aptitude at which he was
surprised himself, for now that he had come into personal
touch with the tools and the honest and patient wood, the
tasks which he did seemed strangely familiar, so that he
could work without undue effort, being filled with a very

complete self-assurance. And Jóusè watching his robust little son, would consider himself to be more than lucky, for had he not already one excellent apprentice in poor Anfos whom he had trained out of kindness? And now here was his own fine flesh and blood bidding fair to become a skilled carpenter who would carry on the family tradition—for Jóusè came of a long line of men who had earned their bread through the bounty of timber. Oh, yes, the good Jóusè was well content these days, and being content he felt pious, so that he prayed a great deal at Mass and seldom missed going to Benediction.

Christophe would be kneeling between his parents, telling his beads with scarred clumsy fingers: 'Je vous salue, O Marie pleine de grâce, le Seigneur est avec vous,' he would whisper, 'Vous étés bénie entre toutes les femmes, et Jésus le fruit de vos entrailles est béni.' And sometimes there would suddenly come to the child one of his flashes of understanding, so that he would glimpse in those momentous words the tragedy and grandeur of God's incarnation— at such moments he would grope for his mother's hand without knowing why he desired to hold it. And presently— if it were Benediction—the triple bell would ring out through the church while the Curé raised the Host in its monstrance; then Marie must glance rather nervously at Loup, always fearful lest he should shuffle his feet or in some other way show a lack of attention.

Just across the aisle from the Bénédit's chairs, would be Madame Roustan beating her breast for the sins which she had never committed. Beside her would kneel her only son, and he gazing up at the Host with eyes that glowed with a sombre light of anger; for child though he still was the sight of the Host would always remind him of his Saviour's wrongs, so that as they walked back to their homes after church he must open his fierce young heart to Christophe, inveighing against those who did not believe as he did, with a vigour amounting to violence. But the cousins met rather less often these days, for while Christophe worked in the carpenter's shop, Jan was frequently working in the Curé's study. The Curé was teaching him the rudiments of Latin and Greek, having suddenly come to the decision that when Jan left school at the age of thirteen, he would undertake the boy's entire training for the Grand Séminaire and thus save expense, since Madame Roustan was not blessed with riches.

The Curé Martel had said to himself: 'Here is a really promising student; his school reports are excellent; he has brains, enthusiasm, and courage. But his mother is poor—it is therefore my duty to do what I can to help him to the priesthood.'

And while all this was certainly true, the Curé, who invariably left something out when he tried to arrive at an accurate reckoning, quite omitted to acknowledge that paternal urge which drew him to Jan with so deep an affection—he loved to see the eager and intelligent child poring over the musty old books in his study, and he loved to foster in that combative soul the instincts in which he felt himself to be lacking.

'Ah, yes.' he would say, 'while we must not fail in charity —for that would displease our Lord—we may certainly feel a righteous indignation which will lead us to fight for our faith and our Church; nothing is achieved without enthusiasm!' And then he would talk of the warrior-saints, and would go on to tell of the warlike Crusaders.

Thus it was coming to pass that Jan, who had been an impetuous and hot-tempered baby, was grafting his natural dispositions on to his Christianity, as is not infrequently the way with Christians. He saw his Lord and the death of his Lord through the eyes of a childish but eager avenger. And since all that the Curé now inculcated would fall into line with the boy's own instincts, his tuition continued without a hitch, to the deep satisfaction of himself and his master. But it must be admitted in fairness to Jan, that he was a splendidly conscientious pupil.

2

At about this time the Curé Martel dared to open a much worn and closely written diary, on nearly every page of which there occurred a certain name—Geneviève d'Arlanges. And as the Curé re-read his own words he marvelled to remember his turbulent passion, to remember how grievously he had suffered, and he thought:

87

'After all, I—yes, even I—have not failed altogether to serve my Lord.' Which was surely the truth, in view of that diary. Then he thought: 'Geneviève ... she must now be quite old.' And this gave him a little pang of regret, for even those whom we have long ceased to love—either from a sense of duty towards God, or because of the fickleness of our bodies—even those whom we have long ceased to love, we yet wish to protect from the cruelty of age, although we ourselves may have been no less cruel. 'Yes,' he thought, 'she must now be as old as I am.'

His mind slipped back over the inadequate years at Saint Loup until he was once more in Paris, a man filled with youthful vitality—an ardent lover, an ardent Christian. On the one hand stood a girl with an innocent face and eyes that had never looked upon sorrow; on the other stood a God with a bleeding brow and eyes that were heavy and dim with suffering. And each of these two appeared to be calling—to be calling to him, the young Antoine Martel, as though his youth and vitality were to them a thing of momentous importance, so that he turned now this way, now that, from suffering to joy, from joy back to suffering.

The Curé Martel remembered long nights spent half in agonized and self-abased prayer, and half in agonized yet arrogant longing. And as he fingered the shabby old book in which he had ventured to write many things that a riper discretion must have omitted, he grew lonely and quite illogically sad because he could no longer feel that anguish. Going to his table he found pen and paper, then a cheap envelope which he carefully addressed to a certain Madame la Comtesse de Bérac.

'Chère Geneviève,' he wrote in his clerical hand, 'It is now many years since you and I met, but always I have been your sincere well-wisher, and always I have remembered you in my prayers, as I hope that you have remembered me . . .' The writing paused, then went on more quickly: 'But let me come at once to the point of this letter. Were I going to ask a favour entirely for myself I should hesitate, since why should you grant it? It is not entirely for myself that I ask, it is also for a little boy in this town who I hope may become a brilliant student. His name is Jan Roustan; his mother is a widow who runs a humble drapery business, and he himself was a posthumous child and has thus never known the love of a father.

'The excuse for my importunity is this: the boy is anxious to enter the priesthood, and, as always, we need good husbandmen to work in God's often neglected vineyards. Unless you have very much changed, dear Geneviève, you are still a religious and generous soul who will give of your plenty to those who have nothing. Therefore, greatly daring, I will beg of you a gift; in due course Jan must go to the Grand Séminaire—that will not be until the boy is nineteen, but I want you to promise to provide the money. We need not consider the Petit Séminaire, since I will prepare him for his Baccalauréat; already I am supplementing his studies.

'Doubtless he could take a scholarship with ease, but that would mean his going to a local institution, whereas I wish to make him a priest of the world—for the world needs its priests to help it to heaven. I wish him to go to Paris, Geneviève, or rather to the Grand Séminaire at Versailles; only the best is good enough for Jan who possesses a rarely courageous spirit.

'And now, Geneviève, the better to persuade you, I will gladly humble myself to the dust and will tell you that I have been a great failure. In thirty years I have done very little except to surround myself with books, and these days when I realize my shortcomings, I find it hard indeed to correct them—Geneviève, if your northern son should crave the south, see to it that his visits are of short duration. Yet I do feel that God in His infinite mercy is giving me one more opportunity to serve Him. He is giving me the chance to train this boy who possesses the qualities which I myself have lacked, and which, for a priest, are so very essential.

'I appeal to you, will you compassionate my need? Will you help me to justify myself in God's sight? I am writing not as your spiritual Father, but rather as a tired and ageing man who earnestly begs that you will not refuse him.

'May God bless you. I clasp your hand in friendship.'

The Curé carefully read over his letter, after which he carried it down to the post box.

'If she will only consent . . .' he mused, sighing.

Then, although he no longer felt love for this woman, his thoughts of her became very limpid and sweet—as limpid and sweet as a stream from the mountains. And he visualized Geneviève as Jan's mother, and himself, for the first time, as Jan's fleshly father. And this he did without guile and without sin—unless the paternal instinct be sinful.

Ten days later the Comtesse de Bérac replied: 'It made me very happy to receive your letter, and yet sad. It was all a long time ago but I have never forgotten our friendship, nor have I forgotten you in my prayers. But do not let me dwell too much on myself, for I, like you, belong to the past, whereas your Jan belongs to the future.

'How could you have imagined that I would refuse? Of course, my dear Antoine, you shall have the money—all the money you require to educate Jan and to fit him worthily to enter the priesthood.

'I myself will drive out to Versailles next week and will have a long talk with the Superior who, by the way, is related to my husband. From him I shall learn just how much you will need; but you might let me know the age of the boy. I gather from your letter that he is still quite young. Nevertheless we will prepare things at once; I believe in the saying: "There is no time like the present."

'I would greatly have liked my own son to be a priest, but that privilege God has seen fit to deny me. However, my Fernand is a good and charming man—I have always much wished that you could meet him.

'When I have been to the Grand Séminaire I will write you again, and do not forget to let me know your protégé's age.

'I clasp your hand in affectionate friendship.'

The Curé went down on his threadbare knees, and his eyes were actually full of tears as he knelt before his new crucifix—the one of fine wood that had been carved by Anfos. And his heart was so glad and so thankful for Jan, that he could not find words for his own gratitude, but must just kneel there gazing up at the Christ, while the tears overflowed and ran down his gaunt face, leaving little shining streaks in its furrows.

3

People very soon heard about Jan's good fortune, for the Curé had reluctantly considered it his duty to impart the tidings to Madame Roustan; and now not a kilo of potatoes could she buy, or a bottle of wine, or a bag of greengages but their vendors must hear all about her son who was under the protection of the Comtesse de Bérac.

Jóusè was alternately amused and annoyed: 'It would seem he remarked while feeling the latter, 'that Saint Peter favours the Faubourg St. Germain. No doubt he will ask for our family trees before he permits us to pass into heaven! Do not be so ridiculous, my sister. Is it not enough that you have a good son who could make his way without your fine lady? To hear you so impressed by a noble name is to know that indeed you are humble in spirit!'

At all of which Madame Roustan could smile: 'Ai! las,' she remarked to a neighbour one day, 'what a pity it is that my brother is so jealous.'

Marie was genuinely glad that her nephew should be helped in so kindly and generous a manner; all the same she decided that le tout petit Loup would, in time, excel even Jan in his studies: 'Jan is clever, yes, but our tout petit Loup has the wisdom of an owl and the sharpness of a needle. Tè, what a child!' she laughed to her husband.

And le tout petit Loup who had come in unobserved, must immediately start to show off his wisdom: 'The English walked about naked,' he remarked, 'all they did to keep warm was to paint their bodies, and the paint that they generally used was called woad. But our brave Duke of Normandy made them wear clothes. What a good thing it was that we conquered the English!'

Goundran said nothing when he heard the news. He liked Jan well enough but he thought that the Curé showed great favouritism where he was concerned; all the same, being loath to criticize the Church, he contented himself with shrugging his shoulders.

Eusèbe, however, not only shrugged his shoulders until his head nearly disappeared between them, but he swore so many inexcusable oaths whenever Madame Roustan came within earshot that Jóusè felt himself bound to protest. After which Eusèbe would seize his old broom and sweep like a fiend should she chance to be passing, and the dust would come billowing out through the door of his shop, which, of course, he took care to leave open.

'That widow makes me want to vomit!' he raged, 'always

running off to the Curé to confession, and she as puffed up with satisfaction and wind as a Pope who has eaten too fine a dinner. "Madame la Comtesse de Bérac!" says she, and then she says: "Madame la Comtesse de Bérac!" And then she belches in case she should burst with arrogance over her sacrée Comtesse. Merde! She is surely enough to block one's bile; the mere thought of her always congests my liver.' And he was not alone in his irritation, although others expressed theirs with more refinement.

On the whole Madame Roustan made but small impression upon those who must listen to her wearisome bragging—for the people of Saint Loup cared as little about titles as they did about the Chambre des Députés, governmental disputes, and vain politicians, so that gradually she grew rather depressed, since nothing is less pleasant than being deflated. Thus it was that upon a certain warm night when the port was noisy with voices and laughter, when someone was tinkling a mandolin, and someone was swinging a concertina, and someone was urging his dog to bark because someone else had just started singing, thus it was that despite a studious son who was being protected by so eminent a person, and despite her own sense of superiority which should have made her able to ignore her neighbours, Madame Roustan of a sudden felt extremely depressed, and her thoughts turned towards the Café de la Tarasque.

Now believing as she did in an ever-present devil, it is strange that she could not detect fumes of sulphur, that she could not perceive in her down-hearted mood a state most propitious to successful temptation; that, in fact, she saw nothing ominous in her sudden desire to revisit the Café. For five years she had never been near la Tarasque, although her own shop was but three doors away, as not only did she highly disapprove of the place, but she feared that it might remind her of Goundran. Yet upon this particular summer night, having seen that her child was safely asleep, she proceeded to touch up her hair at the glass, and then to steal guiltily out of the house while the marble clock in the parlour struck twelve—which meant that she also should have been sleeping.

And as though to aid and abet the foul fiend in his crafty

attack upon Madame Roustan's virtue, Mère Mélanie heaped coals of fire on her head by extending a cordial and loudly voiced welcome: 'Mais Madame, vouse étes surement la bienvenue!' And this she said so that everyone might hear, which, although it should not have done any such thing, did in fact make her client feel rather important.

It chanced that there was still room in the Café, and Mère Mélanie found a convenient table; then she plumped herself down at Madame Roustan's side, and Madame Roustan ordered a groseille. The little violinist with the hump on has back was fiddling, but not many couples were responding, for the night was almost too hot for them to dance—so hot that whenever Mère Mélanie moved she broke out into rivers of perspiration:

'And how is your very dear child?' she enquired; 'I see him sometimes when he plays with his comrades—mais oui—I could stand and watch him for hours. A fine boy, I think him exceedingly handsome!'

Madame Roustan savoured the iced groseille slowly, being careful to cock her fourth and fifth fingers, and after she had taken·three elegant sips: 'My Jan is as usual, quite well, thank God—and just now he is to be congratulated. As you no doubt have heard he is going to be a priest, and when he is older he will go to Versailles—to the Grand Séminaire at Versailles, the best in France, which is thanks to Madame la Comtesse de Bérac.'

'La Comtesse de Bérac!' exclaimed Mère Mélanie, who was genuinely overcome with amazement, 'but surely that is a very great name?'

'Without doubt a great name,' agreed Madame Roustan.

And now, comfortably launched, she explained at vast length all that Jan might hope to gain through this lady, who, hearing of his piety, his talents and his charm, had promised to provide for his clerical future. And Mère Mélanie listened with such obvious respect that Madame Roustan's heart warmed towards her, for here at long last was someone in Saint Loup who accorded her news deferential treatment.

Presently the little violinist stopped playing and Mère Mélanie called him over to the table: 'Alexandre! Come here and listen to this! Madame's son will go to the Grand

Séminaire at Versailles and the Comtesse de Bérac will pay, because Monsieur le Curé finds him so brilliant. Ah, what a joy! The child may become a bishop! Madame must indeed be a proud and glad mother.' And she ventured to press her client's plump hand: 'Alexandre, go and fetch us a bottle of porto!'

So the little violinist with the hump on his back went and fetched the port wine, and three very large glasses which Mère Mélanie generously filled to their brims.

'Vot' santé, Madame!' she said, raising her glass.

'Vot' santé!' echoed the little violinist.

'Santé, monsieur-et-dame!' bowed Madame Roustan.

The glasses were emptied and quickly refilled, for Mère Mélanie must drink to the future bishop: 'A votre fils, a l'évêque!' she announced solemnly.

'A l'évêque!' gravely echoed the little violinist.

'A mon bien cher Jan,' murmured Madame Roustan.

Then the little violinist with the hump on his back wished to drink to the noble and pious benefactress: 'A Madame la Comtesse de Bérac!' he exclaimed, inclining his head through respect for the lady.

So Madame Roustan must again fill her glass in order to drink to the Comtesse de Bérac.

Quite naturally all this bowing and scraping had attracted the attention of the other clients, and now a hefty young sailor-man loudly demanded to be told what was happening.

'Is our Mère Mélanie about to be married? Because if she is I also will drink wine.' And he flung himself down at Mère Mélanie's side; 'Garçon, bring *four* bottles of porto!' he commanded.

Several other habitués joined the party, attracted thereto by so princely an order, and as they thought Madame Roustan a newcomer, they must all drink her health a great many times:

'Madame, a vot' santé!'

'Messieurs, a la votre!' for courtesy surely demanded such an answer. So after awhile breaths reeked like a wine-press whose dregs have lain long and thus over-fermented.

Now whether it was some kind of reaction brought about by this highly appreciative welcome, or whether it was the little violinist who most deftly and silently replenished the glasses, or whether it was the great heat of the room which made her feel quite uncommonly thirsty, or whether it was that the strong and sweet wine very soon seemed as harmless as the weak and sweet groseille, Madame Roustan never knew; but the fact remains that she found herself drinking toast for toast in accordance with the finest traditions of the Café. And moreover by the time that she realized in a vague, placid, happy way what she was doing, it seemed to her not only natural but right, and not only natural and right but pleasant.

'Madame la Comtesse de Bérac . . . ' she hiccoughed, 'My dear son a priest . . . and . . . Comtesse de Bérac. . . .'

No one smiled, but the sailor began to chant slowly:

'As tu vu les fesses de ma belle Louise?
As tu vu ses pis qui sont a croquer?'

And many other charms which Louise possessed were minutely described by the now doleful singer, who feeling in great need of sympathy was making sad sheep's-eyes at Madame Roustan.

The little violinist had started to play, so a few who felt sure enough of their legs left their seats and went off in search of partners. And some of the couples must dance cheek by jowl, and in other ways demonstrate their affection.

'As tu vu les fesses de ma belle Louise?' played the little violinist on his teasing fiddle.

Mère Mélanie wiped her beetle brows; then she drained the bottles into her glass, yawned, drank up the dregs, lit a cigarette, yawned again, and finally glanced at her watch—somewhere in the distance a bell was ringing. Mère Mélanie made the sign of the cross very largely upon her ample bosom.

Madame Roustan got up: 'I must go . . .' she said weakly for by now she was feeling both sick and giddy. But she managed to stumble down the long room and out into the disconcerting sunshine.

It was lucky indeed that the spiteful Eusèbe had not happened to wander along to la Tarasque; that Jóusè hardly ever went there these days; and that Goundran was still bent on saving his money. It was also lucky that Mère Mélanie made a rule of never discussing her clients; but luckier still was the fact that Madame Roustan lived only three doors away from the Café.

CHAPTER TEN

I

THE Curé was more than a little disappointed at the way in which his pupil received the news that his future was being provided for. He had thought that the boy would be overjoyed, for he knew very well that Jan was ambitious. But Jan only looked rather thoughtful and grave; and when the Curé eagerly persisted:

'My son, have you realized all this means? Your training will be paid for by the kindest of ladies,' Jan's answer was made in a doubtful voice:

'Yes, I know . . . but what will she do for Christophe?'

So the Curé did his best to explain that the Comtesse de Bérac had only been asked to help Jan because he would enter the Church, whereas Christophe would continue to work with his father.

That night Jan remained awake a long time, for his heart as well as his mind was uneasy. In a dim, childish way he perceived a great difference between being an arrogant leader in games and this real and very substantial advantage which had suddenly come to him out of the blue, and the more he considered it the more he felt troubled, so that his pleasure in the contemplation of going to the Grand Séminaire at Versailles was damped because nothing would be done for his friend—thus he paid his first youthful toll to affection.

The next afternoon, their school being over, Jan hurried round to the Bénédit's house, only to find Christophe working in the shop, which added to that feeling of uneasiness and trouble.

'Cannot you come out?' he asked anxiously. 'The Curé does not want me and so I thought that we might go up to the old citadel—in this heat we are certain to see many lizards!' And this he said knowing that Christophe was bent upon trying to tame the elusive creatures.

Christophe glanced at his father: 'May I?' he enquired, and his voice was so unmistakably eager that Jóusè nodded his curly head:

'Mais oui, be off, my indolent son!' For he could not bring himself to refuse in view of the splendid summer weather.

So the cousins proceeded to dash along the street before le tout petit Loup could join them, Mirèio following as best she might, her ears back, her tail down and her pink tongue lolling. Presently the three of them turned under an archway that had been bequeathed to Saint Loup by the Romans, and that guarded a precipitous path up the hill that led to the ancient, crumbling fortress. And beyond on the hill-side the air was so quiet that the heat lay revealed by a thin but clear shimmer, and the ground was so impregnated with the heat that it burnt through the soles of the boys' canvas shoes, while the sun all but blistered the skin on their shoulders.

'Rampau de Diéu, what a sun!' Jan grumbled.

But Christophe, being in excellent spirits, found nothing to grumble at in the sunshine—his cousin's good fortune had not kept him awake, indeed he had thought very little about it except to feel pleased that something had happened which everyone said was to Jan's advantage. So now he whistled as they climbed the steep path, and he urged Jan to hurry:

'Zóu, zóu,' he kept saying, for Jan was rather inclined to lag, and Christophe was thinking about the lizards.

And sure enough, when they reached the ruin, every other grey stone seemed to hold a slim body which ended in a pair of very bright eyes—in eyes that were not only bright but observant, so that suddenly there were no lizards at all.

'It would seem that your friends have departed,' said Jan, laughing.

Christophe sat down with his back against a rock, while Jan stretched himself on the ground beside him; then Mirèio discovered a patch of shade in which she lay alternately licking her sores, hunting for ticks, and panting loudly; but after a little she dropped off to sleep:

'That is good,' said Christophe, 'we will now sit quite still.'

And Jan did his level best to obey him.

One by one the lizards, hearing no noise, began to come out of the holes and crannies; extending themselves upon the stones and lifting their little reptilian heads to warm the skin of their throats in the sunshine. Then Christophe uttered a very small sound—it was like a soft but compelling summons—and a lizard turned itself quickly about, fixing inquisitive eyes upon him; so once more he made that very small sound, and the creature, still looking at him, moved nearer.

'I am your friend, you know. . . .' Christophe told it.

But just then Mirèio was disturbed by the flies, and she started an incessant and irritable snapping, while Jan suddenly shuffled his restless feet because they so longed to be scaling the ramparts; and the lizard, feeling itself betrayed, mistrustfully darted back into a cranny.

'Never mind, it will come to me again,' said Christophe.

After this the boys clambered about those old walls that had once known the thunder and stress of battle. And Jan pulled off his jersey, which was striped red and white, and he tied it on to the end of a stick:

'Who will follow the banner of the cross?' he shouted, waving the jersey above his head. 'Christophe, come on! We are now crusaders!'

So they played at being in Palestine where Jan, single-handed, slew countless unbelievers; and where Christophe must continually dash to his aid in the face of terrific personal danger. Nor did Mirèio prove less courageous, indeed she was so much excited by the shouting that she quite forgot the eleven long years which had lain all too heavy upon her just lately, and she thought of herself as a hound of war, so must run about growling ferociously in spite of her many sores and her lameness.

But on their way home Jan grew very quiet, for he wanted to say a great many things that somehow refused to get themselves said—he wanted to say how troubled he was because Christophe could not share his good fortune. And since words seemed to fail him he groped in his pocket, producing his biggest and gaudiest marble.

'Allons, take it! I will give it to you,' he mumbled.

'Why?' enquired Christophe, delighted and surprised.

'Because I would very much like you to have it.'

Presently Jan said: 'Supposing I were rich. . . . supposing I were made a bishop or a cardinal and wanted to give you a magnificent present; what would you like best in all the world?' And he waited expectantly for the answer.

But the answer when it came was most unsatisfactory, for without so much as a moment's hesitation Christophe replied, to Jan's great surprise; 'I would wish for a pair of Eusèbe's sandals.'

'Comment!' exclaimed Jan, feeling dashed and cross, 'I thought you would at least want a house like the mayor's that has a big garden with pale blue vases, and a terrace with yellow tiles and a vine.'

'I do not care for pale blue vases,' said Christophe.

'Well, perhaps a fine horse to ride . . .' persisted Jan. 'A fine horse that resembles the one in that book the Curé lent me about crusaders.' For he longed that his cousin should express a desire for some gift that would cost a great deal of money. 'But yes,' he went on dictatorially, 'you would certainly ask me to give you a fine horse.'

'I would not. I would ask for a pair of sandals—I have wanted a pair for a very long time.' And indeed it was true, although until now this craving of Christophe's had gone unsuspected.

Jan frowned: 'Póu,' he remarked with annoyance, 'they are cheap, common things, my mother says so; and besides, they are pagan, my mother says—except of course, when they are worn by the friars; when the friars wear sandals they make them Christian. I insist that you ask me for something else. If you do not like the house of our mayor I might be able to give you a palace; or perhaps a great ship, as you so much love the sea, or . . .' he paused and started to rack his brain, 'or a sword in a jewelled scabbard,' he finished.

Christophe sighed. 'But I do not want any of those things,' and that sigh had in it a suggestion of impatience.

Now by all the laws governing courteous behaviour, Christophe should not have continued so stubborn; but then neither should Jan have flown into a rage merely because of his great disappointment—and yet so it was:

'Imbecile!' he exploded. 'And not only are you stupid, but you do it on purpose! You pretend that you do not care for such things, whereas everyone cares for magnificent presents. Very well, I hope you will always be poor.' And he quite inexcusably added: 'Cochon!'

Christophe flushed crimson right up to his scalp, while his close-cropped red hair seemed about to bristle: 'Cochon yourself!' he exclaimed furiously, 'I will not permit you to call me bad names! And I do not believe you will ever grow rich; and I do want a pair of Eusèbe's sandals!'

At this stage Jan forgot that he might become a bishop, and he said many things that were far from polite, and which he most certainly could not have heard on the lips of the Curé or Madame Roustan—but Jan had long been familiar with the port, where the Provençal tongue is very elastic. As for Christophe his temper was almost as fierce as his cousin's, when aroused through a sense of injustice, so that now they must go at it hammer and tongs, to the great disquietude of Mirèio. Then, just as they were walking under that arch which had been bequeathed to Saint Loup by the Romans, Christophe suddenly hurled away Jan's gift:

'Nothing of yours do I want!' he said loudly, 'no, neither a palace, nor a ship, nor a horse—and I do not want your dirty old marble!'

And so, as will frequently happen in this world, the best of intentions had led to trouble; Jan's impulse of generosity had but ended in a noisy and groundless quarrel. Having talked a very great deal too much, the cousins parted without saying good-bye, and in consequence neither enjoyed his supper. However, these storms which would blow up like thunder over their otherwise cloudless horizon, never lasted for long, and this one had quite passed by the time they were going to school the next morning.

Jan said: 'I am sorry.'

And Christophe replied by presenting his cousin with a brand new marble which might well have been the twin of the one that was lost: 'Please give it to me all over again.'

So Jan solemnly handed him back the marble.

A few days later Jan went to Eusèbe, and he said: 'Christophe greatly desires a pair of sandals. I have only three sous so I cannot pay you. . . . Do you think you could possibly make them for nothing? If you will do this I will pray a long prayer to Sant Jan l'ami de Diéu for your vine-yards.'

Eusèbe rolled his black eye and looked fierce: 'Ho, ho! So our Christophe now wishes for sandals. And what will our Christophe's godmother think?'

'I cannot imagine,' Jan answered gravely. Though indeed he did not very much care at that moment what his mother would think: 'I will pray two long prayers if you wish, Eusèbe.'

But now Eusèbe appeared to be outraged by so unworthy and mean a proposal: 'Not enough, not enough, I must have nine long prayers!'

'Very well, to-morrow I will start a Novena!'

Then Eusèbe laughed, and he patted Jan's shoulder: 'Petit sot, I do not want your long prayers. The good saints are unlikely to be my friends, as I do not doubt your dear maman has told you. Nevertheless I will do as you ask; and when you have become a very fat bishop I will send in my bill and then you shall pay. Meanwhile tell Christophe to come and be measured.'

3

Familiar though Christophe now was with Eusèbe, he had never yet seen him fitting sandals: Eusèbe always turned the boys out of his shop when he was engaged in this manner with a client.

'Go away,' he would order peremptorily; and if he should catch them peeping in at the door, he would glare with so awful and threatening an orb that not one of the three would have the courage to defy him: 'Did I not command you to go?' he would shout at the guilty and swiftly retreating figures.

For just as the immortal Leonardo da Vinci must have felt when it came to the painting of pictures—intolerant, resentful of every distraction that sought to intrude on the realm of his genius—even so Eusèbe felt in his degree, since the spirit is all, when it comes to labour. Thus Christophe went alone to fit his first sandals, much impressed by the solemnity of the occasion; having washed his feet with unusual zeal, then requested his mother to cut his toe nails. And there was Eusèbe with a large sheet of paper spread out on the floor, and with a very fat pencil; and he ordered Christophe to take off his shoes and stand perfectly still on that large sheet of paper. After which he outlined both his feet in turn, squeezing the pencil between his big toe and its neighbour so that Christophe who was ticklish, laughed, despite the solemnity of the occasion.

The drawing completed, Eusèbe gazed at it for a moment with obvious satisfaction: 'A good shape, and no corns or other defects. There are some who come here with their joints sticking out on each side like a couple of rotten apples: "Eusèbe, make me a pair of sandals," they say; but I tell them they can go to the devil! I will fit you on Thursday evening at six, and do not be late; I am very busy.'

The following Thursday Christophe arrived with a punctuality born of impatience. And now he was to see a fine craftsman in the grip of something very like inspiration. Meanwhile, he himself must stand on a block staring down at the top of that craftsman's head, which he could not but observe was extremely dirty.

Eusèbe took up the unfinished sandals, thrusting them deftly into position; then he started to coax and adjust the thongs—one between the toes, one across the heel, and five lying neatly over the instep. And while he worked it seemed he must gabble, either to the sandals or to himself: 'Santouno! But what is the matter to-day? I observe that you are in a bad temper. Do you wish to give him a blister on his heel? You do not? Then get down a little bit lower . . . voilà! And now what about the big toe—I think we are rather short in the strap, mais oui, and that is a very bad fault—gently, gently, it is less than an eighth of an inch! Ah, but look at the lie of you over his instep; your lie is superb, so firm yet so kind. . . . Eusèbe, you are a fine sandal-maker. Eusèbe, you could surely have made for the Greeks and been very well paid, for you know your business.' During all of which Christophe must perch on his block, trying hard not to laugh when Eusèbe tickled.

But at last Eusèbe looked up with a smile which, for him, was very nearly seraphic: 'The fitting is over and your sandals go well. I do not think we need fit them again—you have got the most excellent feet for sandals!'

So Christophe climbed down and collected his shoes, blushing because of this unexpected praise. Then he thanked Eusèbe for the generous gift, but somewhat spoilt the effect of his good manners by turning back when he had reached the door, in order to ask how soon he could have it.

'Not before this day week,' said Eusèbe.

CHAPTER ELEVEN

I

THE afternoon sun streamed into Christophe's attic, slanting across his narrow white bed with the china holy-water stoup above it, touching a picture of the Virgin on the wall and revealing the layer of powdery dust that filmed the shiny black frame of the Virgin. On the well-worn floor-boards this afternoon sunshine had formed itself into a pool of light whose brilliance contrasted sharply with the shadows that lay in the sagging corners of the room; and directly in the middle of this luminous pool, gravely contemplating his toes, sat Christophe.

He knew very well that he should have been working. To be sure it was a half-holiday, but his father had said before leaving the house to attend a sale at a neighbouring coast-town: 'I myself may not get back until late, therefore Anfos will show you how to dovetail that box. I wish you to listen attentively to him, and not to try and persuade him to play because, being half-witted, he is frequently childish.' And Christophe had dutifully acquiesced, but while his lips had said: 'Oui, mon père,' his thoughts had irresistibly strayed to his sandals.

Eusèbe had brought them across after dinner, very neatly tied up in a clean sheet of paper. Jóusè had already gone off to the station, but Marie had offered a glass of red wine to the unexpectedly generous donor, feeling that she could not very well do less. 'Your sandals have arrived!' she had called to Christophe. And hardly had Eusèbe returned to his shop than Christophe had rushed upstairs with the parcel; so now here he was amusing himself when he should have been making a box with Anfos.

He began to turn his feet this way and that, admiring the pattern of the thongs across his insteps, admiring the pliant brown leather of the thongs, and the heavy work-man-like soles of the sandals, admiring the neat little straps between his toes, and the neat little straps that clung to his heels with such gentle but reassuring persistence. Then quite suddenly as he sat on in the sunshine there came upon Christophe a most curious sensation; he who had never worn sandals until now yet felt that they were intensely familiar, and that something else was familiar as well: his great pleasure and pride in receiving this present. It was almost as though it had happened before, even to the minutest personal detail—a new pair of sandals given to a boy of eight years old by his parents' neighbour, and that boy sitting down to examine the gift in a room which was bare but flooded with sun, and that boy very conscious of idling his time when instead he should have been diligently working.

He frowned and began to ponder this thing: 'Yes, but working at what?' he said half aloud.

And the answer flashed into his mind so clearly that he almost fancied the words had been spoken: 'Working at a little wooden box in the carpenter's shop that belonged to his father.' Christophe sprang up, completely bewildered.

Going onto the landing he hesitated—the house struck him as being unusually quiet. Then he started to descend the rickety stairs, his feet making a soft heavy, slapping sound—the sound that is characteristic of sandals.

Voices reached him as though from a very great distance, and he muttered: 'There are Anfos and Loup—I must find them.' But now even their names seemed a long way away, almost as far away as their voices.

He realized that his head was aching, that indeed his whole body felt vaguely uneasy, and since he was a stranger to physical ills he pressed his hands to his throbbing head with a gesture half of fear, half of resentment. Yet even as he did so he became aware of a very great joy that surged up within him, of an indescribable sense of peace that far exceeded his apprehension; and his mind must abandon itself to this peace, fearlessly, trustfully, without question. But the moment passed and he found himself standing at the door of his father's workshop.

Loup was playing rather timidly with Mirèio, and Anfos

was sawing a heavy log. The sawdust sprayed out either side of the saw and drifted to the ground where it gradually formed itself into a little golden hillock. The sun fell on the biting steel of the blade and on the strong, hairy arm behind it; the arm was thickly corded with veins and covered with trickles of perspiration. Christophe stood silent and motionless, watching. And as he stood there, the kind woodland odour of the log upon which the apprentice was working, the more pungent odour of freshly planed planks grown sticky and resinous in the sunshine, the faint but persistent odour of sweat that rose from the straining body of Anfos; the toil, and the heat, and the clean dry litter, his father's tools on the bench near the entrance, indeed all that made up the spirit of that place began to stir in him a startled awareness, began to take on a reality as new as it was surely infinitely old, so that he wondered if what he saw was being actually seen or remembered; and if remembered, with whose memory; and if seen, by whose eyes—his own or another's. . . .

At that moment Anfos looked up and perceived him, and Anfos covered his face with his hands and dropped to his knees with his face still hidden; while le tout petit Loup pushed Mirèio away and sat gaping in wonder at the apprentice. Then Christophe walked over to his father's work-bench, but slowly as one who walks in his sleep, and he took up a wooden mallet and a chisel, and laying the chisel against an oak block he struck it true and strong with the mallet. The chisel moved, tracing a straight, deep line —hesitated—slipped sideways and was finally still; and Christophe also became very still, his whole body grown rigid because of the stillness. Mirèio crept forward and crouched at his feet, but le tout petit Loup tugged hard at his sleeve and spoke to him loudly, receiving no answer. Then something like terror seized le tout petit Loup, so that he started to scream for their mother:

'Maman, come here! Come quickly to Christophe!'

Anfos was still kneeling as Marie ran in, but he rose when he heard her, uncovering his face and laying a finger against his lips: 'Hush, do not dare to intrude . . .' he whispered.

She pushed him aside, going quickly to her child, and

pale and trembling with fear though she was, she managed to speak to the boy quite calmly.

'Christophe,' she said, 'Christophe, look at me, dear one. Listen, enfantounet, your mother is speaking . . . your mother who loves you and needs you so much. Try to hear her and wake up, my little son.' And she placed her hand firmly over his hand: 'Your mother who needs you so much,' she repeated.

His limbs slowly relaxed and he heaved a deep sigh; then he turned and saw her standing beside him. In a moment his arms were around her neck: 'I thought I had lost you . . . lost you . . .' he sobbed wildly.

Sitting down she drew him on to her knee, and when his sobs had become less violent she questioned him with great tenderness: 'Little flower of my heart, try to tell me what happened.'

So he tried, but quite failed to collect his thoughts; one memory alone appeared to have persisted: 'There is something that I must do,' he faltered, 'it is something that makes me feel terribly afraid. . . .'

Marie kissed him, clasping the child to her breast: 'Then you shall not do it, pichounet! she murmured.

But he looked at her out of his pale, bright eyes; 'I will not always feel frightened,' he said slowly.

She saw that her questions only distressed him, for now once again he had started weeping: 'It is that I pity so much . . .' he wept. Yet when she asked him for whom he felt pity, he seemed bewildered and shook his head: 'I cannot remember . . . perhaps Mirèio.'

So she soothed him, stroking his tear-stained face, and drying his eyes on her rough linen apron while she coaxed with the simple and foolish words that in times of trouble are consoling to children: 'Let us now pretend you are once more a baby so that maman has to carry you up to bed,' and lifting him in her strong peasant arms she slowly mounted the stairs to the attic: 'When I have undressed you, my very small son, I will go and make you a tisane de menthe—maman will make it with a great deal of sugar; and then she will sit beside you till you sleep; to-morrow you shall have a fine holiday from school, and perhaps you can go down and bathe with Goundran. Maman is here, and

Mirèio is here, and Loup and Anfos, and presently your father will return—think how many there are to protect you!'

And her words did console, for when he was in bed he stopped crying and snuggled down under the bedclothes. Then: 'Make it very sweet, please . . . you promised!' he urged, as she hurried away to prepare the tisane.

2

By the time the good Jóusè got home that evening, Christophe was sleeping quite peacefully. So his father said: 'It was certainly strange, yet I do not think that we need worry about him—look at him now, he is fast asleep. He may well have had a slight touch of the sun; let us see how he is to-morrow morning, it is rather late to trouble the doctor. Christophe has always been healthy and strong— do I not know it, I, who bred him? And now it is time that we also were in bed, for your husband is no longer so young as your son and when one is my age one feels this great heat. . . . Ah, yes, Marioun, your poor husband is ageing!' Then as though he would contradict his own words he gave her a mighty and bearlike hug: 'Today I have done a superb stroke of business. Segnour Diéu, but I got that timber for nothing! You shall certainly have a new dress for Sundays.'

3

Christophe was perfectly well the next morning. He had slept a deep and refreshing sleep and was rather unusually hungry for his breakfast, but Marie insisted on the holiday from school, although Jóusè thought it unnecessary.

'I promised that he should stay at home,' she said firmly, for she could not bear the boy out of her sight—not just yet—and, divining this, Jóusè consented.

She was very profoundly bewildered and disturbed by what had occurred—a touch of the sun was the explanation that her husband still clung to; but she herself was far from being convinced that this was a plausible explanation; Christophe was so thoroughly accustomed to the sun of Provence, as were all the other children. But she could not give a name to the curious condition which had over-taken the boy in the workshop. She had seen him while feeling that he was not there . . . and surely he also must have felt the same thing, for had he not said that he thought he had lost her? Yet her instinct warned her not to question him again, but rather to let the incident drop as Christophe himself seemed inclined to do—indeed only once did he speak of it that day, and then without any apparent emotion:

'Were you frightened when I went to sleep?' he asked her.

'No,' she lied, 'why should I have been frightened, my son?'

'That is good,' he said slowly, 'but yes, that is good, because I would never like you to be frightened—I was, though I cannot remember why.' Then he went to unchain Mirèio in the yard and she heard him whistling to himself as he did so.

'It cannot have been very serious,' she mused, only too anxious to find consolation, 'he is quite well again, thanks to God and His saints; already he has nearly forgotten all about it. . . . It may be that he really did drop off to sleep. But can a child drop off to sleep like that, standing?'

4

And this was how they finally came to explain it on those rare occasions when it chanced to be mentioned: 'The time when Christophe went to sleep at his work,' for such everyday words sounded reassuring, and le tout petit Loup had been badly scared, so that he needed a great deal of reassuring.

Anfos alone always shook his head: 'That was not sleep . . .' he would mutter in his beard.

Then Jóusè, observing his wife's anxious eyes, would sharply command the apprentice to be silent, so Anfos would obediently hold his peace, being obedient and docile by nature.

Yet despite Christophe's unimpaired physical health and her willing acceptance of his own simple theory, Marie perceived that the child had changed, that now there were times when he seemed much less childish; times, indeed, when he did not seem childish at all but unnaturally wise and grave for his age, as though he had already learnt the gravity of life, and he only a boy of eight years old. . . . It would strike her as being very perplexing.

She would find herself telling this son many things, speaking as though he were already a man, and smiling the while she talked of his father—so large, so foolish, himself scarcely grown up with his great boisterous laugh and his love of good food, and his habit of wearing the heels of his socks into round, gaping holes the size of a duck's egg. And her smile would be tender and full of pride, as who should say: 'Is he not a marvel, my husband?' And then she might thrust her knuckles through a hole: 'Look, Christophe, look what your poor mother must darn! Hóu, but your father is a mighty man and heavy, that is why he always wears out his socks. And you also, I think, will have his big feet—let us hope that your wife will be clever with her needle.'

And Christophe would nod understandingly, detecting in her voice the note of admiration for that deep-chested, curly-headed sire of his, who kept her so constantly darning and mending.

Sometimes she would speak of le tout petit Loup, who although he seemed rather less ailing these days, was still very far from being robust, while growing more and more difficult to manage. 'Ai! las,' she must sigh, 'mon pauvre tout petit Loup, always longing to be active and well, like you, Christophe; always trying to do things beyond his poor strength because he sees how you can work in the shop, and how strong and splendid your arms are already when you help your father to lift the big planks . . .'

And Christophe would know that although their mother had love and to spare for both her children, she was filled with regret for le tout petit Loup, and at moments felt even a little jealous of the strength that had gone to her elder son who already could lift the big planks with his father. So quite suddenly he himself must grow sad because he clearly divined her sadness and because he felt very inadequate whenever he wanted to offer her comfort.

Then, as likely as not, Marie's conscience would smite her: 'But why do I speak of these things to you, Christophe? You are almost as young as le tout petit Loup.' And perhaps she would tell him to go and find Jan, and to have a good game without his small brother: 'Do not take Loup this evening, just play by yourselves . . . I know well that he must often be in the way. . . .'

But Christophe would hear far more than her words, he would hear the voice of her heart always pleading—always pleading on behalf of le tout petit Loup: 'No, no, I will surely take him,' he would answer; and her eyes would be filled with dumb gratitude and would somehow remind him of the eyes of Mirèio.

For now, what had once come in passing flashes, had grown into a profound and unavoidable knowledge of those things that lay hidden in people's hearts: in the heart of his mother, so fearful, so humble; in the heart of his father who also feared lest grief should darken the life of his mother; in the poor, angry heart of le tout petit Loup who longed for a healthful and vigorous body; in the simple, bewildered heart of Anfos who vaguely divined that he was half-witted. And this knowledge was exceedingly hard to bear since the young will quite naturally shrink from suffering. Thus all that was youthful and heedless in Christophe, his will to that personal happiness which is childhood's essential and trusty armour, his will to that purely physical joy which is childhood's true instinct of self-preservation, indeed everything almost that made him a child, would rise up at times and protest very strongly, so that he would find himself filled with resentment against his own strangely pitiful heart which forced him to divine those other hearts. Aye, and to share their pain with the beasts who groaned beneath man's unmerciful burden.

He would speak almost roughly to le tout petit Loup: 'No, you cannot come with me—I do not want you.' And when Marie would start to console the child, and would look her amazement at this swift change of humour, Christophe would stand there dogged and scowling. Then perhaps he would suddenly rush from the house, heedless of Mirèio whose pads were too sore these days for her to run without pain—he would try not to know that she struggled to follow.

Going to the port he would seek out Jan and would find him more than ready for trouble, so together they might untie Goundran's small boat and row her far out, which was strictly forbidden. And other similar things they might do, most of which would be heavily pregnant with mischief, as, for instance, when they blocked up the overflow of the town's highly prized municipal fountain. One fine afternoon they must suddenly decide to go off and visit the Café de la Tarasque—it was well that Mère Mélanie's red amazon had recently gone to the canine Valhalla, for as usual, Mirèio had followed her master.

The boys plumped themselves down at this table, then that, making faces at the little hump-backed violinist: 'Home bosa! Look at his hump!' they bawled, whereupon several other small urchins joined them: 'Home bosa! Home bosa! Look at his hump!' And the sailor-men lolling and drinking near by, laughed loudly, to the children's immense satisfaction.

But the little violinist who had just been endeavouring to drown that same hump in Mère Mélanie's brandy, the little violinist flew into a rage and ordered the pack of them off to God's thunder: 'Anas-vous-en au tron de Diéune!' he shouted, which caused much general amusement.

Mère Mélanie strode forth flushed and protesting, her lusty black locks still confined by steel curlers; and Mère Mélanie was not looking her best, since quite apart from the stiff curling pins, she never troubled herself to wash, or to powder her nose, until late in the evening. But the little violinist now turned to his lady as though she alone could afford him protection; then made bold by her presence he picked up a glass, intending to hurl it at his tormentors:

'Anas-vous-en au tron de Diéune!' he babbled over and over again, that being the only robust malediction which the brandy permitted him to remember.

Mère Mélanie tore the missile away, then she slapped his hand and thrust him behind her. After which she, in her turn, abused the boys, but in much more explicit and versatile language. Finally she threatened to evoke the law: 'Unless you go quickly I send for the gendarme!' Nobody feared the gendarme in Saint Loup, the small boys least of all—he himself had eight children.

But long before Mère Mélanie's final threat Christophe had left the scene of the baiting, angry because he felt pitiful, yet in spite of his anger consumed with pity. And as once, seven years ago, his own father had walked slowly home, his head bowed in contrition while Mirèio limped along at his side all battered and bloody but uncomplaining, so now Christophe slowly walked towards home, and at his side painfully limped old Mirèio. And it seemed to him that in some strange way there was kinship between the bitch and the cripple; between all afflicted and suffering things, were they dumb or articulate, beasts or men—that their suffering constituted a union. Stooping down he fondled Mirèio's head, walking even more slowly to ease her lameness, while something within him started to weep because of the beauty he perceived around him; a beauty of mountains, of sea, and of sky blending into one vast and fulfilling blueness, but a beauty that was shot through and through with pain—the pain of the hunchback, goaded, enraged, hot with brandy and the shame of his ugly affliction; the pain of Mirèio, helpless and dumb, weak with age and long years of neglect and scant feeding.

'Oh, I do not wish to feel pity!' muttered Christophe.

Presently they came to the ancient church, and Christophe went into its cool, quiet shadows. Mirèio lay very still while he knelt before the shrine of the warrior-bishop. Christophe stared up at the agèd saint who is carved out of wood and has time-blurred features; and he thought of Mathilde who seemed almost as old, but who wore a white cap instead of a hat from which the gold-leaf was gradually peeling. Then he thought of Saint Loup's grateful nightingale that had come with the darkness to sing in his garden: 'Praise God in His Golden Saints,' it had sung—his mother had often told him the legend. Saint Loup had restored its life to the bird, so Saint Loup must have known what it felt like to pity.

Then Christophe prayed rather recklessly, so urgent, so great was his need at that moment: 'Oh, Saint Loup, if I have to go on feeling sorry . . . If I have to go on, then please make me feel brave like you must have felt when you drove back the heathen. But I do not want to feel sorry any more—I want to be like all the other boys—and I do not want to know about pain, especially about Mirèio's pain. And I want to leave my brother at home when I play,

H

because he is weak and spoils all our fun; I want him to stay at home, please, with our mother. Saint Loup, you were very different from me, for you were a splendid, powerful saint who could easily have healed poor Mirèio's sores, and made le tout petit Loup grow strong, and taken the hump away from the violinist. But I can do nothing—nothing at all—that is why I am often terribly unhappy. Perhaps you could speak to our dear Lord Jesus and ask Him to let me be more like Jan; Jan is not at all worried about sad things and yet, as you know, he is very religious. Our Lord will undoubtedly listen to you, because you put up a cross near the town to show Him that you had defended the Christians. Oh, but yes, He will listen to all you say, I know He will listen . . . Saint Loup, please ask Him!'

He stopped praying, and finding two sous in his pocket, proceeded to light a votive candle: 'That should help him to remember,' he thought to himself, feeling that a saint who heard so many prayers might possibly need a tactful reminder.

The saint watched him with those motionless wooden eyes from which the years have wiped all expression. Then the candle burnt up revealing a form that must once have been very golden and splendid—in his left hand this soldier of Christ holds a cross, but his right hand is clasped round the hilt of a sword with which he may quite well have smitten the heathen. And now the flame was swayed by a wind that had suddenly started to blow from the desert, from the desolate river bed of La Crau; in it blew through the cracks and chinks of the windows. Light and shade moved alternately across the carved face giving it a startlingly lifelike expression, so that Christophe felt certain his prayer had been heard:

'All goes well,' he told himself confidently, 'it looks as though our good patron were smiling.'

CHAPTER TWELVE

I

DESPITE Christophe's faith in the power of Saint Loup, all was only too far from well that autumn; for that autumn Mirèio's final courage broke, and with its breaking her heart broke also. Old age superimposed upon constant hardships, the film that was gradually dimming her eyesight, the sores that so stubbornly refused to heal no matter how diligently she licked them, the ticks that for years had been draining her strength, these things had at last got Mirèio under. And now came the added torment of growths on those teats that had hung so painfully heavy with the milk that should have been sucked by her young, by the drowned bastard young of her past fruitions. And Mirèio very much wanted to die, and she went with her pain and her weariness to Christophe. She would stand gazing into his anxious face, imploring his pity by her constant whining. Wherever he chanced to be in the house these days, she would make an effort to find him. It was terrible, for Mirèio was unable to die; even the cruel malignant growths were powerless, or so it seemed, to release her.

Heartbroken, Christophe went to his father yet again: 'Father, can you do nothing for Mirèio?'

'Ai! las,' sighed Jóusè, 'what can one do? I have not got a gun nor can I shoot straight—if I tried to shoot I might well only wound her.'

'There is always the vet . . .' suggested Christophe in despair; but this he did rather timidly for he knew that just now they were short of money.

Jóusè shook his head: 'There is also the doctor. Have you forgotten your unfortunate brother? There are also quite a few bills still unpaid—one cannot clothe and feed children for nothing!'

Marie—who when she had time to think did very sincerely pity the creature—was heavy with trouble, for le tout petit Loup had developed something wrong with his breathing, and most nights he must sit propped up in his bed; the doctor had diagnosed it as asthma. Le tout petit Loup now wheezed when he ran and complained that his lungs felt tight to bursting. He would weep, which of course made the asthma much worse, and then he would double up his thin fist and beat his thin chest in a fit of anger. Moreover there was much that he must not do, to say nothing of all that he must not eat. Small wonder that Marie had no time for the bitch, with the cares of a sickly but turbulent child and a household upon her aching shoulders.

She said: 'You should never forget, my son, that although you may love Mirèio very dearly, she is certainly less than your brother in God's sight.' And her voice sounded rather stern and reproachful. So Christophe perceived that the time was at hand when he himself must do his poor best, and he came to a very momentous decision.

Theft—it was surely a deadly sin; he trembled to contemplate his confession. The Curé's low, stern voice through the grille: 'You have stolen a pot of ointment, my child? You say you have stolen it from your mother?' And then his own answer: 'I stole it for our dog.' And then . . .? But he could not imagine what then, it passed the limits of imagination. Suppose he should ask her to give him the ointment, the miraculous ointment that she put on his knees when he scraped them, that she had put on his father's thumb when a chisel had slipped and cut it last winter; the ointment that had driven away the large boil which Anfos had recently had on his neck? But he knew beforehand that she would refuse. Had she not refused to give it already? Had she not said that the chemist was unpaid? And now there was still more to pay to the chemist.

For three nights Christophe sternly examined his conscience: 'It is theft,' he told himself, greatly troubled, 'and theft is a very deadly sin.'

The third night he heard the voice of Mirèio.

The shed in the yard where Mirèio slept was just to the side of his attic window, and Mirèio was whining because of her pain, whining, and turning restlessly—he could hear

116

the unhappy thuds of her body. Then Christophe knew that he meant to steal.

'I am coming,' he muttered, 'only be patient.'

With pounding heart he crept down the stairs; he felt cold and rather sick, but courageous. His bare feet fell softly yet the woodwork creaked twice, so that he had to stand still, scarcely breathing. Presently he went on again, reassured; Loup was the danger, he slept with Anfos and sometimes his wheezing kept them both awake, but perhaps they would be sleeping soundly by now—it was nearly three o'clock in the morning. When he reached the kitchen a shaft of bright moonlight made it easy to find the key of the cupboard; he knew where it was, in his mother's workbasket. He took it, unlocked the cupboard, snatched the ointment, and quickly relocked the cupboard again; after which he put the key back in its place, and cautiously unbolting the door into the yard, stole round to the shed where Mirèio lay whining.

His footsteps had made no sound on the path, but the bitch must have heard them by intuition, for now she was gazing with dim, rheumy eyes at the entrance to the shed, and as Christophe went in she gave him a feeble but thankful welcome: 'You have come to bring me peace,' said her eyes.

'I have brought you the ointment that heals my knees. I have stolen it out of my great love for you,' he answered, misunderstanding her meaning.

Then he bade her roll over on to her side; and this she did, even as she had done long ago when wishful to suckle her lusty puppies. Clumsily and yet with great tenderness he smeared the ointment over her sores, and over those fearful cancerous growths that now rendered her body a thing of pity . . . of pity, but also a thing of horror. And she sighed a deep and most patient sigh as she lay there under his fumbling fingers that gave so much pain to her aching flesh, but balm to her spirit because of their mercy. For she knew that he could not yet understand that for her there was nothing left in this world any more—nothing left but the love of God, the ultimate refuge of every creature. When he had finished she licked his hand, and at this he must suddenly begin to cry, his tears dripping on to her great scarred flank.

'I do love you so much, Mirèio,' he told her. Then he said: 'I will come to you every night. You will see, this ointment will make you quite well; that I know, because it has healed my knees many times.'

Mirèio did not contradict him.

2

Marie never missed the precious ointment which cost the eyes of the head at the chemist, since no accidents chanced to occur just then. For the rest, the household was so much upset by Loup's asthma that it luckily failed to observe Mirèio's coat, which was suspiciously greasy. Every night Christophe kept himself wide awake until it was safe to steal down and tend her; every night he anointed Mirèio's sores and the growths that were eating into her body. But the sores did not heal nor the growths diminish; on the contrary the growths seemed to get larger.

Then Christophe humbled himself to Saint Loup, and as he did this he became a child who must think, and pray, and hope as a child: 'I asked you to make me like Jan,' prayed Christophe; 'I asked you not to let me see pain . . . I will see all the pain, yes, all the pain in the world, if only you will help me to cure Mirèio. I know I am a very great sinner—a thief; I know that I ought to confess to the Curé, but I do not want to confess to him just yet because he might tell me to give back the ointment. Let me keep it a little while longer, please, Saint Loup, in case it should really be good for Mirèio. But I promise that I will go to confession and that I will ask for a very hard penance. I will say to the Curé: "I am vile in all ways." I will read my Examination of Conscience so that I may not forget one sin, and then I will ask for a very hard penance. I will tell him how much I enjoy bouillabaisse, and little new cakes that are covered with sugar, and tisane de menthe that is made very sweet. Then perhaps he will say: "None of these shall you have for a year." Or perhaps he may even say: "Never, never again must you eat bouillabaisse. And remember when you see it, or even smell it and feel hungry because you like it so much, that you stole a pot of ointment from your mother!" And never again will I eat bouillabaisse if only you will help me to cure Mirèio. Think of your nightingale, Golden Saint Loup—it was little and helpless and so you felt pity. Mirèio is terribly large, I know, but I beg you to try and pity her also. Tell our Lord that I do not want to be spared, that I am quite ready to go on feeling sorry. Tell Him that I do not want to be like Jan—unless He would prefer me to be like Jan—and then ask Him to forgive me for stealing the ointment.' In this wise Christophe humbled himself to the saint who had raised a nightingale from the dead—that is if one may credit tradition.

Who can know why Saint Loup failed to answer that prayer? Perhaps he was very much occupied with matters pertaining to more grievous sinners. Be that as it may, Christophe's prayer went unheard and Mirèio's condition remained unaltered. Then Christophe completely lost faith in Saint Loup, and he thought very bitterly indeed about him: 'I do not believe that he loved little birds—I do not believe in his nightingale legend. I do not believe, no, I do not believe! It is time that I tried to find someone kinder.' And all of a sudden he remembered the wolf that, repenting itself of its erstwhile sins, had become as a faithful dog to Saint Francis.

So now night and morning that merciful saint whose hands and feet bore the blessèd stigmata, that saint must lean down from the shining throne upon which his suppliant visualized him, the better to listen to stumbling prayers which were growing more and more incoherent. And the night came when Christophe went to Mirèio but discarded the jar of his precious ointment, when he just sat still with her head on his lap, talking softly but earnestly under his breath, for he thought that his voice and his presence soothed her. And believing that Mirèio could comprehend words, he told her, quite simply, the story of Saint Francis; the story of The little poor Man of God, who having neither purse, nor cloak, nor shoes, had yet given to his lesser brethren a gift that must always be beyond price— the gift of a pitiful understanding.

'And so,' said Christophe, 'you need not feel afraid, for soon this terrible pain will have left you. I cannot cure your body with my hands because I am not a saint,

Mirèio; but I think . . .' he hesitated, amazed at the words that were forming themselves in his mind, 'I think that I can send you to God with my hands, and that God who loves you will surely be waiting.' Trembling, he laid his hands on her head: 'God,' he whispered, 'I ask You to take Mirèio.'

She tried to shift her position very slightly so that she might look up into his face, so that she might tell him with her grateful eyes that in him she perceived the image of God made manifest to her dumb understanding. That in him and through him she had reached a love that was deathless, since it was the love of God which could make the most humble of lives eternal. Then her head dropped gently away from his touch, and over Mirèio there came a great stillness.

Terrified and confounded Christophe stared at her body growing chilly in death, and already unfamiliar: 'Mirèio!' he cried out like the grief-stricken child that he was; 'Mirèio, what have I done?' And he looked at his work-scarred and merciful hands with fear, for now he was very young—a little Provençal peasant boy of eight years old who lived in Saint Loup and who worked at a carpenter's bench with his father.

3

Anfos it was who went to Jóusè and begged his permission to bury Mirèio. Love for Christophe had apparently sharpened his wits, and he thought that the child might well be consoled if he knew that the creature was decently buried.

Jóusè was not inclined to refuse. He had found his son in the shed that morning sitting dry-eyed and speechless beside the body, and something in Christophe's stricken young face had touched the heart of the father in Jóusè. So now he said: 'Caspi, you may bury the bitch, that is if you can manage to get anyone to help you, for I think you will find her heavy enough—her great carcase will be no light weight to carry. But of course you must bury her after dark. One does not parade dead dogs through the streets of Saint Loup by daylight as though they were Christians!'

for Jóusè much disliked ridicule. 'And where will you dig this fine grave?' he questioned.

Anfos hesitated, and then he said slowly: 'I thought at the foot of Eusèbe's vineyards. . . .'

'Ho, ho!' exclaimed Jóusè. 'Well then, mon pauvre bougre, you had certainly better obtain his consent, otherwise he may dig her up again. I advise you to go now at once and consult him.'

So Anfos went over to Eusèbe and tried to obtain his permission also: 'I ask this for Christophe's sake,' he began, which was wonderfully clever for a half-wit like Anfos, since Eusèbe—that cross-grained old sinner—had a certain sneaking affection for Christophe.

Eusèbe frowned, and spat heavily; then he shrugged, and cast his eye up to the ceiling; then he started to roll a small cigarette in dirty paper between dirty fingers; and finally: 'What is all this that I hear? You would plant a dead dog at the foot of my vineyards? Santouno, what next will you suggest, I wonder! No, certainly not. Do you think I grow grapes for the finest red wine in all France from corpses?' For Eusèbe liked to assert himself when it came to the matter of granting a favour.

Poor Anfos could only nibble his beard and stand on one foot and then on the other: 'I had hoped . . .' he faltered, but his courage failed; he was really terribly afraid of Eusèbe. Those uncanny ill-matched orbs filled him with fear; indeed, nothing on earth but devotion to Christophe could have tempted him into the ogre's lair: 'I will go—but at once I will go,' stammered Anfos as he beat a hasty retreat to the door.

'Do not be such an imbecile!' snapped Eusèbe. Of course he had always intended to give in, so that he started to speak less fiercely: 'It may be that I shall not say no after all. It may very well be that, upon second thoughts, I shall find myself much inclined to say yes . . . I do say it. Yes, you may bury the bitch in that bit of waste ground that abuts on my vines, but'—and now he really became terrific —'but the saints protect you if so much as a leaf, if so much as a tendril is touched in the process. Sarnipabiéune! I will strip you of skin! I will pluck the beard from your face hair by hair! I will . . . '

In sheer panic Anfos turned and fled, scuttling away to the port to find Goundran.

Goundran agreed to help willingly enough: 'I will come to-night bringing an old sail with me. Meanwhile you must find a lantern and spade—we shall need a lantern for the moon is still young. How is Christophe taking the death of the bitch?'

'I do not know—he says little,' Anfos told him.

4

When most of the windows of Saint Loup were dark because most of its tired inhabitants were sleeping, Mirèio's funeral procession set forth. Goundran and Anfos were carrying the body very neatly sewn up in the promised sail; Christophe was carrying the spade and lantern. In silence they made their way through the town, and in silence the three of them passed out beyond it and started to climb the steep, dusty hill that led to the foot of Eusèbe's vineyards— to that rock-strewn waste land where Mirèio still lies, the soil being too stony for cultivation. And even the strong arms that carried her ached, for emaciated though she had become, there were always her bones, and her bones were mighty. The new moon hung sideways. Great luminous stars shone over the road and the nearer mountains; while beyond the sterile and sun-parched waste land there lay faintly discerned a fertility so violent, so undisciplined, that the fecund vines must strain their tendrils almost to breaking. Anfos sighed and his sigh sounded loud in the night, for the night seemed wellnigh as still as his burden. And a little ahead walked Christophe, alone, his lantern casting a dim, yellow beam, the spade carried strongly across his left shoulder.

Goundran thought: 'My godson is indeed a strange boy— no word of regret, no emotion, no weeping. And yet I do know how he loved the beast . . .' Then he thought: 'She was very shamefully neglected; I remember thinking that, years ago, when I saw her in the widow Roustan's shop. I remember thinking that I would speak . . . Ah, well, when a man has his work to attend to, when a man possesses a couple of vessels as I do these days, it has meant hard work. Bèlli Santo d'or, she is heavy!'

Anfos thought . . . But Anfos could think of so little that it hardly seems worth the trouble of recording. The effort of the morning had tired his weak mind—his mind would often grow tired in the evening and now it was past twelve o'clock at night, so that what thoughts he had came vaguely to Anfos.

Christophe thought: 'Mirèio is sewn up in that sail— she cannot come limping to find me any longer. Never again will I stroke her big head, no, never again as long as I live . . . and I laid my hands on her poor, big head . . . I felt that there was something strange about them. I think that now I am afraid of my hands because they were able to send her to God. But where is she? Am I certain that she is with God? Jan would not believe that she is with God . . . perhaps that is really Mirèio in the sail; perhaps there was never any other Mirèio at all.' Then he suddenly found himself whispering: 'Please God, do be very kind to Mirèio.'

The digging was hard when they reached the ground. Anfos and Goundran dug the grave by turns, while Christophe stood near-by to light their labour. The grave looked so large that, as Goundran remarked, it might very well have done for a man. And indeed it did appear both wide and deep when seen thus in the uncertain flame of the lantern. But at last Goundron wiped the sweat from his brow:

'Here, give me the bitch'; he said, 'all is ready.'

So Mirèio who had trodden that Provençal earth ever since she had been a rough, lumbering puppy; who had trodden it in gladness, who had trodden it in pain, was now to find her rest in that earth; and doubtless, had she been able to speak, her courageous old heart would have chosen none other. Thus, as frequently happens in this world of ours which appears to possess strange concepts of logic, Mirèio was more honoured and cared for in death than she was during all her long, faithful lifetime. Had not Goundran and Anfos borne her through their own town, and she cleanly sewn up in a shroud of canvas? Had they not dug a grave large enough for a man in such obdurate ground that their brows had been sweating? Had not Eusèbe permitted her to lie on the boundary of his cherished and profitable vineyards? And had not Jóusè agreed to it all, while dreading the ridicule of his neighbours? Yes, assuredly she was more cared for in death, having justified her existence by dying.

This then was the funeral and burial of Mirèio, the gaunt yellow bitch, who eight years before had brought forth her large litter of lusty puppies in the sawdust and shavings of the carpenter's shop belonging to Jóusè Bénédit—in great anguish and joy she had brought forth her puppies.

5

The next morning Christophe said to his mother: 'Here is all that is left of the ointment which I stole from your cupboard to rub on Mirèio's sores.' And he waited, quaking a little, for her answer.

Marie was scrubbing the kitchen table. She looked up in surprise: 'What is that, my son? But how did you get it? The cupboard was locked.'

'I found your key and unlocked it,' said Christophe.

She dried the soap from her hands on her apron, as was always her habit when hurried or anxious. After which she glanced into the grimy jar that her son was holding out for inspection. There was scarcely a quarter of its contents left, and that quarter was stuck thickly with stiff, yellow hairs.

'You had better throw it away,' she told him. Then she said, but quite gently: 'You were wrong to deceive me. Am I so stern and unkind a mother that you could not have asked me to give you the grease? Is it likely that I would have refused your request? Another time come and ask, pichounet. And now kiss me . . . I am glad that you have spoken the truth. Eh bien, we will try to think no more about it.'

So Christophe kissed his mother on both cheeks, realizing that she had completely forgotten her refusal to give him the ointment in the past, and this because she was now very weary.

Then he sought out his father: 'I have stolen,' he informed him: 'I stole the ointment from mother's cupboard in order to cure Mirèio's sores.'

Jóusè looked up from the plank he was planing, and his

124

eyes were unusually soft and kind: 'Have you told your mother?'

Christophe nodded his head.

'And what did she say?

'That I ought to have asked her . . . That I ought to have asked her to give me the grease.'

Jóusè grunted. 'Well then, I say just the same thing.' And he turned once again to the plank he was planing.

That evening Christophe went to confession, and this was indeed a tremendous ordeal, for he dared not hope that Monsieur le Curé would be as lenient to him as his parents: 'Give me your blessing, Father.' he began, as he knelt on the hard little wooden shelf, 'I have sinned. . . .'

The Curé blessed him and waited.

Then Christophe plunged desperately into his recital, sparing himself and the Curé no detail, not excepting his loss of faith in Saint Loup and his angry thoughts of that warrior-bishop. And while he accused himself of his sins in an agitated and somewhat hoarse whisper, he unconsciously touched a long disused chord in the heart of his tired and south-drugged listener. For the Curé had once been quite fond of dogs, having had a dog of his own in his boyhood. Bobby, he had called it, because at that time he had been not a little proud of his English, and now Bobby had suddenly come into his mind—a plucky, upstanding, curly retriever.

Said Christophe: 'I think I had better say also, that I promised Saint Loup to ask for a penance which would be very hard. I much love bouillabaisse, perhaps you would rather I did not eat it—though I do not think I love it quite so much now,' his voice trembled a little; 'I do not think that I love it so much since the death of Mirèio. But I made that promise to Saint Loup when I told him that I would not go to confession just then in case . . . in case . . .' Christophe hesitated, 'in case you should tell me to give back the ointment.'

The Curé's lips twiched very slightly in the darkness: 'Is that all, my child?'

'Yes, all except this: I laid my hands on Mirèio's poor head and I prayed that God would be kind and take her . . . Then she died . . . and now I am afraid of my hands.'

'That is presumption, my child,' said the Curé.

And he went on to add that whenever God chose he could end the lives of all mortal creatures, so that Christophe must not be a foolish boy and presume to think that his own weak hands had caused the death of the dying Mirèio. And that if he had wanted the ointment for the dog he should have gone straight to his mother and told her, because it was always wrong to take things which belonged to others without their permission; but that nevertheless his intention had been kind—he had wanted to do Mirèio a kindness. These and other very similar remarks he made, and all the while he was thinking of Bobby. 'Bien,' he concluded, 'if you have confessed every sin that you find yourself able to remember, then make a good act of contrition, my son; and for penance say three Hail Marys in honour of the Holy Trinity. And now I will give you absolution.'

When it had been given Christophe thanked the priest.

'Say a little prayer for me,' murmured the Curé.

So Christophe went forth absolved of his sins, and having received the Curé's blessing. The light lay golden over Saint Loup, golden over the red-tiled Provençal roofs that covered the houses at such queer angles, golden over the warm and tideless sea, golden over the stern but protective mountains—for as those who have been to that town will remember, the light is generally golden in the evening. Yet although he was now feeling brand new throughout, the result of so good and careful a confession, although the Curé had been very kind, quite as lenient and kind, indeed, as his parents, Christophe sighed as he turned his steps towards home, because in his heart he was terribly lonely; and because when he tried hard to think about God and the saints he kept thinking about Mirèio.

6

In his study the Curé sat pretending to read. He was tired by his evening of hearing confessions—they were always the same in the town of Saint Loup which, praised be the saints, had not many great sinners. Yes, but always the same little ugly sins—sloth, greed, the neglect or the scamping of prayers, the uncharitable thought, the injurious word, the absence of Christian love for a neighbour. Although sometimes, it was true, there were graver transgressions, bred of overmuch liquor and overmuch sunshine —those shatteringly sudden lapses from grace, which at first had so greatly perturbed the Curé.

'Alas,' he murmured, 'pauvre humanité. How immeasurably distant we all are from heaven.' Then he thought: 'Christophe Bénédit and his dog—I remember that he said something to me about it. That was . . . let me see . . . quite a long time ago. I fully intended to speak to Jóusè, but somehow what with my parish and the heat . . . And how odd that business about the boy's hands, about laying his hands on the creature's head—very odd. And what curious eyes he has; they haunted me one day, I could not forget them . . . Ah, mais non, I, too, become imaginative, Christophe is just like every other boy, he is constantly in and out of mischief with Jan; all the same, I am glad I was a little severe regarding those foolish fancies of his—one is always afraid that the young may grow morbid.' Then the Curé yawned loudly; he was really tired out, for the wind was blowing again from La Crau, which invariably depressed and fatigued him: 'Alas,' he repeated, shaking his head as he closed the book that he was finding so dull, 'how immeasurably distant we all are from heaven!'

CHAPTER THIRTEEN

I

GOUNDRAN's life had hitherto run very smoothly. A hard worker and of a saving disposition, he had managed to avoid financial troubles. Both his fishing vessels were free from debt so could hold their sails high in fair or foul weather, breasting the waves as proudly as they pleased, which was thanks to their careful and thrifty master. Moreover he possessed the placid temper that went with as yet unawakened senses, and had thus avoided those sudden squalls which were apt to blow up at the port over women. And if he missed something of the light of the moon; missed the warm, soft trickle of wine down his gullet; missed the warm, soft weight of a girl on his knees, and the hard throb of blood on those nights in summer when tempers were short while knives could be long; missed the shrill, teasing tunes of the little violinist—if he missed all these things he was yet content, being quite unconscious of what he was missing. Small wonder then that his well-ordered life had hitherto run with unusual smoothness.

But a few weeks after the burial of Mirèio there occurred the death of another old creature, for Mathilde died sitting up in her chair, died as neatly and cleanly as she had lived—no illness, no pain, no chemist, no doctor. Yet her going, so simple a thing in itself, brought about a most mighty disturbance for Goundran, since what was to become of the youthful Elise who was now left without a single relation?

Elise, who had been devoted to her aunt, must naturally do a great deal of weeping. Goundran would find his own eyes full of tears, and would rack his brains for something to say that might be expected to give consolation. Mathilde had bequeathed her small house to the girl, as well as her tiny personal fortune, but Elise was too young to live all alone, such a thing would have outraged every convention. Goundran, of course, found new lodgings at once, having sent in a kind-hearted female neighbour, but the woman could not remain very long; it certainly was a distressing situation.

Goundran said to this neighbour: 'I am deeply perplexed . . . I have known Elise since the days of her childhood, yet I cannot decide what she ought to do. . . . Perhaps you will advise?'

'Mais oui,' nodded the neighbour, 'it is perfectly clear what Elise ought to do, what every young girl ought to do—get married.'

'Have I not said so already,' he sighed, 'but she seems completely indifferent to men; as you know she refused that fine fellow, Bertrand.'

Then he went to Marie and sought her advice: 'The girl has not even a distant cousin—it is sad to be so much alone in the world—do you think that perhaps she might enter a convent? Do you think that she possibly has a vocation?' For now he was really at his wits' end.

'I think her vocation is marriage,' smiled Marie.

So off he must go in search of Jóusè who, as ill luck would have it, was completing a bed for a couple just entering into wedlock; and Jóusè laid down his tools and looked wise while he listened to Goundran with careful attention.

After a little: 'I think,' remarked Jóusè, 'that Elise is much in need of a husband. A young girl with a house and fortune of her own yet no man to protect her . . . pecaire, the poor child! She may soon be exposed to God knows what danger. You have asked my opinion; very well, there it is.' And he stared rather meaningly at his friend.

'Now why is he staring like that?' fretted Goundran.

As he left, Eusèbe was standing in his doorway: 'So Mathilde has at last joined the saints!' he said blithely, 'And what is to happen to her pretty young niece who is not yet, I take it, quite ready for heaven? Tell me, what is to happen to that pretty young niece?'

Goundran shook his head: 'Ah, that is the problem, and she naturally turns to me for help. . . . '

'I do not doubt that she does!' winked Eusèbe.

I

Ignoring the wink which might, after all, have resulted from nothing more gross than an eyelash, Goundran went on to pour forth his woes: 'But how can one hope to cure the child's sorrow? Mathilde was a mother to the little Elise, and now all day long she does nothing but weep, and when I am near her she weeps more loudly, so that I cannot think how to act. . . .'

'Then you must be a cretin,' remarked Eusèbe, 'There is only one cure for a virgin who weeps, quite a simple cure —her immediate deflowering.'

Goundran turned and left him in angry disgust—a lascivious pig of a fellow, Eusèbe!

Yet wherever he went Goundran heard the same thing expressed in less unconventional language; the girl ought to marry and marry at once; what she needed was a strong and protective husband. And everyone seemed to be talking at him as though he were to blame, which was surely unfair. Had he not taken his friend to the house, the excellent Bertrand who was such a fine captain? Had he not taken him many times, always doing his best to egg on the courtship? And had Bertrand not wished to marry Elise? But yes, he had wished to marry Elise! Then why, in God's name, had she been so stubborn? If those two had only been safely married, all this miserable worry could not have arisen.

But the worry augmented by leaps and bounds, for poor Goundran must learn that a lion at bay is a lamb when compared with an amorous woman who, instead of a child, has conceived a grievance. Madame Roustan had waited more than eight years, but now at long last she could take her revenge through the spreading of purely fictitious scandal. It was easy enough, since who can be certain of what transpires in the house of a neighbour? Goundran had shared a roof with the youthful Elise, he being a man, she being a woman, though as Madame Roustan was careful to insist, Elise was more sinned against than sinning. A crippled old aunt almost totally blind had naturally not proved an adequate protection; why, they might have made love right under her nose—they had done, according to Madame Roustan! But what would you? the girl was as ripe as a peach on a southern slope, while as for Goundran. . . . Ah, well, there it was, and all terribly sad; but Elise was more sinned against than sinning.

At first Goundran could not believe his ears, it seemed too monstrous a thing for credence; however, before many days had passed, his ears were burning with indignation. Yet what could he do? It was like a pest that once thoroughly started, must spread its infection, and quite soon the story had reached the port, where it promptly afforded immense entertainment. The men from the tartanes grew merry indeed. Ho, ho, a dark horse, a most crafty devil! No wonder he went out so seldom at night—Mathilde's house had provided sufficient amusement. Sacré Nom d'un Nom, and he to pretend that he could not see the attraction of women! Oh, le fourbe! And then they must start to guffaw while sharing the yarn with their boon companions. Nor would any of them listen to Goundran's denials for to them he now seemed a very fine fellow. Oh, le fourbe! The jests would fall thick and fast, growing more and more turgid with each fresh remonstrance, so that in the end Goundran held his peace, for what was the use of wasting one's breath when nothing could silence their wit but a knifing?

As for Eusèbe, he was so vastly tickled that he grew aggressively cordial to Goundran, popping out of his shop like a Jack-in-the-box whenever he glimpsed the unfortunate fisher: 'Come and drink to your dear little friend,' he would urge, and then he might start his intolerable winking, or give Goundran a knowing dig in the ribs, or, worse still, make a gesture pregnant with meaning. It seemed fruitless for Goundran to turn his broad back and stalk on as a sign of contempt and aversion, Eusèbe's skin could be thicker than his hides when he did not desire to become offended, so that finally Goundran avoided the street, unless he were going to the Bénédit's, and would take his strolls in another direction.

There were people, however, quite a number of them, who looked far less lightly upon moral lapses; and who, whether they had believed that Mathilde was enleagued with the Lord or enleagued with Satan, were shocked at the thought of the youthful Elise having suffered so callous and base a betrayal; and these people were able to make themselves felt to some purpose, when mustered by Madame

Roustan. Goundran shrugged his shoulders and went his way, telling himself that since he was guiltless the accusation must speedily die, done to death by the very nature of its venom. Still, being a friendly and peaceable man he valued not only peace but friendship, and the knowledge that so many now wished him ill was making his heart grow increasingly troubled. Indeed he became very deeply depressed, falling into a kind of grim melancholy.

Yet two friends he had who never for a moment mistrusted his honesty and his honour—Marie and Jóusè remained quite unmoved in their faith. When questioned regarding the scandal Marie said always much the same thing: 'Goundran is the godfather of our Christophe; we chose him because he is upright and good; one has only to see him to know that he is good.' Then Jóusè would nod his large head many times: 'Mais oui, long ago we discovered his goodness.' But alone with his wife he would be less restrained, for Jóusè was bitterly angry with his sister and could scarcely tolerate her in his house, averse though he was to family ruptures. 'Do I not know the woman?' he would rage, 'Càspi, I do. All my life I have known her. If Goundran is Christophe's father-in-god then Germaine is surely his mother-in-the-devil. A vicious-tongued, lustful old hyprocrite with her weekly confessions and her Comtesse de Bérac and her: "*my* son is going to enter the priesthood; *my* son is going to the Grand Séminaire at Versailles." *Her* son, I pity a boy who has such a mother as Germaine. Quelle putain!'

And although Marie greatly disliked gross words, she nevertheless forbore to reprove him.

2

At last Goundran managed to muster the courage to go off and seek out Elise one morning: 'I pray you, leave us,' he said to the neighbour, who now viewed him with marked hostility, having recently visited Madame Roustan.

'If you need me you have but to call, pauvre enfant,' she remarked with a threatening glance at Goundran.

Elise was darning a black cotton glove, but she laid it aside as Goundran approached her. And now there she sat with her tremulous hands clasped tightly in order to still their trembling; and now there she sat with her honest blue eyes turned anxiously in Goundran's direction.

He said, diving head foremost into the subject lest by waiting his small stock of courage should dwindle, he said: 'There is something we two must discuss; but first I will ask a most serious question. Have I ever wronged you, my little Elise?'

'No. How could you possibly wrong me?' she asked him.

'There are ways . . .' he hesitated and flushed. Did she know? Had she heard of the scandalous gossip? 'There are ways . . . or so it would seem. . . .' he stammered, for her inocence made him feel ashamed when he thought of Eusèbe and the men from the tartanes.

'I know of nothing in you that is wrong—that could ever be wrong,' said the youthful Elise; and the blue of her eyes became so profound that it suddenly made Goundran think of the ocean. 'No, nothing in you could be wrong,' she repeated.

Then he noticed the shabby black cotton glove with a very big hole in the tip of one finger, and somehow that glove brought a lump to his throat, because as it lay there it looked so humble: 'Surely your birthday is to-morrow, Elise? I will buy you a pair of kid gloves,' he promised. He had come there to warn her of what was afoot, very tactfully, very discreetly to warn her, but instead he found himself holding her hand: 'Oh, the poor little hand, so cold, so cold . . . and so thin, Elise. Oh, the poor little hand!' Which was not at all what he had meant to say, since it certainly did not sound like a warning. And after a minute he must start to reproach her: 'Why, oh why, could you not have married that Bertrand? A fine man, a fine sailor and my very good friend; handsome, too, and with money saved in the bank. And just see what has come of your great foolishness, here you are unmarried and in consequence lonely. God knows I did everything in my power. . . . Ai! las, why could you not have married that Bertrand?'

'Because,' said Elise—and wonders of wonders, her voice did not shake and her hands ceased to tremble—'because there is only one man in the world, yes, only one man in the world I will marry. And if he will not take me I shall dedicate all the rest of my life to the Blessed Virgin. For surely it is better to remain alone than to mate without love—is that not so, Goundran?

Now whether it was the kind-hearted Saint Joseph who is known to be very propitious to marriage, or whether it was Our Lady herself who may well have been grieved by the girl's situation, or whether it was that Elise's blue eyes had suddenly made Goundran think of the ocean, who shall say? But the fact does undoubtedly remain that an urgent new longing welled up within him, a longing to love, to possess, to protect, to justify his fine well-tempered manhood, and he said:

'I would like you to tell me his name. Who is it that you would be willing to marry?'

She answered gravely: 'His name is Goundran.'

'No, no!' he exclaimed, still a little afraid of betraying his faithful and lifelong allegiance, 'No, no, Elise! Why, I am thirty-six—in another few years Goundran will be forty, and the sea and the south take a pretty big toll. If you look at me closely—closely, Elise—you will see that already my skin becomes wrinkled.' And he turned himself and faced the light. 'Come, stand up and look closer, my girl,' he commanded.

She obeyed and stood gazing into his face which to her seemed a thing enveloped by glory, so that she thought: 'In the image of God—ah, but yes, in the image of God created.' Aloud she said: 'What are the years to love? Love is sronger than time, stronger even than death.' Which some may think showed that she was indeed youthful. Then she laid both her hands on his broad, neat shoulders: 'I have tried to explain very often,' she told him; 'I have tried to explain by making small cakes in the shape of a heart. Do you not remember?' And even as she spoke she was greatly amazed at her own unexpected courage and calmness.

'Is it possible. . . .?' he murmured, 'Is it possible, Elise, that those small heart-shaped cakes were intended for me?' And his voice sounded hushed and almost awed, yes, almost awed because of those cakes—or was it because of what they had stood for?

After this neither spoke for quite a long while. Goundran was once again holding her hand, but now he was lifting the fingers one by one absent-mindedly, scarcely seeing her hand or her any more, so hard was he thinking.

Then: 'Goundran, will you marry me?' said Elise.

He looked up and caught her abruptly in his arms: 'Elise, will you marry me, dear?' said Goundran.

3

They were joined together very quietly and simply, for Goundran had wanted a simple wedding, and besides, there was always the death of Mathilde. Only Marie and Joùsè and Christophe were present in addition to Jan—now a a server at Mass—and of course the indispensable Curé.

The Mass ended, they walked back again to the house that had sheltered them for years, and they walked arm in arm. Goundran was rather unusually flushed and Elise very pale; in all other respects, however, they seemed like an old married couple—so collected, so unhurried, and Elise's grey dress so staid with its black velvet belt and white collar.

But that night the lover and lord of the sea became lover and lord of a mortal woman. And he found it unexpectedly gracious to rest his head on her firm young bosom; to be one with her ardent humanity; for when all was said and done Goundran was human.

4

Joùsè was well pleased with Goundran's marriage. It seemed to him wonderfully right and natural that so comely and stalwart and honest a fellow should mate and, God willing, produce many children.

'Mais oui,' he remarked to Marie the next evening as he fondled a hand grown rough in his service; 'mais oui, marriage sometimes brings sorrow, Marioun—sorrow and anxiety, that I admit,' and he glanced across at le tout petit Loup, 'but it also brings comfort along with sorrow, for a burden that is shared between two loving hearts only serves to bind them more closely together. I rejoice that Goundran has wedded Elise, and may she make him as brave a wife as my Marioun has made her Joùsè!'

So saying he pressed his lips to her palm, a thing that

he had not done for years, not indeed since the days of their earliest mating. And she blushed, recalling those more ardent days, while their eyes as they met became heavy with memories, for this wedding had made them think of their own, so that now many long-forgotten emotions looked out from their faithful toil-strained eyes—curiosity, reverence, diffidence, fear; but above all the imperative summons of life, the urge to beget in triumph through pain, a primitive, brutal, tenacious urge. Aye, and the joy of enduring pain. . . . Thus they saw each other across the years as courageous, forceful, and pregnant with meaning. And standing there they forgot their children in those irresistible thoughts of creation; forgot Loup who was playing at dominoes with his brother beside the lamp on the table, forgot Christophe the splendid first-fruit of their love, the seed of whose body they had sown in passion and prayer and in hope that had long been deferred—even him they forgot because they remembered.

But presently Loup must begin to cough: 'Maman, my chest hurts—it *hurts!*' he said loudly; and he swept the dominoes on to the floor, 'I will not play any longer, Christophe. You cheat. Many times I have seen you cheat!' For le tout petit Loup loathed the pain in his chest and must seek to wound someone, himself being wounded.

Christophe frowned; then noticed his mother's eyes that had once more grown pleading, tired and maternal. He wanted to hit le tout petit Loup, to give him a mighty hard clout on the ear for the spiteful, bad-tempered child that he was, always meanly untruthful when he was losing. But instead he went down on his hands and knees and collected the dominoes under the table, for what else could one do when beneath it all one perceived the infinite pathos of the creature, and the pleading that lay in his mother's eyes? Nothing, except to swear softly to one's self as one groped about:

'Sarnipabiéune!' swore Christophe.

5

Towards Christmas Goundran arrived one morning to announce his intention of doing up his house: 'For,' said

Goundran, looking important yet sheepish, 'you see how it is: when a woman is married she needs many things that a girl does not need—many little new comforts about the home. I would wish to provide my wife with these comforts. And then I would like the whole place to look gayer. I had thought a nice pink both inside and out; the walls are all terribly stained and dirty. And the paint of the shutters ought to be green, a bright, cheerful green like the vines in spring.'

Jóusè nodded: 'That can surely be done,' he told him.

'Very well, then, I want you to come down at once and consult with Elise regarding the colours. There is also the question of cupboards and so on. There are also the doors that the wind has jarred, and the rats have devoured the boards in our bedroom, and Elise says we need a new water butt. Ah, yes, there are many small things that we need— but I myself will help with the paintwork as the weather is too rough to go to sea.'

'It is also too dusty to paint,' warned Jóusè.

But his client was firm, they must start at once, for Goundran was childishly fond of painting.

Meanwhile Christophe, who was planing a very dull plank, looked up from his work with envious interest, and seeing this Goundran evolved an idea: 'Why should not Christophe assist?' he asked Jóusè. 'He is just going to start the Christmas vacation and the devil finds work for all idle hands. Is that not so, my hefty godson? Well, what do you say, shall we colour the walls like pink roses in honour of my little Elise? Shall we paint all the woodwork green like the vines? Shall we, in fact, make the house very clean and ourselves very dirty? Allons, what do you say?'

'I say yes — but a million times yes!' exclaimed Christophe.

'And suppose I say no—what then?' Jóusè enquired. But this he did only to tease the boy, and Christophe knew well that his father was teasing.

Thus the day arrived when Christophe appeared in a very old pair of fisherman's trousers rolled well up in order to fit his legs and gathered into the waist by a strap which Elise had managed to find in the attic. A sail-cloth blouse took the place of his shirt, the sleeves having been cut to above his elbows, and he carried a bucket of distemper so pink and so foamy that he suddenly wanted to eat it. The bucket, in its turn, must carry a brush of such magnitude that the distemper flowed over; a downright, broad-beamed, workmanlike brush with soft thick bristles and a stout wooden handle. Thus armed he attacked the sitting-room; slap, slap, dip and slap; slap and dip, dip and slap, while the rosy distemper ran back from the brush and splashed on to the floor off his dripping fingers.

'Santo d'or!' sighed Elise, 'and upstairs in our bedroom my Goundran works with scarcely less vigour. The floor boards will soon be far pinker than the walls, and already there are big daubs of pink on the bed. God be praised that I thought of covering the mattress! Ai! las, you men when you wish to be useful make more mess than a woman would make in a lifetime. You are careless, you men, as I tell my own man.'

But her lips were smiling indulgently, and Christophe must try to swell out his chest at hearing himself thus coupled with Goundran, and must grin and shrug his shoulders and spit, then apply his huge brush with so manly a flourish that a splash of distemper flew into his eye which he rubbed with a dripping but diligent finger.

Said Elise, displaying true feminine tact: 'If it will not disturb your work for a moment, I have a clean handkerchief here in my pocket—but I do not want to disturb your work. All the same—if you care to come to the window. . . .'

So Christophe held up his face to Elise who first moistened the handkerchief with her saliva, then carefully cleansed his long-suffering eye.

'I thank you, Elise,' he said very politely, and stooping he touched her hand with his lips, precisely as he had seen Goundran do when, one day, she had bound a cut on his finger.

But fine as it was to distemper the walls, it was even finer to paint the woodwork—although Goundran was selfish about the front door: 'No; I wish to do that by myself,' he insisted. 'You shall do the lower shutters, but not the door.' And he handed Christophe a new pot of paint. 'Do not waste it, enfantounet, it costs!' he cautioned.

Oh, the smell and the gloss and the green of the paint, and the way it slid over the battered old shutters! Christophe was happier now as he worked than he had been since the death of Mirèio. The dust rose in clouds, for the port was being swept by a vicious and very persistent mistral; and the dust made a rash come out on the paint which, however, did but prolong the pleasure, since he merely added coat upon coat, applying them always thicker and thicker. One thing only gave him cause for regret—Jan was too much engrossed by his books to take part in this orgy of house decoration. He had said rather sternly: 'I cannot lose time: I must think of the Curé and Madame de Bérac.' And then he had shown Christophe a rosary that the Comtesse de Bérac had sent him for Christmas. 'When one has obligations as I have,' he had said, 'one cannot lose time dabbing other people's shutters.' Christophe had certainly felt impressed, for those beads had looked very grand and expensive. Moreover Jan was quite right about Time: it did seem incredibly easy to lose it. It was here, it was gone, and before you could turn round. With every full chime of the church clock went an hour of the splendid and memorable Christmas vacation. Strive though he might Christophe knew very well that his painting would have to be left unfinished, and that Goundran would then take over his job.

'Time is thieving and stingy and jealous,' thought Christophe, trying to ignore that relentless clock; 'it is angry because I am feeling so happy.'

But more jealous than Time was le tout petit Loup; yes, indeed, he was far more angry and jealous: 'Why may I not also have fun?' was his question; and there he would stand in the wind-swept street with a scowl on his brow and his hands in his pockets. 'You paint very badly indeed!' he would shout. 'If I had that brush I could show you something!'

So one afternoon Christophe gave him the brush, after which he immediately snatched the paint-pot and proceeded to breathe rather hard as he worked, feeling anxious lest they should doubt his skill and remind him of his incessant bragging; and he breathed in the noxious fumes of the paint which very soon brought on his troublesome asthma. Tears sprang to the eyes of le tout petit Loup, but he rubbed them away and continued painting; a lump rose in the throat of le tout petit Loup but he swallowed it down and continued painting; phlegm worried the chest of le tout petit Loup, producing a loud and most painful wheezing, so that Christophe who heard it besought him to stop, but he shook his small head and continued painting. In the end Goundran took the paint-brush away, and Elise marched him firmly off to the parlour, whereupon he was promptly sick on the floor, for the fumes had also affected his stomach.

'All the same,' bragged le tout petit Loup the next morning as he managed to nibble a morsel of breakfast, 'all the same I paint better than Christophe does. When he paints he leaves nothing but ridges and bubbles. My work is like Goundran's, all glossy and smooth.'

'Mais oui, you are probably right,' consoled Christophe.

CHAPTER FOURTEEN

I

The religiously minded in the town of Saint Loup were not only prayerful but extremely busy, for presently would come the month of May when their offspring would make their First Communion. For the past seven months a feud had been raging between those who agreed with the Holy Father—the saintly and simple Pius X, who argued that as his Lord loved little children, Communion might well be received very young—and those who agreed with the conservative clergy who argued that until a child was eleven or thereabouts, it could not receive its Lord with the requisite understanding; an opinion which was also held by the Curé. And thus it had happened that Christophe and Jan had not taken advantage of the Quam Singulari, but would make their First Communion in May when both of them would be just over eleven.

Endless candles now burnt at the shrine of Saint Loup: 'O golden saint, make our dear children worthy.' Endless candles were lighted for the Mother of God: 'O Mary Virgin, thyself a mother, make our sons acceptable to thy Son.' In this wise prayed many a mother these days, for the women always found time to pray in spite of their arduous household duties, whereas the men must smoke at off times, and must stretch out their long legs as they basked in the sunshine or drank a small glass with Mère Mélanie. But what would you? That was the way with all men, their wives must make their peace for them with heaven! Except upon days of obligation, the most that the men ever did—and they fathers—was to clump into church looking awkward and large; and then, having signed themselves with the cross, to clump out again and light cigarettes —still, that was obviously better than nothing, and as Marie remarked with some truth to a neighbour who complained that husbands were not famous at prayers: 'After all, it is they who earn money for our candles.'

In the ancient houses had begun to appear many yards of white net and of fine white muslin. Sewing-machines tapped and whirred in the evenings—one could hear them as one walked past the open windows. And, as likely as not, bending over her task, her work-stained hands sharply contrasting with its whiteness, a woman would be seaming the muslin dress in which her daughter would kneel at the altar—the gentle and innocent wedding dress to be worn by a youthful bride of the spirit. But the veil, ah, that must be made by hand with a prayer for every so many stitches. The dress might be altered and worn again—since needs must when a household was short of money—but the veil would be carefully laid away wrapped in sheets of elegant pink tissue paper, with perhaps a few sprigs of lavender between, or some petals trodden brown by the priest who had carried the monstrance at Corpus Christi. The veil would be shown to intimate friends, to relations who came on a family visit; and, who knows, perhaps to the as-yet-unborn: 'Vois donc, petite Angèle, le voile qu'avait ta maman pour sa Première Communion. Mais oui . . . elle aussi a été toute jeune. . . .' And the lavender sprigs grown bare and scentless, and the petals grown brittle and dropping to powder; for alas, time has little respect at best, and none at all when we become sentimental.

But it must not be thought that the mothers of Saint Loup were guiltless of less exalted emotions; no, indeed, there was much heart-burning these days regarding the texture of net and muslin, the quality and merits of white suède shoes, and the price of the white cotton roses for wreaths. Above all did the faces under the wreaths very frequently give occasion for pride, that subtle and most trusty weapon of Satan. Thus already, although it was now only March, tittle-tattle and gossip were rife between neighbours: 'Ai! las, that the poor little Rosseline should suffer so much from those very disfiguring pimples; to wear white a child must have a good skin—my Sophie, thank God, has always possessed one.' Or: 'That daughter of Madame Perron's grows fat, a real pity it is, yes, a real disaster. And

I hear that her mother complains of the price of net."Ah, mais non," I said to my husband, "if one cannot spend two sous upon our dear Lord. . . . Imagine such a thing, for the child's First Communion!"' Or: 'I was astonished to remark that the Girals were buying those cheap canvas shoes for their daughters instead of white suède—both the girls have big feet which already is surely a great disadvantage. Our Céline has got very small feet and hands; all the same I would not risk those cheap shoes, they would make even her tiny feet look enormous.'

And so the old Devil had occasion to smile more than once as he groomed his tail in the sunshine, or polished his hooves with the snippets of muslin he had found cast away in some family dustbin, or pricked up a furry and impious ear as he strolled by a gossiping group at a corner. But meanwhile the weather was warm and most pleasant, and that blueness of sky and of sea and of mountains which is such an integral part of Provence, appeared bluer than usual, and so did the incense that rose at High Mass, and so did the eyes of Jóusè whenever they rested on Christophe— for Christophe was growing apace these days and would surely become a fair, mighty man; yes, a fair-skinned and mighty man like his father.

2

One night Jóusè sat up long over accounts, frowning and grumbling and chewing his pencil. Goundran always paid and paid handsomely but others did not—a most tiresome business. That couple who had ordered the marital bed, had they paid? Not at all! They had taken their pleasure and much of it, if Jóusè was any judge, yet the good, honest oak of their couch went unpaid for. And then there was that new counter for Germaine; she would cling to her money till the very last minute. There was also that fowl-house up at the farm—oh, but that was all right, they were trustworthy people who never kept a man waiting for his bill; in a week or so now they would pay for that fowl-house. Ah, but Loup . . . the chemist, the doctor, the food . . . so much butter and milk to make him grow fatter, so much bouillon to make his weak limbs grow strong; and the jellies carefully flavoured with wine because his small appetite had to be tempted. Ai! las, ai! las, le pauvre tout petit Loup, coughing and wheezing and complaining of his chest and his stomach and his meals and his home and his brother, yet doing so remarkably well at school—as sharp as a razor he was, the imp. And now if he was not learning to carve! His fingers were far more crafty than Christophe's. Christophe was good at big, simple jobs—the sawing of planks, the hacking of timber. He used his tools as to the manner born, with precision, with strength, with foresight, with knowledge. But le tout petit Loup possessed something that he lacked, a kind of ingenious impertinence, which made him not only clever but daring, so that he had gone to his father's prized hoard and had dragged out a Gothic panel to copy—the impudence of it, a child of his age! But, pecaire! he had not copied it badly.

How totally different they were, the two boys—since their earliest infancy they had been different; and this difference was very much marked now at school, for Christophe was not at all a good student. Christophe was so stupid about learning from books that the thing had begun to puzzle the master. Of course, he, Jóusè, had never liked books, yet he could not remember that when he was at school his lessons had been so difficult to him. Monsieur Roland declared that by word of mouth the boy could learn quickly, but not from print. This was grave, for an overworked master lacked time and patience to make an exception of Christophe, and already his brother had passed him in the class—oh, that imp, he was surely as sharp as a razor! Yes, Marie was right, Loup was cleverer than Jan in spite of the Grand Séminaire at Versailles and that sacrée Madame la Comtesse de Bérac!

Would Germaine pay soon? How soon would she pay? He really must settle down to accounts and stop thinking about less important matters—Christophe would be making his First Communion and clothes had to be bought for the solemn event. . . . How soon would that Germaine pay for her counter? Germaine had received a measurement card sent from Paris by Madame la Comtesse de Bérac—she was showing the thing all over the town—Madame la Comtesse would give Jan his suit—a fine suit he would have for his

First Communion. Sacré Nom; then Christophe should have a fine suit! Sacré Nom, he should have a suit finer than Jan's—a count's suit he should have, a duke's suit, a prince's! He, Jóusè, knew of a shop in Marseille where they kept all such things—a magnificent shop, frequented by the children of prosperous merchants. Their cut was superb, their materials glossy, their prices enough to make a man blink. He, Jóusè, had blinked but had then used his eyes and had seen those rows of wax figures in the windows—lifelike they had been, they had almost moved, boys of Christophe's age too with real hair on their heads; yes, and actually with real rings on their fingers! But that was not all; he had passed there in May and had stood before one particular window—little girls in beautifully soft muslin frocks with wreaths and long veils and white ivory prayer-books; little boys in immaculate black broadcloth suits, flottant ties, and with white favours worn on their sleeves—and especially had he observed their shoes, so rich, so unserviceable, so useless. Elegant black patent shoes they had worn—and that window had been labelled: 'PREMIERE COMMUNION.'

Bien, his Christophe was going to have one of those suits. He should have it if the devil ran away with the business; if Saint Loup himself stumped out of his niche in order to counsel economy—if his namesake had to go without bouillon! Ah, mais non, not that . . . le pauvre tout petit Loup! All the same he was going to buy one of the suits from that window labelled: 'PREMIERE COMMUNION.'

Beside Christophe, Jan would cut a mean figure, in spite of those costly clothes sent from Paris, in spite of his elegant nose and fine eyes, and what Germaine described as his scholarly forehead. A mere wisp of a boy, no physique, no strength; why, to give him a plank to lift would be to break him, whereas to see Christophe lifting a plank was to know that you had not betrayed your manhood. A lovely sight, Christophe lifting a plank, with small muscles already upon his young arms and rippling out on his sun-burnt shoulders. . . . What a son to have made! And what sons he would make, in his turn, when he gave his old father grandchildren!

Jóusè got up abruptly and went to the drawer where his

wife kept her pen and ink and notepaper: 'Messieurs,' he wrote in his thin sprawling hand, 'I desire to purchase the very best suit that your firm can provide for my son's First Communion. I shall also require a fine linen shirt and the kind of collar that the English call It-ton, and a white flottant tie of very good silk, and a white ribbon badge to be worn on the sleeve, and a pair of first quality black woollen stockings. I shall also require patent leather shoes of the sort I have seen displayed in your window. Messieurs, should you know of anything else that is now being worn on this solemn occasion—know of any small extras that would add elegance—then I beg that you will at once inform me. Meanwhile kindly send me a measurement card—my son is nearly eleven years old but large for his age, having very broad shoulders. His mother will fill in the card with great care and return it to you at the earliest moment. . . .' Then he added some pompous courtesies and finally signed his name with a flourish.

'Allons,' he muttered, wagging his head as he wiped the pen on the seat of his trousers, 'allons we will see if a son of mine cannot go suitably clothed to Jesus.'

CHAPTER FIFTEEN

I

I T was during the long preparation for Communion upon which the Curé always insisted—those months of endless religious instruction which, in spite of his habitual indolence, he felt it his duty to give the children—that Christophe began to study the gospels with a new and curiously personal interest.

Far into the night he would read and re-read their simple yet poignantly tragic story; and the while he read he would grow aware of an uneasy feeling of apprehension, illogical, strange, and until now unknown. He would think:

'Why should I be feeling afraid? It all happened a very long time ago . . . and besides, Christ was God.' He would cling to this thought, so familiar and in consequence so reassuring.

But another strange thing would bewilder the boy: he would want to find something that was not in the gospels. His mind would grope about helplessly trying to understand its conviction that a link had been lost, a link with the divine, and that thus what remained was less than perfection.

'Such thoughts are great blasphemy,' he would decide; 'I had better confess at once to the Curé. It may easily be the devil who tempts because I shall soon make my First Communion.'

But he neither confessed nor spoke of those thoughts, for just lately he had grown very shy and self-conscious. The south and his unusual physical strength were forcing their will on his anxious body—he was coming to an early maturity with all that that holds of diffidence, of despondency, and of introspection. There were days now when the sadness he had grown to resent would refuse to give way before his resentment, when he could not go forth, as he had in the past, intent on some mischievous adventure, but must work at the bench in his father's shop even after there was no further need for working, until Jóusè observing his scowling face would scowl in his turn and might even speak sharply:

'I have told you to stop for to-day and be off—my timber and I like a cheerful apprentice!'

Then Christophe would drop his tool with a bang, avoiding the brown, doglike eyes of Anfos that followed him about with anxiety; and perhaps he would wander across to Eusèbe and find him squatting among his hides, intent upon stitching a pair of new sandals.

Eusèbe would look up: 'Ho, ho, my cabbage, so you visit the scandalous Eusèbe who prefers his vineyards to Holy Mass, and his rolls of hide to a hide-bound Curé! Eh bien, you are welcome as you were in the days when I told you of the terrible Recatadou di Rato-Penado, and of other true things which no doubt you have now grown too wise to credit. Sit down. Pecaire, how enormous you are! One would think you were several years older than your age—ah, yes, you are much too big now for my legends.'

But one evening Christophe said: 'Tell me your legends,' for he longed to be once again just a small child sitting there in the dusk with le tout petit Loup and Jan, while Eusèbe made them all tremble.

So Eusèbe laid a sandal aside, and he turned first his blue-white eye upon Christophe, then his fierce black eye that glowed like a coal, and he told in a solemn and awesome voice of the Recatadou di Rato-Penado. Then he told of the Baumo de la Masco Taven, and Lou Courredou de l'Esperit Fantasti, while the sudden nightfall darkened the shop, so that Eusèbe must light the lamp which gave out so pungent and unpleasant an odour.

'There is still the Cafourno de la Chaucho Vièjo,' he reminded. 'I remember how frightened you became when you first heard about that horrible nightmare—shall we have it?'

But Christophe shook his cropped head, while his pale, bright eyes actually filled with tears: 'No,' he murmured, 'I cannot feel frightened any more . . . not at such things . . .'

'That is sad,' remarked Eusèbe. For something of the wisdom he had gleaned from the earth, and from years of

tending the fruits of the earth, touched his hoary old heart
to a partial understanding, so that his glowing black eye
looked more kind as it rested on Christophe, and he spoke
almost gravely: 'It is that you now have a new thing to fear
—as we grow we must listen to the story of life; mais oui,
mais oui, the story of life—yet who knows but that that
is also a legend. Mon brave, it is better to be like me; I say
to myself: "I have lost an eye, but thanks be to Bacchus I
have still got the other." I say to myself: "Boots and shoes
are not gay, they are clumsy and ugly and dull to make, but
thanks be to Bacchus I can also make sandals." I say to
myself: "I am growing old like my good feather bed; I am
careless and dirty; the girls will not look at me down at the
port, and the men from the tartanes make a mock of my
blindness, thrusting forward their women upon my blind
side—but thanks be to Bacchus there is still the fine wine
and the dreams that come from the fine, friendly wine" . . .
Yes, surely it it is better to be like me. Life was simpler
far when the world was pagan.'

'But then I am not a pagan,' sighed Christophe.

2

Sometimes Christophe would seek out the studious Jan
who, when he was not on his knees in the church, was
engrossed by the books that the Curé had lent him. And
Jan would motion his cousin to a chair: 'Do not go—I like
to feel that you are near me.' Which was true, for despite
his prayers and his books he still felt a very deep love for
Christophe, as did Christophe for him—that tenacious love
which had shown itself first when they two had been infants.

Christophe would gaze at Jan's dark, bowed head, at
his slender figure and handsome profile, and would wonder
how Jan could tolerate him, such a slow-witted, stupid and
clumsy fellow. He would almost decide not to have his hair
cropped, but to wear it as Jan wore his, with a parting—it
was ugly cropped so close to the scalp. But then he would
remember that his hair was red and quite straight, not a
curly red-gold like his father's.

Presently Jan might lay down his book, yawn and
stretch:

'That is quite enough for this evening! Let us go out, it is hot in this room.' So out they must go arm in arm as usual.

Christophe would listen while Jan discussed life with the very complete assurance of childhood. But now when he spoke about his religion his eyes burned as they did when they looked on the Host—all on fire, he was, at the thought of Communion:

'Surely I could kill the people who blaspheme against our Lord's name, who despitefully use Him!' Yes, now more than ever must his Lord be avenged. 'I could kill them—do you not feel like that also? Eh bien, what is the matter? Have you swallowed your tongue?'

For Christophe would answer such outbursts with silence. Jan would turn his accusing young eyes on his friend—a child's eyes yet already those of a fanatic: 'You are lukewarm, you blow neither hot nor cold,' he said angrily one day, falling back on his namesake. 'Is it you who would strike a blow for our Saviour? When I speak of blasphemers your face becomes stupid and dull like a mule's—you are dumb like a mule, like a beast that because it has got no soul is deprived of all feeling and understanding!'

And the walk came near to being a failure, for Christophe must struggle to keep his temper, while Jan must remind himself of the love that he bore this silent and obstinate creature who seemed so unwilling to kindle the fire of a faith that was worthy of him as a Christian.

Thus the weeks slipped by and there came the March night when those tiresome accounts were perplexing poor Jóusè. And that night Christophe sat in his attic alone, reading by the flickering flame of a candle—he was reading the gospel according to Saint Luke very carefully, because its beauty impressed him. And whenever his eyes met the name Galilee, they paused, for to him that name held great sweetness; and now, as was always the case these days, he must picture a green and bountiful country having many deep streams that gushed over rocks, and wide valleys, and ranges of snow-capped mountains.

'Yes, but how do I know these things,' he mused; for even the notes of the singing birds he felt that he knew—there were many such birds—yet he had not been told of them by the Curé. The Curé cared nothing about Galilee beyond what it stood for in scriptural history.

Then after a time, as the boy still read on, he realized that once more he was seeking, but that now he knew what it was that he sought: 'When He bathed His feet in that stream ... where is it? He had cut His foot on a stone and it bled. He sighed a little and took off His sandals; then He blessed the water for cooling His feet ... But where has it got to? Why cannot I find it?' The sweat broke out on his hands and forehead, while something very like panic seized him as he turned from gospel to gospel in search of the incident that had not been recorded: 'He took off His sandals and bathed His feet ... He blessed the water,' he kept repeating.

Pain. He was suddenly conscious of pain—the pain of the body. He clutched at his foot, he stamped it upon the ground: it was whole. Then whose pain was this, his own or another's? But pain. He was suddenly conscious of pain—the pain of the mind. He was deeply discouraged, he was filled with persistent and anxious doubts, his brain ached with a host of unanswered questions—he was doubting himself. Was he doubting himself? Whose doubts were these, his own or another's? Yes, but pain—the searing pain of the Spirit. The intolerable anguish of divining perfection, the intolerable pity for each conscious thing that was yet unconscious of that perfection. The intolerable longing to show forth God as the Ultimate Triumph, the Beginning and the End of all things in Love—in the Love of God that was patient, courageous, invincible, deathless. The longing to lift the whole world up to God. But whose longing was this, his own or another's?

And now he could not any more see the attic, for its walls must give place to luminous visions, to a sunshine more ruthless than that of Saint Loup, to skies that were bluer than those of Provence. And a tall man, he saw, with a small reddish beard; a poorly clad man who looked like a peasant. And this man had made a cup of his hands and was holding a bird, and the bird was singing. Yes, right up into his smiling face the bird sang; Christophe could see its minute ruffled throat, could perceive all the joy that throbbed in that song, could divine the creature's sense of protection.

Then words, heard as though through illimitable space: 'This is my brother — shew mercy to all things.'

And again, on the road to Jerusalem . . . the man had paused, seeing a beast of burden, a pack-mule that stumbled beneath its load—inarticulate, humble and heavy-laden. He had flung the load from its aching withers, and its withers were pitifully galled and bleeding . . . He was healing the galls with the touch of his hand . . . 'This is my brother —shew mercy to all things.'

And now he was in the street of a town, a populous hill-town—its name was Nain. He was kneeling beside a dying dog, a pariah dying in great desolation. The gaunt yellow creature lay stretched out in the sun, too feeble to drag itself into shelter, and its body was covered with festering sores, but its eyes looked into the eyes of the man with an indescribable expectation . . . He was laying his hands upon the beast's head: 'Our Father . . . into Thy merciful keeping . . .'

Christophe sprang up with a stifled cry: 'Mirèio!' he gasped. And again: 'Mirèio!'

It was over. He saw the walls of his room, saw the cheap but familiar print of the Virgin, saw his narrow oak bed with its clean white quilt, saw the stars gleaming in through his dormer window. He ran to the window and looked down the street he had known all the years of his short existence; and while he still stood there an uncertain gleam appeared from Eusèbe's half-open doorway—without doubt he had just staggered home from the port and was fumblingly trying to light a candle. And Christophe felt grateful towards these things, for they came as a balm to his understanding—they were crude, simple, homely, everyday things; aye, even the drunken old sandal-maker.

Then turning he flung himself on to the bed and began to cry weakly: 'Mirèio . . .' he sobbed, for the wound of her passing was not yet healed, 'Mirèio, come back from God; I want you!' But after a little his sobs died away and he lay quite motionless. He was sleeping.

CHAPTER SIXTEEN

I

THE days that followed that strange night of vision were filled with acute anxiety for Christophe. He shrank from speaking of what had occurred with a dread so intense as to be almost morbid, yet something seemed urging him on to speak: 'Tell Jan . . . tell Jan . . . tell him what you have seen.' The words would hammer themselves out in his brain with a kind of heavy monotony, with a patient and irresistible persistence.

His work suffered; he grew duller than ever at his books, for now he scarcely knew what he was reading. He would fancy that he saw those words on the page and would afterwards grow confused during the lesson, so that Monsieur Roland must thump his desk: 'Christophe Bénédit, this is intolerable, shameful! Not a question this morning have you answered correctly.' And turning to Loup, 'Allons, Loup, attention! Kindly tell me the principal victories of Napoleon.' Then le tout petit Loup looking ludicrously small and fragile beside his large-limbed brother, would pipe out the victories victoriously, ticking them off on his brown, skinny fingers. The class would grin as Christophe sat down as red as a beetroot with shame and confusion. But this was not all, his hands lost their assurance, growing doubtful when handling the hammer and chisel:

'Segnour Diéu, what are you doing, my son?' Jóusè would exclaim on a note of impatience. 'Strike more firmly; you will ruin that excellent wood! Do you think the saints send us our timber for nothing?'

So Christophe would steady his chisel and strike: 'Tell Jan . . . tell Jan . . . tell him what you have seen . . . tell Jan . . . tell Jan . . . tell him what you have seen . . .' With a kind of despair he would start hammering wildly in an effort to break that intolerable rhythm.

Marie said to her husband: 'Our Christophe is ailing, he eats little, and I do not like his strange silence. Houi, if our Christophe also becomes ill, he who has always had such perfect health . . . It would seem that indeed the kind saints desert us!' And she looked as though she intended to weep.

'Do not be so ridiculous, Marie!' snapped Jóusè, 'The boy is maturing—it is natural enough—your golden Saint Loup himself cannot baulk nature. . . . At Christophe's age I also felt glum, but that was because I had so many boils. I remember quite well how conscious I became of everything that pertained to my body. Beyond this there is nothing wrong with your son. But keep a sharp look out in a few years from now—he may then catch the deadly distemper called women.' And he laughed, remembering his own precocity, patted her cheek, and went about his business.

But that night when the boy was already in bed, his mother made her way up to the attic; and she smoothed his pillow, and straightened his sheet, and carefully tucked in his old brown blanket. Then she suddenly folded him close in her arms calling him many endearing names—little kind, foolish names that she had used long ago when he greedily sucked his life from her bosom. For her heart was heavy at the thought of this child who was daily drawing further away from childhood towards a future that none might foresee, not even the wise, tender heart of a mother. And because he was barely eleven years old despite the precocious strength of his body, he laid his head eagerly down on her breast, for he also was anxious to hold back the years because of an undefined dread of the future.

'Enfantounet,' she whispered, 'shall I sing you to sleep?'

He nodded in silence, fearing that speech might destroy this foolish yet comforting illusion.

So Marie sang him an old lullaby that had long soothed many a Provençal cradle, and her voice was thin but tuneful and sweet as she rocked the boy who lay in her arms as willingly as though he were a baby:

'Holy Mary, Mother of God,
Will you take my little son into your keeping?'
'Surely I will, for I, too, had a Son—but my little Son
    was laid in a manger.'
'Holy Mary, Mother of God,
Will you cherish my little son through his childhood?'
'Surely I will, for I, too, had a Son—but my little Son
    was forced into exile.'
'Holy Mary, Mother of God,
Will you guide my son's feet in the days of his man-
    hood?'
'Surely I will, for I, too, had a Son—but my Son's feet
    became terribly weary.'
'Holy Mary, Mother of God,
Will you plead for my son at the hour of his
    dying?'
'Surely I will, for I, too, had a Son—but my Son died
    upon Calvary that yours might inherit the Life
    Everlasting.'

She stopped singing, Christophe had lifted his head and
was gazing up into her face intently: 'Enfantounet . . . why
do you look at me so . . .?' she faltered, for she thought
that his eyes seemed strange—very old, very grave, very full
of pity.

2

Jan listened to his cousin with incredulous amazement:
'Comment, you would have me believe you saw Jesus—yet
you cannot even remember His face?'

'No, I cannot remember His face,' said Christophe.

They were sitting in the woods just beyond the town,
near the spot where Jan had slain his last couleuvre, and
the woods were beginning to smell of spring, for March had
recently passed into April.

Jan persisted: 'And you say that He bathed His feet in
a stream and that one of His feet was bleeding? How much
did it bleed?'

'It bled quite a lot—and it pained Him.'

'How do you know that it pained?'

'Because I could feel the pain,' replied Christophe.

'But why should our Lord have blessed the stream as though He were grateful? I do not believe it! The Curé blesses water but that is for us, in order that we may benefit by it; it keeps away fiends when it has been blessed.'

Christophe answered: 'Yet I know that He did feel grateful . . .'

'And you want me to believe that He actually spoke?'

'Yes, He spoke of a bird that He held—it was singing.

'And what did He say?' demanded Jan.

'He said: "This is my brother—shew mercy to all things".'

'And what next?'

'He healed many galls for a mule . . . that was on the road to Jerusalem . . . the mule was cruelly overloaded.'

'And then?'

'He knelt by a dying dog in a street in Nain.

'How do you know that it was Nain?'

Christophe thought for a moment: 'I cannot tell you.'

'And then?'

'He laid His hands on its head and prayed—He was sending the dog to God. It was suffering, its body was covered with sores . . . very terrible sores . . .' His voice sank to a whisper, 'I cannot be wrong for the dog was . . . Mirèio.'

They stared at each other as once in the past they had stared in dumb fear when the blow dealt by Jan to the couleuvre had scarred Christophe's shrinking shoulders.

Then Christophe said slowly: 'These things are all lost— they must have forgotten to write them down, that is why there is something I miss in the gospels.'

'You are mad!' exclaimed Jan, still feeling afraid, 'Only saints and holy martyrs see visions.' Then he flushed, 'But what is that you have said? Who are you to pretend to miss things in the gospels? Are you the four evangelists perhaps? One would think you were all four of them rolled together! Sarnipabiéune, but what conceit! No doubt you know better than Monsieur le Curé, no doubt you know better than our bishop, mais oui; no doubt you know better than the Holy Father!' And now he was working himself into a rage. 'Moreover you blaspheme—you blaspheme about Mirèio. Mirèio was a beast and beasts have no souls, yet you tell me that Jesus sent her to God—it must be that you are both stupid and wicked! In any case she is not very long dead, therefore how can Mirèio have been seen by Jesus? And I do not believe that our Lord healed a mule, he healed only human beings with souls—blind men He healed, and women, and lepers—the people He wished to have with Him in heaven. You are lying, or else you will soon become mad. No, you have not seen our Lord but the devil.' He paused for a moment to recover his breath, then he went on more quickly, spluttering a little: 'Listen to me well, I will now repeat what is said at the end of Revelation: "If any man shall add unto these things, God shall add unto him the plagues that are written in this book." Yes, those are the actual words of Saint John, and that is what *you* have done, added to these things, and therefore you are a very great liar!"'

Christophe said quietly: 'I have spoken the truth. I have told you what I was meant to tell you.'

They faced each other and Christophe's calm eyes met and held the turbulent eyes of his cousin. And now they were not young boys any more—at this moment they were neither young nor old, but just two living creatures irrevocably bound by the bonds of an infinite love that was ageless.

Jan muttered: 'You are wicked because you blaspheme, yet I do not wish to kill you like the others. . . .' Then all of a sudden he burst into tears, and when next he spoke his words were quite childish: 'Oh, oh,' he blubbered, 'what am I going to do? You will go down to hell and then I shall lose you!'

Christophe looked at him, not knowing what he should say, or how he might best hope to give consolation.

They walked home hand in hand as they had been used to walk when they were very small children. They forgot that they had both grown since those days, remembering only that they had quarrelled yet again and must therefore keep close together, for they felt an intangible dread of separation. They spoke little, and when they arrived at Jóusè's workshop they parted without looking at one another, for Jan was feeling ashamed of his tears, and Christophe divining this, tried to spare him.

But that night Jan remained a long time on his knees in front of his crucifix, praying for Christophe.

This particular quarrel although it had passed quickly had made a deep impression upon Christophe; it had strengthened his very unwilling conviction that in some way he differed from other people, and this thought was intensely distasteful to him.

Jan had spoken to the Curé about those visions, and the Curé, it seemed, had not been outraged but had taken the whole matter almost lightly. He had called Christophe into the Presbytery at the end of the usual Sunday instruction, and had listened with a grave and courteous attention to the boy's replies to his searching questions, and then he had remarked that all such happenings were capable of divers explanations. Christophe might well have fallen asleep, and who could account for the strangeness of dreams? Or again, he was probably working hard, having realized that he was rather backward. Bien, a tired brain was often an active brain, but not always a very reliable brain; it played curious tricks, it imagined things that had no importance because no existence. And then there had been the death of the bitch; of course Christophe had fretted about Mirèio. He, the Curé, had once had a dog of his own, a most faithful creature, a curly retriever. One could grow very fond indeed of a dog. . . . Well now, might not that account for quite a good deal? It might surely account for one of the visions. But the visions themselves had been gentle visions—our Lord and the little bird, that had been charming—a charming fancy—quite a picture it made; our Lord with the little bird in His hands . . . but of course Christophe knew all about Saint Francis, that was how things got themselves jumbled up, but no matter. . . . None of it mattered at all so long as one did not allow one's fancies to masquerade as the truths of religion. Christophe had his Church and his Church had Truth. Jan had been silly about the whole business, had given it all too much importance. He, the Curé, had had a long talk with Jan who had promised not to be so impulsive: 'And now, Christophe, put it right out of your head. Do not worry yourself, just be a good boy and pray to the Sacred Heart of our Lord that your First Communion may be very perfect.'

Thus the Curé Martel, who had honestly made a great effort to advise with kindness and wisdom.

But neither Jan's folly nor the Curé's wisdom had been able to dim the memory of those visions, or to rob them of their deep reality—for the tangible is never so entirely real as that which is seen by the eyes of the Spirit.

It was strange perhaps that the boy did not turn to his mother at this time of bewilderment and trouble, or even to the father whose stalwart love made up for a certain lack of understanding, but stranger still that he should have found consolation in the companionship of Anfos. And yet so it was, for to Anfos he went during many a desolate hour in the evening; to Anfos who would often remain in the workshop striving to capture nomad thoughts in the net of his wonderfully skilful carving. Anfos had taken to carving flowers—oleanders, carnations, sprays of mimosa; to carving the tendrils and leaves of the vines, and the fruit that bent the branches of the vines, and the frail winged creatures that swung on the vines. And if any would buy he might sell such work, for Jóusè was a just and good-natured master. So to Anfos the boy would go with some object in which he himself had discerned great beauty—for now he saw beauty in many a thing that had seemed in the past unworthy of notice—the young leaf of a mulberry tree, very green, very neat, and a network of delicate veining; a sprig of wild lavender plant from the hills, quiet and retiring but persistently fragrant; a soft, foolish moth with the eyes of an owl and wings of the intangible colour of twilight—a moth rescued by Christophe's careful hands from a fiery grave in the lamp above Anfos.

'Look, Anfos,' he would say: 'it has down on its wings—a kind of shining silvery powder!'

Then Anfos would lay down his tool and look, his doglike eyes full of profound admiration: 'Bèu Diéu,' he would murmur, for his words were few, so that whenever his heart was moved or his childish mind animated to pleasure, he could only call upon a beautiful God—but this tribute would seem all-sufficing to Christophe. Thus it was that these two, the boy and the half-wit who had knelt to this boy when he was a baby, that these two were now drawn very close by a perception which has little to say to the intellect— the inward and spiritual perception of beauty.

But at times Christophe needed to be alone, and would wander off by himself to the hill on the summit of which stands the ruined fortress. Climbing slowly with his eyes bent upon the ground, while his head felt heavy with unanswered problems, he would finally reach the old citadel, now held by the bright-eyed garrison of lizards. And sometimes he would stretch out a quiet friendly hand, and would make that small sound—that very small sound which was like a soft but compelling summons; and a lizard would lift its throat to the sun, then glance brightly at Christophe's hand and move nearer, then all of a sudden it would be on his hand or his arm, to be followed by another and another—for at last he had won the friendship of these creatures. Yet his heart was so full of trouble these days that he would not always call his companions, but would sit staring down at the roofs of Saint Loup, or away to the sea that spread bluely beyond them, while his mind sought in vain to explain itself and the unsolved enigma of his existence.

Brooding darkly he would conjure up all his troubles: his stupidity at school which perpetually shamed him; his constant and unhappy quarrels with Jan—always quarrels in spite of their great devotion; the thoughts that would come into his head undesired—thoughts of pity, of anxious and eager compassion; his misery over the sufferings and pain of all speechless and thus defenceless creatures . . . that mark on his shoulders when Jan struck the couleuvre. And his hands, the great fear he had felt of his hands since the night when their power had released Mirèio—or had she been actually going to die? Had he only imagined that his touch had released her? And the day when he put on his first pair of sandals . . . that queer falling asleep at his father's workbench . . . that queer waking up with a sense of dread because of something that he must do. But what? he had brought back no memory of it. Then those pictures—Christ holding the singing bird—Christ healing the maltreated beast of burden—Christ laying His hands on Mirèio's head . . . on Mirèio's head? but Mirèio had been now. It was he and not Christ who had laid hands upon her, and the town had not been Nain but Saint Loup, and the place not a street but a shed in the yard, and the time not midday but after midnight . . . Christ and Mirèio . . . Mirèio and Christophe. . . .

He would cover his face and begin to pray: 'Lord, I am only eleven years old . . . I am big and clumsy but my brain feels quite small. I am stupid, I cannot learn anything from books, and I do not understand . . . no, I do not understand what it is that makes me so different from people. Lord, I want to be kind, but I do not like pain, I do not like knowing so much about pain—I have told Your golden Saint Loup this already. And I do not want to see things all wrong as I did when I saw You kneeling by Mirèio, because though I see wrong I feel I see right, and it worries me . . . Jan says that I shall go mad . . .' His prayer would trail off into vague confused words about Jan and Mirèio and his own First Communion.

But one late afternoon as he sat near the ruins trying to pray and but ill succeeding, he uncovered his face rather suddenly and looked down on a green and most bountiful valley, and he heard the rushing and splash of a stream—a soft turbulent sound, and the singing of birds that had never sung on the hills of Saint Loup, yet the notes of whose songs were completely familiar. And beyond, very far away, he perceived not the dark, rugged, unclothed peaks of the Maures, but the peaks of much higher and snow-capped mountains.

Then he spoke, but softly, for some joy is so fragile that it breaks at the touch of our coarsened vibrations: 'Galilee . . . I am looking at Galilee.' And his heart was dissolved in a peace so immense that it passed even his profound understanding, while his eyes filled with slow, reminiscent tears—the tears of a wanderer who had come home to the happy greenness and peace of that valley. 'You are beautiful,' he murmured, 'you are fruitful and kind; you shelter the birds, you nurture the cattle, you have many deep streams at which all may drink. And at evening your mountains are heavy with rest, and at dawn your mountains are the first to praise God . . . to praise. . . .' His voice faltered and died away; then he raised his hand as though he were blessing.

A bell sounded. He saw the town of Saint Loup with the sea lying placid and azure beyond it, saw the dark, rugged, unclothed peaks of the Maures, saw the ancient church with its open belfry and heard the three rhythmic strokes of the bell that proclaimed the lifting up of the Lord at the evening service of Benediction.

CHAPTER SEVENTEEN

I

THE new suit arrived—the suit from Marseille that Christophe would wear for his First Communion. Loup's marmoset eyes all but dropped from his head, so astonished was he at its glossy black splendour. And what stockings! as soft as though woven of silk; and the spotless white shirt of the finest linen; and the funny stiff collar that the English boys wore; and the wide flottant tie, and the wide ribbon badge to be worn on the sleeve—a white satin band with a big round rosette and elegant streamers. And the shoes! so thin, so incredibly shiny, with laces as silky and soft as the stockings; but above all, one truly magnificent thing—the suit in addition to jacket and breeches, had actually got a real grown-up waistcoat, a waistcoat with striped sateen at the back and a manly, neat little strap with a buckle!

Oh, but le tout petit Loup must regret his pert inattention to Monsieur le Curé, his suckings and scrunchings of sweets during class, his sudden and often embarrassing questions, all of which had led to Monsieur le Curé's stern words: 'You are not yet sufficiently serious, my child; I fear we shall have to delay your Communion.' And now here was Christophe dressed up in the suit, and examining himself in their mother's best mirror, then complaining that the shoes felt too tight for his feet and begging to wear his ugly old sandals. And now here was Christophe thrusting a finger down the funny stiff collar that the English called It-ton, and declaring that it felt all wrong on his neck, while he, Loup, could scarcely contain his desire to see his own neck rising out of that collar. It was indeed a real cause for regret that he had been pert to Monsieur le Curé.

Marie said: 'You may now take the suit off, my son, and she started to unbutton the magnificent waistcoat.

Then Christophe unfastened the collar with a plop and divested himself of his shoes and stockings, then his jacket, while Marie dragged down the breeches and carefully drew the shirt over his head, taking pains that it should not get creased in the process. With a sigh of relief Christophe thrust his brown legs into shorts made from Jóusè's old linen trousers, and his head into a sleeveless striped cotton vest, and his feet into the pliant, well-contrived sandals.

'You are not what the English call: "Gen-tell-men," ' scoffed Loup, 'you behave like what the English call: "Com-mune" ' for Monsieur Roland had once been to Hull, and would sometimes discourse with his pupils of England, dropping a word here and there by the way, just to show how conversant he was with the language.

Said Jóusè: 'Well, this I can surely affirm: no boy will be better dressed than our Christophe. You may very well hold your head high, my son, the suit fits superbly, while as for the cost. . . . But your mother is of my opinion, I know—there are certain occasions upon which one spends money.'

'Mais surement, surement . . .' Marie agreed. 'And besides, our Christophe has quite a fine figure.'

Le tout petit Loup turned white and then red, while his eyes became less like a sick marmoset's and more like a thoughtful, malevolent monkey's as he watched his mother folding the suit, then the wide flottant tie, then the soft woollen stockings, and finally disposing of the whole in her drawer beneath several clean layers of new tissue paper. And that evening when Marie went up to her bedroom in order to look for a spool of cotton, what must she find but le tout petit Loup with his mischievous fingers among the paper. And while she observed him, herself unobserved, what must she see but le tout petit Loup removing the paper, then stroking the clothes very much as though he were stroking a cat, making small guttural sounds the while in his throat, sounds that seemed less suggestive of asthma than pleasure.

'Who told you to open that drawer?' she demanded.

Did he jump? Not he! All he did was to turn with a smile so seraphic that it quite disarmed her: 'It was that I wanted to touch the suit in which Christophe will visit our

Lord,' he said sweetly, 'Ai! las, that I may not visit our Lord! Maman, will you not speak with Monsieur le Curé?'

Marie shook her head: 'No, I cannot, my son—he alone is the person to judge of your fitness.'

But that night as she lay at her husband's side, she expressed a grave doubt of the Curé's wisdom: 'I think he is very unwise,' she declared, 'not to let Loup receive Communion this year merely because the child fidgets in class. Imagine! this evening he was stroking that new suit because it was going to be worn for our Lord—was that not touching of le tout petit Loup?'

'Maybe—but now I would sleep,' grunted Jóusè.

And indeed it did appear that le tout petit Loup had suddenly grown amazingly religious; he was constantly fingering his holy medals, or telling his beads by himself in a corner, or getting up on week days to go to Mass, or kneeling—apparently lost in prayer—at the foot of his Patron's shrine after vespers.

'So long as you do not make yourself ill . . . that is all I ask of our Lord,' fretted Marie.

But the Curé continued to shake his head. 'Next year, if you are attentive in class, we will then consider your First Communion.'

2

May came in, the month of our Blessèd Lady, the month of the children's approach to the altar. The Curé Martel was puckering his brow and fidgeting his feet as he sat in his study. He was struggling to forget a psychological treatise and to concentrate instead upon his address to the parents of youthful communicants—it would shortly appear in the Parish Journal:

'Soyez-en félicités mes chers parents crétiens, car vous avez donné à vos chers petits enfants le privilège suprème, le privilège sublime, de s'agenouiller aux pieds de leur très-cher Jésus. . . .' He sighed; every other word seemed to be: 'cher'; he was no good at all at this sort of writing. Then he tried to enliven his brain with snuff, sneezed twice, wiped his eyes, blew his long-suffering nose and stained a new handkerchief brown in the process.

Meanwhile, an air of suppressed excitement was very apparent in many a household: little girls with discreet but rather bright eyes; little boys looking sheepish, good and embarrassed; mothers with expressions which were usually reserved for occasions such as funerals or weddings; fathers with a kind of high pride on their brows, as who should say· 'See what we have done for the Lord by creating such handsome and excellent children!' Oh, yes, it was very apparent indeed, this air of suppressed but undoubted excitement.

May the first. Marie getting out Christophe's fine clothes and tweaking the buttons—she mistrusts shop sewing—then flicking a speck off the breeches with her thumb, then laying the suit back again in the drawer and covering it up with the new tissue paper.

May the second. Jóusè and Marie disappearing after many loud, conspiratorial whispers. They are seen going into a shop near the port where a galaxy of Prayer Books is displayed in the window.

'This is not of real leather,' the salesman explains, 'mais Madame, croyez moi, it is even better—observe, too, the charming little cross on the binding—and the clasp. There is also a very fine picture of Saint Aloysius at the altar rails, Saint Aloysius receiving Communion,' and he quickly exhibits that youthful saint.

'Yes, but what would *real* leather cost?' Marie asks him. She is told, and Jóusè shakes his head sadly: 'No,' he murmurs, 'too much, too much, Marioun.'

'Ah, well,' consoles Marie, mustering a smile, 'as Monsieur here says, this Prayer Book is charming—and strong, Monsieur says—is that not so, Monsieur? With a fine clasp and all—then think of the picture!' For the poor are wonderfully patient at times when it comes to foregoing some innocent longing.

So the Prayer Book that is not of real leather but of something that Monsieur has said is even better, is duly purchased and carried away. And that night it is carefully inscribed by Jóusè—but upstairs in the bedroom lest Christophe should see: 'A notre très-cher fils Christophe, de la pàrt de ses parents à l'occasion de sa Première Communion,' writes Jóusè, protruding, as he does so, the tip of his tongue—the small page is terribly awkward to write on.

May the third. Christophe's suit is hung in the air in case it should smell a little of camphor. Le tout petit Loup still telling his beads, but out loud instead of in a sibilant whisper. Anfos sweating right down into his straggling beard because he is afraid of being late with his present—a carved plaque depicting the Chalice and Host surrounded by a choir of birds and much glory. Marie lighting candles to the Mother of God: 'O Mother of God, make our Christophe worthy.' Jóusè also saying a prayer at her side, and near-by quite a handful of other parents. Jan as pale as a wraith with his dark burning eyes—Jan looking as though his eyes must consume him. He kneels in front of the shrine of Saint Loup, and his face is turned up to the warrior-bishop. Madame Roustan, diligently beating her breast, as always, for the sins she would like to commit but which, alas, she has never committed. Goundran passing the church and deciding to look in—why not? might as well say a prayer for one's godson. And the Curé galvanized into activity by what is going to take place on the morrow, the Curé goes padding around the church, counting the hassocks, fidgeting with chairs, pinching the wicks of the votive candles. He looks worried—that paternal address is not ready, he will have to stick at it all night if need be; and meanwhile his handsome aquiline nose is somewhat inflamed by excessive snuff-taking, and his prominent eyes look distinctly moist—he has grown much addicted to snuff just lately.

At la Tarasque Mère Mélanie feels sentimental. It is only, as yet, early afternoon, so the stained marble tables boast very few clients; this gives her a great deal of time for thought and she sits behind her bar-counter thinking. Madame Roustan has been in for a Sirop-de-menthe, and has talked about Jan and his First Communion. Jóusè has stopped to buy cigarettes, and has talked about Christophe and his First Communion. Madame Perron's young brother, an artist from the north, has drunk more than one petit verre already; he is now rather sleepy but before his lids drooped he complained that the house was like a ship in a tempest—such rushing about, and no meals, if you please! 'Why? because the white muslin dress of my niece does not fit; it is found to be much too tight, and to-morrow she makes her First Communion.'

Ah, the dear little children—the dear Mother of God—the dear Jesus—it is all so terribly moving. Alas, that she, unhappy Mère Mélanie, has never been granted a child by heaven—a girl child who could wear a white muslin dress, white suède shoes and a wreath of white cotton roses. So many years of men, always men, and they as alike as two peas in a pod and with only one idea in their heads. . . . And they strutting and crowing like cocks in a barnyard: 'Mais, ma chérie, if you think you have known the real thing before you met me, only wait, I will show you! Mais non, you have never yet known the real thing!' And they as alike as two peas in a pod—lascivious, selfish and clumsy; quels salauds! But one put up with men for the sake of a child. Ah, the dear little children—the dear Mother of God—the dear Jesus—it is all so terribly moving.

Mère Mélanie gropes about in her bag; she finds lipstick, a small box of soiled face-powder, the key of the cellar, some unpaid bills, an odd curling-pin and a piety medal; and at last, tucked away in a fold of torn silk, her handkerchief heavily scented with chypre, and with this she quite openly dabs her eyes several times—it is all so terribly moving.

Christophe sits alone. He has climbed once again to the old citadel with its garrison of lizards. The lizards run over his feet and hands but he does not see them for his eyes are closed. He is not asleep, he is only very tired—too tired to think much, to feel any emotion. To-morrow he is going to receive his Lord, he and Jan are going to receive their Lord. . . . But Christophe is too tired to feel any emotion.

CHAPTER EIGHTEEN

I

THE next morning the Bénédit household rose at cock-crow, for Marie wished to prepare déjeuner and tidy the rooms before dressing for Mass. It was obvious, of course, that upon such a day there must be neither undue haste nor confusion. Moreover, Madame Roustan had expressed a desire that the two families should start out together; she and Jan would come up to her brother's house and then they could all walk down to the church, and Marie did not choose that her sister-in-law should find their home other than in good order.

'What a woman,' grumbled Jóusè as he dragged some old trousers over his night-shirt, 'for ever interfering! One would think that living as near the church as she does, we might have been spared this procession, but no. However, it is all very clear, she wishes to show off her marvellous Jan his marvellous clothes that have come from Paris—"Madame la Comtesse de Bérac," sacré Nom! Are we all to parade the streets like a circus?'

But Marie looked shocked: 'Let us try to be calm.'

'It is that I wish to be calm,' frowned Jóusè.

Anfos was hanging about on the landing; he was grasping a pair of very old scissors: 'I would . . . like . . .' he stammered, and pointed to his beard.

Jóusè nodded: 'Come along then, come into the workshop. But mind, you must sit very still while I trim. And have you brushed up that old suit which I gave you? And the shoes, are they cleaned?'

'I have done all,' said Anfos.

Jóusè thought that he seemed more half-witted than usual; his lip sagged and his brown eyes looked rather frightened.

'Are you not well?' Jóusè asked him kindly, for he often felt pitiful of his apprentice. Le pauvre bougre—he was now nearly thirty years old, yet remained as a child in all things save his work.

'So glorious . . . so terrible . . .' muttered Anfos.

'What is terrible?'

But Anfos made no reply

'It is better not to worry him,' Jóusè decided as he quickly and deftly trimmed the thin beard. Then: 'Voilà, it is finished, and you look like a duke! Now go and show yourself off to Marie.'

In the bedroom upstairs the bed had been made, and on it Marie neatly laid out Christophe's clothes; he should dress himself in her room for Communion—that was something she would like to remember. Having seen that nothing was missing from the outfit, she closed the door gently and going downstairs proceeded to finish the rest of the housework. Christophe helped her in a clumsy, inadequate way, a thing that she had never known him do before, and it suddenly struck her that his offers of help arose from a great desire to be near her.

'It is natural,' she mused, 'he is nervous, no doubt,' and she let him go blundering on with his tasks. 'After all, he is only a child,' smiled Marie.

Meanwhile Jóusè was putting away his tools, for no work would be done that day in his workshop, while Anfos had been sent to sweep up the yard so that when they returned even that should be tidy.

Then quite suddenly Marie glanced over her shoulder: 'Where is Loup?' she enquired, 'Was he not here just now? I thought he was saying his Rosary.'

'I think I can hear him above us,' said Christophe, 'I think I can hear him walking about in your room, I do not think he is praying.'

Marie listened: 'You are right.' Then an awful premonition made her hastily fling aside her duster, 'We must see what he is doing,' she said breathlessly, 'I feel that we must see at once what he is doing!' So together they hastened up to the bedroom.

There are some things in life that one never forgets, that impress upon the mind indelible pictures. Neither

Christophe nor his mother was ever to forget the apparition of le tout petit Loup that greeted their eyes a minute later. He was standing quite still in front of the mirror admiring his reflection, having rigged himself out in the clothes that Jóusè had bought for his brother.

'Hèi—Bono Maire de Diéu!' breathed Marie.

She did not know whether to laugh or to cry, whether to pity or to feel very angry, so grotesque was the effect which he had produced, yet so obvious was his self-satisfaction. Ai! las, ai! las, le pauvre tout petit Loup, the short breeches hung almost down to his ankles, the jacket appeared to be resting on sticks, while the fine manly waistcoat, in spite of its strap, stood out hollow and stiff from his concave stomach. Ai! las, ai! las, le pauvre tout petit Loup with his wisp of a body—he looked like a scarecrow.

But now Jóusè had suddenly appeared on the scene: 'What is this?' he roared, standing transfixed in the doorway.

'It is that I am going to Communion!' piped Loup; and he resolutely turned and faced his parents.

'Ho, ho!' rumbled Jóusè deep in his throat. 'Take those clothes off at once!'

'I will not,' Loup informed him, folding his ridiculous twig-like arms.

Santouno, what a way to speak to his father!

Said Jóusè: 'You need a mighty hard beating, you have crumpled Christophe's shirt, a very great outrage, but because you know well that you are too small to beat you become more intolerable every day.'

Loup nodded: 'I know that I am too small to beat—if you beat me it would surely bring on my asthma.' And he wheezed a little to give point to his words.

'I command you to take off those clothes!' thundered Jóusè.

Marie ran quickly and closed the window: 'Not so loud,' she warned, 'Eusèbe will hear you; already he stands at the door of his shop with his head on one side as he does when he listens. I think he is growing deaf of one ear; all the same if you shout like that he will hear you.'

Jóusè breathed hard: 'I care not a sou; I care neither for Eusèbe nor the devil. Here have I bought magnificent clothes for Christophe, clothes that have cost me the eyes of my head, clothes that have come all the way from Marseille —from that grand and expensive shop in Marseille—and this impious child puts them on, spoils the shirt, and leaves the mark of his thumb on the collar. But look at the collar where his black thumb has been!'

'I think it will come off with bread,' murmured Marie.

'That may be—I doubt it—but one thing I swear, I will not be defied to my face by my children. I order you, Loup, to undress yourself.'

'Then how can I go to Communion?' Loup asked him.

Ah, no, that was too much! Jóusè stamped on the floor, so enraged that he himself became childish, for le tout petit Loup, with diabolical craft, was gently but firmly fingering the collar.

'Come, Loup,' said Marie in a still, small voice that should surely have reminded him of his conscience, 'come to mother and let her undress you at once.'

'And for God's sake stop touching that collar,' groaned Jóusè.

But le tout petit Loup merely turned his thin back on them all: 'To-day I am going to Communion.'

The daring, the incredible daring of the imp, defying his parents, defying the Curé—a mosquito, a gnat, a midge of a child, and dressed in a suit that was sizes too large so that everyone who saw him must laugh, yet declaring that he would go to Communion. And what did he think the Curé would do when he saw such a figure approaching the altar! Well, but what could he do? Make a scene in the church! Oh, the imp of Satan, the midge, the mosquito! Jóusè tugged at his beard and ruffled his hair; box Loup's ears? but no, a finger would break him. Then what? Compromise by offering a bribe—some sweets, or that little toy boat from the bazaar? Malavalisco, a nice situation! Then a gleam of hope shot into Jóusè's eyes—perhaps he would take off the clothes for Christophe.

'Christophe,' he whispered, looking rather shame-faced, 'Christophe, ask him to take them off for your sake—but speak gently, for one never knows what he may do . . . remember we have only got one collar It-ton.'

The tactlessness of men, the obtuseness of men, the blundering imbecility of them. Marie realized just a moment too late that Christophe was going to appeal to his brother—was appealing:

'Loup, I very much want my new clothes, please take them off . . . they are my clothes for Communion.'

It was done; the match was set to the fuse and the fuse burnt quickly, then came the explosion. Le tout petit Loup whisked round like a flash, wheezing and coughing and choking with temper: '*Your* new clothes,' he spluttered, '*your* this and *your* that. Your fine stockings and shirt and your grand English collar. Everything for you and nothing for me. You paint Goundran's house, but I may not paint; you bathe, but I may not go near the water; you play dominoes, and I may not win. And why do I not win? Because you cheat. And now also, it seems, I may not go to Communion. Everything you take, even Jesus you take, you are greedy and mean, even Jesus you take. . . .'

'Hush, oh, hush! You say terrible things!' gasped Marie.

But le tout petit Loup waved her off with his hand: 'Perhaps you all think me an imbecile?' he challenged. And now had he been the Pope himself he really could not have spoken more calmly. 'I have studied the laws of my Church,' he informed them, 'and our Holy Father Pius X— who they say will surely become a great saint—has drawn up . . .' he hesitated a moment, 'has drawn up. . . . Well, that really is of no importance, whatever he has done is called: Quam Singulari.' Oh, the imp of Satan, he had got it all pat! 'Yes, Quam Singulari,' he repeated grandly. 'And the Quam Singulari says that I, Loup, may go and make my First Communion this morning. I have long attended the Curé's classes and have therefore received the needful instruction. If he says that I have not, the Curé lies—and this he may do because I suck sweets which Christophe gives me to help my asthma. And if Christophe can have a fine suit so can I; I shall therefore go in his suit to Communion.' He stopped speaking, and pale but immensely triumphant, he hitched up the sagging legs of the breeches.

You might well have heard a pin drop in the room, for you could not have seen three more paralysed people than those who now stared at le tout petit Loup—that mosquito, that gnat, that midge of a child with the eyes of a wizened, malevolent monkey. There was only one thing that they might have said—they all thought of it, too, at precisely the same instant. They might have said: 'Look at yourself in the glass; not just at the top of yourself but at the whole!' Yes, they might have, though naturally none of them said it.

But a sly and insidious foe had poor Loup, which was always lying in wait to undo him. And it lived in his lungs, this insidious foe, which gave it a very unfair advantage. All in a moment he was fighting for breath, and a really alarming attack it was this time. So Christophe must take off the shoes and stockings while Marie deftly removed the collar, trying not to spoil the white flottant tie. Then she handed the jacket and waistcoat to Jóusè, and one way and another they got him undressed and to bed, where he lay like a sick marmoset, much too suffering to resemble a malevolent monkey. Then Marie must run out in search of a neighbour, and the wife of the corn-chandler promised to come and remain until they should get back from Mass.

'Very well,' sighed Jóusè, 'very well, that is settled. And now I think we had all better dress; it is late, and one cannot keep the good God waiting.'

'You and Christophe be off, then,' said Marie rather crossly, 'go and wash and get into your clean underclothes. I must try some stale bread for this smudge on the collar.'

2

In due course Madame Roustan arrived with Jan; she was wearing a heliotrope coloured voile dress, mauve gloves, and a mauve hat with white ostrich tips—the costume very ill became her stout figure. But Jan in his beautifully cut Paris clothes—the cloth of which Marie observed was not glossy—with a bow that was certainly smaller than Christophe's, and a sleeve badge that had certainly much shorter ends and in consequence looked less showy but neater, with a missal of finely tooled crushed morocco, the gift of Madame la Comtesse de Bérac—Jan indeed seemed well worthy of the Church parade that had been so adroitly contrived by his mother, and Marie was ashamed to hear herself sigh as she glanced from this mirror of fashion to Christophe. Was Christophe's white bow just a trifle too large? Ai! las, what a pity that all her stale bread had not moved that greasy mark on his collar. And his Prayer-Book . . . oh, well, as Monsieur had declared . . . still, she did wish that it could have been of real leather!

She herself had had scarcely any time to dress, and she now felt dowdy in her faded blue foulard. Loup had kept her, then Anfos had needed her help, and so, of course, had Christophe and his father. But how smart Jóusè looked in his striped brown suit and new made-up tie—that at least was a comfort. And how honest and manly her Christophe looked—he possessed a far finer figure than his cousin.

Madame Roustan was speaking: 'He is lucky indeed in having a friend like the Comtesse de Bérac. Such a missal! I tremble to think of the cost! And the suit, I believe, was made by the tailor who makes for Madame la Comtesse's son—as you may have heard, Jóusè, he is in the army, Cuirassiers, I believe.'

All these damned repetitions! Jóusè turned and slapped viciously at a mosquito.

The cousins eyed each other and smiled. Jan said softly to Christophe: 'Show me your Prayer Book.' Then: 'I really like it much better than mine—mine has too much gold, but do not tell mother. And yours has a clasp; I wish mine had a clasp! All the same, she is kind, that lady in Paris.'

They both felt extremely self-conscious in their clothes, a fact which seemed to draw them together. Christophe's shoes were pinching abominably, and he greatly disliked the feel of a waistcoat, though Jan's gentleness more than made up for it all—he could be like this sometimes, wonderfully gentle, and perceptive too, as he had been about the Prayer Book.

But now Madame Roustan was impatient to start: 'Come, my son, we will lead the way,' she said firmly, and taking Jan's arm she stepped out into the street.

What could Marie and Jóusè do, therefore, but follow with Christophe between them? And they all three eclipsed! 'Ah, how like her, the insolent female,' thought Jóusè. Then to make matters worse, Anfos trod on their heels, in his doglike desire to keep close to Christophe.

Yes, but what of Eusèbe? The effrontery of him! His callous, nay outrageous lack of fine feeling! He was actually beating his old feather bed as hard as he could from his bedroom window; grinning and beating his shameful old bed while the air became thick with its moth-eaten feathers.

'Will you stop that?' shouted Jóusè, shaking his fist as a feather lit upon Christophe's shoulder, 'Will you stop that? We are being smothered in your filth!'

'Eh, what?' croaked Eusèbe, turning an ear and pretending that he was almost stone deaf, 'Go on beating, you say? Beat harder, you say? But surely, my friend, I will go on beating!' And he nearly tore the bedding in half, so mighty a blow did he give with his broomstick.

Madame Roustan ignored these unseemly proceedings, but Eusèbe could never ignore Madame Roustan: 'Hòu,' he shouted at her dignified back, 'Madame has decked herself like a peacock; and yet I have heard it said that fine feathers do not necessarily make a fine bird; and, moreover, that vanity comes from the devil!' Then he hoicked and spat recklessly into the road—he was in a diabolical mood, that morning.

They continued a slow promenade to the church, for Madame Roustan, who was setting the pace, had decided that there was no need to hurry. And now down the narrow and tortuous side-streets came girls in long billowing white tulle veils, walking carefully to spare their expensive suède shoes, and occasionally patting their wreaths of white roses. Christophe noticed a couple of boys that he knew, classmates who marched stiffly beside their parents; but by common consent they passed without a word, too embarrassed and shy to exchange a greeting. Then came more boys, all wearing white flottant ties and white sleeve-ribbons in accordance with custom; then more girls, until the whole town seemed alive with these solemn and rather touching young creatures. While away in the open belfry of Saint Loup the bells were playing a very old hymn somewhat stiffly because they themselves were so old: 'Jesus Christ, the Shepherd, the Lamb, and the Victim. . . .'

Jóusè was thinking as he walked by his son: 'I have surely much cause to be humble towards God this day,' for the plaintive lilt of the tune had driven the irritable thoughts from his mind, so that he no longer observed Madame Roustan or Jan in his beautifully cut Paris suit, but only the boy who was close at his side. 'It is true,' he mused, 'I have much cause to be humble and yet proud when I think of my firstborn offspring; yes, and of God, who is also a Father, and of Mary the immaculate Mother of God, and of Joseph my very dear patron saint who became the pure spouse of that immaculate Mother. . . . It is not always easy to understand these mysteries: one can only be humble and grateful.'

'Jesus Christ, the Shepherd, the Lamb, and the Victim . . .' chimed the bells, 'the Shepherd, the Lamb, and the Victim. . . .'

Marie was thinking as she walked by her son: 'May my child's Communion bring me faith and courage, so that I can say to our blessèd Lord with an honest, courageous and truthful heart, "I leave all to Thy infinite wisdom and mercy. . . ."'

Christophe suddenly slipped his hand into hers.

'Jesus Christ, the Shepherd, the Lamb, and the Victim. . . .' chimed the bells, 'the Shepherd, the Lamb, and the Victim. . . .'

And now they were mounting the steps of the church.

'Jesus Christ, the Shepherd, the Lamb, and the Victim. . . .'

And there was Goundran upon the church porch, very seemly and grave in his best Sunday clothes, and beside him Elise who was heavy with child so must wear a long cloak for modesty's sake, even although her eyes must proclaim the great joy that would presently quicken within her. And near Goundran stood several young fishermen friends; big, brown-skinned fellows with a smattering of faith and more than a smattering of superstition. They had come because they believed that good luck followed those who attended a First Communion; that their presence would please Mary-Star-of-the-Sea.

'Jesus Christ, the Shepherd, the Lamb, and the Victim. . . .'

And there was Madame Perron's young brother. He was hurrying after his sister and niece, despite the fact that when he was up north he refused to believe in God or the devil; despite the fact, too, that the previous night his thoughts had been more than a little unruly, and his conduct none too chaste down at the port.

'Jesus Christ, the Shepherd, the Lamb, and the Victim. . . .'

And there was Mère Mélanie ready to worship, but also to weep on the least provocation; and there was Mère Mélanie's hump-backed violinist who only last evening had grinned as he played: 'As tu vu les fesses de ma belle Louise?' and similar songs on his shrill, teasing fiddle. And there was the woman who sold cherries in the street but who did not always give you fair measure; and the wretch who was said to be fabulously rich, to have sacks full of gold hidden under his bed while pretending to be a destitute beggar. And there was the pious youth from the shop in whose window appeared so many fine Prayer Books: 'This is not of real leather,' he had said many times, 'mais Madame, croyez moi, it is even better!' Was it better, or would it wear out in a month? N'importe, it was all in the good cause of business. The butcher, the baker, the candlestick maker, some bringing their children, some coming without them; for the most part respectable citizens enough, who paid their just dues to the Church and State, who married and gave their offspring in marriage; for the most part well-soaped and appropriately garbed in honour of this impressive occasion.

'Jesus Christ, the Shepherd, the Lamb, and the Victim. . . .'

The bells stopped abruptly, and now in their stead the ancient hymn was pealed out by the organ, and at this Mère Mélanie started to sniff, then to dab at her eyes conspicuously, then to glance at her little hump-backed violinist.

But in spite of Mère Mélanie's facile tears and the brandy-soaked breath of her crooked companion; in spite of Madame Roustan's foolish conceits—her sins and her son and her Comtesse de Bérac; in spite of those large-limbed men from the sea, whose faith was submerged by their superstition; in spite of the folly, the meanness, and the sin that will enter even the holiest place where two or three are gathered together—yes, in spite of it all, there was something abroad that was infinitely above and beyond those people, and yet, as it were, in the midst of them . . . perhaps God's incurable optimism flaming up at the sight of the kneeling children.

The Mass had begun. At the foot of the altar the Curé was making his public confession and the children were dutifully striking their breasts: 'Mea culpa, mea culpa, mea maxima culpa.' But Christophe was clutching·the back of the chair upon which he knelt, and his staring eyes were not on the priest but were turned to the wall against which stood a life-like Crucifixion—a large agony fashioned from wood and paint with much skill by the hands of some bygone craftsman. And although he had seen the thing many times and had thought of it only as a symbol of salvation, he now saw it as the crucified body of a man, of a man who was very terribly human—the outraged and bleeding body of a man dying slowly as he hung there in torment; while in some incomprehensible and terrifying way this fearful perception seemed to link itself up with him and with his approaching Communion. Cowering down he covered his face with his hands: 'I cannot . . . I cannot . . . I cannot . . .' he thought wildly, scarcely knowing if he were praying or blaspheming.

Time passed, but he was unconscious of time. The triple bell rang out sharp and clear as the Curé offered the Host to God, then the Chalice, for the sins of his congregation. But Christophe heard only the groans of a man, and the man was very terribly human.

It had come; the Curé was striking his breast and speaking quite low but with careful precision, repeating the simple words of his Church very slowly: 'Domine, non sum dignus. . . .' Then a sound, a soft, secretive rustling sound like the sea slipping back over pebbles in a mist, as the children got quietly up from their knees and began to move forward with bowed young heads. Then a voice, rather startled and close to his ear—his mother's voice: 'Christophe, are you ill. . . ? It is time.'

'I cannot . . . but I cannot . . .' he thought he answered.

Yet he found that he must have risen after all for now he was standing close to Jan in the nave, then kneeling beside him at the altar rail—he could feel the touch of his cousin's slim shoulder.

'Corpus Domini nostri Jesu Christi . . .' Jan was passing him the little protective platter. . . . 'Corpus Domini nostri Jesu Christi custodiat animam tuam in vitam æternam.'

White with terror he received the proffered Host, passed
the platter blindly on to his neighbour, then clung to the
rail with a kind of despair—for a moment he had the
sensation of falling.

3

The reactions of youth are not only elastic but they strongly incline towards self-preservation; thus the shock of that
curious First Communion became less acute as the weeks
wore on and the boy's conscious mind strove for explanations
that would make the occurrence appear more normal, He
still could not look at that Crucifixion, it is true, but must
always turn away his eyes from its infinite pathos and
infinite horror, but when next he received the Sacrament he
was able to do so with comparative calmness—a faint,
indefinable shadow of dread was all that remained of his
unreasoning terror. And although this indefinable shadow of
dread did not leave him, as had done the more violent
emotion, he persuaded himself that it might very well be
that everyone felt such a dread at Communion—so solemn
and so spiritually vital an event, and those who received
their Lord, so unworthy. But one did not care to speak
of such things, they were far too private and far too
sacred.

His terror—that was not quite so easy to explain; yet he
strove with all his might to explain it. He had felt very tired;
perhaps he had been ill, perhaps he had even had a high
fever . . . Loup would get a high fever at times and feel
queer . . . perhaps he, Christophe, had been just feeling
queer and had not known that he was actually ill because he
was so unaccustomed to illness. Then would come that
thought of the divinity of Christ, so familiar and in consequence so reassuring. Jesus Christ, true man . . . yes, but
also true God; and he, Christophe Bénédit, less than nothing,
a schoolboy born and brought up in Provence, impossible
therefore that the Crucifixion in the church should have any
personal meaning beyond the promise of spiritual salvation.
That was how he had always seen it before, and that was
how he must see it again—as a symbol of his spiritual
salvation.

179

'Jesus Christ,' he would mutter, 'the Son of God . . . not as I am, but the veritable Son of God. . . . Ah yes, that undoubtedly makes all the difference!'

But one day he must suddenly catch his breath, while his heart seemed to stumble and then stand still, for clear and distinct as the notes of a bugle, as the warning of the triple Communion bell, there leapt into his combative, unwilling mind the momentous words: 'But as many as received Him, to them gave He power to become the sons of God.' And just for a moment he was conscious again of that sickening sensation of physical terror. Then his strong young instinct of self-preservation, which was always so ready to come to his assistance, leapt up, in its turn, to defeat that saying: 'It means,' he thought violently, 'that when we are dead we also may be with Jesus in heaven. That is what those words mean. What else can they mean? Who would dare to make himself the equal of Christ? Not the Curé, not Jan, not even the saints.' And he frowned, 'I must certainly stop all this thinking which the Curé would say leads to great foolishness, and, moreover, to what is far worse—presumption. When I go to Mass I will beg our Lord to make me very simple and humble.'

In this wise Christophe sought to explain those things by which his humanity was sorely troubled.

CHAPTER NINETEEN

I

IT was early in July when Anatole Kahn made his first
appearance in the town of Saint Loup—a stout middle-
aged man with a waxed moustache, whose dark
business suit suggested the north, and whose interest
was so great in all he beheld that it led him to ask
innumerable questions. He was friendly, urbane, and
apparently prosperous, to judge by the wine which he
ordered at la Tarasque—vintage wine, as Mère Mélanie
afterwards confided to her cronies; yes indeed, the best in
the cellar.

The townsfolk were willing enough to talk, rather
flattered and amused by the admiration which this stranger
expressed for their mountains, their sea, their vineyards, their
houses, and their tortuous byways. Thus it was that quite
soon he was able to collect a fine packet of practical information. Among other things which he managed to learn was the
fact that you could not furnish a house save by putting
yourself to the trouble of a journey. You must go to Marseille for your tables and chairs unless you employed Jóusè
Bénédit who, it seemed, was a very remarkable fellow. A
carpenter he was, and a cabinet-maker, managing to ply
both trades with great skill; but then Bénédit was the sort
of man who was clever at anything he turned his hand to—
at a pinch he might even build you a house—ah, yes, a very
remarkable fellow. But slow . . . perhaps he was over conscientious. He was certainly imbued with the pride of his
crafts; nothing but the best must leave his bench, and the
best could not be achieved in a hurry according to him, so
he took his own time. And meanwhile, of course, you just
had to wait, which frequently made you feel rather impatient. All the same, many people employed Bénédit,
nearly everyone did, he was quite a tradition. Moreover it

seemed foolish to get into a train and go to Marseille—
train journeys cost money.

'But this Jóusè, has he no apprentice?' asked the stranger.

'Well, yes, but the poor Anfos is half-witted. He is
willing, but he needs to be treated like a child; he cannot do
much without Jóusè's supervision.'

'Then,' said Anatole Kahn, 'it comes to this: if I wish to
obtain . . . now let me see . . . say a drawing-room suite
upholstered in satin, or a nice little ornamental clock, or
rugs, or pictures, or perhaps a brass bedstead I must trouble
myself to go to Marseille.'

'Yes, Monsieur.'

'Ah,' he murmured, 'that seems a real pity.'

He remained for more than a week in Saint Loup,
staying at the small hotel near the station. And during this
time he was joined by three friends who were thought to be
business men of some kind and who, judging by the labels
on their trunks, came from Paris. Where he himself came
from no one could guess, since his luggage consisted of a
solitary hand-bag.

But on the whole they aroused little interest, these
strangers, for the weather was unusually oppressive. A vast
indolence had taken hold on Saint Loup so that even the
bells of the church sounded drowsy, while as for the Curé, he
was finding it hard not to doze as he sat in his airless box
hearing those dreary and monotonous confessions.

All the same, one person there was whose interest was
thoroughly aroused, and this was Madame Roustan. She
had chanced to look out of her bedroom window and had
seen the four men examining the shop next her own, the
shop that had belonged to a grocer but was now up for sale,
he having retired—and a fine shop it was, too, just on the
corner. Then the very next morning they had entered the
shop, having doubtless obtained the key from the baker;
and that same afternoon a fifth man had arrived bringing
with him a long foot-rule and a note-book. He had also
brought many patterns of paint—little bright-coloured
strips on a bit of cardboard. The strangers had stood
together in the street pointing at the premises of her ex-
neighbour, making notes, holding patterns of paint against
the door, measuring the frontage, and the Lord knew what-

all! After which they had turned and strolled off down the quay apparently engaged in earnest conversation.

Presently it was said between coffee and cognac, between slicing onions and frying potatoes, that the property was sold to that man who had stayed for a week at the hotel— there would be a new grocer. Bien, they hoped that he was honest and above all cheap, not a usurer like his predecessor. Who was he? Well, his name was Anatole Kahn—he had told the baker that he was an Alsatian. Where was he? Ah, ça . . . very possibly in Toulon arranging about the title-deeds which was always a long and fatiguing business. Then yawns, and the matter was melted from their minds by the wellnigh intolerable heat of the weather.

Workmen came and began to torment the old shop; its protests could be heard from morning till evening as they tore down its groaning interior walls, ripped up boards and laid pipes for a water supply which was destined to feed nothing less than a bathroom. At this people really did open their eyes pretty wide with amazement, in spite of the heat-wave. A bathroom, if you please! And the privy in the yard being dug up with a great deal of swearing and stinking because Monsieur must have his closet indoors! But what next would he have? He was doubtless a marquis! Well, they wished he was there to enjoy the stench, and the blowflies, and the clouds of full-bellied mosquitoes. And what was the marquis proposing to sell? Perfumery, perhaps —God knew it was needed! No, but truly, what was he proposing to sell? He was making himself a marvellous showroom, and was actually painting the cellar walls . . . Putting in the electric light, too, at vast cost. Why, only important places had that—the hotel and the railway station for example. Most sensible people were content with lamps, which were not only far less dangerous but cheaper.

Madame Roustan was irate. All this hubbub and stench; quite enough, she declared, to ruin her business. And the brick-dust flying about in her shop, and the rubble piling up in front of her door, and the drain-pipes piling up against her back fence, and the ladders jostling her decrepit old gutters. So secretive they were, too, the whole lot of them, from the architect down to the dirtiest workman. Not one word could she get as to what was afoot, no, nor any redress, only shrugs and smiles and vague answers to her loud and indignant questions. As for Jóusè, he was utterly unconcerned. What cared he for the wrongs of his widowed sister! All he asked, it appeared, was to be left alone: 'Do not worry me, Germaine, I cannot attend—not now—I am really extremely busy.' A nice brother! But then naturally he was unaffected by the dust, and the stench, and the droves of mosquitoes. Nor was the Curé much better, she decided; all he did was to counsel restraint and patience; while Goundran was entirely taken up with Elise—such a fuss about her approaching confinement!

'Surely a woman without her own man to protect her is pitiful indeed,' sighed Madame Roustan.

Then one day who should come strolling into her shop but the cause of all this outrageous disturbance, Monsieur Anatole Kahn with his waxed moustache, his thick northern clothes, and his middle-aged paunch across which was suspended a handsome gold watch-chain.

'Ah, Madame,' he said suavely, 'I very much fear you must greatly dislike your troublesome neighbour. But quite soon I am hoping that the work will be done; meanwhile I apologize for any inconvenience. Believe me, Madame, I have had to be absent myself upon very important business; the fault is my architect's, therefore, not mine. I am deeply distressed to observe that your gutter has been bent—yes, very deeply distressed. Madame must permit me to provide a new gutter.'

He had large ox-like eyes and a very red mouth—the skin of his lips looked as soft as satin. On each of his plump, blunt hands he wore rings, though his nails were habitually soiled and bitten. A vulgar and over-dressed little man with his light cloth-topped boots, and his purple necktie, and his hat that appeared too small for his head; but his eyes were resting on Madame Roustan with a gentle, persuasive yet appraising expression.

'Madame will forgive me, I trust,' he murmured.

Now not only had Madame Roustan intended to express herself forcibly when she met him, but she had actually drawn up a very long list comprising each real and imaginary grievance—the stench, the mosquitoes, the blow-flies, the dust, the noise, and the damage to her gutters and fencing; every crack in her walls, every scratch on her doors she had carefully, if not always truthfully, noted; yet here she was growing quite flustered and coy because of Monsieur Kahn's ox-like eyes with their gentle, persuasive, yet appraising expression.

She said: 'Eh bien, Monsieur, I will admit that I and my poor little business have suffered. However, if the work is now nearly complete and Monsieur is prepared to replace my bent gutter. . . .'

'There is nothing I am not prepared to replace for you, chère Madame,' he assured her suavely.

'Ah, Monsieur is too good.'

'Not at all, chère Madame, my wish is that we should be excellent neighbours.' He sat down. 'You see how it is, Madame: I come here to the south because of my throat— I unfortunately suffer from tonsilitis. I come here as a stranger, so I go to Marseille and instruct a good firm to send in careful workmen; and I also employ a first class architect to whom I repeat a great number of times: "No inconvenience, if you please, to my neighbour; everything must be done to allay the dust; to avoid all bad smells when removing that privy; use strong disinfectant," I am careful to say. He ignores me—there are smells but no disinfectant. For two months they have idled; it is now September. Early in October I must open my shop because I, like yourself, have to work for my living.' He paused, and she asked him:

'What will Monsieur sell—if that is not an indiscreet question?'

'By no means, Madame,' he replied with a smile, 'I propose to sell everything for the home—in Paris I had a furnishing business. I think that Saint Loup is a coming place, and that therefore it provides an excellent opening.' And he smiled again, gently stroking his moustache. 'Yes,' he repeated, 'a most excellent opening.'

Madame Roustan was completely taken aback: 'But Monsieur, we are poor, and our tastes are so simple . . . my brother. . . .'

He waved these objections aside: 'Saint Loup will not always be poor, I assure you. Chère Madame, believe me,

the day will arrive when your charming Saint Loup will
become the fashion. A fine beach, a warm sea, cheap wine,
cheap fruit, much sunshine and really exquisite mountains.
What do you think brought me here, chère Madame—
apart, of course, from my tonsilitis? A small picture, it was,
that brought me here, a picture of the harbour with the
mountains beyond—I discovered it on the Rive Gauche in
Paris. I said to the salesman: "How much does he want?"
And he answered: "Not much, he is quite a poor artist."
Then I said: "I will take his name and address, in addition
to which I will buy his bad picture." Madame, the thing is a
masterpiece; you shall see it, I have it in my portmanteau.
Bien, Madame, this spring when I visited the Salon there
were two more pictures by that same artist, pictures of the
little side-streets of your town—very cleverly done, very
clean, true colour. The man's name is Beauvais; I believe he
is young and that those were his first important exhibits.
But the point is this; his pictures were attracting a very
great deal of admiration, so that doubtless this Beauvais
will come here again, and through him may well come other
good artists, and through them the town of Saint Loup will
get known—they will do all our advertising for nothing. Ah,
Madame, forgive me if my tongue runs away, the fault lies
with my great enthusiasm. Already I see Paris gowns in
your window, and fine lingerie, and gay bathing cos-
tumes. . . .'

'In my window?' she asked him incredulously.

'But surely, Madame—in your window, why not? It
will be but a step from the drapery business.'

'It sounds like a marvellous dream . . .' she faltered.

'But a dream that is going to come true,' he told her.
Then he got up: 'Madame, I have kept you too long. I talk
too much, it is my greatest weakness.' And he gallantly
pressed a kiss on her hand. 'I go now to give orders about
that new gutter.'

She watched him as he hurried away down the quay, no
doubt going in search of his absent foreman. Such ideas; she
was feeling quite upset, and yet withall rather pleasantly
excited. Then she thought: 'Why not? The man may be
right . . . we certainly have the most excellent bathing.
Bèlli santo, our Saint Loup as a summer resort, frequented

by rich and fashionable people . . . and I selling Paris models in my shop, and fine lingerie, instead of bone buttons! Ah, mais non, he is mad, that poor Monsieur Kahn . . . yet who knows, such things must have happened before . . . there must surely always have been a beginning. . . .' And she suddenly decided to find Mère Mélanie and discuss these surprising possibilities over a small cup of coffee at la Tarasque.

2

That evening Madame Roustan went to visit her brother. She found the Bénédits in the parlour; Marie was darning a pair of socks and Jóusè was quietly reading his paper.

'Ah, Germaine,' said Marie. Then: 'Loup, bring up that chair, Christophe, go and fetch wine and biscuits from the kitchen, but keep your greedy hand out of the tin! They are fond of sweet biscuits, my sons,' she said smiling.

Jóusè laid aside his paper: 'Good evening,' he grunted.

Madame Roustan began the moment she sat down: 'I fear I am the bearer of very grave tidings. I fear . . .' there ensued a long, meaning pause.

Then Jóusè said with a malicious grin: 'Do not tell us that you have been excommunicated!'

'That remark is in very bad taste,' she informed him. 'and I do not propose to discuss religion. I have come to tell you that Anatole Kahn is about to open a furnishing business.'

'And who may he be?' enquired Jóusè blandly.

'That you surely must know, for the whole town is talking. He has bought the big corner shop next to mine, the shop of Monsieur Dubois, the grocer.'

'Attendez . . .' murmured Jóusè, pretending to think hard, 'I remember, he has just installed a fine bathroom. The sea was too small for him, I have heard—not sufficiently wet, not quite enough water. . . .'

'He will also install many other fine things, and more is the pity,' Madame Roustan said tartly. Then before her brother had time to reply, she plunged into an animated description of the future of Saint Loup, according to Kahn, and of all that this prophet would most certainly sell in his handsome and up-to-date shop on the corner.

'But' said Marie, interrupting, 'who will buy his cheap rubbish when my husband here gives such fine value for money? Honest tables and chairs and all made by hand. . . . I fear that your poor Monsieur Kahn is foolish. In Saint Loup we know where it is wise to spend.' And she laughed a little, nodding her head. Then: 'A small glass of wine, Germaine?' she suggested.

But Christophe was not deceived by the laugh: 'She is frightened,' he thought, 'she is really very frightened.'

Jóusè said, as he yawned and stretched his great legs: 'You come here, my sister, with what you imagine—I do not say hope, I say what you imagine—are unpleasant and perhaps even evil tidings. But believe me, I shall live to see my son Christophe carry on this old and honourable business. Your friend may sell a few musical boxes, or perhaps cuckoo-clocks—that I think more than likely. I myself will buy one of his cuckoo-clocks if only to amuse the poor, childish Anfos. For the rest, he is doomed to failure, your friend; our people know the value of well-seasoned timber.'

'But,' she argued, 'suppose many strangers should come, suppose they they should come in summer for the bathing and need things in a hurry—beds and tables and things. . . .'

'Rubbish, you are talking rubbish!' laughed Jóusè, 'Where would they live, these fine people of yours? Do not be so completely ridiculous, my sister. No, no, I shall not sleep a wink less well because Monsieur Kahn will open his shop with a firework display some time in October! On the contrary, Germaine, I am really quite pleased—it may be that his little venture will prove useful. Rugs you said he would sell, among other things; eh bien, Marie needs a new rug for this room. She and I will be his first customers, for I fear that he will not last very long, it would therefore be wise to purchase our rug before the inevitable disaster.'

Madame Roustan thought: 'Is my brother a fool? Or is Monsieur Kahn, and not he, the fool? So much money that poor Monsieur Kahn must have spent . . . yet I cannot believe quite all that he said . . . I cannot quite see Paris gowns in my window. . . . And, moreover, Jóusè is correct in one thing: if those grand people came to us where would they live? They could not well live in tents on the beach, and our only hotel is exceedingly small . . . to accommodate tourists one must have many houses.' Aloud she said: 'Let us hope you are right—it is naturally more serious for you than for me. I do not myself make tables and chairs, I sell buttons and tapes to gain my living. And then, I have only one son to think of, and he is already provided for, thanks to the Church and Madame de Bérac. Ah, yes, it is more grave for you than for me. But no doubt the good saints will hold you in mind, remembering that you have a wife and two children, and the one child so ailing that he costs a small fortune what with his diet and his doctor's bills . . . ai, ai, . . .' After which encouraging words she got up, kissed Marie, and took her departure.

When she had gone Jóusè slapped his big knee and guffawed: 'Oh, that sister of mine, she is comic! She comes here full of hope that we shall all weep. What a woman, the breath of her nostrils is affliction. She is one of those who carry a ready-made cap to fit fears: "Put it on," she says. But I answer: "Your neat little cap does not fit me!" "It is graver for you than for me," she says, "*you* have a wife and two children to provide for; but no doubt the good saints will hold you in mind, remembering that one child is always ailing." Ah, mais non, she would pick the eyes out of a corpse; a positive vulture she is, my sister! Well, now, I say this: let Anatole Kahn, or whatever his name is, go to the devil. I am Jóusè Bénédit, born and bred in Saint Loup as my father was born and bred here before me, as his father was born and bred here before him; and always we have lived by the honesty of wood, by the honesty and skill of our brains and our fingers. Birth and death, death and birth our good beds have sustained, to say nothing of fine, sturdy Christian mating. There are beds in Saint Loup that my grandfather made, as sound this night as the day when he made them. Does that count for nothing? Sant Jan l'ami de Diéu, it counts for a lot in the eyes of our people. I am willing to put my trust in our friends—for that matter in all who have had dealings with me. Am I, Jóusè Bénédit, to shake in my shoes because some mad upstart arrives from nowhere with yarns about the growth of a town which has not grown one inch in two hundred years? We shall next be hearing that the bells of Saint Loup have jumped out of their belfry and run off to Paris; that the good saint himself has hopped down from his niche and is drinking a petit verre at la Tarasque—so progressive, so modern have we become with our furniture emporiums and our grand summer season! Ah, no Marioun; do not look so pensive, you shall eat bouillabaisse for many a day—yes, the bouillabaisse blanche shall you eat, and chicken. Never fear, Marioun, but that Jóusè will provide, as he always has done, for his wife and children. Your Jóusè believes in the good sense of his clients and his clients will continue to believe in your Jóusè. And now kiss me, my wife, and you also, my sons; then let us go happily up to our beds and dream of that cuckoo-clock which I shall buy in order to give a little pleasure to Anfos.' So saying he gave them each a rough hug, kissed them each on both cheeks, and then took his wife's arm: 'Come, my dear, or I shall not get up in the morning.'

And indeed he did suddenly feel very tired, after this, for him, long and eloquent speech which had set him perspiring from head to foot. But that night he slept not one whit the less soundly because of the advent of Anatole Kahn who was going to provide all things for the household.

CHAPTER TWENTY

I

PRECISELY as the clock struck two p.m. on October the second Kahn would open his shop, and this because two and two make four, which he always considered his lucky number. From an early hour on that autumn morning a youth was distributing circulars announcing the event to all who would take them; a stranger he was who had come from Paris, and his open-necked shirt exposed a skin of such whiteness when compared with the sun-bronzed skins of the south, that it looked positively indecent. However, he was smart enough at his job and by noon nearly everyone down at the port had received the news that Anatole Kahn would display a superb and unique collection of furniture at popular prices —Louis Quinze and Louis Seize not excepted.

Goundran smiled rather ruefully to himself as he scanned the long list of advertised objects; he must keep Elise's hand out of his pocket. But all the same he took the thing home.

'We will go,' said his wife with unusual decision. Then: 'I see there are clocks. . . .'

'Yes, and pictures,' added Goundran.

'And brass bedsteads'; sighed Elise, 'it is foolish, I know, yet how much I long for a really nice bed made of brass.'

Goundran thought: 'And her time is so near, it has almost arrived . . . could I possibly afford it?'

Marie—who while doing her morning shopping had stopped to chat with the corn-chandler's wife about the prices of food, Loup's persistent asthma, and the corn-chandler's son who was Jóusè's godchild—Marie had a circular thrust into her hand by the young man from Paris.

'What is this?' she enquired.

'If Madame will give herself the trouble to read it. . . . And you also, Madame,' he said nonchalantly as he handed another to the good Madame Simon.

The corn-chandler's wife clipped on her glasses: 'Tè, it is Kahn, that new man at the port who will open his shop this afternoon. I think I must go, it may well be amusing. Not that we have any money to buy, Guillaume's business college has cost a great deal, but the boy is so clever that one does not regret . . . and now that he will come home and help his parents. . . . Such a fine boy he grows; and he sent his love to his godfather when he last wrote from Marseille: "Give my love to Papa Jóusè," he said. Now what have I done with that dear child's letter? I thought I had it here in my bag. . . .'

But Marie, excusing herself on the plea that she would be late, turned and hurried away with the circular feeling like lead in her pocket.

Arrived home she went in search of her husband. He was waiting about in the kitchen with the children; Loup was peering into a simmering saucepan and sniffing its contents, Christophe was reading, and Jóusè was staring out of the window.

She thought suddenly: 'My man . . . his back looks quite old . . . he is ageing, my man.' And this thought was so painful that the stab of it made her speak almost sharply: 'Kahn has many fine things to sell,' she announced, 'and moreover he will sell them at popular prices. Look at this,' and she held out the circular, 'it is being distributed all over the town—he is going to open this very afternoon!'

'That I have already heard,' said Jóusè. He read the announcement, then he laughed very loudly: 'Louis Quinze, Louis Seize, this thing says he will sell us! Yes, no doubt, Marioun, but then who will buy? That is what I ask you. Ah, mais non, Louis Quinze!' And crushing the circular in his hand he hurled it, still laughing, into the corner.

But le tout petit Loup had now pricked up his ears, for he much wished to know the contents of that paper, so he promptly retrieved it, spread it out on his knee and read in his turn: 'Gramophones . . .' he murmured.

'What is that?' enquired Jóusè, swinging heavily round.

'Gramophones, and I wish to possess one,' announced Loup.

'Ah, really, and what else do you wish to possess?' Jóusè's voice sounded suddenly ominous.

'Many things that I find in this list,' Loup told him.

Christophe nudged his brother, then he trod on his foot with rather more vigour than he had intended.

'Why are you treading on my toe, imbecile? Get off it!' bawled Loup, as he doubled up his fist.

'Do not threaten me like that with your fist!' flared Christophe.

'Then keep your enormous feet out of my way.'

'I will not!'

'You have feet like an elephant's!'

'Ah, bien, you have feet the size of a bug's!'

'Maman, maman, Christophe has called me a bug!'

'Oh, be silent, both of you,' exclaimed Marie. 'Santo Ano d'At! I am late as it is. Stop quarrelling if you wish to remain in my kitchen.'

Jóusè shrugged his shoulders: 'Such a hubbub,' he muttered, 'and a man who has worked for long hours feels tired—since five this morning have I been at my bench, and now nothing to eat, the food is not ready!' Turning, he blundered out of the room.

'He looks tired, that is true enough,' thought Marie. Then she snatched Kahn's announcement away from Loup, opened the door of the stove and burnt it.

But Christophe sat as stiff as a ramrod in his chair, for his eyes were suddenly aching with tears: if he moved by so much as an inch they must fall, and at his age one did not shed tears, it was childish.

2

Much secrecy had been observed by Kahn with regard to the arrangement of his fine new shop and the dressing of his two spacious plate-glass windows. The goods, when they had come out of their vans, had been swathed like so many sacred mummies, and once they had entered his premises all the doors had been locked and the blinds drawn down before anyone had started unpacking.

'No doubt with his grand electricity he can well afford to dispense with mere daylight,' people had jeered; but nevertheless there was quite a large crowd in front of the shop a little before the hour of the opening.

Two strokes from the clock and up went the blinds, while the doors were flung wide with a princely flourish. And there stood the youth of the circulars with a big bobbing bundle of air balloons, bearing the inscription: 'Galeries Kahn' on their taut, rotund sides of many colours.

'Prenez, Madame! Prenez, Messieurs et Dames, pour vos enfants. Voilà, ma petite! Encore un? Encore deux? Mais voilà! Joli, hein?' And he dexterously disentangled the bundle.

Then Anatole Kahn stepped forward with a bow. Very smart he was, wearing a pearl in his necktie, wearing pale grey trousers with heavy black stripes, and a flower in the buttonhole of his jacket. He felt honoured, he said, indescribably honoured by the presence of so many distinguished clients. As a stranger to their beautiful town of Saint Loup he knew himself to be at a real disadvantage, yet he dared to hope for their patronage on the strength of his honest and untiring endeavours to deal fairly by all—five hundred francs or one franc, they would find it just the same thing when it came to receiving good value for their money. The most trivial purchase was an honour conferred, and would thus receive his personal attention.

And now came the strains of the *Marseillaise* from a large gramophone at the back of the showroom. Most stirring it was, they all had to admit; such a fine record, too, a real military band—Boudiéu, one could fancy one saw the men marching! And that over, came a jolly new popular song, words and all, from the Folies Bergères in Paris. Then the ballet music from Faust—Boudiéu, one could almost fancy one saw the girls dancing! The devil must be in it! These gramophones . . . Mère Mélanies' hump-backed fiddling friend would undoubtedly have to look to his laurels!

They jostled and laughed and flicked the balloons and fingered the stock and examined price labels. They went down to the cellar which was brilliantly lighted and contained an assortment of rugs and mattings. They swarmed up the stairs to the first-floor showroom where cots and new-fangled perambulators suggestively elbowed double-bed-steads. But beyond an insignificant trifle or two—a vase, a small tray and suchlike objects—they apparently had not come there to buy, in spite of the really surprising cheapness of much that Anatole Kahn had to offer.

Goundran stood gazing at a flashy brass bed which possessed a particularly striking mattress—green and white ticking with a small orange line; and beside him, clinging to his arm, stood Elise: 'Ah, que c'est ravissant!' she kept saying.

And hearing her, Anatole Kahn stepped forward: 'It is also exceedingly cheap'; he assured them, 'the best hair and wool, the best lacquered brass. Then Madame has doubtless remarked the design, dignity with lightness, quite le dernier chic—such bedsteads are now all the rage in Paris.'

But Goundran shook his head: 'Not to-day, my friend—even the cheapest article costs money. We must think it over; is that not so, Elise?' For Goundran was a thrifty if devoted husband. Yet he thought: 'How much I should like to purchase that bedstead for the little one's coming confinement . . .' And he gently pressed his wife's arm as he whispered: 'Do not despair, I may buy it for you yet; we will go into our banking account this evening.'

It was not until late in the afternoon that Jóusè arrived upon the scene, and with him came his wife, his two sons, and Anfos. Jóusè moved with a kind of majestic precision, squaring his heavy and ageing shoulders. His chin with its thick curly beard was thrust out, his eyes and his lips were quietly smiling.

'Let us see what this mountebank has to sell,' he remarked to no one in particular as they stopped in front of Kahn's largest window.

Oh, that plate-glass window of the Galeries Kahn—the meanness, the blatant untruthfulness of it! The drawing room suite à la Louis Quinze, thin gilt already beginning to rub, cherry-coloured, half-cotton, deceitful satin; the in-adequate tables with spindle legs, and joints that would gape at the least provocation; the marble-topped, bow-fronted chests of drawers that had nothing substantial about them but the marble; the cabinets with flimsy untrustworthy locks and glass that distorted because of its cheapness;

the plush piano-covers with appliqué flowers and borders of tinsel that a breath would tarnish. . . .

There were rugs of so-called Oriental designs that had never known the Orient or its weavers; there were clocks whose outsides suggested Buhl, but whose insides suggested an operation; there were trays made for Europe by a crafty Japan who was careful that she herself did not use them; there were joss-sticks whose smell would have brought a blush to the cheeks of the most hardened heathen idol; there were pictures in iniquitous machine-carved frames, pictures covertly suggestive and crudely sentimental. And hanging in the very midst of it all—a most lovely, simple, and truthful conception—was 'The Angelus' framed in grave, quiet oak, looking as helplessly out of place as a nun who should find herself in a brothel.

Jóusè stood with his hands thrust deep into his pockets while his eyes grew incredulous and then angry; a man who had toiled for many long years he had earned a right of kinship to that picture, to the humble yet unparalleled dignity of patient, enduring, and honest labour.

Marie asked him timidly: 'Shall we go in?'

He nodded, and they turned and entered the building.

Kahn saw them and pushed his way through the crowd: 'I am proud to make your acquaintance,' he said suavely, and he held out a hand which Jóusè ignored.

'I have come here to buy a rug for my wife—and a cuckoo-clock,' Jóusè told him briefly.

'And a gramophone!' chirped le tout petit Loup, glancing out of the corner of an eye at Christophe.

They made their way down to the now transformed cellar accompained by Anatole Kahn in person: 'I repeat,' persisted Anatole Kahn, 'that I am most proud to make your acquaintance, Monsieur Bénédit, to know so distinguished a confrère.'

Jóusè stared at him and the stranger fell silent; whereupon Marie hastened to select her rug which Jóusè, still without speaking, paid for.

Then Anfos unexpectedly lost his head. Perhaps he was subconsciously feeling the tension, or perhaps it was merely that the noise and the crowd and the somewhat rash promise of a cuckoo-clock had thrown him into a state of excitement:

be that as it may, he proceeded to cuckoo. And so exact were the notes he produced, so wonderfully clever his imitation, that people turned round incredulously.

'Yes, yes, in a minute—hush, my dear,' implored Marie.

He caught hold of her hand like the child that he was—like the great bearded child that he was, le pauvre bougre: 'But you promised!' And now he was tugging at her hand.

'This way, if you please,' remarked Kahn quite gravely.

There were only two cuckoo-clocks it appeared, the one very big, the other very little. The price of the larger was much too high; Jóusè muttered that it was out of the question. The price of the smaller he could well afford, and this he decided to give his apprentice. So the clock was taken down from the wall and placed by Kahn in the arms of the half-wit.

'Bèu Diéu!' murmured Anfos softly.

Then le tout petit Loup felt that his turn had come: 'And where is my gramophone?' he demanded loudly. 'Why may I not have my gramophone? Am I not of more importance than he is?' And he pinched Anfos so that the clock nearly fell.

'Do not hurt me . . . Ah, do not hurt me,' implored Anfos, his brown, dog-like eyes growing suddenly frightened.

'Leave him alone!' ordered Christophe sharply.

But Loup scowled; he was thoroughly out of temper. Owing to the lateness of their arrival he had not even managed to get a balloon, the supply, by that time, having been exhausted: 'I will surely break his ridiculous clock if I may not have my gramophone!' he threatened.

'In that case you can go without your supper,' remarked Marie.

3

They made their way home in comparative silence, Anfos diligently nursing his cuckoo-clock; Marie keeping a watchful eye upon Loup; Christophe apparently lost in thought, and Jóusè staring down at his shoes.

But after a while Jóusè looked up grinning: 'I did not observe much fine business, Marioun; Louis Quinze and

Louis Seize are still on their thrones, and I fancy they are perfectly safe to remain there. What a scrap-heap—what rubbish! Yes, but also what an insult to the common sense and good taste of our town. I felt almost sorry for the impudent fellow.'

'I will break that ridiculous clock!' repeated Loup.

'No . . . no . . . it is beautiful . . .' Anfos whispered.

But that evening poor Anfos broke it himself, for he could not resist its affable inmate who burst open his door, bowed, flapped his grey wings, and then cuckooed in such an ingratiating manner that Anfos must jump up and down for sheer joy, and must move the hands of the clock round and round so that he might go on hearing the cuckoo. This he did such a number of consecutive times that the kind little bird became quite exhausted, and finally stuck half in and half out with his head at a very reproachful angle.

Then Anfos began to murmur strange names, strange endearing names of his own invention; then he started to whistle the soft double note wherewith he had used to attract the wild birds when he lived in that village high up in the mountains; then he kissed the cuckoo's minute pointed beak: 'Talk, talk to me—talk again!' he entreated.

But the cuckoo answered never a word, for the fragile spring of his life had been broken.

And so joy was miserably turned to tears—large tears trickled down the half-wit's thin cheeks and mingled with the straggling hairs of his beard as he stood there and gazed at his own destruction. And knowing that any emotion was harmful, Marie coaxed him gently upstairs to his bedroom, and undressed him, and put on his coarse linen nightshirt. Then she promised to bring him a tisane de menthe—a tisane de menthe made excessively sweet like the one which had once helped to comfort Christophe—but this only if Anfos would be a good child, get into his bed, and try to stop weeping.

CHAPTER TWENTY-ONE

I

CHRISTMAS came and went, the mistral subsided, the sea grew placid and warm in the sunshine. The vines showed illusive suggestions of green, and the mulberry branches began to make leaves wherewith they would nourish industrious silk-worms. The sturdy, peeled brown trunks of the cork-trees appeared to take on a more intense colour, so that they matched the people's tanned limbs, and the brown honest face of Goundran who smiled—always smiled, these days, because his wife had presented him with a fine infant daughter—and the brown, monkey face of le tout petit Loup, and the brown sardonic face of Eusèbe.

Eusèbe was feeling lazy this spring; he dawdled about a great deal in his vineyards, neglecting his work and his clients alike, while his bedroom became unspeakably dirty. He drank deep of red wine and thought many deep thoughts of a somewhat undesirable nature: 'Ah, this wonderful land of my birth—' he would chant, 'this wonderful land of vines and plump women. Is there anything lacking in this Provence of ours? We have grapes, also plump, and the grapes have juices and the juices are squeezed into casks of our making. Why, the very trees strip themselves of their clothes in order to provide us with corks for our bottles! Only look at her beautiful naked brownness—she resembles a woman that superb Chêne Liège! And like a woman the more you strip her the better she is, the finer she grows; leave her intact and she withers away . . .' And one evening he was actually seen to embrace the stout, unresponsive waist of a cork-tree. What a scandal, the lascivious, drunken old rogue! Could nothing be done with that shameless Eusèbe?

The weeks passed; scarlet cherries were sold in the

streets, and baskets of succulent, moist, green almonds. The maquis began to smell vital on the hills, while the rhythmical whirr of enamoured cingalas in the Curé's garden so distracted his mind that he shut all his windows when writing a sermon. To the thickets came endless nightingales, singing snatches of song even while it was yet daylight, in memory of the kindly act of Saint Loup who had once restored its life to a fledgling: 'Praise God in His Golden Saints,' they sang, 'Praise God . . . in . . . His Golden . . . His Golden Saints.' For whatever the Curé might choose to think, all the birds of Provence believed in that legend. The couleuvres, irresistibly drawn to the sun, slid out of the woods and began to uncoil their handsome and conspicuous lengths—most unwisely. Christophe's lizards up at the old citadel lay sprawled on the stones, their throats palpitating, their eyes ablink, their tongues darting for flies; while below, through the tortuous streets of the town lumbered farm carts drawn by cream-coloured oxen.

And meanwhile there was always Anatole Kahn dressed in his unsuitable northern clothes which, for some strange reason, he never discarded. Ah, yes, there was always Anatole Kahn, affable, smiling, but growing more insistent, for slowly but surely he was making his way with these good-natured, indolent southern people. His shop was so very conveniently placed, and then it was easy to buy from a shop—such a saving of time, such a saving of trouble. Moreover they liked what he had to sell; he was not perverting the taste of his clients, but rather was he dexterously bringing to light a desire for his goods which had always existed. Quite a number of people had secretly envied that shiny, mock-mahogany suite purchased by Madame Roustan's late husband; and now similar suites could not only be seen any day and bought by those who had money, but this could be done without catching a train, without incurring the least inconvenience.

Yes, but Anatole Kahn meant much more than this: he meant more than the saving of mere inconvenience, than the pleasant indulgence of extravagant desires on the plea that his goods were ridiculously cheap, his delivery prompt, and his terms quite easy, for Anatole Kahn had begun to mean romance—the unromantic romance of the pocket.

Oh, but he was tactful, Monsieur Anatole Kahn, with his soft brown eyes, and his over-red lips from which he would let fall words as of honey. Never a suggestion that could lead them to feel that they had been slow-witted, indolent sluggards; by ignoring their lost opportunities he had all the more time to devote to their future. And the future was what mattered, said Anatole Kahn, the future of the beautiful town of Saint Loup that would shortly become known all over France as a summer resort of the first importance. And when he spoke thus his soft eyes would gleam as though with the flame of inspired prevision, while his voice would take on the emotional timbre of a man who knows himself for a prophet, so that those who heard him would go home much impressed in spite of themselves:

'Hòu, what ideas! Yet one must admit that he carries conviction. But then who will come to our town in the heat—always excepting a few crazy artists? A bathing season, he would have us believe, and in consequence business, and in consequence money. . . .'

He was patient, he listened to every objection, he frowned, rubbed his chin and appeared to consider. He frequently nodded: well, they ought to know best, yet he could not but feel that a few pretty villas just beyond the town on the road to the hills . . . or say down near the beach to the left of the port. The road-bed was not bad—as the place became known people could easily reach it in motors. Why not? The mountains? Well, but what of them? People could reach Saint Loup by the Corniche. But he did not wish to appear too aggressive—after all he was only a recent arrival—still, he did feel that great possibilities having once been foreseen should be carefully prepared for. The shortage of houses was a drawback, of course—a most serious drawback when it came to tourists.

And as though fate were playing right into his hands, who should arrive that summer but Beauvais, the very man whose picture he had bought, and who since that purchase had sprung into fame, thanks to those first exhibits at the Salon. And following like a tail in the wake of a comet, came quite a fair number of lesser artists, all eager to paint, all willing to pay within reason for decent accommodation. Why, the little hotel near the station was crowded, what with their models, their wives, and their easels, a happening that had never been heard of before—the proprietor was beside himself with excitement.

At la Tarasque much vermouth was consumed after bathing, but at night as the moon came up drinks grew stronger. They were young these arrivals, they were spend-thrift and gay, so things started to hum when, their work being over, the little violinist with the hump on his back teased their feet to dancing, and Mère Mélanie's brandy plus his fiddle turned their scatter-brained thoughts to women. But how witty they were; ah, yes, and how friendly —promising to paint the walls of the café with all sorts of amusing fantasies. And then, thanks to them, her business was booming.

There was only one tiresome fly in the ointment: the fishers greatly resented this invasion, while the men from the tartanes had begun to scowl darkly on finding that all their tables were taken—it was lucky, perhaps, that Mère Mélanie's new friends did not understand the Provençal language. Indeed, one evening there was quite a to-do when a giant called Ravous stalked into the café supporting a comrade who was heavy with wine, and demanding that they should be given a table.

'Malan de Diéu!' swore Ravous-the-mighty; and once launched there gushed from him invectives so amazing that Mère Mélanie began to grow nervous for her guests, and above all for her little hump-backed violinist. Moreover, in spite of those strong beetle-brows which gave to her face such a virile expression, and in spite of that glorious and memorable night when, unaided, she had vanquished a drunken seaman, Ravous's bulk was so vast that no two men in the room could have budged him an inch without his permission.

Said he, having finally run out of insults: 'My comrade is being grossly insulted! He is drunk, you say, well then, I tell you, no! And if he is drunk, then I ask you, what of it? I also am now about to get drunk, very drunk, and for that I require a chair, and a table on which I can rest my bottle. Yes, and what I require I intend to take!' And he threw back his shoulders and bulged his muscles, 'Uno, dous, tres!' he boomed ominously, 'Who, I wish to know, is going to get up before I trouble myself to remove him?'

No one trembled, since no one had understood a word, his furious face merely causing much laughter; but the little violinist was now really afraid, and this not without reason perhaps, knowing Ravous. Sidling across to Mère Mélanie: 'Coax him, ma chérie—try coaxing,' he whispered.

So Mère Mélanie patted the monster's cheek, then she ruffled his hair: 'Sois gentil,' she entreated, 'do not threaten your poor little Mère Mélanie who has always felt a tenderness for her big Ravous. Is it kind to bully your Mère Mélanie who depends upon clients to gain her a living? Come and kiss your little Mère Mélanie. . . .'

'Ah, that no!' growled Ravous, looking suddenly scared.

'Tafort!' hiccoughed his comrade, 'Go and kiss the old whore!'

Ravous scowled, then he gulped hard, closing his eyes: 'Bono Maire de Diéu . . .' he groaned as he kissed her.

The room rang with applause. To Mère Mélanie's relief, her clients appeared amused and delighted. They were artists of course, and no man in Saint Loup was more picturesque in appearance than Ravous with his faded check shirt, his red neckerchief, his bare tattooed arms, and his little gold ear-rings; it was therefore advisable to welcome him, perhaps. . . .

'Go and bring in a table from the kitchen this instant, and make haste about it!' she bawled to the waiter.

So Ravous was placed at the end of the café and was given a generous portion of brandy as was also his comrade, by now half asleep, but continully being roused up by Ravous who wished to assure him that he was not drunk, and that if he were drunk he was drunk with honour.

'The honour of my friend is my own,' he declared many times, 'for I, Ravous, love my dear friend . . . ah, how much I love him . . . my very dear friend . . . I would die for my friend.' He was fast growing maudlin. And presently, he supporting his friend, they danced, upsetting two chairs in the process.

But some of the fishers—although less aggressive than the men who sailed the seas in the tartanes—some of the fishers were also less forgiving, and from that night on they transferred their custom to the café farther along the port, the café that belonged to Mère Mélanie's rival.

It was only natural that Anatole Kahn should desire to become acquainted with Beauvais; had he not recognised the man's greatness and in consequence bought that picture of the harbour for next to nothing when its painter was starving? Yes, assuredly, for Anatole Kahn possessed the Jew's fine appreciation of art despite those iniquitous plate-glass windows—he sold in order to grow rich and buy, what he sold being very different indeed from what, should he prosper, he would care to purchase. Then, again this Beauvais, this now wealthy fellow with his genius, his sudden fame, his admirers, was a valuable asset to the town of Saint Loup and thus to Anatole Kahn's ambitions; nay more, to his dreams, for, strange though it may seem, there were moments when Kahn became a dreamer. And if he dreamed cheaply and hideously, if he dreamed of a town outraged and disfigured, if his dreams like his shop were directly opposed to the spirit that clung to a small oil painting which could now be sold for a large sum of money—enough money to acquire quite a nice bit of land—it must not be forgotten that the mind of man is a mass of distressingly strange contradictions.

To meet Jacques Beauvais was not at all easy. Kahn racked his ingenious brain to no purpose. He knew him by sight, a most elegant person wearing white silk shirts and tussore silk trousers; a young man with a handsome, weak face, fair hair, slim flanks, a jade cigarette case and a mistress. But he could not very well accost him in the street, nor could he present himself at the hotel on the grounds that the celebrated Galeries Kahn would amply repay the trouble of a visit. And yet, after all, it was the Galeries Kahn that chanced to come to the help of their founder.

Beauvais needed some drapery for a background: 'Well, and what have you got?' he demanded crossly, ' I cannot find anything but striped umbrellas in this town—even a dark table-cloth would do.' Then glancing about him: 'My God, what horrors! This shop did not exist when I was here last. It ought not to exist now—I think I will burn it!'

Kahn smiled an indulgent, paternal smile: 'Ah, monsieur, we others we also must live, and to do that we must give people what they desire. Is this table-cloth suitable? Its colour is dark, and if monsieur can manage to hide the border. . . .'

Beauvais frowned, then he laughed, and his laugh was so youthful and so pleasant a thing that it went very ill with eyes already somewhat marred by dissipation: 'So you do not admire its fine border?' he enquired. 'You do not admire your own stock-in-trade—those exquisite Louis Quinze chairs for instance?'

Anatole Kahn shrugged deprecating shoulders: 'I will answer that question in just three words. Monsieur asks me if I admire those gilt chairs, and I answer in just three words —I sell them!'

'Then you ought to be ashamed of yourself,' grinned Beauvais.

The cloth purchased, Anatole Kahn said gently: 'If monsieur will spare but a few more moments I will show him something which I do not sell—a thing of very great beauty, of genius. I am poor, yet this treasure I do not sell although it is now worth a great deal of money.' And he led the way into his simple office, bare save for a roll-top American desk, a stool, a shallow cupboard and a picture.

'So,' said Beauvais, 'so it was you who bought it!'

Kahn nodded: 'Yes, at Fleuret's, monsieur.'

'For five sous because I was needing bread and you, apparently were a good judge of art. And now it is worth . . .'

'To me nothing in money, monsieur, because I will never sell it.'

Beauvais stared at the middle-aged over-dressed tradesman: 'Then you must be an imbecile,' he remarked, 'Or an idealist, which is much the same thing. Who can say how long my price will keep up. To-day I am famous, to-morrow . . . who knows! The mistral is not more erratic than the critics. Take the money, my friend, take it while you can get it!' advised Beauvais who since he had become a rich man was assuming the air of a hardened cynic. In reality he was both flattered and pleased, for if those beloved of the gods die young, those beloved of the arts live on as children. Turning, he studied the picture with interest: 'Fine,' he murmured, 'ah, yes, it is really fine! There is splendid technique in the treatment of that sunshine . . .' Then he suddenly seated himself on the stool: 'I have reason to be grateful to this town, I suppose, though my nature, thank God, is very ungrateful . . . still, Saint Loup has undoubtedly buttered my bread, and I find le pain bénit de la gaieté tastes less stale when it is spread thickly with butter! Is it not strange that the more we have in this world the more we are always needing? At one time I was glad to get clean in the sea, whereas now I am missing my Paris bathroom. The hotel is abominable—bad food, hard beds, and a waiter who perpetually stinks of garlic, and yet only a very short time ago I thought myself lucky to be staying there at all . . . I suppose that you do not know of good rooms, or a decent flat somewhere down by the port— a flat with a bathroom and clean sanitation?'

Kahn appeared to consider. Then: 'I fear not, monsieur, our Saint Loup is still in the Middle Ages.'

'And therein lies its charm,' said Beauvais, sighing. 'Why is it that nothing is ever quite perfect? Why cannot I have a medieval Saint Loup, a comfortable bed and an agreeable bathroom?'

'I see no reason at all,' replied Kahn, 'monsieur has but to build himself a villa.'

Beauvais looked up from staring at his shoes and his eyes were suddenly bright with interest: 'En voilà une idée! I had never thought. . . . But of course that is what I am going to do! A mas in the ancient Provençal style; but inside—ah, mon ami, what modern comfort—three bathrooms at least!' He was often like this, childishly elated over some passing fancy. 'And my garden shall end in the sea,' he announced; 'there shall also be a vineyard and an orchard of peach trees.'

'Some good ground might be had to the left of the port, monsieur—it belongs to Hermitte, the baker, but perhaps he could be induced to sell . . . if monsieur bought that ground he would also buy vines.'

'And peach trees?'

'Alas, no, but they grow very fast . . . however, my friend may not wish to sell.'

'I insist that he sells it to me!' exclaimed Beauvais.

A few days later the news spread like wild-fire. 'Beauvais has purchased a large piece of land from Hermitte—they say he will build a fine villa. In any case he has paid a fine price, and what for? The vineyard is utterly worthless. Hermitte is rubbing his hands, I can tell you! It was Anatole Kahn who arranged the deal; that man has a marvellous head for business. Hermitte will pay him a commission, and why not? That seems only fair when one thinks of the price he received, and the vineyard utterly worthless. . . .'

Marie said to her husband: 'If this Beauvais comes here every summer it may very well bring other people . . . perhaps that will help us with money, Jóusè . . .' But this she said rather timidly, for Jóusè, these days, never spoke of such matters.

They were sitting over their midday meal; he looked up from his plate: 'There is nothing wrong with my business, nothing whatever,' he said loudly, 'there have always been months when work has been slack; in my trade one must take the good with the bad—a good month, a bad month— they balance each other. Are you and my children not well clothed and fed that you meddle with things that do not concern you? One would think that my children went short of food!' His face flushed and his eyes looked suddenly angry.

She sighed. Le tout petit Loup did go short of his bouillon, his milk and his wine-flavoured jellies these days, because she could not pay the chemist, and the chemist was a very unpleasant man—he made pointed remarks when they kept him waiting. And then there was Christophe who was growing so fast that his broad brown chest was splitting his jersey—always he seemed to be needing new clothes; and then there was Jóusè who wore out his socks so incredibly fast; and then there was Anfos. Four bodies to clothe and four mouths to feed, and that cold weight of fear that lay on her heart. . . .

'It is that I must pay the chemist . . .' she faltered.

'Has he not had enough? Let him rot!' growled Jóusè. He pushed back his chair but he did not get up and hurry away as had once been his custom. Anfos went off to the workshop alone. 'Your Beauvais has given me an order,' he told her. 'I must put a cheap fence round his precious land, and a board to announce that the land is private! Maybe he will ask me to build a dog-kennel, or if that is too costly perhaps a hen-coop; yet they say that the land was sold, thanks to Kahn, for double its value—there is no lack of money.'

'I also have heard that,' Marie assented.

After this they fell silent, he scratching his chin through his beard with slow, meditative fingers; she nodding to Christophe, then glancing at the clock to remind him that he and Loup would be late: 'It is time that you started for school,' she whispered.

So Christophe and his brother stole quietly away, for even the turbulent tout petit Loup did not dare to disturb his father at that moment.

But when they had gone Marie faced her husband: 'Jousè, I must have the money for the chemist, and a few francs over to buy Christophe a jersey. Génas will not wait, he is pressing us hard, and Loup cannot exist without asthma powder. As for Christophe . . . you can see for yourself how it is . . . he grows hourly. There is also Eusèbe's small bill; it is time he was paid for that last pair of sandals; although that is far less urgent than the chemist.'

Jóusè got up slowly; he moved slowly these days, and she noticed with a pang the white hair on his temples, the white hairs in his beard . . . he would soon be quite white . . . an old man . . . but she must have that money for the chemist. Had he got it? Oh, that cold weight of fear on her heart; and the question which she had not the courage to ask: 'Jóusè, is it Kahn who is making us so poor?' If only she dared . . . but she lacked the courage.

He was changing, her man, he was growing more silent, he no longer shouted his jokes to their neighbours as he worked half in and half out of his shop. Even Anfos felt the change in his master and would come to her whimpering like a small child who was scared and in need of consolation. Then the days, growing always more frequent of late, when Jóusè's diligent hands would be idle, when he would wander about the house, or rummage among his old bits of carving, or pretend to repair the fence of the yard that so obviously did not need repairing: 'It is good that I have a free hour, Marioun, this fence would have blown away in a mistral . . .' and sometimes he would whistle when engaged on such tasks, or hum to himself if he thought she was listening. What was wrong? He was still an excellent craftsman, a most honest, careful and capable worker, yet just lately so few people needed his work when it came to the matter of cabinet-making—oh, yes, they would call on him for odd jobs, repairs to a door or a rat-eaten skirting, but not for the things in which he excelled. Was he wilfully blind to what was happening? Was Jóusè wilfully shutting his eyes to the fact that his business was steadily declining? Yet surely with so many unpaid bills . . . with so much expense and so little money . . .

Anatole Kahn . . . the Galeries Kahn . . . just under a year since the shop had been opened. No, it could not be that . . . the time was too short . . . besides Jóusè did not work for the whole of Saint Loup; he never had worked for the whole of Saint Loup; there had always been those who bought ready-made rubbish, his own sister, for instance, who had gone by train to Marseille if she needed a new chair or table. And yet Kahn was prospering; why, only that morning she, Marie, had seen a drawing-room suite being purchased from him by Madame Hermitte, and the Hermittes had been Jóusè's customers once—he had made nearly everything in their house, including the cradle for their first baby. Madame Hermitte had appeared to be much occupied, much engrossed the moment she had caught sight of Marie. Anatole Kahn of the Galeries Kahn, so crafty in business, so persuasively gentle: 'Ah, Madame, I hope that your dear little son suffers less from his asthma in this fine weather . . .' 'Ah, Madame, I have but one heartfelt regret and that is that your husband appears to dislike me; cannot you induce him to be more kind? I much need his goodwill, I who come as a stranger . . .' Anatole Kahn of the Galeries Kahn, so brilliant a salesman with so handy a shop, and everything ready, no need to wait, and everything clearly marked with the prices, no need to work out the cost of a chair or a table or a bed—no need to bargain. Goundran had bought Elise a brass bed, Goundran was buying from Kahn . . . even Goundran.

She stared at her husband as he stood there before her, very big, very strong still but growing much thinner. At his age it was not a good sign to lose flesh, his skin looked distressed somehow—it was sagging. And his eyes, what was it they reminded her of now that they were not any longer angry? Ah, she had it! They were like the eyes of a dog. . . . And that sigh . . . it was like. . . . Her mind groped about for something she had heard a long time ago and then only partially, vaguely perceived. A profound, resigned sigh . . . it was like Mirèio.

'Jóusè, let the chemist's bill go—he must wait. Let him wait, my beloved—do not worry. . . .'

But Jóusè quietly shook his great head: 'No, no, leave it to me—I shall find the money.'

CHAPTER TWENTY-TWO

I

Autumn; the artists returning to Paris with their comet, their models, their wives and their easels. Saint Loup busy with its numerous activities but gradually ridding itself of strangers. The Curé labouring his wearisome sermons which tended to lengthen as the weather grew cooler; Jan working strenuously at his Latin to the satisfaction and pride of his tutor; Madame Roustan painstakingly looking for sins— her own but also those of her neighbours; Mère Mélanie abstaining on Fridays from meat but not always from her little violinist; Eusèbe trying to catch up with lost time by drinking less wine and stitching more sandals; Goundran fishing, looking after his prosperous affairs, making love to his wife and playing with his baby. Marie more anxious than ever about Loup who had recently developed palpitations; the chemist part-paid and part-pacified; the doctor unpaid, but so kindly a man that he was fast becoming as poor as his patients; Jóusè still silent; Anfos still scared, and Christophe growing more and more stupid at school, oppressed by a sense of approaching disaster. Thus the autumn gradually passed into winter.

The winter found Anatole Kahn well content, his venture having more than justified his judgment. The profits were unexpectedly large—there seemed little doubt, therefore, that the Galeries Kahn were providing their clients with just what they wanted. Sitting at his roll-top American desk their founder wrote long, self-satisfied letters, enclosing elaborate sheets of accounts to certain business friends living in Paris. And since nothing succeeds in this world like success, he was now regarded in Saint Loup with admiration, nay more, with respect; his staunchest adherents being Mère Mélanie and Madame Roustan.

He said—and surely with some justification: 'Did I not tell you that Beauvais would return to the town that has undoubtedly made his fortune? Did I not tell you that others would follow, and that through them Saint Loup was bound to get known? They came, ah, precisely, but what did they find? One hotel, one miserable little hotel that does not even possess a bathroom. Moreover they were crowded together like sardines, there was not sufficient accommodation. With Monsieur Grimaud I have nothing in common; he is stupid and he runs his hotel very badly. He says: "What has once been is still good enough," and I answer him: "Let the past bury the past, our affair is solely concerned with the future." Then he shrugs his shoulders and looks imbecile; I am weary of that fat old carp, Monsieur Grimaud. However, there remains you, dear Mère Mélanie, and you are an intelligent and enterprising woman, so to you I say: what about all those fine rooms? No less than two floors of them over your café! To you I say put in a bathroom at once, and a couple of comfortable water-closets; there must also, of course, be electric light; et voilà, you become the Hôtel de la Tarasque! "Hôtel et Café de la Tarasque" you become and in consequence greatly extend your connection.'

Mère Mélanie listened delighted yet fearful. But would it not cost a vast sum of money? What did her dear little Alexandre think? Did he think they could possibly manage to afford it? Of course it was bound to pay well in the end, this had surely been made very clear last summer; yes, and meanwhile that brigand farther on down the port who had stolen quite a few of her fishermen from her—God pity their stomachs, such foul liquor he sold—that brigand would receive a slap in the face, and so would those surly, ungrateful clients. Hôtel de la Tarasque . . . a bathroom . . . Santouno! Yes, but could they, dared they venture to afford it?

The little violinist with the hump on his back thought they dared, but he left the decision to her, she being such an excellent business woman: 'Mais, ma chérie, it is you who will have to decide—I am only a child in matters of money.' For the little violinist knew his Mère Mélanie; if he urged this grand scheme and it happened to fail, she would very probably turn round and beat him; so he said yet again:

'You will have to decide,' and slipped quietly off for a glass of brandy.

Kahn seemed confident of obtaining good terms from the firm in Marseille that had worked for him—Mère Mélanie could pay them so much every quarter. It would surely be very well worth their while in view of the splendid future of the place; he would tell them to call on Mère Mélanie at once so that all might be finished in time for next summer. Might he tell them to call? 'Ah, Madame, do not lose this great opportunity, I entreat you. You have courage, Madame; success follows the brave. May I tell them to call?'

Mère Mélanie nodded.

So that night as Mère Mélanie lay abed by the side of her little hump-backed violinist, their propinquity was quite without blame, since nothing was thought of but current accounts and how much they would venture to take from her savings.

2

Spurred by Mère Mélanie's enterprise, Madame Roustan discovered a couple of rooms which could well be spared for letting to boarders; what furnishings were needed she purchased from Kahn who eagerly did his best to advise her. Next came Hermitte, the baker, at one time a man too lazy to care very much about money, but now so impressed by his balance at the bank—resultant upon selling his land to Beauvais—that he wanted to see that fat balance increase, and was fast bidding fair to become a miser.

He said to his wife: 'We have surely an attic that we also can let next summer to an artist? It is foolish the way we pamper our children, the four of them can perfectly well sleep together during the season, and that they shall do. I am not prepared to forgo a fine profit.'

'Both the attics need whitewash,' said his wife doubtfully, 'especially the small one. Shall I send for Jóusè? There is also a leak to the left of the roof.'

'I will do what is needed myself,' snapped Hermitte.

Madame Simon went bustling round to see Marie, and her husband it seemed, did wish for assistance; 'Just a few small repairs to our top back room; the woodwork is not very strong round the window, and the door requires a new handle and lock; Jóusè will work for us cheaply, I know; after all, your Jóusè is Guillaume's godfather. And to tell you the truth we have not much to spend, what with Guillaume's college and now his wedding. . . . Yes, in the spring . . . a most charming girl, her father is a notary in Marseille, but of course a wedding is always expensive. Guillaume is coming to see you himself—ah, yes, he has always loved Papa Jóusè. However, what with this thing and that, I said to my husband: "Why should we not let our back room to some nice young couple next season? The old sacks can go down to the cellar," I said, "and if Jóusè just casts a look at rat-holes . . . . It seems a real pity to waste that room." '

'He shall go and see you to-morrow,' promised Marie.

Meanwhile Kahn enquired of Eusèbe one morning: 'Have you not got a cupboard that you can furnish? You will have to indulge in a good spring-cleaning before you put anyone into your cupboard, but after all, that will do you no harm, and I think if you only take my advice and prepare in time, you will make some money. We are certain to have a great number of artists again next summer, and whatever you require the Galeries Kahn can supply at small cost—I am anxious to help you, that goes without saying.'

Eusèbe's black eye began to glow hotly: 'What is this? A devil of an artist in my convent? My slumbers disturbed by some young vermenoune who comes crawling in drunk every night from the café? His absurd contraptions all over my shop; paints squeezed on my floors, my walls and my ceilings? And your vile, cheap rubbish polluting my home? By the vomit of that bilious dragon la Tarasque, you have made a very insolent mistake! You are speaking to one who is called Eusèbe, and he greatly despises you, Anatole Kahn, for what you are doing to line your own pockets. You are canaille, and you have the brain of a bug; that is why you are hoping to make of this town a place that is only fit for canaille. If I had my way I would drown you at once, I would stuff you head downwards into my cesspool.'

This was awkward indeed, for Kahn had arrived intending to ask a particular favour. He wanted to rent a small bit of ground in order to put up a monster board advertising the charms of the Galeries Kahn, and as ill luck would have it the ground was Eusèbe's—it happened to be on the Corniche Road and was therefore extremely well placed for Kahn's purpose. But Anatole Kahn had long since decided that quarrels were always a bad investment and that pride was the rich man's prerogative, so now he said, gulping down his annoyance:

'Do not anger yourself. I am not what you think me, an adventurer; no, I am quite the reverse—a quiet and well-meaning business man. And to show you that I bear not the slightest resentment I am actually going to entreat your assistance. I desire to rent a few yards of that land just beyond your vineyards where the road joins the Corniche—I want to put up a species of board. I am fully prepared to pay well,' he finished.

Then Eusèbe opened his mouth and bellowed so that the very hides trembled. The lid of his white eye puckered and twitched, while the ball of his black eye blazed like a furnace as he swore certain mighty Provençal oaths, so terrific that few save he dared to use them.

'Ah, well,' sighed his visitor, turning to go, 'I deeply regret this misunderstanding. If you should change your mind . . . bien, you know where I am.' And lifting his hat he sauntered away.

'Bèsti malestrucho—ignorant beast, hell-toad, may you fester!' growled Eusèbe.

3

It took Kahn just two days to secure his ground from a woman who spent her life boiling silkworms. While not quite so well placed it was yet good enough, being in a fairly commanding position. It took Kahn just two weeks to procure his board from Marseille; a colossal, flamboyant erection advertising his wares in the following words which were painted in decorative red and black letters:

MESDAMES!!!   MESSIEURS!!!

VISITEZ L'ANCIENNE VILLE DE SAINT LOUP-SUR-MER.

ARRÊTEZ VOUS SURTOUT AUX GALERIES KAHN.

VENEZ VOIR NOS AMEUBLEMENTS DU DERNIER CHIC.

MOBILIERS DE STYLE À PRIX MODÉRÉS.

OBJETS D'ART, GARNITURES, TAPISSERIES, TENTURES.

The good folk of Saint Loup stood and gaped with amazement. What a man! What a brain! Why, to see such a board was to think they were living at Monte Carlo! Well, perhaps they would be having a Casino quite soon; why not? With Kahn there was really no telling. The women exclaimed; the men laughed and winked, tickled by that appeal to the newly wedded, and everyone felt very proud of their town. Only look at the splendid advertisement—it began on the ground and reached up to heaven! Even the Bénédit's oldest friends were too much excited to notice their absence, while as for Eusèbe's . . . oh, well, he had no friends and, if one might believe him, did not want any.

But one evening Eusèbe walked forth alone to visit that detestable board by moonlight; all alone by the light of a scandalized moon he walked, intent on relieving his feelings. And just how he relieved them need not be told—it can safely be left to the imagination.

CHAPTER TWENTY-THREE

I

DURING December Kahn was absent for a fortnight, his shop being left in charge of the youth who had offered balloons on the day of the opening. Where had he gone to now, the great man? Here, there, and everywhere, that Anatole Kahn! And he knew how to keep his own counsel when he chose; however, later on they might hear all about it.

When he returned Kahn was closeted with Hermitte for quite a long time, and they shouting and scolding just as though they were not now the dearest of friends since Kahn had helped Hermitte to sell his land—incidentally, for less than half its value:

'Preposterous, disgusting, you would actually rob me! How can I pay the high price Beauvais paid you? Am I wearing silk shirts? Am I keeping a whore? Am I thinking of building a white marble palace?' And Kahn chewed the end of his fat cigar, then spat, so immense was his indignation. 'Who found you a buyer?' he went on still more loudly, 'Who helped you to empty that simpleton's pockets? Who told him that if he bought that land he bought vines? Sacré Nom, and your vineyard for years has been sterile! Who told him that he was getting a bargain; who lied—yes, I ask you, who lied out of friendship? I, Anatole Kahn. And what is the result? You prove grossly ungrateful and endeavour to rob me!'

Hermitte swallowed and blinked and made swift calculations on his blotting-paper with a violet lead pencil. Never had he felt more excited in his life, and yet never more wretched, because undecided. Ought he to let this new land go for less than the last lot? It actually adjoined Beauvais' boundary, therefore why should he have to sell it for less, when the world might contain other crazy artists? But those swift calculations were going to his head, for at times strong drink is less raging than riches; only think of the proportions his balance would reach could he but bring himself to accept his friend's offer! Think of seeing the total in neat black and white whenever he cared to open his bank-book! And supposing he refused and then could not sell after all— supposing no one else wished to buy? What a strain it was this amassing of wealth: it was really enough to drive one demented. Poor Hermitte alternately ruffled his hair, bit his nails, and sucked at his violet lead pencil; avaricious yet doubtful he mentally writhed on the horns of this distressing dilemma. In the end they came to a compromise, Kahn agreeing to pay him five hundred francs more than the price which he had originally offered; whereupon Hermitte puffed out his cheeks and looked sly, considering himself a very shrewd fellow.

And now people were talking from morning until night, Kahn's name being constantly heard at the cafés. Ho, ho, but he must be exceedingly rich; a grand shop all done up at his own expense, and then land upon which he was going to build villas! And what if he did not attend Holy Mass, he sent generous subscriptions to Monsieur le Curé—this they knew for a fact. A good fellow he was, and anxious to further everyone's interest. Saint Raphaël indeed! very proud of itself, very proud of its train de luxe from Paris. Pòu, wait a bit—just wait a few years till the bathing was in full swing at Saint Loup; Saint Loup had a much finer beach than Saint Raphäel. Yes, and wait until Anatole Kahn had a word with the mayor about proper electric lighting. The mayor was a stubborn and slow-witted fool; what they needed was a mayor with an eye to progress, what they needed was a mayor like Anatole Kahn who would put good money into everyone's pockets. Why, the local authorities were nothing but brigands, neglecting the town and pur-loining the taxes. Imagine such a thing! filthy cesspools that stank and disgorged themselves over the vegetable gardens. Santo Flour, if the visitors came to suspect they would surely start thinking about typhoid fever. Santo Flour, if Saint Raphäel should come to suspect. . . . Outrageous the way they were all being robbed! They had reason to be grateful to Anatole Kahn who had shown them how they and their town were neglected.

Thus they talked; scowling ominously at the mayor in the very streets of Saint Loup, should they meet him; refraining from lifting their hats when he passed, which had long been their courteous and friendly custom; making loud-voiced remarks about cesspools that stank, whenever he happened to come within hearing, since progressive ideals not infrequently oust that charming though less profitable virtue, politeness. But the mayor of Saint Loup was so old, so near-sighted, so deaf, and moreover so benevolent a person, that he went on his way with serenity, quite unconscious that anyone had been scowling.

2

New Year's Day brought with it magnificent weather; the sky was cloudless, the air like crystal. People almost forgot their grievances as they stood to gossip at windows and doors, feeling pleased with themselves and with most of their neighbours. And Anatole Kahn was feeling pleased with himself as he hurried along the street swinging his cane—he was going to pay a visit to Jóusè.

A pity that Jóusè so greatly disliked him, but this state of affairs must no longer continue, for he needed the fellow's help now in his schemes, and moreover Jóusè would doubtless consent to work cheaply in view of his financial position. Then again, if other good workmen existed anywhere in the district Jóusè could find them; his influence, too, should go a long way, for his name was still very greatly respected. With Jóusè as foreman the building would run smoothly, no thieving, no exorbitant demands, no quarrels; and all done with the minimum of expense, since the men would be living hard-by their work which would save the cost of board or train journeys. Of course there remained the question of time; the best of these southerners worked very slowly and one villa at least must be ready by June—on that point he would have to be firm and emphatic.

Arrived at the Bénédit's house he knocked briskly; 'Bonjour, chère Madame. Can I speak with your husband?'

Marie said: 'My husband is resting, Monsieur. It is fête; will to-morrow not do as well?' and her gentle brown eyes were hostile and watchful.

'Alas, no; my business is pressing,' he told her.

She hesitated, hating the man with all that her gentleness could muster of hatred; yes, but also fearing this soft-spoken stranger who was bringing her husband's business to ruin. And seeing her hesitation he stepped in and passed her quickly:

'Ah, pardon . . .' he murmured.

Jóusè was sitting alone in the parlour with drooped head and closed eyes: he appeared to be sleeping. Kahn coughed and Jóusè sat up with a jerk, saw him, and lumbered on to his feet: 'Monsieur, what is the meaning of this intrusion?'

'Business, Monsieur.' And Kahn glanced round the room noting the signs of disintegration; the worn, sagging couch, the much-mended blind, the pane of broken glass in the window. Then he let his gaze rest on Jóusè's frayed shirt: 'Is business unwelcome, Monsieur?' he asked gently.

'That depends with whom it is transacted,' frowned Jóusè.

Without more ado Kahn seated himself: 'Bénédit,' he began, now dropping the monsieur, 'Bénédit, let us talk as man to man. From the first I seem to have incurred your dislike—I who have always desired your friendship. But alas, it is only too natural perhaps, for in this world because we must struggle to live we are apt in that struggle to injure each other. I may well have injured your trade, Bénédit . . . I have injured your trade, let us face the truth.'

'That is not the truth,' Jóusè told him sharply.

Kahn held up his hand: 'Have patience, my friend; I do beg that you sit down and listen with patience.'

'Gramaci, and if I prefer to stand?'

'It must be as you wish, but I beg you to listen. Bénédit, I fully intend to succeed, the Galeries Kahn are as yet in their childhood; they will grow, they will spread out on every side, they will add department after department. A department for this, a department for that—perfumery, lingerie, ladies' dresses; hats, stockings, boots and shoes, garments for men; there shall also be a juvenile department. You have been to the Galeries Bleues at Marseille?' Jóusè nodded. 'Very well,' his visitor continued, 'you have visited the Galeries Kahn of the future. This town will grow also, its boundaries will extend, we may take it that they are extending already for Beauvais' villa will be built on the outskirts. Other villas will follow to the west of the port in the wake of his—my new premises with them. Ah, yes, Bénédit, the growth of Saint Loup has become my dearest, my most cherished ambition. And this brings me to what I have come here to say—that colony of villas is about to be started.'

'I care nothing for your colony of villas,' remarked Jóusè.

Kahn gazed at him out of his soft, ox-like eyes: 'And yet I would wish you to benefit by it. I am here to offer you work, Bénédit; I am here to suggest that you build those villas.' And then before Jóusè had time to reply: 'But you understand they must be built quite cheaply; I have only a certain amount to spend and my money must bring me in a fair profit. For instance, our timber need not cost a fortune; I imagine there is . . . well . . . timber and timber. Then our walls, why make them obtrusively thick as the villas will only be used in the summer? And the paint, why be foolishly extravagant with paint? Why put on four coats where two are sufficient? Provided some bright colour covers the deal, those who purchase will never be any the wiser—at least not just at first—after that, eh bien, after that it ceases to be our business. But of course we must naturally bear in mind that the villas should have an attractive appearance; they should look, eh bien, I will be perfectly frank, the villas should look better built than they are . . . it is always my rule to speak frankly in business. But then you know well how it is with building; a little touch here, a little touch there, a small balcony say, or a curve to a window and immediately you have obtained your effect, the pleasing effect that catches a client. And now about the question of time; one villa at least must be ready next season. I would like it to be ready at latest by June and sold,' he smiled quietly, 'sold by August. A quick sale is very essential, my friend, and therefore this matter of time is important. But being a man of intelligence and foresight you may ask who is going to purchase my villas; you may wish to know what I propose to do in order to bring them to the notice of the public. My idea is to use

Beauvais' land as a bait; I shall publish the fact that the celebrated artist has acquired a large piece of ground near the port and will very shortly be building a mansion. Our first little nest shall cling close to his fence, which I seem to remember you yourself put up for him. Ah, yes, he should prove very useful indeed, a celebrity is always a valuable asset. Well, those are my plans; have I made them quite clear?'

'Very clear indeed you have made them,' said Jóusè.

Kahn nodded: 'That is good. Now about your profit: I propose to advance you a reasonable sum on account, you to find reliable workmen and yourself to work under my architect who will doubtless suggest a small monthly payment. I shall tell him that you are well acquainted with these parts and that therefore I wish you to act as foreman. The precise amount which you will eventually receive must depend on the cost of materials and labour. But this I do promise: for every two sous that you save, one shall find its way into your pocket, and surely I cannot be fairer than that, or do more to show how much I wish to work with you.'

Kahn stopped speaking and the room grew heavy with silence. Jóusè stared out of the broken window. He was wavering; this offer meant regular work, months of regular work for him and Christophe—Christophe was nearly thirteen years old, and so would be leaving school in the summer. With the prospect of more than one villa to be built, the boy could very soon begin earning—and then there was always le tout petit Loup who continued to cost a great deal of money. Yes, despite his antagonism to Kahn, Jóusè, because of his children, was wavering. But suddenly into his tired blue eyes leapt the dogged, determined look of the peasant—the look that even to-day fronts the world with a stubborn pride in passing traditions; the look that has in it something primitive and fine and courageous, yet also something pathetic. There he stood fast ageing but still undaunted, still clinging to his faith in himself and in those who for years had given him honourable employment, still unable or unwilling to admit defeat, still unable or unwilling to envisage the future. And that pride handed down to him by his forebears, that will to uphold the integrity of labour, that deep love for those things which the hands have made and which thus have become a part of the craftsman; aye, and the memory of brave old dwellings once seen in the narrow by-ways of Lisieux, dwellings that had stood for the dignity of home, for the honesty and skill of their master-builder, must now all combine to delude the perceptions of this man whose soul was not of his time, but rather of some simpler and more stalwart era. Standing there staring out of his broken window, clad in clothes that were daily becoming more shabby, he yet fancied himself indestructible; as firm and enduring he felt as the arch bequeathed to the town of Saint Loup by the Romans.

He swung round and faced the apostle of progress: 'It is that you would make of me a robber'; he thundered, 'it is that you would have me build lies, all lies, in order that you may sell them as houses. Green wood I must use because it is cheap and will therefore procure you a larger profit. And the walls need not be obtrusively thick, nor the paint, it would seem, because those who buy, being fools, will not be any the wiser. And sell quickly, you say; but yes, you are right, it will surely be better to sell very quickly, for such kennels as you have asked me to build will be blown to the ground by the first honest mistral. Well, I answer you, no! Build your kennels yourself, do you hear? And now get out of my house!'

Kahn said softly: 'Yet I would not have war between us. . . .'

'It has always been war between us,' replied Jóusè.

CHAPTER TWENTY-FOUR

I

KAHN's first villa was not begun until April. Joúsè having refused to help with the project, Kahn had naturally turned to the firm in Marseille who, however, had proved to be much too expensive. In vain did he point to his first princely order and the fact that they had not been kept waiting for their money; in vain did he point to Mère Mélanie who had given them work on his recommendation; the firm in Marseille remained adamant when it came to their price for building his villas.

Irritating it was to hear Mère Mélanie bragging loudly about her new water-closets; declaring with something very like pride that the chill which had recently sent her to bed had been the result of her spacious new bathroom: 'I could not resist; so charming it looked. "You are foolish, ma chérie," Alexandre warned me, "a bath is always a perilous thing, those who take one should afterwards sleep in flannel." Mais oui, he was right, the result was most grave; in future I shall leave my bathroom to clients!'

For the Hôtel de la Tarasque was now ready and waiting; neat bedrooms, electric light, sanitation, while Kahn's villas by which he had set such store were as yet barely struggling into existence. Moreover the thrifty Mère Mélanie had not purchased as much as Kahn had expected, having found a great number of odds and ends stored carefully away in one of her attics, so that on the whole the Galeries Kahn had not benefited to any extent by the rise of the Hôtel et Café de la Tarasque; however, Kahn cloaked his irritation in smiles and proceeded to scout up and down the coast for a firm whose demands would meet his resources. In the end he discovered a humble contractor who lived in the neighbourhood of Menton, a Frenchman in the eyes of the law, it was true, but in every other respect an Italian, as were also the talkative, good-looking youths who had been sent along from the frontier as workmen. Having deftly erected a few wooden shacks for themselves they appeared to lose interest in building, spending most of their time making eyes at the girls, drinking quarts of red wine, and brewing black coffee; and although the sun by now was quite hot, they shivered at the first intimation of a mistral: 'Tempo da cani, signore!' they would say, rubbing their hands as though it were freezing. Then speaking in their hideous bastard French, they would go on to grumble that the wind dried the ground and thus rendered it harder to dig foundations. One morning, however, it obligingly rained, but it seemed that this was not propitious either, for when Kahn went along to urge on the work he found them all crouching under umbrellas while one of them strummed on a mandoline in order to cheer his depressed companions.

Bitter although Kahn felt towards Jóusè who had wilfully hindered his impatient ambitions, he none the less spoke of him with regret, carefully curbing his rising anger—as one who had been very grievously wronged spoke Kahn, and his voice was patient and gentle: 'It is not that he wishes to harm us, the good Jóusè, but rather that his outlook is retrogressive. He possesses, alas, the obstructionist mind— the mind that is always an enemy to progress. It is sad, for what would become of this town of Saint Loup if there were many more like him? Then again, he will not keep abreast of the times, and thus he condemns our new methods of building. He forgets that we do not build castles these days, that is why he so much disapproves of my villas. But, bon Dieu, we must give people what they require, and what they require are villas not castles. Yet I sympathize with him for I also love strength, and beauty, and timber the size of an oak tree. I also love spending a very great deal, but I do not love asking exorbitant prices and thus driving the tourists away from a town whose future is solely dependent upon them. Later on when Saint Loup has become better known, I shall aim at building commodious mansions with terraces leading right down to the beach. But we must not run before we can walk; patience, I say; that shall be for the future. And meanwhile let me build a few small, summer

225

P

homes and sell them to people who come here from Paris; to people who will go back and talk of this place, for, believe me, their tongues will make all our fortunes. I explained this to Joùsè but he grew very angry, so angry that he did not pause to consider; he behaved as though his hatred of me had made him blind and deaf to all reason. I will not dwell on his final insult—as you know he ordered me out of his house, and why? Because I wished to employ him! His goodwill would have greatly assisted us all . . . ah, well, there it is, we must get on without him. But my deepest regret is the fact that my workmen are not, as I wished, the men of this district; the money which I am about to spend must now find its way into strangers' pockets. I am all for spending our money at home; why, I ask you, should we benefit men from Menton?' In this manner spoke the soft-voiced Anatole Kahn to all who would listen, and they were many.

So now those who had recently spent on repairs because they believed in Saint Loup's rich future—Madame Roustan, Madame Simon the corn-chandler's wife, Hermitte the baker and a number of others—began to feel very deeply aggrieved at the attitude being adopted by Joùsè, began to fear that in hindering Kahn he might also be hindering their personal interests. While as for Mère Mélanie the progressive, whose improvements were being paid for out of savings, Mère Mélanie cut Joùsè dead in the street, and so did her little hump-backed violinist.

'Ah, mais non,' she protested, 'that Joùsè is crazy, he would have us all back in the Middle Ages. He is fast becoming as bad as our mayor; very well, from now on I refuse to know him. I consider that he has played Kahn a mean trick—but doubtless it arises from a lack of education.'

Madame Roustan took her grievance off to her brother: 'Here have I spent much money doing up those two bedrooms, and now you have seen fit to quarrel with Kahn upon whose enterprise we are all depending. A few pretty villas will improve the whole town; what can have possessed you to refuse to build them?'

Joùsè shrugged and yawned: 'That is surely my business; and in any case, Germaine, why are you whining? Those who cannot find villas will look for rooms—I have probably helped you to let your apartments.'

Madame Roustan, however, remained obdurate: 'It is vital that Saint Loup should spread,' she persisted, 'there will always be those who prefer to take rooms, but such people do little or nothing for trade, trade is only supported by those who own houses. You know very well that I depend on my shop and that life is always hard for a widow; as it is I can scarcely make two ends meet. . . .' She nagged on until Jóusè's temper gave way:

'Oh, for God's sake let me alone!' he exploded.

But even Goundran must forget to be loyal, this in spite of that time just prior to his marriage when the Bénédits had stood forth as his friends in the teeth of much hostile public opinion. Even Goundran went about shaking his head and declaring that Jóusè had been very foolish. For Goundran, these days, had grown dotingly fond of his eighteen months old daughter Aurano, and Aurano loved good things to eat and toys, which were promptly procured for her by her father. Kahn's villas, once lived in, would provide a fresh market for such delicacies as turbot and langoustes which could always be sold at excellent prices. There would also be cod to sell for la brandade—Goundran had noticed that visitors ate the rich Provençal dishes with remarkable gusto. So now he must go about shaking his head and protesting that Jóusè had been very foolish. Yet in justice to Goundran it should be admitted that his deep disapproval was not purely selfish. He considered that Jóusè in refusing Kahn's work had inflicted a very real wrong upon Christophe. He had wilfully deprived the boy of a friend who might well have proved useful to him in the future.

Goundran said to his cronies: 'I am grieved for my godson. Jan has got the Curé and that Madame de Bérac, but Christophe has no one to help him along, and his father's business is practically ruined. I do not say that I respect Jóusè less, not at all; I think everyone should respect Jóusè for an honest, courageous and Christian man, but I think he is wrong upon this occasion. Pecaire! why such a to-do about the walls and the planks and the paint of a few little villas? Only God himself can erect perfect walls, and those He reserves for our mansions in heaven! In this world we must all live as best we may and be thankful for a roof to cover our heads. Moreover a married man cannot indulge his whims, he has ceased to be his own master. Do you think that I would throw good money away. Not I, with Elise and our pretty Aurano!'

Once a lover and lord of the sea he had been, then the lover and lord of a mortal woman; but now he was the slave of Aurano's blue eyes which were bluer far than his own or her mother's, of Aurano's minute but imperious hands that grabbed at his hair and his gaily striped jersey, of Aurano's delightful chuckling laugh that tumbled over itself with enjoyment. There she was, an actual bit of his body, yet a creature whose beauty he thought so amazing that whenever he touched her soft white limbs he could scarcely believe that his crude seed had made her, and must worship this transfiguration of himself, for when all was said and done Goundran was human.

But meanwhile people noted what Goundran was saying, for had he not been a close friend of Jóusè? And so what with his speeches, and Mère Mélanie's ire which had led to the cutting of Jóusè in public, and Madame Roustan's unceasing wails, and Madame Simon's pained criticisms, and Hermitte's terror lest Jóusè should join with the mayor in a plot to rob him of money, it was not surprising that those who had begun by feeling aggrieved were soon feeling resentful.

2

This disaffection of their neighbours and friends had begun to weigh heavily upon Marie. It was not that people said much to her face, but rather the things that she knew they were thinking, and she dreaded her morning shopping, these days—dreaded the carefully guarded words which veiled the rising resentment against Jóusè. For now among those who had known him for years, one friend only remained unswervingly loyal, one friend only, it seemed, had nothing but praise for Jóusè's firm stand against Anatole Kahn, and that friend was none other than Eusèbe. Lustful, intemperate, blind of an eye, and openly proclaiming himself a pagan; never setting his dirty foot inside the church, or giving a centime to Monsieur le Curé; a disaster, a veritable thorn in the flesh with his filthy old bedding hung out of the window so that all who passed by might see for themselves how complete was his unconcerned degradation, Eusèbe now frequently wandered across to the Bénédit's house after work in the evenings, and Jóusè seemed anxious to make him feel welcome.

They would just sit there talking scarely at all, yet conscious of the bond that had sprung up between them, the bond that binds those who belong to the past; for each of them knew that he hated the present, and yet each of them knew that the past was dead, and moreover that time can have no resurrection; yes, and each of them knew in his own separate way a nameless and at moments very deep sadness. And so they would drink, for the coming of Anatole Kahn, a vulgar and over-dressed stranger whom both could despise for the thing that he was, had yet made them grow conscious of their isolation. Nay more, this aggressive middle-aged man who was so persuasive in all his aggressions, this man with the soft voice and ox-like eyes who when insulted merely lifted his hat in polite and undisturbed salutation, this man who when they stood barring his path would arrive at his goal from another direction; this man who himself was no longer young, who possessed neither physical charm nor vigour, was making them feel unaccountably old, and what was still harder to tolerate, helpless.

So Eusèbe must tilt back his chair and laugh hoarsely: 'Ho, hoi, there is always good liquor, and good liquor makes the blood run faster than girls! If you ask me: "Eusèbe, which shall it be, a wench for your bed or wine for your stomach?" I will answer: Give me the comfort of wine, and let me lie down by a fruitful vineyard—it pays better and costs less than a fruitful woman!'

Marie would order her sons off to bed, and Anfos must go at the same time as Loup whose sleep was disturbed if he followed later. And presently she also would seek her room, leaving Jóusè before a fresh bottle of wine, his eyes clouded, his chin sunk on to his breast—he who had used to berate Eusèbe for an impudent, dirty, drunken old sot who disgraced not only himself but his neighbours!

Poor Marie would open her Prayer Book at random and would read many prayers to the blessèd Virgin, or perhaps to the Sacred Heart of our Lord, or perhaps to Saint Joseph, Jóusè's patron; for her peasant mind would feel dull with grief, so that she must seek among printed words for what she herself lacked of inspiration. But alone in his attic her elder son would be staring miserably into the darkness, for such nights would bring with them neither visions nor prayer, but only a new and devastating doubt—the doubt of a merciful God's existence.

Christophe would be thinking: 'My father had courage, yet his courage it is that has turned against him. Can courage sometimes be too heavy for us? Because of his courage my father is breaking.' And this would seem monstrously unjust to the boy, as he lay staring miserably into the darkness.

One morning he must leave the house very early in order to seek out Monsieur le Curé, for he felt an intolerable emptiness, as one who had suffered some deep bereavement: 'Is it a part of myself that has gone, or is it . . . ' But he could not complete this thought; when he tried to do so the thought would elude him.

He discovered the priest alone in the church: 'Mon père, I wish to confess,' he said gravely. So the Curé slipped on his cotta and stole, and together they entered the dark confessional.

'Mon père, something dreadful has happened to my faith. . . .'

'Go on, my child,' said the Curé, calmly.

'I cannot say my prayers. . . .'

'And why cannot you pray?'

'Because I no longer believe in God.'

There ensued a short pause, then the Curé murmured: 'And yet I think God still believes in you, and perhaps that is even more important.' He could be, at times, quite a wise confessor.

'But supposing that we only imagine a God . . .' faltered Christophe at the end of his painful confession. 'Supposing that He has no existence at all, that we think He is there just because we need Him?'

'And who put that great need in our hearts, my child? Surely that need is God,' said the Curé. Then he told the boy to remain and hear Mass in order that he might draw near to his Maker.

So Christophe received the little white Host with that

curious feeling of apprehension which was all that remained of the terrible fear that had gripped him during his First Communion. Very reverently he received the Host from the Curé's delicate, scholarly fingers.

But the sense of doubt and bereavement persisted, so that Christophe grew more and more melancholy, eating little, and walking with drooping head; while at moments he would find himself almost tearful because the mountains looked unusually blue, or the olive trees unusually silver, or the stars unusually bright and friendly; for if there was no God to thank for such things, there could be neither meaning nor hope in their beauty. Thus April passed gloomily on into May, and the cloud did not lift until one May morning when Christophe was once again plunged into sin, this time through losing control of his temper.

There were boys at the school who took pleasure in baiting, and although they liked Christophe well enough on the whole, they must now ape their parents' resentment of Jóusè by repeating remarks they had overheard, and which they embellished in the repeating; all of which Christophe treated with the large disdain he accorded to the buzzing of flies and mosquitoes. But the day came when someone went a step too far; it was André, the eldest son of the chemist, a pimply, bullying lout of a boy who started to gibe during recreation.

Said André, speaking unusually loudly: 'Your father owes us a very large bill, and yet he is too lazy to work and earn money, without doubt because he now drinks so much wine! Eh bien, I say that your father is a thief. When people do not pay what they owe, it is thieving!'

The blood sang in Christophe's flaming ears, his scalp pricked, his muscles tightened for action, and he felt enormously, joyfully strong—strong with rage, a most uplifting sensation: 'Fiéu de baudrèio! Panto! Gusas! Malavalisco à vous!' he shouted. 'Liar, you who call my father a thief! Take that!' and he suddenly shot out his fist, striking his enemy full on the mouth, 'And now that!' and he struck him full on the nose, so that André gave a loud yell of pain, lost his footing and promptly fell over backwards. And never did a boy produce quite so much gore as this pubescent, full-blooded son of the chemist.

What a hubbub. Loup frisked about like a lap-dog: 'Kick him! Kick him hard in the stomach!' he kept yapping, while Jan fell upon a couple of other youngsters who had recently been making themselves offensive. Then everyone started to fight at once, for no reason except that the thing was infectious.

Out strode Monsieur Roland, very red in the face: 'Silence! Have you gone quite demented?' he thundered. Then he caught sight of André who continued to bleed, while Christophe stood glaring down at him in triumph: 'Bon Dieu!' exclaimed the master, 'Someone get me a sponge and a bucket of water. Stop squealing, André.'

3

The end of it all was more trouble for Marie. Christophe had got off comparatively lightly, for although Monsieur Roland was often severe, he was also a just man and very observant. Having lectured the culprit for half an hour he dismissed the whole affair with a warning. But the chemist was bent upon making a scandal: his André, he said, had been brutally battered; struck in the face he had been several times, and this without the least provocation. Jóusè should pay and pay handsomely for the boy's damaged clothes, the shock, the ointment, the lint, the bandages, and the doctor; otherwise . . . bien, one always had one's redress, there was always the law, one could start a procès. Jóusè shrugged his shoulders and capitulated; the chemist was very essential to Loup who, indeed, could scarcely have lived without him. But Marie secretly heaved a deep sigh, for the money would have to be taken from savings.

That evening Jóusè said to his son: 'Consider the expense you have put us to, Christophe. No, but really I cannot understand this affair. Why did you strike that André in the face? Will you not explain? It was very unlike you.'

Christophe shook his cropped head and looked stubborn. He was sorry that his father should be put to expense at a time when money was so hard to come by; but explain the cause of it all? Ah, ça non! There were things that one did not say to one's father.

'If you tell him the reason,' he threatened later, having

followed le tout petit Loup into his bedroom, 'if you tell him the reason, I shall be very angry! Jan has promised not even to tell Aunt Germaine. And now you will promise to tell no one at all. Allons, vite, I am waiting. . . .' And Loup actually promised.

So once again Christophe must seek out the Curé, but this time his confession was wonderfully cheerful, all things considered: 'Mon père, I have sinned. I have given way to ungovernable temper. I called André Génas several bad names, and I put a malediction upon him because he said that my father was a thief, and I hit him twice, as hard as I could. Ah, mon père, he lay there and bled like a pig! And perhaps I ought to tell you, mon père, that I felt very happy while I was hitting. And . . . mon père . . . I once more believe in God. . . .'

'God moves in mysterious ways,' thought the Curé.

CHAPTER TWENTY-FIVE

I

At a time of great strain and unhappiness a comparatively insignificant event may discover the chink in our armour; an event connected, as likely as not, with an equally insignificant person and thus it was Madame Simon's son, Guillaume, who became all unwittingly instrumental in causing the first sign of faltering in Marie.

A good fellow, a kind-hearted fellow this Guillaume, with a tender and perhaps over-scrupulous conscience, so that from very anxiety not to injure or wound he frequently blundered. Then again, at the moment he was tactless with love of Clotilde, the notary's scatter-brained daughter. Clotilde had sharp, impertinent eyes, and lips that were harshly defined by lip-stick. Her hair was crimped, her handkerchiefs scented, and her nails too shiny, too red and too pointed. All of which Guillaume found intensely alluring; and if his parents felt doubtful at moments they were careful to keep those doubts to themselves—the daughter of a Marseille notary was a match of considerable social importance.

The wedding had been postponed for two months owing to the trouble in finding an apartment, since Clotilde considered that parents-in-law were only endurable at a distance; nothing would induce her to share their roof, and this she had made very clear to her fiancé.

'I will not live over a shop,' she had stated, 'especially a shop that harbours large rats that will come and nibble my toes in bed! Moreover there would be your father and mother.'

Ah, yes, Clotilde was going to be difficult to please and the town of Saint Loup had little to offer—no cinemas, no dances, no milliners' shops, no zoological gardens, no brightly lit boulevards along which to stroll of an evening with friends—indeed it had little to offer but Guillaume. And knowing this, Guillaume must tread warily, so that when he had ventured: 'You remember my godfather whom you saw at la Tarasque that afternoon? I would wish him to make our marriage-bed for us, and also, perhaps, one or two other things . . .' he had quickly succumbed to Clotilde's protests, eagerly agreeing that what they required was a modern bedstead with blue cretonne curtains, a drawing-room suite of gilt and cerise, and a dining-room suite of carved ebony— or at least of something that looked very like it.

Clotilde had wanted their furniture to be bought in Marseille, which perhaps was quite natural; but then had arisen the question of means: the notary was willing to pay for their apartment but not, it appeared, for what they put in it, so Guillaume had gone to see Anatole Kahn to arrange for a certain amount of credit. Kahn had promptly agreed to quarterly payments; he was only too pleased to help the young couple, they might choose what they liked, he was only too pleased . . . of course there would be just a little percentage. So one evening towards the beginning of June, Clotilde arrived to stay for a night with Guillaume's respectful but nervous parents—this in order to visit the Galeries Kahn the next morning with an equally nervous Guillaume.

It was surely the devil's own luck that Marie should have chanced to be passing at the time of their visit, that the door of the shop should have chanced to be open with Kahn and his clients standing just inside it. And what could have possessed so seemly a woman to pretend to be gazing at Kahn's front window, so that she might overhear what was said, and know the precise extent of the order? What possessed the soft-voiced Anatole Kahn to raise that soft voice as he ran through the items, loudly checking off first this purchase, then that, can undoubtedly only have been the devil. For hearing him Marie went red and then white as she clutched at her shabby old shopping basket, while the lump that rose in her throat was so large that just for a moment she could not swallow. Many others now patronized Kahn, as she knew, yet somehow, to-day, this young man's desertion must loom larger than all that had gone before— it is frequently less the event than the moment. Turning quickly she hurried along the quay, but not before Guillaume had looked up and seen her, and not before Guillaume had flushed to the eyes: 'I will not be a minute', he whispered to Clotilde, 'you wait here.' And off he dashed in pursuit, the kind-hearted, tactless, blundering creature.

Had Guillaume been just a little less kindly . . . but no, he must speak, must try to explain and thus only succeed in wounding more deeply. Having come up with Marie he stammered and blushed like a schoolboy caught out in some grave misdemeanour: 'Listen . . . I want you to know how it is—the time was so short before our wedding; the delay in getting a suitable apartment . . . and then Clotilde . . . she is young and she loves pretty things; ah, no, no, not that, it was really the time, otherwise I would surely have wished papa Jóusè . . . but the time was so short. You do understand. . . ?'

Marie answered: 'I will tell Jóusè what you have said.' And still clutching her shopping basket she left him.

In and out of the shops she went calmly enough, even managing to smile as she gave her small orders: 'But yes, perfect weather, not yet grown too hot . . . I think I must have some potatoes this morning.' 'Loup seems better, I thank you. When will Christophe leave school? Next month. Yes, please, half a kilo of sugar.'

But once back in her home she could no longer smile. Perhaps it was the sight of her husband sitting idle with his hands hanging limply between his knees, perhaps it was those scared, anxious eyes of Anfos, or perhaps, it was the gasping of le tout petit Loup who, knowing quite well that he ought not to run, had yet felt the urge of youth in his bones and had raced home from school far ahead of Christophe. Be this as it may, she must now start to tell them about Guillaume Simon's open desertion; and then she must cover her face and weep with a kind of childish, disconsolate weeping:

'He called you papa Jóusè,' she wept; 'it is . . . that he . . . called you . . . papa Jóusè. . . .'

Jóusè jerked clumsily out of his chair: 'Stop, stop, Marioun; I cannot support it!' and his voice sounded unfamiliar and strained: 'Stop crying, Marioun . . . stop crying, I tell you! Will you stop it, Marie!' and he stamped his foot, 'I have told you that I cannot support it.'

But she could not stop crying. Her tears once released flowed forth like a stream that had long been ice-bound, dripping down through her fingers on to her lap as she woefully rocked herself backwards and forwards: 'And he called you papa Jóusè . . .' she repeated over and over and over again with a desperate, unreasoning monotony: 'ai, ai, and he called you papa Jóusè.'

2

Nobody came to Saint Loup that summer apart from the usual handful of artists. Beauvais had apparently forgotten his land—he was said to be wandering about in Spain, and his satellites were presumably with him. Mère Mélanie managed to let two bedrooms and Madame Roustan had one humble boarder, but the Simon's spare room was unoccupied and so was the attic of Hermitte the baker.

Kahn's first villa was still very far from completion and could not be finished before the autumn, yet he went about smiling his confident smile: 'Remember that Rome was not built in a day. Believe me, my friends, I have no misgivings.'

And they did believe him, the more so, perhaps, because he himself was continuing to spend, having recently turned a commodious shed into something not very unlike Jóusè's workshop. The Galeries Kahn could now undertake repairs thanks to a joiner whom Kahn had imported, and whom people were finding both skilful and sprack, so that doubtless this venture, also, would prosper.

Eusèbe, however, was content with the fact that despite the fine weather the town remained empty: 'It would seem,' he remarked with a satisfied grin, 'that the fat golden calves prefer other pastures. Possibly our watchful dragon, la Tarasque, objected to so much insolent browsing; a fine beast she remains, a most worthy beast, in spite of that Marthe and her holy water! In any case we are now left in peace; I told you how it would be, my good Jóusè.' Then as Jóusè neither looked up nor replied: 'Eh bien, I shall take myself off to the café until the black crow on your shoulder has flown. . . .' And Jóusè did not attempt to detain him, for these days he must brood for hours on his wrongs, filled with a slow, fundamental anger.

He had not believed it, the big stupid peasant, he had not believed that his honest brown hands would be scarcely able to earn him a living, that his honest brown oak and his sweet-smelling pine would lie idle against the walls of his workshop, that a life spent in ceaseless labour and thrift could result in so galling a poverty, might even result in stark destitution. No, not until Marie had wept had he believed—her tears had washed away his illusions. So now there had come that slow, fundamental anger, and at times his resentful eyes would grow bloodshot, while his face would be stained by an ominous flush that grew deeper with every deep swallow of wine—the strong, comforting wine from the vineyards of Provence.

'Marioun, fetch more wine. . . . I am tired to-night; but yes, at my age a man needs support. Did you hear me, Marie? I said fetch more wine!' And sick at heart his wife must obey him.

He would sit with his chin resting on his left hand, the hair of his beard spraying out through his fingers. His right hand would be slowly fingering the glass which every few moments he raised to his lips, and the liquor would fan his anger to flame, augmenting his bitter sense of injustice:

'Marioun, he will starve us, that Anatole Kahn; he will starve us craftily, little by little. And they help him to do it, our friends, Marioun—may God send the lot of them down to hell!—they buy the man's filth because it is cheaper. Houi, the good truthful oak, the fine oak, there it lies despised, spat upon, Marioun—a great pile of it lying despised near my work-bench! He has come here to snatch the very bread from our mouths, to ruin the old and honourable trade that I learnt from my father in this very house, that he learnt in this very house from his father; yes, and always have we been honest workmen. But now honesty counts for nothing, it seems, the honest can starve so that Kahn may prosper. "Bénédit," that swine says to me in the street, "Bénédit, I hope that you find yourself well. How is your wife, Bénédit?" he says, "I hope that your wife is well, and your children. Remember, my friend, that I bear you no grudge. . . ." Bèsti! I could batter the mouth off his face! I could batter until there was nothing left, no mouth and no

treacherous soft brown eyes . . . when I look at those treacherous soft brown eyes I feel as though I were treading in cow-
dung!' And the flush would spread up until it reached Jóusè's
brow, the veins standing out like cords on his temples.

Marie would do what she could to calm him, as she strove
to recapture her own faltering courage: 'Listen, my Jóusè,
we are not starving yet, nor do I think God will permit us to
starve.'

But her husband would seem not to grasp her words:
'Starving! Yes, yes, we shall soon be starving!'

Le tout petit Loup would begin to wheeze, for fear
never failed to react on his asthma, and his father's heavy,
congested face with the beard stained by wine that had
spilled from the glass, would throw him into a kind of
panic: 'Maman—oh, maman . . .' the boy would gasp,
unnerved by that fear and the pain in his chest. Then
Marie would gather him into her arms, while her sorrowful
eyes turned slowly to Christophe.

And sitting there speechless yet acutely attentive as though
being forced to rivet his mind, nay his very soul on this
ruin and suffering, Christophe would find himself seeking
for words which although familiar would always elude him—
words that he seemed to divine had a power to heal not only
the flesh but the spirit. Torn by pity, by his terrible comprehension of the misery that was engulfing his father, of the
dumb plea for help in his mother's eyes, of the nervous
tremors shaking his brother, the boy would suffer a kind of
triple anguish that at moments became almost physical, and
so poignant that it appeared past endurance. Calling up
every ounce of his strength and courage, he would try not to
feel appalled by this thing which so greatly exceeded his
understanding; and as he sat on there white-faced and rigid,
he would fancy that he heard the words he was seeking
being spoken by someone a long way away, so that he could
not hear them quite clearly. Then would come the strange
thought: 'Distance does not exist, it is all here and now, it
has always been here; there is neither time, separation nor
distance. It is all here and now, it is all in me . . . they are
me, I am them, and we are . . . we are. . . .' But the thought
would waver, grow dim and go out like a light that a sudden
wind had extinguished.

A great feeling of helplessness would possess him bringing with it, quite often, an angry resentment. He would set his young lips in a stern, bitter line, refusing to meet his mother's eyes, refusing to see his father's flushed face or the miserably labouring chest of his brother; for just as he had tried to shun pain in the past, even so he still struggled at times to shun it. And occasionally it almost appeared as though he had managed to stifle his pity, and when this happened he went to his bed without saying 'good-night,' hard of heart and triumphant; without saying his prayers he went to his bed, blowing the candle out very quickly and hiding himself underneath the quilt, lest he see his mother's eyes in the darkness.

3

At this time there was seldom a tranquil evening, for now his parents frequently quarrelled. They quarrelled over things that in prosperous days would have seemed to them both the merest trifles: the lamp would gutter, die down and go out because Marie had felt too tired to refill it; or the kitchen door would refuse to close because Jóusè had felt too disheartened to mend it, or the sink would prove to be stopped up with grease because Anfos had sailed a boat in the sink instead of using his rod to cleanse it. And such happenings would get themselves all out of focus, appearing as veritable disasters, so that Jóusè would turn and reproach his wife and Marie would turn and reproach her husband. For their love must submit to their nerves these days, to the tyrannous sway of their ailing flesh, and the quarrels might grow very angry and loud to the great perturbation and wonder of Anfos.

On one such occasion he covered his ears and was off before any of them could catch him; and so wild did he look as he rushed from the room, that Jóusè stopped shouting to drink more wine—a fresh tumbler of wine because he felt anxious: 'Pecaire, now where has that imbecile gone? He ought to be in his bed,' he scowled. 'Christophe, go after him, go at once and bring him back here—he deserves a good hiding!'

Christophe got up and fetched a light, and sighing he went in search of the half-wit.

He found Anfos crouching down in the workshop among the odds and ends of old carving; utterly limp and dejected he looked: 'He resembles a suffering dog,' thought Christophe. Then he suddenly felt his eyes stinging with tears, for seeing him there the creature crept forward and rubbed a gaunt cheek against his hand, making inarticulate, animal sounds of love and distress—it was like Mirèio.

Christophe said: 'Tell me what you are doing here, Anfos, you seem so unhappy—come back to the kitchen. We were worried about you, that is why I have come. Moreover it is late, it is time for bed.' And he fondled the man's thick, dusty hair; 'Come back, it is time for bed,' he persuaded.

But at this Anfos gazed at him almost sternly, and when he spoke his voice sounded accusing: 'The words!' he said loudly, 'The words! the words! Master, where are the words? Why will you not speak them?'

Christophe shivered and pushed him roughly away: 'What words? I tell you they do not exist!' And panic-stricken he fled in his turn, leaving Anfos alone in the darkening workshop.

But dreadful as were those discordant evenings, there were times when the days seemed almost more dreadful, when Christophe, now no longer at school, must try to invent fictitious tasks in a fruitless effort to soothe his father. For Jóusè would have the boy at his side although one pair of hands had become one too many, and observing his son's pretence of work he would often speak with great bitterness, as though venting his anger and pain upon him: 'Ho, ho, you are very busy, my son, we prosper, my Christophe is very busy. He appears to be whittling a little stick, or perhaps he is making a little whistle! Ho, Anfos, why are you wasting your time? Come and help, this task is too heavy for Christophe.'

One morning he looked up from his bench with a grin: 'My son, here is something well worth your attention. Observe how I smooth the sides of this hole, observe the graceful curve of this hole, and its smoothness—not a notch in the deal, not a splinter. Fine work for a cabinet-maker, ah, yes, this is fine work indeed—such great skill is needed! Do I hear you say that your father makes beds? Do you say that your father makes oak chairs and tables and

Q

cupboards and chests? Is that what you say? because if so you lie, you lie, my son; your father makes deal seats for stinking privies! And this afternoon you shall carry this jewel of cabinet-making to the farmer, Gaston; you shall walk through the town with it under your arm so that all may observe how the Bénédits prosper. "Tè!" they will exclaim, "There goes Jóusè's son with a handsome new seat for old Gaston's privy." It is well to exhibit our prosperity to those who now buy at the Galeries Kahn, in case they should fancy we miss their custom!' Christophe stared at him with miserable eyes, and seeing this Jóusè spoke all the louder: 'Ah, yes, there is also a fence to mend; the Simons require a new slat in their fence, it would seem that the dogs can enter their garden. Madame Simon requests that you mend her fence, but on the instant, you must please understand, on the instant. The charge will be one franc fifty!' And this sort of thing would go on pretty often, for Jóusè was not his own man these days; the wine would have soured in him during the night, so that his head throbbed and ached the next morning.

With infinite patience Christophe would try to do what he could to comfort his father: 'After all,' he might urge, 'we may outlast Kahn. Kahn may suddenly find himself tired of Saint Loup—one can see that the town is quite empty this summer. And then do not forget that the Curé has ordered six rush-bottom chairs for Our Lady's Chapel; I have noticed such chairs at the Galeries Kahn, yet the Curé prefers to come here to us, and something tells me that this is good luck—I have the idea that our luck is changing.' These and many similar things he would say, while secretly feeling that they availed nothing.

And meanwhile Anfos would just sit and carve—always carving he was these days in his corner. Strange pictures now grew up under his tools, having in them a kind of disorderly beauty. Figures half-human and wholly demented: beasts, birds, wide circles and swift, flashing lines, wings and claws, a goat's head, the head of a fish, inextricably tangled with human bodies. Or perhaps he would seek to humanize flowers, giving some flower the torso of a woman—of a woman he could only have seen with his mind, could only have visualized by instinct. And men he would carve with the heads of trees: 'Look,' he would babble, 'they have kind green heads; they think kind green thoughts; they listen to birds all day and all night, and the birds are wise, very wise. . . .' And then he might start to whistle. Sometimes he would fashion angular landscapes having mountains that never rose on this planet, having seas that never washed earthly shores, having ships that never sailed earthly waters. And when he did this his brown eyes would shine with a light that seemed to proceed from the spirit, so that his face became quite transformed by the rapture he felt at his own imaginings:

'Look, look! little master, this is where I go when I fly, when I fly away, little master. Farther and farther to no one knows where but Anfos. . . . Bèu Diéu, and up . . . up . . . up!' And then he would make as though to fly, flapping his arms and his great red hands, 'My feet are too heavy . . .' he would mutter.

Mad. Christophe knew that Anfos was mad these days, that their trouble had tipped the scales, turning the half-wit into a madman. Jóusè would curse and Marie would fret, observing that he grew always more strange, but Christophe could probably have restrained him. Yet he lacked the heart to forbid those wild carvings, divining the longing from which they sprang—the longing of one whose hope lay beyond, whose fulfilment must be in another existence. Anfos was mad with the pain of the world, with the pain of his own maimed, distorted life, and was striving to fashion a world of dreams into which he might escape from despair— he was striving to conjure beauty from madness.

4

There were days when the boy could endure it no longer, and then he himself would have to escape from the man who was mad with the pain of the world, and from that other man with the bloodshot eyes and the beard now habitually matted and stained. He would think: 'I, too, must get away for awhile. If only for an hour I must get to the sea; I must let the sea wash me clean of it all.' Then without a word he would lay down his tools and go off to some lonely spot on the shore, there to give himself body and soul to the water.

With a kind of rapture Christophe would swim through the vast, impersonal depths of blueness; a mote, an atom, a thing so minute by comparison that he scarcely existed. And this feeling of being intensely alive yet obliterated, would give him great joy, a sense of great peace, completion and joy such as many an one has claimed for Nirvana. He no longer wished for the sea as a friend, was no longer conscious, indeed, of its friendship, but rather he rejoiced to find it aloof, and completely divorced from human emotion. To be no more himself because one with the sea, that would seem to him entirely fulfilling.

Time would pass and still he would swim on and on, a competent, skilful and fearless swimmer. And as he swam thus his whole being would grasp at elemental and primitive things—the sea, the wind, the incalculable sky—at such things he would grasp with all his might, plunging his head in and out of the water, flinging his body from side to side in the ecstasy of his sudden revolt. Soulless he would feel and completely disburdened, like a creature reborn into liberation. And the sun would begin to swing to the west, then to drop very slowly towards the mountains, then more quickly until on a sudden it had sunk, a red disc behind the black peaks of the Maures, leaving the sky and the sea to flame, so that the wings of the homing birds would be touched with a transient, unearthly glory. Looking up the boy would observe the stars, faint as yet because of the after-glow, and turning he would start to swim back to the shore, but regretfully and without resignation.

5

In such moods Christophe often sought out Eusèbe, and together they would walk up to the vineyards. To reach them they must pass by Mirèio's grave, now hidden beneath a tangle of shrubs—those aromatic Provençal shrubs whose perfume still faintly disturbed the Curé. No stone marked the place where Mirèio lay but beside it there rose up a round, grey boulder, so that Christophe could easily find the spot, only sometimes these days he would not want to find it and would turn his face resolutely aside—there was pain in the memory of Mirèio.

Eusèbe would watch the boy with interest: 'Càspi!' he would murmur which meant very little; he frequently murmured 'Càspi' to his vines when he peered at them, taking stock of their progress, and now he would peer at the boy at his side, attentively but never unkindly.

Christophe was allowing his cropped hair to grow, and released from the clippers it sprang up quite briskly. Its colour had darkened since his earliest youth; Eusèbe observed that it looked almost auburn. He also observed that Christophe's pale eyes in his sun-bronzed face were queerly attractive, that his features though rough-hewn, held a look of power, that his brow was low and wide and convincing, but above all his figure pleased Eusèbe, so strong it was, and of such excellent proportions. Eusèbe considered himself a fine judge, for had he not been born in the town of Arles, and had Arles not been born in the lap of the pagan? And had he not worshipped pagan art at the Musée Lapidaire many a time? He had, and so now he would think to himself:

'The boy is magnificent, what a torso! It is really remarkable how much he has changed for the better; and already he looks quite mature. Ai! las, that he cannot become a Greek athlete.'

One day he remarked: 'We are all very ugly, we have grown very ugly and our bodies are mean—even here in Provence which at one time was pagan. But you, Christophe, remind me of those who live on in marble, of those I have seen thus at Arles. Your features are too rough and that is a pity, but presently your body will be like theirs, a thing of great strength and of perfect balance. Now look at me, Christophe, a poor dwarf with one eye, and then think yourself lucky to possess such a carcase. Houi, but the women will be round you like bees!' Christophe smiled rather vaguely, knowing nothing of women.

What he liked was to wander among the vines, for their greenness gave him an exquisite pleasure, and he loved the contented and earthy smell which seemed to haunt all Eusèbe's vineyards. Eusèbe would stoop down and pinch the grapes, but gently as one pinches the ear of a baby, and then he would talk to them playfully as Christophe had heard him talk to his sandals. Or perhaps he would want the boy to admire:

'Come and look at these bunches, are they not beauties?
Only see how they flush, only see how they swell. Bigre!
already they are heavy with juice. This year I shall certainly
make a nectar that the gods will not despise at their table!'

So, stooping, Christophe would look in his turn, and when
he must suddenly think of his father he would thrust the
thought firmly out of his mind, praising the grapes to please
Eusèbe. Then slipping his hand through the old man's arm:
'And now tell me again all about your vineyards.'

Nothing loath Eusèbe would start to explain the reasons
why his vines invariably prospered: first came Bacchus, that
lusty god of the grape, but then came Eusèbe a very good
second. Winking and grinning and waving his hand he
would tell of his craft, his care and his knowledge; of his
truly amazing patience and skill—none so skilful, said he, as
the old Eusèbe. Oh, yes, there were others who thought they
grew grapes—pòu, their grapes were shrivelled and worthless. If you wished to obtain any juice from such grapes you
must first blow them out to bursting with spittle! While as
for their wine—Santo bèlli Mariniero! to drink it was to
have an attack of the colic! No, no, Eusèbe alone could grow
grapes; if he chose, his vineyards could become world-
famous, but he did not choose, sarnipabiéune, not he! What,
degrade his beautiful vineyards with placards fifteen feet
high? Why, the grapes would turn in their skins with sheer
horror at such a proceeding. Why, Bacchus would literally
belch with rage. Càspi, such doings must be left to upstarts
like Kahn and his ilk—Ah, the venomous toads, degrading
and fouling the face of the country!

On and on he would gabble while Christophe listened
amused, feeling thankful for the distraction, while he drew
the fresh upland air into his lungs and sniffed the strong,
happy smell of the earth, determined that he would be
happy also. And sometimes he must laugh and remind
Eusèbe of that day when he had lured them all from their
parents—Christophe and Jan and le tout petit Loup—
giving them bunches of sweet grapes to eat and rough
bread, and milk to drink at the farmhouse, telling them
stories about the old gods, and about the nymphs who so
dearly loved honey; must remind him of Loup's remark that
same evening when, sitting beside his mother at supper, he

had loudly declared that his name had been changed by the nymphs, so that now he was not Loup but Bacchus. Eusèbe would chuckle and slap his thigh—that incident never failed to delight him: Ho, hoi, what an imp le tout petit Loup! As clever he was as the black lamp of Satan! And from this they might fall to talking of things that belonged to Christophe's earliest childhood, for the boy liked to dwell on those happier days since they seemed to provide an escape from the present. But one event he would never discuss, to the great annoyance of old Eusèbe who having been generous longed to be praised—he would never discuss his first pair of sandals.

CHAPTER TWENTY-SIX

I

PEOPLE began to shake their heads, declaring that Jóusè was going to pieces. What a fool he had been to refuse Kahn's work, what a fool not to keep abreast of the times—all the same they were feeling a little uneasy. It was shocking, said they, that a Bénédit should have let himself go down hill so quickly; degraded he looked with his ill-kept beard, his frayed, dirty shirt, and his shuffling gait—a changed man, and frequently not quite sober. His poor wife; it was terribly sad for her yet even more sad, perhaps, for the children. Take Christophe, a tall strong boy like that should be put to some steady, lucrative work, instead of which he just hung about idle. Ah, mais non, his father was greatly to blame with his hatred of Kahn and of all forms of progress.

And indeed Christophe longed to find lucrative work, any work that would help them by bringing in money; but Jóusè had harshly refused his consent, becoming enraged at the very suggestion: 'That, no!' he had stormed, 'You will stand by your trade; you will stand by your trade if you starve in the process. It shall never be said that he has driven you out! It shall never be said that a son of mine has been forced to accept some mean, dirty job by a base-born impostor like Anatole Kahn!' For immense was becoming this man's unreason.

And seeing the flush that spread over his face as the anger swept up through his large, ailing body, Christophe had suddenly held his peace, warned by a swift premonition of danger.

There were others, however, who felt it their duty to interfere in this grim situation, and among them the Curé who was worried lest Jan should suffer through fretting about his cousin; he also had left school and was now engaged upon grave and extremely important studies.

Jan had suddenly announced: 'I would give up the priesthood if Madame de Bèrac would be kind to Christophe and look after his future instead of mine . . . but yes, I would even give up the priesthood if Christophe would consent to enter the Church. Mon père, do you think we could make him do so? Do you think we could make him become more submissive and less foolish about imagining things that he says have got left out of the Bible?'

The Curé had looked at him very sternly: 'You have spoken as the young will speak in emotion. No, Jan, God has chosen you for His priest, and we cannot decide such matters for God who may well have plans of His own for Christophe.' But the next day he went to the Bénédit's house, having made up his mind to speak to Jóusè.

'It appears to me,' began Monsieur le Curé, 'it appears to me that it would be better if you let Christophe look for employment elsewhere. He is really surprisingly strong for his age, so perhaps he could get a job at the station, or else on the line beween here and Saint Raphael; I see they are making extensive repairs. . . .'

Jóusè answered: 'My son is a carpenter, he is neither a luggage-porter nor a navvy.'

The Curé curbed his rising irritation: 'Yet I know that your son is anxious to earn money in order to do what he can to help. Christophe, is that not so?' And he turned to the boy.

'Mais oui, I much wish to earn,' murmured Christophe.

'Christophe's place is here with his father,' said Jóusè; 'My son is a Bénédit, Monsieur le Curé, and a Bénédit does not turn tail and run from his duty because he fears for his stomach. Many years we have worked for this town of Saint Loup—my father, his father and his father's father. Timber brought us success and through it we will fail if we must, but we will not give up our tradition. My son is being trained to follow our trade, and so long as there is even a fence to mend I intend that he shall continue his training. While I am alive he remains at his bench. That is my decision, Monsieur le Curé.'

But now the Curé in his turn was stubborn, thanks to his anxiety over his pupil, and he started to argue quite vigorously, pointing out the gross and unparalleled folly of preventing Christophe from taking a job when, as everyone knew, things had come to a pass that was forcing Jóusè to fall back on his savings: 'Bénédit,' he concluded, 'you are terribly wrong. God helps those who help themselves, remember, and although you are suffering for what you have felt to be right, for upholding an honest tradition, you are also suffering for pride's sake, my son.'

'Then I will continue to suffer,' frowned Jóusè.

The Curé got up, at last convinced that his arguments were utterly fruitless, and taking his hat he walked out of the house: 'In another moment,' he said to himself as he went, 'I must surely have lost my temper.'

Goundran came: 'I am worried about my godson. Why not let me make a sailor of Christophe? Listen, Jóusè, I am going to buy a new boat so shall soon be needing a sensible lad. Only say the word and the matter is settled—may I have him?' But Jóusè shook his grey head. 'He is dulling his brain with drink,' thought Goundran.

Madame Roustan arrived; she knew of employment. Monsieur Bled at the Bazaar was wanting a boy to run errands, carry parcels and deliver newspapers. Not all boys, she explained, were so lucky as Jan, not all boys could be patronized by a countess! Should she tell Monsieur Bled that Christophe would call?

Tron de Diéune! she might tell Monsieur Bled what she pleased; but meanwhile she could take herself off to the devil or her Comtesse de Bérac—Jóusè did not care which. Had she heard him? She could take herself off to the devil!

Simon père turned up looking worried and awkward. He wished to find someone to unload sacks of grain, and to do little odd jobs about the place . . . Christophe now . . . he was strong, and a good-tempered boy. . . . Surely Christophe would be just the very fellow. The pay was not famous but still, it might help. What about it . . . considered as a beginning?

What about it? Why nothing, nothing at all, And Jóusè proceeded to spit on the floor, then to rub the sole of his shoe on the spittle.

Even Hermitte the baker sent his spouse to suggest that Christophe might be taught the intricacies of baking. It seemed that her brother, a pastry-cook of Toulon, was very anxious to find an apprentice. Christophe could live with her brother and his wife who were prosperous, quiet, and kindly people. This would be an advantage, for Jóusè would know that the boy was properly housed and fed; it would also mean that he was looked after.

But Jóusè laughed loudly: 'Ah, yes, no doubt, and get my son's services thrown in for nothing! No, I thank you, Christophe has his own home; he has also a trade which is not that of baking.'

Madame Hermitte quite naturally felt aggrieved, and in this frame of mind she returned to her husband.

Hermitte was furious when he was told of the way in which Jóusè had spurned his wife's offer: 'Zóu,' he remarked, 'very well then, so be it, As for me, I am done with the whole ugly business. When a man has no money wherewith to buy food and yet plenty of money to drink himself silly—yes, and when in addition he insults my wife, he cannot expect my consideration. It is time that he paid for the bread I provide; I am poor and so greatly in need of his riches!'

And now everywhere Hermitte went he complained to those who were nursing a similar grievance; and they listened eagerly, nodding and shrugging as who should say: 'We have done what we could, we are free from all blame, the fault lies with Jóusè.' And since human nature is at times only human, they were greatly relieved to find an excuse for ridding themselves of that uneasy feeling. Even the Curé and Goundran shrugged; the one going back to his books and his pupil, the other to those boats that were so spick and span, and that brought in the fishes that brought in the money which, in its turn, was spent on Elise and Aurano.

'What will you?' said Goundran, fondling his wife, 'I cannot support more than one family, and since Jóusè sees fit to ignore my suggestion. . . .' Then he lifted Aurano high into the air: 'Ah, bon!' he shouted, 'We go up . . . we go down . . . with the breeze in our sails, with the breeze in our hearts. Up . . . down. Up . . . down. O! lou brave ventoulet!'

2

Although the Curé urged Jan to study almost ruthlessly because of a love which was fast bidding fair to become an obsession; although he talked much of the Master's work, of those plentiful harvests awaiting the reaper, and although he endeavoured to reassure Jan and himself by insisting that Christophe's life could safely be left in the hands of his Maker, Jan was not reassured for he also loved, and love sometimes demands a great deal of reassuring. Thus it was that once more he must lie awake, very deeply distressed because of his cousin; and wise though he certainly was for his years—bookwise in such things as theology and latin, as dogma and ritual, as legend and fact pertaining to saints and to reverend persons—he yet thought at these times with the mind of a child who, himself loving food, would dread to go hungry.

That Christophe now often went hungry he knew, the best being saved for his ailing brother, and so Jan would lie on his bed and scheme how to get cake and fruit while having no money; for the matter of that how to get bread and cheese wherewith to fill Christophe's rapacious stomach. Christophe's appetite was whale-like these days, so remorselessly was his young body growing—he would even go foraging up in the hills, on the look out for sweet and edible berries. Why, when Madame Roustan asked him to supper, this because her son had stamped and insisted, she declared that the larder was cleared for a week, that her housekeeping purse was completely flattened.

'Santo Flour,' she would grumble, 'he eats like a pig. No, I cannot but feel that Christophe is greedy!'

But apparently Jan had become greedy also, for whenever he visited Hermitte the baker he would gaze with big, longing eyes at the wares: 'U . . . m, that looks good, very good . . .' he would murmur. And if Hermitte was serving this was met by a frown, but if Hermitte's fat wife was behind the counter Jan might easily go off with two or three cakes, or a couple of rolls shaped like glossy brown crescents. And so it would be when he passed the greengrocer: 'Good morning, Madame,' he would say politely, 'surely your peaches are extra fine? But enormous; I have never seen anything finer!' For he knew that this woman possessed a kind heart, and moreover he fancied that she rather liked him.

And so she did like him. Her own son having died she had grown indulgent towards all budding saplings; and then

Jan's handsome face was hard to resist as he eagerly scanned her fresh, sun-warmed fruits:

'Tè, you shall taste them, mon gars,' she would smile, remembering the son who had dearly loved peaches.

But wherever he went it was now much the same; he appeared to think of nothing but eating: 'Càspi, I am hungry,' he would say, getting home, 'Maman, give me some cheese and a fat chunk of bread. I cannot endure to wait until dinner!'

'You are worse than Christophe!' his mother would snap.

Then Jan would shock her by being disgusting: he would laugh and protest that a ver solitaire was a very exacting and active worm, requiring to be constantly nourished and pampered: 'Otherwise it will bite!' he might say with a grin, 'So please hurry before it becomes really angry.'

And while she prepared the impromptu meal he would quietly slip away to his bedroom, there to put the peaches under the bed together with the gifts from fat Madame Hermitte. And these would be joined a little later by cheese and thick bread from his breeches' pocket. As crafty as any conjurer he grew at decieving his grumbling and stingy mother: 'Look, it has gone!' he would suddenly exclaim, 'All gone! Pecaire, my poor worm was famished.'

It might be the next day that he sought out Christophe, or perhaps it might be the very same evening: 'Let us hide ourselves,' he would mutter darkly, as though they were once more playing at pirates, 'let us hide and examine my ill-gotten spoils—I bulge with them.' So off they would go to the attic.

Then Jan would produce the food he had hoarded, somewhat flattened and bruised but none the less welcome; and seeing the peaches Christophe would pause, knowing well that they ought to be saved for his brother. But in the end conscience would have to give place to the ravening claims of that growing body; skins and all, he would quickly devour the lot, scarcely waiting to spit out the rough, stringy stones—this to Jan's never failing distress and amazement.

'Ah, Christophe, ai! las, ai! las . ...' he might say, no longer able to feel light-hearted.

But Christophe would heave a deep sigh of content as he turned his attention to bread and cheese, or to Hermitte's sweet cakes and delectable croissants.

Jan was becoming much gentler these days, for now he in his turn was stirred by compassion, so that when the feasting had come to an end he would often listen with patience and tact to much that he privately thought must be fancy. Christophe would tell of those glorious swims, and of how when he gave himself up to the water he would feel like a creature without a soul, like a part of the sea and completely happy. And then he would tell of those walks in the vineyards, of the untroubled vines with their lovely greenness, of the earth that knew neither sorrow nor pain, of the smell of the earth that was full of contentment. Yes, but then he would tell of the madness of Anfos, of his father's bitter, destructive anger, and of all that was devastating their home, turning peace to turmoil, achievement to ruin. And one evening he tried very hard to tell of those words which possessed the power of healing.

'You see, they are in me, Jan,' he said gravely; 'yet often I seem to hear someone speak them who is very far off. But then comes the thought that there is no time and no distance; it is all here and now . . . it is all only ONE, but I do not know what. . . .' His pale eyes sought Jan's face, 'It is all only one, just one,' he repeated.

Jan said anxiously: 'It may be that you are hungry. I have read that those who need food will imagine many things—I must try to bring you more food. Perhaps I can even bring you some meat, although that is less easy to get from my mother.' In his heart he was thinking: 'He will never make a priest. Supposing he should talk in this queer way to sinners, supposing he should suddenly start to preach about there being no time and no distance, about everything being only one thing; they would think he was mad—even madder than Anfos.' But when Christophe insisted that it was not hunger, divining the doubt in the heart of his cousin, Jan found his hand and held it in his: 'I am going to pray to our Lady of Good Counsel, for I cannot myself comprehend what it means any more than you can, and perhaps she will help. God is three and yet one—do you think it means that?'

Christophe shook his head: 'More, oh, a great deal more; and sometimes it seems to come very near, but then it goes back and I lose it again.'

'Goes back?' murmured Jan.

'Yes, back into me . . . deep down . . . and when it is very deep down it is lost because I can no longer think it . . . because. . . .' He hesitated, bewildered.

And now his strange eyes looked almost beseeching so that Jan made a last rather desperate effort: 'I have it!' he cried, 'I now know what it means; the oneness you speak of means your Communion. By receiving the wafer you receive our Lord. Of course that is what it means, your Communion.'

Christophe's hand turned suddenly icy cold as it lay in the firm, warm clasp of his cousin, and he shivered a little: 'No . . . not even that. It means more than receiving the Host—even more. But I cannot, ah, no, I cannot explain; only sometimes I feel that its meaning is—dreadful.'

Jan said solemnly, 'Nothing can mean more than God.'

'Yes—but what does God mean?' whispered Christophe.

CHAPTER TWENTY-SEVEN

I

TIME went by: it was autumn, it was winter, it was Christmas. Jóusè confessed that he drank too much wine, that his heart was consumed by bitterness, that he frequently felt a hot uprush of anger. Striking his breast he mumbled these things, his bulk disposed awkwardly in the confessional which was shallow and cramped, so that Jóusè's big feet stuck out ludicrously from its green serge curtain. The Curé rebuked, advised and forgave, sighing because of his penitent's sins but also because his own back was aching—he was now sixty-six and his body grew stiff when he sat for too long in the same position.

'Make a good act of contrition,' he sighed. And Jóusè made an act of contrition.

After this he lumbered away to his home, resisting an overwhelming desire to turn in for a minute or two at la Tarasque, trying not to think of past Christmas Eves that had been so prosperous, happy and peaceful, but above all trying not to hate Kahn: 'Ai,' he muttered as he took his way past Kahn's shop, 'it is hard indeed to be a good Christian.'

At the midday meal he abstained from liquor and in consequence grew so deeply depressed that the house seemed stifled beneath his depression. A large, desolate, penitent sinner indeed, whose confession had brought him no comfort or peace, but only a sense of renewed desolation. And what could they do? It was dreadful to see him sitting hunched in his chair and he near to weeping. Marie racked her brains for encouraging words, Christophe tried his best to distract and amuse him, even Loup became docile and ate the food that his mother had prepared, without complaint; but Jóusè's whole being was one immense ache for the solace that lay so close to his hand . . . the strong comforting wine from the vineyards of Provence.

Then quite suddenly Anfos began to laugh, and he laughed and laughed, losing all self-control, so that he choked and spat out his soup which ran down his beard and the front of his shirt—a thick, greasy trickle mixed with saliva. Clutching the tip of his beard he sucked it, still choking and gasping and spluttering with laughter, until in the end he must hold his side and his belly: 'O! O! Ai . . . ai . . . O! O!' And he rocked himself now this way and now that, 'O! O! . . . Ai . . . ai; ai . . . ai . . .' spluttered Anfos in a kind of agonized ecstasy.

Without warning, Jóusè leant forward and struck him.

2

Midnight Mass; the altar blazing with candles because once long ago a solitary star had served the wise kings from the East as a beacon. Midnight Mass; the church fragrant with clouds of incense because once long ago the reek and the steam of cattle, the sweating of anxious peasants, incredulous, frightened and wholly amazed, had lain heavy upon the air of a stable. Midnight Mass; the Curé robed in white vestments of satin embroidered richly with silver, because once long ago a Child had been born very crudely and harshly into this world, with scarcely a fold for His swaddling. Midnight Mass; God's atonement, man's reparation.

From the organ-loft came the voices of children, hesitating, uncertain—Adeste Fideles.

'Ye faithful, approach with joy and with triumph.' Then suddenly everyone singing at once in the prayer-book-latin they had known since their childhood: 'Come ye; oh, come ye, to Bethlehem. Come and behold Him, born King of the angels.'

'Oh, come let us worship; oh, come let us worship,' sang Jóusè, his voice booming up from his chest, 'Oh, come, let us worship, Christ the Lord. God of God, Light of Light . . .' The high-sounding words came loudly and confidently from his lips, but his mind was disturbed because of a bruise that was staining the drawn, puzzled face of Anfos.

R

'Lo, He disdains not the womb of the Virgin. Very God, begotten and not created. . . .' Anfos was slowly stroking his hurt and wailing painfully out of tune, 'Oh, come, let us worship Christ the Lord.' The notes wavered, growing jerky, confused, as Anfos still stroked, then prodded his cheek; and he missed out the final lines of the verse, got scared and began all over again, 'Ye faithful, approach with joy and with triumph. . . .'

Then some impulse made Jóusè look at his son. Christophe was standing unnaturally still, his lips closed, his eyes fixed on the blazing altar; and as Jóusè looked his voice died in his throat. Ah, but no, this was only some trick of the candles! Curse them; why must they blow about in the draught, making grotesque and preposterous shadows? It was only a shadow on the boy's left cheek. What else could it be that seemed so like a bruise. . . ?

Anfos found his place and finished the hymn: 'The Word of the Father has appeared in our flesh. Oh, come, let us worship Christ the Lord.'

3

The Mass was over. They made their way to the Crèche, Marie holding Loup by the hand, Jóusè following with Anfos and Christophe.

'Hurry, hurry!' hissed Anfos in Christophe's ear. He was greatly excited because of a lamb that Jóusè had allowed him to carve for the Curé.

The Crèche had a corner all to itself, and around it was gathered a crowd of the faithful. Some were selfishly trying to tell their beads while others must wait, craning over their shoulders. The rocks of the cavern that had served as a stable, were of cardboard covered with painted paper. The Christ was of wax, with a waxen smile; Mary and Joseph were made of plaster as were also the three wise kings from the East, the shepherds, the sheep, the ox and the ass, so that the lamb carved from Jóusè's fine oak by Anfos, had quite a distinguished appearance.

Jóusè pushed his way forward to where Madame Roustan was reciting The Five Joyful Mysteries, without joy but with obvious determination: 'Pardon, Germaine, my wife also would kneel,' he muttered; whereupon Madame Roustan glared, then reluctantly ceded her place to Marie.

And after awhile there was room for them all to kneel down, so Anfos could see his lamb which the Curé had been careful to place in the foreground: 'Bèu Diéu,' remarked Anfos with deep admiration, 'Bèu Diéu,' and he eagerly stretched his hand across the low railing and stroked the creature.

Marie caught the hand and held it in hers: 'The lamb now belongs to Jesus,' she whispered, 'and He may not wish you to play with His toys.'

'But I also belong to Jesus,' said Anfos. Then he suddenly remembered the pain of his bruise and fell to prodding his cheek once again.

'Càspi! Now why must he do that?' thought Jóusè.

Loup started to fidget; his knees were so thin that they generally ached a good deal when he knelt, and moreover he had come to the end of his prayers which were briefer than those of his aunt, Madame Roustan. So now he could think of nothing to say—that is nothing that seemed to fit the occasion—for his thoughts had grown somewhat undisciplined and were dwelling upon Eusèbe's legends. He sighed noisily, shifting from knee to knee, biting his nails and dropping his Prayer Book, so that Marie released the apprentice's hand in order to put an arm round Loup's shoulders. And as she did this she remembered the time when he had lain helpless upon her bosom; so small he had been, le pauvre tout petit Loup, and because of his smallness so deeply appealing. Nor was she the only mother that morning to indulge herself in such gentle remembering as she looked at the Baby of Bethlehem who must lie upon straw from the corn-chandler's warehouse—Simon always sent up the straw for the Crèche, it represented his Christmas donation.

A crude and primitive thing that Crèche, having much that was pitifully childish about it; having neither imagination nor skill; having neither dignity, art, nor beauty. Yet to those who looked upon it with faith, to the work-worn women who must bear many children, to the work-worn men who must ceaselessly toil, it appeared very natural and reassuring because, somehow, so much a part of themselves.

Mary and Joseph . . . no room at the inn. . . . Ah, yes, there was often no room at the inn for those who were not possessed of riches. Pecaire, and the Child just about to be born! Ah, the poor blessèd Mother . . . no room at the inn. And surely she must have felt terribly tired, for had she not come a very long journey? Thus they saw in that primitive Crèche at Saint Loup many things that suggested their own situations, and would frequently leave it greatly consoled, so that what it lacked in artistic worth it made up for in the worth of the Spirit.

And to Christophe also there came consolation as he knelt with clasped hands in front of the Infant. For he seemed to divine many simple hearts; nay more, to divine that all goodness was simple with the wise and courageous simplicity of a God indivisible from His creation. And seeing the sheep, the ox and the ass who had given their Lord their humble manger, he perceived that they, too, the dumb patient beasts, had been lifted up on that day of salvation; that the Christ who had willed to be born in their midst had thereby acknowledged a brotherhood which must stretch far beyond the limits of time, since He who conferred the grace was eternal. So now Christophe prayed very confidently, and the prayer that he offered was for Mirèio, who greatly loving had greatly fulfilled the law of her lowly but faithful existence: 'I would like You to keep her with You,' he prayed, 'until I come, Lord . . . until I come. She was very obedient when she was here so I do not think You will find her much trouble; but she may feel a little bit lost without me because, as You know, we were never apart. Please Lord, do not let Mirèio feel lonely.' Then he suddenly added, 'And take care of Anfos.'

CHAPTER TWENTY-EIGHT

I

SPRING came, and as though the hopeful season only served to make Jóusè more hopeless by contrast, his fits of sudden anger increased as did also those moods of despondent brooding. Not for long had he managed to keep from wine after that sterile Christmas confession, but now when he drank there would follow remorse—a fresh scourge for tormented, drink-sodden nerves and arteries growing always more brittle. At such times he could hardly endure to see Anfos with his mouth sagging open as he bent to his carving, and yet he must stare at the ungainly sight as though it possessed some grim fascination:

'Diéu!' he would mutter; 'the man looks like a beast; that face of his has become scarcely human.'

And conscious of those watchful, hostile eyes, Anfos would often jump up in a panic, letting the carving slip from his knees as he scuttled away to hide himself in the attic, the shed, or even the privy. Then Jóusè would heave an unhappy sigh and turn to his son as though dumbly appealing: 'What am I doing?' he would seem to ask, as his bloodshot and hostile eyes grew remorseful.

In silence Christophe would leave the workshop, bent on consoling the luckless apprentice, and the man would cling to him desperately: 'They will send poor Anfos away, little master, and what will become of him all alone? No one cares for him but you, little master.' And one morning he said a curious thing: 'Mirèio and Anfos . . . I think, the same . . . because of their love . . . because of God's love, your love, God's love . . . I think, somehow, the same. Do not send us from you. . . .' And he dropped to his knees looking up into Christophe's compassionate eyes.

Then Christophe in his turn said a strange thing:

'Where you are I am; where you go I shall come. There is no separation, no going away. . . .' He paused, bewildered by his own words.

'Bèu Diéu! Ah, Bèu Diéu!' smiled Anfos.

And true it was that Jóusè had been thinking of ridding himself of his mad apprentice—a dark thought that had lately possessed his mind, though he knew that the unhappy creature was harmless. But Anfos made one more mouth to feed, one more body for which he must somehow find clothing while his own two sons went ill-fed and ill-clothed; and then there was now that growing aversion.

He said to Christophe quite casually one evening when they were alone in the workshop together: 'I shall have to get Anfos put under restraint. He is mad, and we are too poor to keep him. I shall of course ask our Curé's advice, for I would not wish him unkindly treated, but I know that many asylums exist where such penniless people are cared for free. I shall also have to consult the doctor.' He did not look at his son as he spoke, but busied himself about his bench. 'Say nothing as yet to your mother,' he finished.

It had come, the thing Christophe had long been dreading; the thing that the madman himself had known through the strange intuition of the insane, the thing that had made him beg for protection. And yet Christophe could see that judged by the world, by the common standards of human reason, his father would surely be justified, for their stock of money was fast decreasing. But judged by something that was far more profound, by the reason that animated the spirit, this desertion of Anfos was terrible indeed, though less for the servant than for the master.

'My father,' he cried, at that moment unable to pause and consider what he was saying, 'my father, it cannot, it must not be. Anfos would die of grief if he left us. You dare not betray him because of our want. Ah, but listen, my father, Anfos feels love, and those who feel love—even if they are mad—become one with God. Will you drive God away? Will you make Him suffer because we are poor?' The words sounded preposterous, ridiculous, crazy, and hearing them Christophe came near to despair: 'I cannot put it quite clearly . . .' he stammered.

Then Jóusè turned with rage on his son: 'But yes, but

yes, you have put it too clearly. Very well do I understand what this means; you care more for that madman than for your parents. You care more for Anfos, it seems, than for Loup who goes short of his food because of the man. A fine story! Would you have me believe that your God expects me to starve my own flesh and blood in order that I may nourish a stranger? Bien, then I say that you also are mad! I will not keep the fellow, no, by God I will not, if I have to drive him into the street, if I have to fling him out with these hands. . . .' The rasping voice suddenly choked and stopped as Jóusè pitched forward and crashed to the ground like a tree beneath the last blow of the woodsman.

They heard the thud of his fall and rushed in, Marie and Loup and the terrified Anfos. And a mighty man indeed Jóusè looked, lying there with his bulk outstretched on the floor near his work-bench among the sawdust and shavings. Marie knelt down beside him, stroking his forehead with fingers that neither faltered nor trembled, and when she spoke her voice sounded cold, for some anguish defies all human expression.

'Loup, go at once for the doctor, my child.' Then: 'I think we must try to get him upstairs. Run, Anfos, and ask Eusèbe to help us.'

Pale to the lips Loup hurried away, glad of any excuse to escape from his father's face, for now there was blood on the beard; Jóusè had grazed his chin badly in falling.

Poor Anfos dashed headlong across the road: 'Come . . . come . . . come and help us, she says,' he spluttered, tugging at Eusèbe's sleeve and forgetting his erstwhile fear of the man in his eagerness to make him move faster; 'so big, so big, so enormous, so . . . quiet.' And Anfos suddenly started to sob, while keeping his grip on the grimy sleeve as he dragged its owner towards the doorway.

In this fashion they returned to the Bénédit's house, Eusèbe protesting and Anfos sobbing. But when Eusèbe saw what had occurred he flung out his arms: 'Houi!' he exclaimed, his black eye very wise and full of compassion. 'Houi! Now here is a terrible thing to have happened to so good and stalwart a fellow!' And because he was deeply distressed, he spat.

'I would wish to get Jóusè to bed,' Marie told him.

So Eusèbe seized Jóusè's thick shoulders and tugged, tripped over his long leather apron, cursed loudly and started to tug again.

'Ah, but gently . . . move him gently,' begged Christophe, going to the small sandal-maker's aid, as did Marie and the still weeping apprentice.

How they finally got Jóusè up the steep stairs Marie never knew, for her husband's weight seemed incredible, unendurable almost. His head drooped limply, jerking a little from time to time with their stumbling movements, so that she felt that her heart must break to see him so dumb, so afflicted and helpless.

'Ai,' she thought, 'and my Jóusè would jest about Death! Ai, ai, it is foolish to jest about Death, for who can be sure that he is not listening.'

When at last Jóusè lay stretched out on the bed Eusèbe stood looking down at him grimly. Then he rubbed a trickle of sweat from his eye, and a tear that had somehow got mixed up with it: 'Tron de Diéune!' he swore angrily under his breath, surprised and disgusted at his own emotion. After which he departed without more ado and made his way down to Mère Mélanie's café.

2

The doctor arrived to find Jóusè still unconscious : 'Your poor husband has had a stroke,' he told Marie, 'but I think he will live—yes, I think he will live; though we cannot yet know the extent of the hæmorrhage.' It appeared that little or nothing could be done except to wait with courage and patience.

Towards dawn Jóusè suddenly opened his eyes: 'Where am I? What is it?' he mumbled thickly; and he tried to raise himself in the bed. 'My left side, all gone; all gone . . . my left side.'

'Hush, belovèd, you must lie quite still,' Marie warned him.

But Jóusè was restless: 'I want my son . . . not Loup, I want the other . . . not Loup. . . .'

Christophe said quietly: 'I am here.' And he laid his cheek on the tumbled pillow.

Jóusè tried to smile: 'Ah, bon, you are here . . . What happened? I cannot . . . seem to remember.'

Then Christophe thanked God in his grief-stricken heart: 'I am close to you always—but always,' he whispered.

Very slowly Jóusè found the boy's hand, and raising it to his lips he kissed it.

3

Later on that morning Marie said to Christophe: 'You two were alone; tell me just what happened.'

'It was Anfos . . .' he faltered uncertainly; 'I did not want him to be sent away, for he needs us so much . . .' And then he told her.

She listened to him in absolute silence, but when at last he had finished speaking she said: 'That was not your father, my child—your father is kind and courageous and generous. Did he not beg poor Anfos to share our home? Did he not go and bring him down from the mountains when you were still a small baby in arms? It was surely not your father who spoke of turning him out, but your father's illness. We say many strange things when we are ill, and the saints who are good and wise do not listen—or if they do listen they always forget. Let us also forget as your father has forgotten. And now I must put some fresh ice on his head.'

Thus did Marie release her son from blame very simply, even as she released her husband.

CHAPTER TWENTY-NINE

THE Curé stood tall and erect in the pulpit. His brown and slightly prominent eyes which of late had been dulled by advancing years, now blazed with fanaticism. Extending an arm and a long white finger he pointed down at his congregation who stared back at the finger with something like awe as their pastor continued to address them. The Curé's voice rang out like a challenge. It was virile, the voice of a man of twenty whose physical passions were clamorous, who could love and hate with intensity should passion once get the better of reason.

A deep hush brooded over the ancient church, brooded over those pallid upturned faces, for the Curé was gripping them one and all. He whose bloodless sermons they had slept through so often, was now skilfully playing upon their emotions as a master will play on a violin, so that beyond a few gasping sighs his words struck sharply on silence.

'Rise up! Rise up!' cried the Curé Martel, 'Defend yourselves against the blasphemers! The barbarians have invaded France, our belovèd soil is beneath their heel, and like Attila they will show no mercy. Ah, my brothers, my sisters, the soil of France is sobbing and looking to you for deliverance. The very stones are crying aloud for deliverance, yes, but also for vengeance! The German hordes are defiling Liège, they are raping and slaying women and children. Belgium weeps this day side by side with France, they two are united in the bonds of affliction. Their daughters are outraged, their sons are slain, their holy places are being polluted. It is surely the Anti-Christ who has come. In the name of the true Christ, rise up and destroy him!

'Ah, my brothers, my sisters, I stand here before you as your priest, but I also stand here as a man who is filled with a righteous and enduring anger. And as priest and man I solemnly declare that for us this war is a holy war against a people possessed by Satan. Yes, and this I declare in the name of peace, as one who has given himself to Christ's service: there can be no Christian peace in the world, no peace that is truly pleasing to God until Germany lies defeated in the dust and burnt in the flames of her own damnation! Therefore listen you who are the fathers of sons, give your sons without stint, give them nobly, gladly, for to-day there is only one Father—God; and God it is who demands them of you. And you who are the mothers of sons listen also, give your sons without tears, give them splendidly, sternly, for to-day there is only one Mother—France; and France it is who demands them of you. And you who are in the first pride of your manhood, leave all for the sake of God and your country; for the sake of a noble and honourable cause, for the sake of our hard-won civilization. As I look upon you I feel my own youth rushing back to me through your superb young valour. I feel your strength entering into my arms, and into my voice, and into my heart; and I say to the Christ: "Here are those who will fight for the cross upon which You were crucified!" And to France I say: "Behold your defenders!"'

The Curé made the sign of salvation and left the pulpit—the sermon was over.

2

Marie walked home between her sons and her brown peasant face was patient but puzzled. A momentous disaster had fallen upon France, this they had all known before that sermon; indeed they had known it for seven long days, talking of little else in their homes, in the streets and in the cafés. And yet Marie's face was patient but puzzled as she strove for a fuller understanding of what this momentous disaster might mean and, still striving, fell far short of realization. For in spite of the Curé's impassioned outburst, August brooded placidly over Saint Loup, filming the distant mountains with haze; while down in the harbour not a vessel stirred, so immeasurably peaceful and blue lay the water.

She said: 'That was surely a very fine sermon—very fine.'
But her voice was lacking in conviction. She was tired and
the war seemed a long way away; much farther away than
the large pile of laundry which should have been finished
on the previous evening—for now Marie must earn by
washing for neighbours. Then she said: 'It is strange how
trouble breeds trouble. Only four months ago came your
poor father's seizure, and it may be that never again will he
stand; then comes this terrible German invasion.' But
Christophe knew that her thoughts were less of the German
invasion than of his father.

He nodded, finding no adequate answer, conscious only
of a wellnigh unendurable sadness, of a kind of inexplicable
grief which had come upon him all unawares as he sat in the
quiet, familiar church and listened to that unfamiliar voice,
so unlike the monotonous voice of the Curé. He had been
deeply stirred by those eloquent words, catching fire from
the man's fanatical anger, so that he also had felt enraged
against those who had planned to destroy his country;
enraged and elated because of his rage, and because he might
one day go to the war unless, as some thought, it were
quickly over. He had seen himself fighting shoulder to
shoulder with Jan while the regiment cheered their courage.
A vision of glory had obsessed his mind as he pictured the
battlefields of France with all a boy's childish but courageous
illusions, with all the chivalry of his youth and a certain
stubborn simplicity bequeathed to him by his peasant
forebears; but then had come that strange feeling of grief
for which he could still find no explanation.

His silence, however, passed unnoticed, for le tout petit
Loup was intensely excited and was trying to walk with a
martial stride as though he already felt himself to be marching—he was making the best of his four foot eight by craning
his neck and squaring his shoulders.

'Tron de Diéune!' swore le tout petit Loup in his piping
voice; 'I will kill any German who dares to show his face
in our town. Ai! las, that I am not a few years older! But I
grow. Maman, am I not growing quite fast? I shall soon be
tall enough to enlist; I shall tell them that I am nearly
eighteen and then they will let me become a poilu. Already
I can smoke without being sick . . .' And he suddenly

produced a bent Caporal from his breeches pocket, and proceeded to light it.

Marie snatched the cigarette out of his hand: 'What is this? Who has taught you to smoke?' she demanded.

But le tout petit Loup shrugged his shoulders and grinned: 'One cannot remain a baby for ever. At my age one smokes as a matter of course; moreover I find that it helps my asthma. And as I get up at half-past five every morning in order to sweep the bazaar for that pig of a Bled, I certainly feel that I am entitled to spend a few centimes on a packet of cigarettes now and then.' And he actually winked quite a large wink at Christophe.

Marie sighed. It was true enough that he worked before school in order that he might assist them, and this fact had made him exceedingly proud—it had also made him exceedingly daring. More daring than ever had Loup become, and so defiant that she could not control him.

Christophe worked these days at Jóusè's old bench with Anfos to help whenever work offered, struggling to keep the business afloat in spite of his youth and his limited training, for he knew how much this meant to his father. And a number of people had rallied to the boy, doing all in their power to give him simple employment, so shocked had they been by Jóusè's stroke, but in spite of their kindness the burden was great for such young and inexperienced shoulders. Yet to hear Loup talk was to think that he only was willing and smart enough to earn money. A scandal it was the way the imp bragged as he jangled a couple of sous in his pocket, as he told how he cheeked the fat Monsieur Bled and had once dropped a dust-pan on to his corn for the fun of hearing him howl with anguish:

'Hoi! but he howled!' bragged le tout petit Loup, 'Yes, and now he is careful to leave me in peace, for of course he could see that I did it on purpose.'

Ai! las, ai! las, le pauvre tout petit Loup; he must cough while he swept for all his fine bragging. The dust would get into his treacherous lungs and the impudence would be smothered by coughing; and when he got home for his scanty meal before going to school, he might have palpitations because so much coughing had tired his heart which was less pugnacious, it seemed, than its owner. And knowing these things his mother was indulgent, as indeed she always had been in his case, for if Christophe was still the apple of her eye, le tout petit Loup remained the fruit of her compassion. So now she pretended not to notice the wink, or the fresh cigarette which he took from a packet and jauntily stuck behind his small ear, in spite of the fact that the day was a Sunday.

'We must hurry, my children,' she said amiably. 'Your father will be wanting to hear the news. He will also wish to be told about the sermon.'

<h2 style="text-align:center">3</h2>

Jóusè was lying on the massive oak bedstead upon which his father had lain before him. Here his parents had consummated their love, bred children, and finally passed to the beyond. And here he himself had deflowered his wife, bred children, and would almost certainly die—in accordance with the Bénédit tradition. The bed was so large that it dwarfed the room, leaving but little space for its neighbours—a washstand, two chairs and a small chest of drawers were all that could find accommodation. Above the bed hung a crucifix, and beside it, very quiet but watchful, crouched Anfos.

Jóusè sighed, and Anfos stumbling up went and fetched his master a glass of water, holding it clumsily to his lips while the water spilled itself over the quilt and splashed down the front of Jóusè's nightshirt: 'Cool . . .' said Anfos, sticking his finger in the glass and smiling.

'Ah, yes . . . it is cool,' agreed Jóusè.

The room was heavy with the heat of summer. The small blind seemed unable to quench the sunshine, the small window unable to let in fresh air, so that what air there was smelt of clothing and illness—the smell peculiar to poverty and to those among the poor who are ailing. Anfos returned to his place on the floor, shaking some drops of sweat off his brow like a dog that has just scrambled out of a pond. From a cork-tree in a neighbouring yard came the ceaseless creaking drone of cingalas.

Jóusè's body was so still that it might have been carved in the oak of one of his own blocks of timber. His left hand must perforce remain motionless, but even his right hand lay without motion; only his eyes seemed possessed of life as they turned and rested upon the door with a questioning, anxious expression of waiting. It would often be thus, he would lie for hours with his eyes on the door when Christophe was absent; and if Marie and both the boys left the house the faithful madman would crouch beside him, clumsy but solicitous, demented but mild—indeed Jóusè must sometimes smile to observe how diligently he strove to be gentle, for now he bore Anfos no resentment.

Had Jóusè forgotten? They could never be sure and were careful that nothing should occur to remind him. The rest of his past he remembered clearly; Mirèio he remembered, and Anatole Kahn who had come from the north to ruin his business, and his own despair which had led him to drink, and then his awakening to consciousness towards dawn on the fearful night of his seizure. Two things only his mind appeared to have mislaid—his repugnance to Anfos and his quarrel with Christophe. But even those other memories would now often seem like dreams to Jóusè; like dreams sometimes sweet, sometimes brave, sometimes sad, and sometimes shot through with a searing anger . . . but dreams. . . . Perhaps all life was just dreams? Lying there the paralysed man would wonder.

The front door banged. Ah, bon, they were home at last. They were coming upstairs: 'Christophe . . . Christophe!'

The name sounded blurred and Jóusè frowned; he was now much troubled by a thickness of speech which he had some ado to endure with patience. This and his sores were his greatest cross; he had dark, inflamed sores at the base of his spine—the doctor said it was because he lay heavy.

Christophe came in with Loup and Marie, and as always he was struck by his father's whiteness; Jóusè's hair and beard were as white as snow, and the flush which had long since died from his face had left behind it a waxen pallor. No colour anywhere save in his eyes; his eyes had grown wonderfully young and clear, and as blue as a patch of sea in a mistral. But above all the hands that lay on the quilt never failed to rivet the boy's attention. Those once capable hands tanned by wind and sun and hard manual labour to the colour of bronze were now as waxen as the skin of the face; and delicate they looked, like a bedridden woman's.

Christophe said: 'It goes better with you, my father?'

Jóusè nodded: 'But yes, it goes better with me, except for that sore on the right of my back—I have christened him Job!' And he smiled a wry smile. Then: 'I wish you would come here and touch my back; something in your touch seems to ease the pain.'

A long pause ensued, and when Christophe spoke he was shocked by what he heard himself saying: 'That is nonsense! There is nothing in my touch to ease pain; it must surely be your imagination. There is nothing, I tell you, to ease pain in my touch.'

But Jóusè looked at him quietly: 'Imagination . . . reality . . . Is there then so great a difference between them?' And his eyes held a kind of solemn reproach.

'Eh bien, I will do as you wish,' sighed Christophe.

Helped by Anfos he turned Jóusè on to his side, then placed a timid hand over the sore, feeling all the while very greatly afraid, because he must remember the death of Mirèio. Afraid, yet conscious that his touch did, in fact, possess some incomprehensible virtue which fear went far to deprive of its power, and this knowledge but served to make him the more fearful.

Marie was diligently dusting the room, and as she dusted she told of the sermon, then went on to give Jóusè the news of the war: 'It appears so impossible, so unreal that I do not seem able to grasp it,' she finished.

Jóusè listened, closing his eyes and his lips; the latter in case he should be tempted to tell her of the things that his eyes had actually seen as far back as 1870, on the bitter and terrible field of Sédan. He had never spoken of those things to his wife although sometimes he had shown her his medals. Ah, well, here he lay only half alive; old, paralysed, and with sores on his loins; unable to lift so much as a finger in defence of France . . . Jóusè groaned aloud.

'Am I pressing too hard?' Christophe asked anxiously.

'No, my son; no, no, it was something inside. Marie, get me those medals out of the drawer. They should be under my best black tie; or perhaps I left them under my pants . . . Have you found them?'

'Yes, they are here,' she answered.

Le tout petit Loup sidled up to his mother: 'Let me hold them,' he pleaded, 'just for a moment.'

'Well, only for a moment then,' Marie warned, 'No, Loup, I forbid you to put them on!' But Loup was already in front of the mirror.

'Be careful! Ah, be careful!' Jóusè exclaimed, 'The ribbons are frayed, they may easily break.' And his speech was more laboured and indistinct because he felt worried yet utterly helpless, and because he was beginning to realize that a bedridden man who survives too long may outlast the regard accorded to illness. For le tout petit Loup ignored him completely, twisting the medals this way and that, in order that he might admire their effect: 'I have said . . . do not do it . . . the ribbons will break. Put them down. I have said . . . put them down,' stammered Jóusè.

Then quite suddenly Christophe could bear it no longer. swinging round he grasped Loup's shoulder and shook him: 'Will you give me those medals?'

'I will not!' Loup snapped.

'But I say that you must.'

'And I say I will not!'

'Ah, bon, I shall have to take them,' frowned Christophe, dumping his brother onto a chair and proceeding forthwith to unfasten the medals.

A fine hubbub to break out around a man's ears! Loup yelled as though he were being murdered: 'Bèsti!' he yelled as he struggled and fought, working himself into one of his rages, 'Bèsti!' And he managed to slap Christophe's face with all the strength that his weak arm could muster.

Hit him back? Christophe dared not hit such a wisp. He was cowed, as Jóusè had been, by Loup's weakness. All he could do was to rub his cheek; half angry, half pitiful, half amused: 'It would seem that your muscles improve,' he murmured.

And meanwhile Anfos had started to moan, slowly and rhythmically rocking his body as though he were keeping time to the dirge of his long-drawn-out and lugubrious moaning.

Marie clasped her hands in a kind of despair: 'Boudiéu! what a way to behave—what a way! Loup, I command you, be silent this instant!'

But le tout petit Loup continued to storm, though his fury had brought on a fit of coughing: 'I think I will hit him again,' he choked, glaring defiantly at his mother.

A fine hubbub to break out around a man's ears! Jóusè tried to shift his position but failed—his sore was aching again quite badly. The sun burnt his eyes even through the blind, even through his eyelids when he had closed them, and his paralysed side felt as heavy as lead—like a corpse he told himself that it felt, and must start to wonder about this, dumbly. The noise and confusion had worn him out, so that his face showed the slight distortion that had been bequeathed to it by the stroke; his mouth sagged a little, downwards and open . . . If only that sore would leave him in peace . . . if only Anfos would try not to moan . . . if only Loup would stop coughing and storming. . . .

In the end Marie pushed Loup out of the room and turned the key on him: 'Ai! las,' she sighed, 'he grows more impossible to manage every day. Ai! las, what is going to become of my Loup? So small he is, yet with such immense rages.'

But Christophe had turned to look at his father; and he noticed the mouth with its unconscious sagging, and the terrible stillness of the stricken side, and the terrible patience of the closed, wrinkled eyelids; indeed all that was pitiful he must observe with the keen and relentless sight of the spirit, scourging himself for his own harsh words, for the fear that he seemed unable to conquer even in the presence of so mighty a need: 'I am surely a very great coward,' thought Christophe.

Then he quietly walked across to the bed, trying as he did so to move with precaution lest the crazy old boards of the floor should creak, and he laid the worn medals in Jóusè's hand with a gentle and very courteous respect.

'Pin them onto my nightshirt . . . ' Jóusè mumbled.

CHAPTER THIRTY

I

As the fearful summer of 1914 dragged its festering wounds on into the autumn, Marie grasped the meaning of war all too well, for war preyed like a vulture on northern France and even on peaceful and distant Provence. The abortive recapture of Alsace and Lorraine with its triumph and subsequent humiliation, the grim fighting retreat of the English from Mons, the bombing of the cathedral at Malines, the tales of outraged and slaughtered civilians, these things gathered over Saint Loup like black clouds, menacing its homes with sorrow and death as the women of Provence gave their men—a proud but very terrible giving.

Marie Bénédit looked at her sons, and strive though she might to put her country before even them in this hour of its need, she yet thanked God that her sons were so young; God and His Golden Saints she must thank, for while man created the patriot, it was God Himself who created the mother. Kneeling at the shrine of the warrior-bishop, which now blazed with perpetual votive candles, she prayed that peace be restored to the world, that the days of their tribulation be shortened. And beside her might kneel the plump Madame Hermitte who also had sons and they older than Marie's, or the Simons whose Guillaume had gone to the front, or Elise whose husband was still of the age and the disposition to see active service. Madame Roustan, as likely as not, would be there, grown a trifle pale and a trifle subdued because her Jan was four months Christophe's senior—even a few months might count later on, might make all the difference between life and death, supposing the war were of long duration.

In and out of the church went Monsieur le Curé, rejoiced by the sight of those blazing candles; and quite often he would be accompanied by Jan, sometimes bent upon prayer, sometimes bent upon tasks in connection with the vestry, or perhaps the altar. Jan's face had an eager yet stern expression, for his mind was obsessed by the Curé's preaching. Stern, too, were the prayers that he offered up as he knelt on the punishing stones of the aisle, feeling glad that the stones should bite into his knees, since those who might be privileged to fight must first begin by subduing their bodies. And meanwhile the clouds grew more ominous as the German guns crept nearer to Paris, so that scarcely a home not already bereaved, but was overshadowed by the threat of bereavement. A mighty torrent of anguish and death was sweeping over France and her people.

2

Goundran said to his wife: 'In a few weeks' time I may well be catching some very fine fishes—steel fishes with big, ugly German snouts! Thank God, I am not yet grown too old.' Then his eyes turned and rested upon the child, and all of a sudden Goundran fell silent.

Elise was carefully darning the jerseys which she knew he would never wear in the navy, but which none the less she must wash and darn because, in a way, this task was consoling. The jerseys were so much a part of himself and their life together that they seemed to protect him by forming a close link with a past that had nothing more deadly to fear than the mistral.

She looked up: 'I would like you to take these with you . . . when you go . . .'

He nodded: 'But surely I will. Why not?' And once again there was silence.

Presently he said: 'About Aurano. There is still that money untouched at the bank, and of course there would also be some small pension. And then there are my boats; they should fetch quite a lot . . . I must speak of these things.' He flushed awkwardly because one's own death was an awkward subject, especially to discuss with one's wife.

'I will try to remember all you say,' she promised.

Leaning forward he kissed her diligent hands, and at

276

this she must bend lower over the needle in case he should see the dread in her eyes, and the tears.

'Kind and very dear hands . . .' he whispered. Then because his own eyes were not guiltless of tears, he started a boisterous game with his daughter: 'Ho, hoi! what a monster we have in our net! I believe we have netted some species of dragon! Shall I tickle him under his scales—like this?' And Goundran tickled the child's small ribs.

Aurano wriggled, squealing with laughter.

*   *   *

Madame Simon sat reading a censored letter from Guillaume; he was somewhere fighting for France. Yes, but where? If only they might know where! She said: 'I would very much like to have his address—it would comfort me to have his address.' For her mind, even now, was not quite war-wise, so that sometimes she said little foolish things, still thinking in terms of safety and peace. 'Never would he fail to give me an address when he went away even for a night,' she finished.

Simon sighed as he looked at her, shaking his head—like Jóusè he had once fought against the Prussians. When a lad he had stood on the fortifications of Paris, so that Simon knew all about war and the way it had of ignoring mothers, the poor souls . . . the poor, anxious, pitiful souls . . . 'Our son's address is: La Patrie,' he told her.

She acquiesced meekly: 'Mais oui, you are right. I am stupid—I think I am growing old. Guillaume sends you his love—but read for yourself. It appears they are full of courage and hope, not at all down-hearted, our Guillaume says. And he wants us to know that he is quite well, that the life seems to suit him—that he is happy.'

*   *   *

At la Tarasque Mère Mélanie opened much wine, and not always, these days, would she accept payment.

'Non, non, mon brave! Keep your francs for yourself. And now give your Mère Mélanie a good kiss—yes, and write to her sometimes when you get the chance. Alexandre! Hurry up, Pierre waits for his wine. And be careful not to slip on the cellar stairs—you know what I told you, a bottle of porto.'

Mère Mélanie must frequently wipe her eyes, fishing her handkerchief out of the bag that contained the piety medal and the lip-stick. And the more they joked and kissed her and joked, and swore to come back, if only to please her, the more she must fish in the untidy bag. Ah, the lovely fellows!

'Alexandre! Bring champagne, a couple of bottles. Did you hear me, Alexandre? I said bring a couple of bottles of champagne; and after that you can give us some music.'

So the little violinist with the hump on his back would fetch the champagne and then begin playing. And now he played tunes that had come with the war, some of which had been brought to France by the English: 'It's a long, long way to Tipperary,' he played—rather lugubriously, it is true, for he thought this particular song melancholy.

And sometimes the clients would have none of it, but must shout instead for a hoary old favourite: ' "As tu vu les fesses de ma belle Louise?" Tafort, Alexandre! "As tu vu les fesses. . . ." '

Then the little violinist would try to grin: 'As tu vu les fesses de ma belle Louise?' he would play, swaying lightly upon his toes as the insolent ribaldry pranced from his fiddle.

Eusèbe would sit and dream in his corner; very drunk, very old, and dirtier than ever. And his dreams would be of more splendid wars, of more splendid men, of more splendid women. Helen of Troy he would love in his dreams while the wine made a mock of his unruly senses and kindled his long since impotent desires into besotted, virile illusions. Nay, even Venus he would love in his dreams, and he coming at her with the thunders of Jove . . . or was it Apollo? Or was it Ulysses? His mythology grew somewhat vague at such times, but no matter, the result would be much the same, and to Eusèbe quite satisfactory.

Then those who were about to lay down their lives might start to jeer at the old sandal-maker; less crudely, perhaps, than the men from the tartanes, but nevertheless they might start to jeer: 'Bon soir, mon général. How goes the war? Superbly, no doubt, since mon général snores! Boudiéu, what a scarecrow! We will take you along to Berlin in order to frighten the Kaiser.'

And perhaps Eusèbe would open his eyes and just stare at them blankly, vouchsafing no answer. One evening, however, he jeered in his turn: 'How goes the war? You may very well ask. "Kill!" you say. "Hate and kill, kill and hate!" you say. But I thought He told you to love one another . . .' Then he drifted back again into his dreams.

'Do not anger yourselves,' begged Mère Mélanie, 'he is drunk, mes enfants, that is why he raves.'

And because they could see that Eusèbe was drunk, they humoured her, shrugging and taking no notice.

* * *

Anatole Kahn was alone in his office. It was midnight, yet his desk was still littered with papers, for just lately he had slept very badly indeed—too many thoughts would he have in his head, and those thoughts were not always by any means pleasant. Business was staggering from blow upon blow. No one spent because no one would part with their money, so the stock he had purchased just prior to the war seemed likely to become shop-soiled in his windows. And not only this, but the villa was unsold, while its neighbour remained scarcely more than foundations. At the first crack of doom the young men from the frontier had been snatched away without adequate notice, nor had others been sent to continue the work; not the slightest effort had been made to replace them. The contractor had remarked: 'C'est la guerre, monsieur.' After which he had turned a deaf ear to all protests. For the matter of that Kahn's own men had gone; he now possessed neither joiner nor salesman.

But even before the declaration of war, the season had fallen far short of expectations, and the usual handful of artists who had come to paint the most picturesque parts of the town, had left almost as soon as the men from the frontier. They had packed up their brushes and canvases and easels with a speed that Kahn had found really astounding —some had even forgotten to pay their bills, so keen had they been to fight for their country. Thus two years in succession rooms had gone unlet to everyone's immense disappointment.

Kahn sighed; then he re-read a letter, frowning: 'We have got ourselves to consider,' ran the letter. 'Roux, as you know, we cannot consult, nor does one worry a man on active service, but on his behalf as well as our own we must remind you that the money we invested in your ventures gives us every right . . .'. .

He flung the thing down with a grunt of disgust. Already so scared and the war just begun! Fine friends, the despicable, cowardly fools! But the moratorium, ah, that was his friend, it might save him yet and with him his business. There remained the affair of the villas, pretty grim, but after all even that was not hopeless. La Sociéte Foncière du Midi could not press for interest so long as hostilities continued, and with peace there would come a house shortage, of course. Taking up his pen he began to write:

'Cher Albert. Here and now I refuse to submit . . .' No, that would not do; he tore up the sheet. 'Cher Albert,' he began all over again, 'I can only entreat you and Edouard to be patient. Of course I regret having bought that new stock, but how could I possibly foresee what has happened? And that being so I must beg yet again that you will not delay in sending the cheque; I cannot keep this place going on nothing. You say that you have all risked your money in my shop, but while the shop prospered you prospered with it, and surely to despair at the first small reverse in our fortunes, at a time like this, is bad business. Have courage, I implore you to have courage, my dear friends; with your help I can steer the ship through the storm, I can bring our venture to ultimate success . . .' In this vein he wrote on for page after page until his hand ached, and his head and heart with it.

At last he addressed the envelope. Heaven knew when the letter would reach them in Paris—the posts from Provence had always been bad, and now they were fast becoming abysmal. Then he suddenly dropped his head on to his arms. Dieu, but he was tired! perhaps he could sleep. He would try to sleep just where he sat—at his desk; better this than to risk the insomnia that generally set in after undressing.

CHAPTER THIRTY-ONE

I

THE months passed bringing neither mercy nor respite, but only fresh hatreds to corrode the heart as war swept civilization aside and men bred and reared up in the knowledge of peace were now forced to the fearful knowledge of killing. One after another such men left Saint Loup, for the most part simple, ignorant fellows who had seen only quiet and seemly death, if, indeed, death had ever crossed their vision; and one after another they must kill or be killed, since not always are battles won by ideals—they are sometimes won by self-preservation. And yet through the welter of anger and blood, of agony, mutilation and horror, there would shine out triumphantly many a deed of selfless and thus very perfect courage, as the finite claims of the quaking flesh must give place to the infinite claims of the spirit. And in this there would be neither friends nor foes, but only those who gave of their best and became as brothers because of that giving.

Completely bewildered by his own emotions which grew daily more violent and more contradictory, Christophe struggled to find the inward peace that Jan and the Curé Martel had found; what they had attained to, Christophe must seek with something approaching desperation. For now there were times when he could not endure a compassion that seemed to be all-embracing, a compassion that saw but one suffering whole on those terrible blood-drenched battlefields, that perceived neither warring rulers nor nations but only a pitiful suffering whole rushing on to destruction because of its blindness. Even love itself seemed to resent such compassion, the deep love that he felt for his native Provence; he would think that the very soil cried out, raising its voice in protest against him.

'Cannot you understand?' he would mutter, 'I love you—but cannot you understand?' And yet as he spoke them, the words would sound vague and unconvincing because he himself lacked not only conviction but understanding.

He had now little work to occupy his mind since orders were growing scarcer and scarcer, and so he would wander alone for hours through the country that he had known from his childhood, through the olive orchards climbing the hills, through the thickets of maquis and out beyond to Mirèio's grave and Eusèbe's vineyards. And wandering thus he must often indulge in imaginings that were becoming fantastic: he would hear his own name in the songs of the birds and would fancy that like the soil they reproached him.

'You are right,' he would tell them, 'it is I who am wrong. I will tear this great foolishness out of my heart—I will tear it out and trample upon it.'

Perhaps a stray mongrel would follow in his footsteps, for although he himself went short of food yet he could not endure that a beast should go hungry, and this the poor starvelings had come to know, so that one or another would slink at his heels hoping that once he had left the town he would fling a crust of bread from his pocket. The mongrel would always be covered with sores, yes and with that dreadful humility which incites the world to persecute its outcasts, and seeing this Christophe would sit for a while and fondle its head, and make it lie down in order to ease the pain of its limping.

'There was once a dog called Mirèio,' he would say, 'she also was lame and had sores, like you. Her body is buried not far from here, but the real Mirèio is safe—very safe.' And then he would tell the mongrel about God, and about the Little Poor Man of God who had spent his life in preaching God's mercy. And if he had brought his midday meal with him he would give it to the purulent, cringing creature, and because he was able to lighten its burden by even so much, his own burden would lighten.

Then something, perhaps the expression in its eyes as the dog looked up, still hungry but humble, would remind him of all that was pitiful: of Mirèio who had learnt to fear life more than death: of the harmless and persecuted couleuvres; of his father who lay on the massive oak bed;

of his mother who toiled without rest or hope; of le tout petit Loup with his labouring lungs; of Anfos who carved mad, unearthly dreams as he strove to conjure beauty from madness. And the vision must widen until it embraced those unknown millions who struggled and suffered; until he perceived but one suffering through perceiving the anxious bewildered soul that looked out of the eyes of a starving mongrel. Groaning, Christophe would cover his face, conscious that his moment of respite was over.

There were days when he mustered all the strength of his will to strangle compassion beneath feelings of hatred, when he flung his imagination into space and pictured the ruin wrought by the invaders: pictured the blasted and blackened orchards, the pastures whose greenness was torn and trampled, the cornfields ploughed by the harrow of death, the streams whose waters were polluted by carnage. He would suddenly cry out and shake his clenched fists, for the deep and enduring anger of the earth, thus outraged, would seem to leap forth and possess him.

Then his hands would drop again to his sides: 'It must be that they do not realize,' he would think; and that thought would persist until, in spite of himself, the anger had vanished.

In such a mood as this he sought Jan one evening, knowing that in him he would find what he needed—the conviction that at times it was right to hate, that pity could only mean spiritual weakness. Jan welcomed him gladly and, as always, he talked of the sins committed against their country. The Curé, said Jan, had spoken the truth in proclaiming the advent of Anti-Christ.

'Have they not destroyed Reims Cathedral?' he demanded; his voice shaking, his fanatical eyes ablaze. 'Do they not seek to destroy our Lord Who is no longer left in peace on His altars? And is this not the work of God's enemies?'

Christophe nodded: 'Yes, yes, of God's enemies. To pity them therefore is surely a sin. . . .'

'Those who pity are either cowards or fools, or worse! But who pities them? What do you mean?' And Jan looked at him sharply.

Then Christophe lied: 'Not I!'

'Ah, bon, for a moment I thought. . . .'

'You may keep such thoughts to yourself;' scowled Christophe.

* * *

That night as he lay on his bed Christophe wept very bitterly, not knowing why he was weeping. He knew only that never before in his life had he felt such a sense of complete desolation, such a sense of betrayal, such a sense of grief, such a sense of loneliness and desertion.

2

The war passed into its second year, and now there was no one who dared to predict when the end would come or upon which side would lie the ultimate victory. The seasons came and went in Saint Loup bringing with them wind and sun and fruition, but few men remained to care for the land; Eusèbe must work himself in his vineyards, sweating and swearing as he sprayed and dug and felt the weight of his age on his back which ached fiercely after a hard day's digging.

'Sarnipabiéune!' swore Eusèbe, 'I will bottle my wine if I rupture my kidneys! Are my grapes to rot because all men are knaves and imbeciles with their hideous war? If I tread my grapes on the coals of hell my wine shall be not only bottled but sold!' And he angrily deluged a quaking plant till its leaves turned blue with sulphate of copper.

In the streets of the town might be seen the wounded, who had wandered along from a neighbouring château: the château was now a convalescent home being run by a patriotic lady. And quite often these wounded would stop and gaze at the ancient church and the picturesque houses, or exclaim with delight at a group of palms, or point to the tall eucalyptus trees, for many of them were clerks from the north who had passed their lives upon office stools which had only been left for the mud of Flanders. Now they limped, supporting their weight upon sticks or swinging a shattered leg between crutches, or trying to light a cigarette with a brown-gloved hand, palpably artificial. Some wheeled themselves in invalid chairs, manipulating the wheels with much skill as they eased them over the uneven cobbles; while others coughed carefully, having been gassed and sent to Provence because of its climate.

All things considered they were really quite cheerful and would often visit the Café de la Tarasque where they generally ordered a lemon squash, an iced groseille or a cup of black coffee. And if Mère Mélanie in her own private sanctum occasionally produced something stronger, the doctor was spared any consequent grief—what the eye doesn't see the heart doesn't grieve over. At the café there might also be those home on leave who were drinking their fill and a little bit extra, for when men have made a long sojourn in hell it is not surprising that they should feel thirsty. Then the whole and the maimed would grow merry together, their jests being bandied from table to table in the anatomical argot of war with which even civilians were becoming familiar.

But the little violinist with the hump on his back must often sigh as he looked at the wounded, and that sigh would not be because of their wounds but because he was actually filled with envy—it was better to have a useless leg, an ersatz hand, or a lung that was hardening, for the sake of glory, than an inglorious hump because one's father had kicked one's mother. And now when he played, in spite of his efforts the fiddle would sound as though it were wailing, so that Mère Mélanie when he came to her bed must box his ears for an indolent lout who no longer put spirit into his tunes, although there was plenty of it in his belly:

'To hear you is to think of a hearse,' she would rage. 'Mon Dieu, you have cause enough to rejoice that deformed as you are, you need not fight. The least you can do is to earn your keep!' And then she would suddenly box his ears, for the sight of him often aroused her anger.

However, he would seldom reply to such gibes, even when his belovèd chastised him severely. What was the use of trying to explain? And in any case he would be fuddled with brandy.

3

During November Goundran returned on the briefest of leaves. He was browner than ever and apparently he had caught many fish, though he seemed disinclined to talk much about them. He never patronised Mère Mélanie, for long absence had made of this husband a lover, and then in addition to his wife there was the child, and then in addition to them both there was the money. Goundran must save even out of his pay, just in case . . . No good spending money on drink, it must all be put by for Elise and Aurano. He lived happily during those few peaceful days, lying long abed with Elise beside him; and perhaps in the morning their couch would be shared with their energetic four-year-old daughter. Aurano would climb on to Goundran's chest and tug at the chain of his large holy medal; an entrancing medal of Saint George with a spear whose point was down the throat of a dragon. There was also a ship upon the reverse and waves, and Jesus stilling the waters.

'Donne! donne!' she would order imperiously; so Goundran would slip it over his head and lay it in her acquisitive hand, whereupon Aurano would start to kiss it.

The time was too short to be wasted on friends—Goundran's home had become very precious to him. All the same they went to the Bénédits, for he could not help worrying himself about Christophe. He found little hope and great poverty, and since there seemed nothing that he could do except grieve, he did not repeat the visit, speaking quite frankly that night to his wife, for Goundran had always despised self-deception.

He said: 'I must live in the midst of war, therefore when we are together I want to forget that the world contains so much failure and sadness. Perhaps I am wrong, unchristian even, but in any case that is the way I feel, so I think that I will not see them again until I am once more back upon leave.' Then he took Elise roughly into his arms, seeking forgetfulness as he held her.

Guillaume also came home upon leave that winter, but he had less cause to rejoice than Goundran, for Clotilde had been trying to heal the wound of his absence by a series of wild flirtations; indeed gossip regarding her conduct was so rife that Guillaume went off to consult his mother.

Madame Simon sighed, but she did what she could to reassure the unlucky young husband: 'Clotilde is foolish, that I admit. Yet I cannot think that she means any harm.

Do not worry about it too much, my son.' For her only desire these terrible days was to keep all trouble and sorrow from Guillaume.

Very thin he had grown; and his eyes looked strained—there was something haunted and scared about them: 'Ah, what I have seen . . .' he would say and then stop, hastily lighting a fresh cigarette with fingers that not infrequently trembled. A sick man he was in body and mind, for Guillaume was far too gentle for war; if he lived the misery of it would break him. So now to his poignant distress about Clotilde, he must add quite a number of lesser distresses; his mother's hair had turned almost white, and this struck him as not only pitiful but tragic, he continually fretted because of her hair, and because his father also was ageing. He went often to church yet he seldom prayed; he would just sit gazing down at his boots in a sort of humble, helpless dejection; and when he got home he would sometimes ask his mother if he had harmed anybody:

'I have always wished to be kind,' he would sigh, 'but it seems that in life we fail to be kind, very often. I know that I hurt Papa Jóusè.'

'Nonsense, my child, you are kindness itself—and good.'

'No, no, I hurt Papa Jóusè.'

Indeed the thought of his godfather's illness and poverty was becoming an obsession: 'I think of him when I lie down to sleep; I think of him even out there at the front, and of how I gave in to Clotilde about Kahn . . . It was weak, I ought to have been more firm, Papa Jóusè should have made our marriage bed. I believe that my weakness brought on his stroke. . . .'

'That is folly, Guillaume,' Madame Simon would tell him.

Then perhaps his father would take a hand: 'Allons, mon gars, such thoughts are morbid; and you a fine fellow in uniform, defending us all, and you brave as a lion!'

But one evening Guillaume burst out abruptly: 'Not brave, a coward—I am always afraid!' For he had not yet grasped that the bravest man may very well be the man who is frightened.

Poor Guillaume, he was certainly one of those whom nature had fashioned for kindlier business. A bad soldier he made, always slightly bemused, always slow, and at moments intensely stupid; the despair of his sergeant, the despair of himself, and the butt of his less sensitized com-companions. He hated his life and would sometimes think that the poilus who got themselves killed were lucky. The noise of a battle shattered his nerves, the stench of its carnage sickened his stomach, but the cruelty of it went deepest of all, for that struck at his shrinking, horrified spirit.

From his wife he derived but small sympathy; she admired the warriors who took warfare more lightly, and who when they came home had got just two ideas in their pates: much wine and violent love-making. Guillaume wanted to make violent love, it is true, but his methods now often seemed to her childish; why, once he had burst into tears and sobbed immediately after having possessed her. Shaking and sobbing Guillaume had lain, nor had he vouchsafed any clear explanation, so that in the end Clotilde had been terrified and had spent the rest of that night in the kitchen.

On another occasion he had been quite unable to satisfy her clamorous body: 'But what is the matter with you?' she had asked. 'You are well, you have not even been wounded!' And Guillaume had felt himself flushing with shame as he pleaded that war was a tiring business. His leave was not at all a success, although he had longed for it so intensely.

Before he went back to the firing line he begged Marie to let him speak with her husband; and Marie consented: what else could she do? It was not in her kindly heart to refuse him.

Guillaume stood awkwardly at the bedside; he was speechless at first because of the shock of Jóusè's greatly altered appearance.

Then Jóusè said: 'Ah . . . so at last you have come.' And this struck the young man as an odd way to speak, for it sounded as though he had been expected.

'Mais oui, I have come, Papa Jóusè,' he faltered.

'I knew you would, Guillaume,' Jóusè went on, 'you are worried about going to Kahn. You think that I find it hard to forgive—but I cannot any longer feel really angry. Ah, no, when a man must lie on his back all day he has surely time to forgive; and in any case it was a small thing, my godson.'

But Guillaume was bent on accusing himself: 'Nothing is small that wounds,' he said slowly. 'If I wounded you then I did a great wrong for which I can only ask your forgiveness. I have witnessed many terrible sights, and now I desire to be kind—always kind. Many very terrible sights I have witnessed. . . .'

'Yet it seems that you see beyond them,' murmured Jóusè.

Stooping, Guillaume kissed the quiet, paralysed hand: 'All is happy between us then? All is forgiven?'

'But yes,' Jóusè smiled, 'all is happy indeed; and listen, I am going to tell you something: I feel that when next we two meet I shall walk. . . .'

'Pecaire,' thought Guillaume, 'the poor hopeful man; never will he walk in this world any more. Aloud he said: 'God grant that you are right. And now it is time that I went, it grows late. Bless me, Papa Jóusè.'

And Jóusè blessed him.

*　　*　　*

In the workshop Guillaume said good-bye to Christophe, and he fancied that he was seeing this boy for the first time in his life, and that what he saw was somehow unreal and yet convincing. Great beauty he saw, and pale, luminous eyes that were looking at him with such vast understanding that he longed to lose himself in their depths, to bathe his spiritual wounds in their mercy.

'It must be that I am imagining things,' he thought, 'and that will not do at all. Is this not Christophe, the carpenter's son whom I have known since he was a child? Yes, surely this is Christophe Bénédit—there is nothing whatever unusual about him.'

Christophe said: 'I am glad that you came here to-day.' And his voice was so natural that Guillaume felt relieved; it was breaking and therefore a trifle gruff, which only made it the more reassuring.

'I also am glad that I came . . . ' answered Guillaume.

After which there ensued an awkward silence, for youth is shy of expressing emotion and neither of them could find just the right words, so that in the end they gravely shook hands and Christophe turned again to his work-bench.

CHAPTER THIRTY-TWO

I

Few things happened to break the monotony of misfortune that hung over the Bénédit household as savings dwindled to vanishing-point and could thus no longer augment scanty earnings. Even the war grew monotonous, so that at times it seemed to Christophe that the world must always have been at war, the streets always full of the mutilated, the church always filled with black-clad figures who knelt to pray for the souls of their dead—the women hiding their tears beneath veils, the men dry-eyed and grim in their stiff new mourning.

Scarcely anyone came to see Jóusè these days, for in spite of a genuine sympathy people were growing used to his illness. And what was that illness of his, after all, when compared with the scourge that was decimating youth? The paralysis of an ageing man had ceased to stir the imagination.

Eusèbe would come and sit with his friend, but now Eusèbe was always complaining. He had rheumatism, he declared, in his loins, the result of working among his vineyards, and whenever he moved he gave a deep groan, gripped his back and started cursing the Germans. Jóusè suspected that Eusèbe was not quite so suffering as he pretended, that the groans were in order to get sympathy—although this was certainly very unlike him. Indeed Jóusè had begun to wonder of late if this barefaced pagan sometimes felt lonely; disregard of neighbours might be all very fine so long as a man retained physical vigour, but when aches and pains came to stiffen the joints and the lumbar muscles then it was that most men acquired much more respect for the world's opinion.

Madame Roustan occasionally visited Marie, but these visits of hers were extremely unwelcome. She had always managed to thrive upon woe, and just now she had more than enough to thrive on. She would sit there dilating upon the stroke that had prematurely removed her own husband:

'Ai! las,' she would sigh, 'he died at his post like a soldier, he was actually measuring ribbon. I myself was behind the desk counting change when I suddenly heard a sound like a gurgle. Ah, bon Dieu, what had happened? A gurgle I heard, and there was my Geoffroi lying flat on his stomach across the counter with his head hanging down. His face was as red as the ribbon in his hand. . . . I distinctly recall that the ribbon was red . . . red satin at one franc fifty the metre.' And from this she would go on to give all the details of poor Monsieur Roustan's post-mortem appearance: of the manner in which they adjusted his jaw and combed his beard and parted his hair; and of how they had not liked to keep him too long before screwing him down, because of the thunder. In the end she would always say much the same thing: 'Mais, ma chérie, I am thankful Geoffroi was taken. It is surely a million times better to die than to linger on in a living death.' A truth that her listener would find far from cheering.

Sometimes Jóusè would thump the floor with the stick which they always put on the bed beside him, and hearing this Madame Roustan would go, but dolefully as though leaving a funeral.

'Eh bien,' Jóusè would say when his wife appeared, 'has she plucked the eyes from the dead man's carcase? Never mind, Marioun, you are rid of her at last.' And then he would laugh his thick, difficult laugh, for his sister could no longer arouse his ire, he had grown to think her too trivial a person.

But one evening there arrived at the Bénédit's house a person who was far from being trivial. Monsieur Roland arrived, no one less, if you please. And why? To discuss le tout petit Loup, his abilities, and his possible future. Loup had now left school and was working long hours at the Bazaar Bled as general factotum, and this Monsieur Roland appeared to deplore while admitting that it must go on for the present.

Said he: 'Loup was always an excellent pupil and I cannot but think he is being wasted; however, Madame, I quite realize that money is none too easy to come by. But after the war I think Loup should go in for the higher examinations, and then I would like to see him train as a teacher. Once the war is over I can do several things: I have one or two friends who are influential and I mean to interest them in our Loup so that he may continue his education. A little assistance, n'est-ce-pas, chère Madame? Enough to replace his earnings perhaps, so that he can be free to go to the Sorbonne. No, no, do not thank me, I do this for myself quite as much as for him; it is good for my prestige, it is also good for the prestige of the school. A really promising pupil is rare, and when one is discovered there are those who will help him. Of course there arises the question of health —Loup is not over-strong and that is a drawback; still I think that we ought to take the risk. . . . In any case I am willing to take it.'

Christophe and Marie stared in amazement; they could scarcely believe their ears; were they dreaming? Imagine such a thing, le tout petit Loup so clever that he would become a teacher! Imagine such a thing . . . le tout petit Loup!

'Ah, Monsieur . . .' they began simultaneously.

Then Marie said: 'This is a miracle. This is surely the work of his dear patron saint.'

But le tout petit Loup said nothing at all, maintaining a rather ominous silence.

When Monsieur Roland had taken his leave, Marie hurried away to inform her husband that le tout petit Loup was already made: 'Did I not say that Jan might be clever that all the same our tout petit Loup was as wise as an owl and as sharp as a needle?'

Joúsè nodded: 'And the Sorbonne is quite as fine as the Grand Séminaire, I believe,' he informed her; 'nor do I doubt that the good Roland's friends are quite as fine as Madame de Bérac! When next Germaine comes you can tell her this news; but first bring her up here—I would see her face. Boudiéu, I would not miss Germaine's face when you tell her this news for a thousand francs!' And since Joúsè was still only human, he chuckled.

Then into the room marched le tout petit Loup, his cheeks flushed, his monkeyish eyes bright with temper. At his heels followed Christophe looking perturbed:

'Loup is greatly upset,' he whispered to Marie.

And undoubtedly Loup was greatly upset. Spinning round he stamped his foot at his brother: 'Stop whispering, will you? It gets on the nerves. I cannot support your eternal whispering. If you want to say something then say it out loud. You will drive me mad, hissing there like a snake! And in any case, why are you interfering?'

'Santo Ano d'At!' his mother exclaimed; 'Santo Ano d'At! Now, what is the matter? Here is heaven showering blessings into your lap and you take this occasion, it seems, to be rude. You ought to thank God for all He has done. Why, you did not even trouble to thank your master.'

But le tout petit Loup flung up his small head, clenching his hands in an effort not to wheeze as he valiantly choked back a fit of coughing: 'I refuse to be a fat Monsieur Roland,' he spluttered; 'I refuse to sit on my behind all my life and wear glasses that make my eyes look like marbles; I refuse to grow bald and have rolls of pink flesh at the back of my neck bulging over my collar; I refuse to scrawl things on a blackboard with chalk and then rub them off again with a duster; I refuse to teach fools who do not want to learn, and who when they have learnt still remain imbeciles. Moreover I have chosen my future career. My mind is made up: I shall enter the army. And kindly do not call me le tout petit Loup. Do you hear? I say I will not be called. . . .' He sat down abruptly, clutching his side, 'Not le tout petit Loup . . . no . . . no . . . not that . . . not le tout petit . . . I tell you I hate it!'

But in spite of his angry, protesting spirit, Loup must submit to a physical body, must submit to being laid flat on the floor by Marie while Christophe rushed off to get water, must submit to Jóusè's solicitous warning that when one possessed so feeble a heart one could ill afford to give way to temper.

'Try to be calmer,' entreated Jóusè; 'it is very unwise to become so excited.'

Ai! las, ai! las, le pauvre tout petit Loup—though when Christophe returned he was already better. He had still got youth to fight on his side and these sudden attacks were of short duration:

'Take your arm away,' he said peevishly as he gulped

down the water. And then to his mother: 'Stop dabbing my forehead; it is nothing at all. I do wish you would stop and leave me in peace—so much fuss about nothing at all, it is childish!'

Getting up he made his way out of the room very slowly, and still slowly he went downstairs, thrusting his knuckles into his eyes because tears were unthinkable for a soldier.

Marie tried to follow: 'He will surely die'; she wept, 'Bèlli Santo d'or, we shall lose him.'

But Christophe laid his hand on her arm: 'I think he would rather be alone,' he told her.

2

As time went on Christophe could but wonder at his father's wellnigh amazing patience. It was like a bright rift in the clouds of despair that gathered about Jóusè's suffering—a strange outcome, it seemed, of so bitter an illness. Jóusè must frequently lie for hours like a log because no one was at hand to move him, the weight of his bulk pressing down on his sores, but in spite of this he seldom complained, only his eyes would betray his anguish. Most pitiful he was, the patient giant; Christophe could often have wept to see him stretched there so helplessly on the bed; and yet something told Christophe that all was well, oh, but very well indeed with his father. He had lost his former craving for liquor, and moreover he had grown exceedingly simple. His mind remained clear, his brain unaffected, but his mind took great pleasure in simple things; he would like the feel of a spray of mimosa and would stroke it tenderly with his sound hand. Indeed he who had never looked twice at flowers now seemed to discern a new meaning in them.

'God is cleverer than I am,' he would say; 'as for me, I could never have made mimosa.'

Jóusè dreamed vividly these days, uncertain if he was sleeping or waking, and he liked to discuss these dreams with his son; Christophe could see that they gave him pleasure. The dreams were concerned with bygone things; he seldom if ever dreamed of the present. Of his childhood he dreamed and must sometimes laugh because of a childish peccadillo; of his youth he dreamed and of budding manhood, happy years when he took great pride in his muscles, when with three mighty blows he had felled a tree, and a hefty fellow at that, he told Christophe; and then of his courtship of Marie he dreamed, he would constantly dream that they two were courting.

'Ah, my son, to-day I was wooing your mother. So young she was and a little bit frightened. Ah, my son, there was not a line on her face, nor a single white thread in her thick black hair. She was wearing a comb I had given her; there were many small scrolls of gold upon it. It had once belonged to my great-grandmother—the one who was loved by a Spanish sailor; but she would not have him, caspistello, she would not! She preferred an honest joiner from Provence.'

But of all his recurrent dreams there was one that Jóusè affirmed to be the most persistent. Mirèio would come padding up to the bed and would lay her great paws upon his chest, the while she looked at him very intently; and [then she would suddenly lick his cheek and look at him again. Jóusè always declared that Mirèio was trying to tell him something. And one evening Jóusè said to his son:

'I think I now know what she wishes to tell me. It is that she wishes to say she forgives. . . . I am glad she forgives me that terrible beating. Ai! las, the poor beast, I must have been mad, for I beat her until she was bleeding and spent. . . .'

'You beat her?' breathed Christophe, grown suddenly pale.

And Jóusè nodded: 'Yes, yes, I beat her; and this I did for your sake, my son; I did it because I thought she might harm you. I beat her although she was covered with sores. . . . Ai, ai, if her sores were throbbing like mine. . . .' And Jóusè went on to tell of that night when he had rushed round to Madame Roustan's and had found the bitch crouching near-by the cot: 'She was savage with love as I now know,' said Jóusè, 'but then I did not comprehend how it was; I thought that my son might well be in danger.' At great length he spoke of his brutal deed, concealing nothing—it was like a confession. And when Christophe besought him to say no more Jóusè held up his hand, compelling attention: 'I want to tell you the truth, the whole truth; for a very long time I have wanted to tell you.' Then Christophe knew that his father must speak, that the words were wiping a bruise from his spirit.

And as he listened with tears in his eyes and great pain in his heart for Mirèio's suffering, he was conscious of that sense of oneness again, suddenly perceiving that the pain in his heart was not for the suffering Mirèio alone, but also for the man who had caused her to suffer. At that moment Christophe came very near to a more perfect understanding of God; but the moment passed, leaving him desolate, and he hid his face against Jóusè's shoulder.

CHAPTER THIRTY-THREE

DURING the autumn of 1916, that never-to-be-forgotten autumn when France bled from a thousand unstanched wounds, Anatole Kahn faced ruin.

Many urgent letters had followed that first warning letter from his business associates in Paris, but now had come one that he could not ignore, that he dared not ignore—it was brutally final. The Galeries Kahn must be offered for sale and their contents would have to go under the hammer. No more pouring of money into a sieve, no more bolstering up of a worthless business. Kahn's associates had consulted, it seemed, and were quite determined to cut their losses. They went on to state that for more than two years they had foolishly pandered to his importuning, but that as he had now clearly lost his head they themselves would conduct all the final arrangements. The shop would be put in an agent's hands at once, while the auction would be left to a firm of well-known auctioneers in Toulon. The original scheme had been his, all his. It had not succeeded; he had over-spent outrageously, he had squandered their money; very well, he must be prepared for the fact that they did not any longer intend to support him. No more demands for money would be met beyond the very barest obligations until such time as the property was sold. As for Kahn he would get his fourth share in the proceeds of anything that was saved from the wreck, but they wished him distinctly to understand that once this venture had been wound up they intended to sever all business connections. It would surely have been far more honest and wise had he seen fit to tell them the true situation instead of insisting each time he wrote that the business was just on the verge of reviving. He had known that one of them was at the front, while the others were engrossed by important war-work and on this they all felt that he had presumed; indeed they were not sure that after the war they would not immediately start a procès unless he fell in with their decision at once, abiding in every respect by their wishes. These and many other statements that letter contained, none of which was very easy to stomach.

A nice kettle of fish and no mistake. Kahn twisted and turned like a rat in a trap, while feeling himself to be utterly helpless. They were three to one, they were adamant, and the Galeries Kahn would have to go—he was overwhelmed by an immense self-pity. And true it was that every centime he possessed had been risked for the sake of those dreams of his, quite as much as for personal ambitions. Those dreams had already cost him his savings, his rings, his gold watch, even Beauvais' picture. Yes, even the picture had been sold in the end to a disagreeable and close-fisted dealer. Nor had Kahn shrunk from subduing the flesh, cutting down his food and wine and tobacco; denying himself the society of a certain large-hearted lady at Saint Raphäel; for into the conception of the Galeries Kahn as into that of those jerry-built villas, had gone something of the man's very body and soul; he had fathered them as men father their children. They had leapt in the womb of a sorry ideal—an ideal that had meant more to him than women.

Anatole Kahn looked around his shop. He looked at the gilt that the salt air had tarnished, at the cheap cerise satin and cheaper plush that the careless sun of the south had faded, at the clocks whose oil had dried on their wheels, at the Japanese trays that had lost their sheen, at the joss-sticks that no one had bought for months, at the fly-blown frames of the sentimental pictures; and all that he beheld showed the hatred of Time for the soulless and would-be time-serving craftsman. Nor was anything else in much better case; upstairs the moth had got into the bedding, and downstairs in the cellar the damp had returned, injuring the rugs and some large rolls of matting. Single-handed Kahn had been no match for Time whose whirligig had brought in its revenges. And how much would this shop-soiled stock fetch when sold? Very little indeed, its owner decided, not enough to keep a man going for long. Then what did it mean? Destitution . . . starvation?

Anatole Kahn made his way to the villa that was to have been the forerunner of many. There it stood an unlovely and unloved thing, a home that no one apparently wanted. Its walls were already cracking and stained, its wrought-iron bell-pull already rusted; while some urchin had used his catapult with devastating results to its windows. And as though this were not enough, it appeared that the land—which sloped sharply downward from Beauvais'—was enleagued with the always incalculable sea, and had thus from the first been a bad proposition. The sea, resenting the villa no doubt, had oozed itself into its very foundations, creeping up through the boards of the dining-room floor upon which it had left a species of fungus. The whole structure exuded an atmosphere of failure, neglect and disintegration.

Kahn suddenly collapsed on a heap of rubble that some careless workman had left in the kitchen, then he buried his face in his shaking hands. Such vast sums he still owed the Société, and no money wherewith to pay the high interest. That the moratorium had saved him so far he now considered but a small consolation; the war over, his property would be seized, and even this war could not last for ever.

'Quelle misère . . . mon Dieu, quelle misère!' he moaned, as large, womanish tears trickled through his fingers.

2

Gossip had always been rife about Kahn since the days when he had first divulged his grand schemes, and now it was raging throughout the town; everyone knew of his desperate straits despite his efforts to throw dust in their eyes, for all little communities seem to possess a mysterious bureau of information.

For some time his fame as a man of affairs, as a prophet and apostle of progress had been waning. For some time they had held aloof from his shop, partly because they had not wished to spend but partly because they had begun to feel mistrustful; the goods he had sold them had not worn well when compared with Jóusè's stalwart productions. Then again, they considered that his prophecies had not only been very misleading but expensive. A prophet, they jeered, should have foreseen the war and in consequence not urged the spending of money. They were bitterly disappointed in Kahn who had raised such high hopes only to dash them. And as frequently happens to those who serve their own ends by augmenting the greed in others, Kahn himself became the first victim of that greed—people whose pockets he had failed to line had very naturally come to dislike him.

But now that he was bankrupt, now that everyone knew he had only possessed a fourth share in the business, that in fact he had never been wealthy at all, the dislike of him blazed with surprising vigour. Ah, the fraud, and he talking of all his fine schemes, and of all he would spend, as though he had millions! And he ruining Jóusè Bénédit and bringing about that incurable illness; Jóusè Bénédit who had been born in Saint Loup, who belonged to Saint Loup, who was a part of the town, a tradition as his father had been before him; what an outrage that was, when one came to think, one's own neighbour rolled in the dust by a stranger. There were even some folk who remarked that Kahn's name was, to say the least of it, highly suspicious, who declared that he might very well be a spy, this in spite of the fact that the gentle old mayor insisted that such a suspicion was foolish: 'You do not believe it yourselves,' said the mayor, which was true enough, no one really believed it. The fact was that nerves were badly on edge; it had been an appalling spring and summer with the enemy pressing on every side and causing an indescribable slaughter. The fate of the Allies had hung in the balance, and now there had come the French counter-offensive with its long lists of missing, wounded and dead; small wonder that nerves were badly on edge as death swept like a whirlwind over France, devastating the peaceful homes of Provence. And then there were those who could honestly say that Anatole Kahn's advice had misled them; Mère Mélanie, for instance, who had run into debt through making extravagant alterations, and Hermitte who now never ceased to wail that restoring his attic had cost him a fortune, and Madame Roustan who had done up two rooms in the hope of obtaining a substanital profit. No denying that Anatole Kahn was to blame; no denying, either, that most people blamed him.

But strangely enough his worst enemy was a gentle and very innocuous person. It was Guillaume Simon who harmed Kahn the most and this, as it happened, he did by dying. He had died of wounds at the battle of the Somme, and Saint Loup had elected to make him its hero, although why, not a soul in the town could have told—there had never been anything heroic about him. However, he served as a most handy scourge wherewith to lacerate Kahn's shrinking shoulders; there was neither rhyme nor reason in the thing, but then war itself is a monstrous unreason. So now there were many who muttered dark threats whenever they passed the unfortunate tradesman, who shook their clenched fists as they walked by his shop—presumably for the glory of Guillaume; who chalked up: 'Herr Kahn' on the shop door at night, yes, and other extremely unpleasant things, to the great indignation and fear of its owner.

Only the Bénédits and old Eusèbe seemed unmoved by this explosion of public feeling. Eusèbe shrugged, spitting contemptuously: 'The beast has not changed his species,' he remarked; 'a pig will always remain a pig.' After which he went off to buy flannel in the town—red flannel, that infallible cure for lumbago.

Madame Roustan visited Marie in vain, nor could she get much satisfaction from Jóusè. Marie said: 'But we do not think him a spy, and as for his business having come to ruin—eh bien, that cannot make Jóusè walk; there is nothing healing about Kahn's misfortune.'

And her husband nodded: 'You are right, Marioun, I cannot run off to join in the rejoicings; moreover two failures do not make one success.' Then he yawned very loudly and closed his eyes as a hint to his sister that he would be sleeping.

But if Jóusè had ever desired revenge, then very assuredly he now had it, for at night Kahn would lie wide awake in his bed listening to sounds, always listening to sounds, most of which were produced by imagination. At other times he would think he smelt smoke and would ransack the place from garret to cellar, shivering because of his horror of fire—supposing they should burn him alive as a spy? Such a thing might occur at a time of war-madness. Getting back into bed he would start to think while still hearing those sounds and still smelling that burning; amazing how acute his perceptions had become, and all able to function at once—amazing. Hark! Was that someone at the front door . . . ? He had told Hermitte that he was an Alsatian, he distinctly remembered having told the fool; then why did not Hermitte come out and say so? An Alsatian he was. All the days of his childhood had been passed on his father's farm in Alsace; he could see the house now, a poor sort of shack surrounded by poor, unproductive acres. Curse that smell, it had got itself into his nose; yes, but where did it come from? that was the question! Why had he thought that it gave him importance to wrap himself round with a cloak of mystery? Why, oh why, had he been so secretive, so careful never to answer their questions? He might have told them about that farm, and about the time that had followed in Paris when at last he had climbed to comparative success, had amassed quite a tidy bundle of savings. Savings? Where were they now . . . they were gone. . . . Surely that was a strange sound near the window? A sly sound like someone smothering a cough . . . a sly, choking sound . . . over there near the window. But why had he invented that ridiculous yarn about having come to Saint Loup for his throat? Never in his life had he had tonsilitis. He had told Madame Roustan that ridiculous yarn. Had she believed it? Very probably not, in which case she had doubtless resented the lie and was only waiting to do him a mischief. And why had he ruined Bénédit, why had he not been more patient, more subtle? As a stranger he had arrived in this town and had ruined one of its most revered natives; an unwise, a foolhardy thing to have done, which might well result in his own destruction.

On and on would hammer those merciless thoughts, those vain regrets, those hysterical terrors. He must fling himself at the feet of the mayor and implore the old man to give him protection—the mayor knew quite well that he was no spy. Yes, but the mayor knew other things also: they had wanted to make him, Kahn, their mayor—perhaps the old man had felt angry and jealous. He might even deliver him over to be shot; people were shot as spies every day, even women, and upon the slenderest suspicion. He must leave Saint Loup quietly after the auction, must slip out of the town before they could catch him. But where could he go, he, a ruined man? He would get no more help from those scoundrels in Paris, and at least he still had a roof over his head in Saint Loup, and that was better than nothing. No shop would sell quickly at such a time, and surely they would hesitate to turn him adrift until it was sold? Edouard would not do that—perhaps he might ask to remain as caretaker. No, he could not face tramping the streets for employment; he had done it once many years ago, but then he had been a strong youth from Alsace. Closing his eyes he could still feel the pain of his boots as they rubbed on his blistered heels, of his stomach as it seemed to devour its own entrails, so famished had he been in those early days when he tramped the Paris streets for employment. But now he was soft and past middle-age—his skin had grown soft and so had his muscles. His feet ached if he went for a really long walk. How old was he . . .? Bon Dieu, he was nearly sixty; too late for a man to make a fresh start, to go begging for work from door to door—a man could not beg with distinction at sixty!

On and on would hammer those merciless thoughts, growing always more urgent but more bewildered as Kahn listened and sniffed and longed for sleep, yet feared to close his eyes for an instant. His aggressive assurance had left him completely, he was now little better than a deflated bladder. He could see only destitution ahead, this in spite of the fact that never in history had more jobs been open to men of his age who were able and willing to make themselves useful. Immense chagrin, humiliation and terror were combining to rob the man of his senses; no shell-shocked, battle-torn wreck from the front could have been less capable of clear thinking.

3

Kahn never knew at what precise moment after the auction he evolved the idea of going to see Jóusè Bénédit, nor did he trouble to analyse his motive. Was it a sudden belated desire to render the stricken Jóusè a service because

Kahn had learnt what it felt like to fail? Or was it partly self-preservation—the wild hope that by serving the man he had harmed he would gain some small measure of toleration? Who shall answer, since all human motives are mixed and are seldom more palatable for the mixing.

With bent head Kahn walked slowly away from the port, away from the littered and empty shop with the notice: 'A Vendre' pasted up on its windows, away from the scene of his desolation. With bent head he knocked on the Bénédit's door, then waited, not daring to knock again so fearful was he anent his reception.

The door opened and Marie stood in the entrance: 'You . . .' she breathed, 'You, Kahn. . . .' And then she fell silent.

'Yes,' he muttered, 'it is Kahn. I have something to say . . . I have something that I must say to your husband.'

Marie stiffened: 'I do not know what that can be, but whatever it is you shall not say it. Ah, no, I will not let you into this house in order that you may once more insult Jóusè. Never again shall you enter our house.' And she made to close the door in his face. 'Enough misery you have brought us,' she told him.

But at this Kahn thrust his foot through the door with a sudden gesture of desperation: 'Let me in!' he clamoured; 'I am here to bring help. I am here to undo a very great wrong, I am here. . . .'

At that moment Christophe came from the workshop.

Marie turned to him: 'This man demands to come in; he pretends that he wishes to offer us help, that he now feels regret.'

'Let him come,' said Christophe.

Marie stared at her son, incredulous and angry, then she stood aside and allowed Kahn to pass her, not knowing why she obeyed the boy, conscious only that his gaze was resting upon her.

'It is your father I want . . .' faltered Kahn.

'My father it is who wants you,' answered Christophe.

He led the way up the rickety stairs and into Jóusè's comfortless bedroom: 'Father, I have brought Anatole Kahn. There is something he very much wishes to tell you.'

Jóusè automatically tried to rise, as always when he was

agitated, but the effort failed and he lay white and still. 'Sit down, Anatole Kahn,' he mumbled.

Kahn pulled up a chair, and as he did so he was conscious of a new and distressing sensation, for self-pity is easier far to endure than the pity a man must feel for another.

'Bénédit . . .' he stammered, 'it is . . . it is. . . .'

'I think that my father knows,' said Christophe.

Then Kahn began to speak rather wildly: 'Bénédit, I am ruined, I have lost all my money, and moreover I am hated and loathed in this town; not a soul but whose hand is now turned against me. They pretend that I am a German spy. Bénédit, there is only one man who can save me and that is a man whom I have harmed. For his sake they may leave me in peace, Bénédit; they may leave me in peace if they know I can help him. Ah, but will he do this thing . . . will he forgive?'

Jóusè said: 'What is it you would have this man do— this man whom you say you have harmed?' And he waited.

Kahn edged his chair nearer: 'I would have him employ me. I would have him let me manage his business; I would have him let me do what I can to make it a going concern again. I would have him let me work with my hands. . . .'

Jóusè frowned and his whole face suddenly darkened: 'You to work with your hands!' he exclaimed bitterly, 'You who have wished to destroy all beauty; you who have lived by soulless machines; is it likely that you could work with your hands?'

Kahn answered: 'And yet I was trained as a joiner.'

In the pause that followed it seemed to Christophe that the room was alive with conflicting emotions. He could feel the despair of Anatole Kahn, the fear, the remorse, the awakening of pity. He could feel the resentment in Jóusè's heart, the rekindling of that slow and terrible anger.

'Ah,' Jóusè said thickly, 'so you were of my trade; very shameful indeed then was your betrayal.'

Christophe looked at his father, and as he did so Jóusè's eyes must turn and meet those of his son; slowly, reluctantly they must turn to be held as by some relentless will that dominated and claimed his whole being, that refused to permit of any escape—a will whose strength lay in unquenchable mercy. And neither of them marked the passing of

U

time; it might have been hours, it might have been moments that they strove together this parent and child, eye to eye, mind to mind in absolute silence. Then Christophe sighed as though physically tired.

'Zóu, I accept your offer,' Jóusè muttered.

And thus it was that the renegade Kahn came back to the work he had long deserted; to the quiet, simple and honest work of those who gain their living through timber. Very gravely they consulted for over an hour, deciding that Kahn should see what he could do, assisted therein by Christophe and Anfos, and that meanwhile he should be given his food—this until the profits had arrived at dimensions sufficient for him to share them. And as they talked there came upon Jóusè the peace which is only found in forgiving, and that curious wish to protect and befriend the creature whom one has at last forgiven, the creature who because he has much received and is therefore a debtor, confers a blessing.

Before Kahn left they told Marie his plans and his hopes, and she seeing her husband's face was greatly amazed, for Jóusè smiled as though he were very well pleased and contented. And since his contentment had always been hers Marie held out her hand to Anatole Kahn:

'Monsieur, you are very welcome,' she said.

'Madame, I am at your service,' he answered.

CHAPTER THIRTY-FOUR

I

THE astonishing advent of Anatole Kahn marked a turning-point in the Bénédit's fortunes; it was not very long before Christophe discovered that Kahn was a thoroughly competent joiner. For awhile he had seemed rather shy with his tools as though uncertain of regaining their friendship, and the tools in their turn had rubbed his soft skin until his palms were covered with blisters; but a few weeks had set all this to rights, so that now he gripped the chisel or saw with the strength and complete assurance of an expert — well grounded Kahn had been in his youth before he deserted the carpenter's bench to seek a more lucrative career in Paris.

At first people refused to believe the news. What, Anatole Kahn employed by Jóusè! Anatole Kahn taking charge of affairs on behalf of the man he had set out to ruin! Incredible, preposterous: Jóusè would not consent to such an arrangement; it must be a lie. And yet there was Kahn in Jóusè's own workshop as large as life, and with Christophe beside him, so that finally they accepted the fact that many strange things can happen in war-time. Then quite soon it was even being said that if Anatole Kahn really did know his job, Jóusè might well have made a good bargain; Christophe was young to assume full control and, as everyone knew, Anfos was a half-wit. Oh, that Jóusè! He was shrewd and no mistake: in losing his legs he had not lost his shrewdness. Having found out that Kahn had been trained as a joiner he had commandeered him to build up his business. It was surely a case of the biter bit; a great scheme, and one not devoid of humour. Well, well, they must see what this joiner could do, this prophet who now worked at a bench in his shirt-sleeves, this apostle of progress who had meekly returned to the use of the hand-saw, the plane and the hammer, this millionaire who disdaining the sea as too common a thing, had required a bathroom! And since even Death cannot hope to destroy the endless daily needs of the living, since anxiety cannot repair a back-door, and grief cannot mend the leg of a table, and, moreover, since many such necessary tasks had of late been either forgotten or neglected, Kahn found himself suddenly snowed under with orders, some of which were inspired by curiosity, and some by an admiration for Jóusè. Oh, that Jóusè! He had just been biding his time; the revenge was indeed unusually perfect! Gone were his enemy's smart northern clothes, his scarf-pin, his rings and his opulent watch-chain, and in their place was a soiled check shirt and a pair of cheap, ready-made linen trousers.

'Bonjour, Monsieur Kahn. Will you kindly come round at once and repair the lid of our cesspool? It is split and permits the stench to escape.'

'Mais oui, Monsieur, I come on the instant.'

He would bow with his paunch bulging over his belt, and his waxed moustache as stiff as a poker, and his smile apparently quite self-assured, just as though he had not been sold up for a bankrupt. That they could not rile him was very annoying; still, they had to admit that his work was satisfactory.

And indeed it was very remarkable to observe how Anatole Kahn kept his temper, how completely he managed to shed his grand air while appearing neither down-hearted nor humble. The truth was that he felt so immense a relief at finding himself in comparative safety, that he cared not a pin for their childish jeers which could neither roast him alive nor shoot him. Every morning he arrived at the Bénédit's house in time for coffee and a slice of dry bread; every night he returned to the Galeries Kahn which, except for his bedroom, were deserted and empty. Thanks to Edouard, he was allowed to stay on until such time as the place was disposed of. Yes, but now when he went to his bed he slept, and that sleep seemed to him like a boon from heaven as it came flooding peacefully over his mind, great waves of it, waves upon waves of sleep, until consciousness lay submerged by oblivion. On awaking his mind would feel placid yet vital, no longer submitting to thoughts of failure, so that while he shaved he would think of new schemes whereby he could help himself and Jóusè:

'Is it likely that I cannot win through!' he would exclaim to the soap-daubed face that looked out of the mirror.

His first scheme was to bait harmless traps for the wounded who would frequently stand staring into the workshop. He and Christophe made cigarette boxes of oak on which Anfos was set to carve popular generals from their pictures that Kahn cut out of the papers. The generals were crude but then so were the times; the boxes were simple but then so were the wounded. Cigarette cases followed with great success; upon these there appeared the flags of the Allies which le tout petit Loup embellished with paint. Since his earliest childhood he had been neat-fingered and now he spent hours with a box of oilpaints which Kahn had ordered for him from Marseille. Every evening he coloured the Allied flags; his brows knit, the tip of his tongue protruding:

'Do not joggle my arm, clumsy animal! And stop breathing warm wetness into my ear; it distracts me,' he would scold at the spell-bound Christophe.

There were also wooden blotters having views of Saint Loup, for Anfos must cease from his carving of dreams and content himself with the peaks of the Maures, and with ships that sailed upon earthly waters. And pin-trays there were, and photograph frames together with other gifts suitable for ladies, so that he who possessed the requisite price could send a souvenir to his sweetheart. The entire collection was neatly displayed upon trestle-tables set out in the roadway. But one morning Anfos abruptly remembered the crucifix he had made for the Curé, and he started to carve many little Christs from fragments of wood that Kahn had discarded—with incredible speed he carved little Christs, then nailed them on to their miniature crosses. And as he did this he moaned and wept, keeping up a perpetual loud lamentation, flinching each time he adjusted a nail and tapped it lightly in place with his mallet.

'Ai! paure pichounet, ai! ai!' he moaned, as though he lamented over a baby.

Kahn became impatient, but Christophe whispered

that he must not try to coerce the apprentice lest this fit of
madness grow more acute: 'It is that he wishes to dream,'
explained Christophe, 'and that when we will not permit
him to dream he tries to hide himself from us with God;
but to-day he is finding God very sad.'

Anfos looked up with red-rimmed eyes: 'God is always
sad, as you know,' he told Christophe.

After all, the crucifixes sold well; quite a number of
wounded soldiers bought them: 'Dis donc, les petits
crucifix . . . combien?' And having been informed, they
would finger them shyly. Then: 'Alors . . . oui.' And off
they would go with their purchases tucked away in their
pockets.

But Anatole Kahn had larger ideas than this making of
what he considered mere trifles. Why not visit the convalescent home and offer to work for the patriotic lady?
Through her he might hear of other such homes, having
first obtained her recommendation. So what must he do but
tramp off to the château, and having arrived there become
so insistent that the lady he sought hurried into the hall,
demanding the cause of such loud conversation.

'Ah, Madame,' explained Kahn, 'I am here to entreat
that you will accord me a brief interview.' And he handed
her one of the battered old cards that Jóusè had used upon
rare occasions.

'Bénédit . . .' she said thoughtfully; 'Bénédit. Mais oui,
I think I have heard about him. Surely his case is terribly
sad? Did I not hear that he was paralysed?' And her face
became very solicitous, for she was kind-hearted as well a
patriotic.

Kahn sighed: 'Paralysed, as you say, Madame; paralysed,
with a wife and two children to keep.' Then he quickly
explained how essential it was that for Jóusè's sake she
should give him employment: 'Already one child is so
fragile,' he went on, 'that a puff of wind would blow him to
heaven; he cannot digest our coarse peasant food, a mere
mouthful and he immediately vomits, yet how gentle, how
patient, how resigned he is. . . .'

'But what sort of work can you do?' she asked.

'Almost anything Madame requires,' he said boldly.
'I make back-rests for those who need such supports, and

cradles for those who have injured legs, and strong little tables that take the places of trays—very useful when a man must have meals in bed. Yes, all manner of comforts I make for our heroes. Perhaps, also, Madame would consider a shelter, a charming shelter out there in the sunshine. Ah, Madame, what a haven of peace that would be!'

She smiled: 'But, Monsieur, we have many shelters.'

'Yet I feel that Madame requires just one more,' he coaxed. 'I can see its exact position!'

The end of it was that she gave him an order for a couple of back-rests and three bed-tables: 'It is true,' she admitted, 'that we need several things, and the transport grows always more difficult. Perhaps I will ask you to build that new shelter, but first you must let me judge of your work—you will naturally have to work to our patterns.'

Kahn thanked her, then bowed himself humbly away, but his face was flushed and his eyes bright with triumph.

And so in addition to cigarette boxes, pin-trays and the like, Jóusè Bénédit's workshop began to produce quite a number of objects that the kind-hearted lady required for her patients; and since she was very well satisfied Kahn obtained his much-longed-for recommendation. All day might be heard the sound of the saw and the rhythmical tapping of hammer and mallet; all day might be heard the sound of Kahn's voice as he lustily shouted for this and that tool, or sang some lively song of the cafés. And all day Jóusè, hearing these cheerful sounds, must lie on his bed and ponder deeply:

'Surely,' he pondered, 'God's ways are most strange, yet most kind.' And then he would talk to God, but familiarly, using the Provençal tongue as though he spoke with some well-loved friend towards whom he had every cause to feel grateful.

2

At about this time Kahn began to pay board from his share of the sum realized at the auction. It was not a large sum, since owing to the war there had been a very meagre attendance; there had also been the question of depreciation. The bulk of the stock had been bought by a man from

Marseille representing the Galeries Bleues—people said he had got it for practically nothing. Still, after Kahn had settled his debts to the townsfolk there was certainly money left over, for he calmly ignored the obvious claims of La Société Foncière du Midi.

'Let them go to the devil,' he remarked; and then grinned, remembering the incalculable sea, 'they are welcome to take my land with them,' he added.

Not quite honest? Perhaps not. But now Anatole Kahn had become enamoured of his repentance. He could see little else save Jóusè's need and his own obligation to build up the business. The Société, he argued, was rolling in wealth and could quite well afford a doubtful venture, therefore why pay it interest out of his funds which, in any case, would be quickly exhausted? Like most enthusiasts Anatole Kahn saw only his latest enthusiasm, its predecessors appearing as dross when compared with the inspiration of the moment; but then, after all, he was not alone since even the righteous have limited vision. So now as well as paying his board he bought many new tools that were badly needed; some more delicate than those that Jóusè had used, some more up to date and thus more convenient. He also purchased a brand-new bench, wishing Christophe to have the use of his father's, and that, for him, was a great courtesy which let us assume was remarked on in heaven. Oh, yes, he was doubtless making his soul, though with somewhat less skill than he made bed-tables.

Sometimes Jóusè protested that Kahn was too generous, that indeed he was far exceeding their bargain. But Kahn knew very well how the profits had grown: 'That is nonsense,' he said; 'I shall pay myself back in less than a year; I know what I have spent.' And with this Jóusè must perforce be contented.

As for Marie she accepted it all thankfully, not daring to question, for le tout petit Loup could once again have his jellies and bouillon. It was never safe to talk of good luck; better light many candles to one's patron saint and leave the rest to God's understanding.

But Jan did not share Marie's superstitions, and he openly rejoiced: 'Christophe you grow fat; your face is becoming as round as the moon!' Then all of a sudden he hugged his cousin. And because his mind was so greatly relieved Jan prayed with renewed enthusiasm—he had started the Thirty Days' Prayer for Kahn lest he fail in this new role of benefactor.

Even the cross-grained Eusèbe accepted Kahn as a necessary evil, that was when he thought about him at all, for just lately his thoughts had become occupied by another and far more interesting person. Æliana, his granddaughter, occupied his thoughts, for now at long last he was forced to concede the claim which the years pressed so heavily on him—that lustful black eye had been growing dim, and he trembled remembering old Mathilde who he knew had been threatened with total blindness. He would often come wandering over to Marie and work on a pair of sandals in her kitchen, adjusting the soles and the thongs by feel, since his sight was sometimes too blurred to see them. And while he did this he must talk and talk about his own youth and his only daughter who, like Germaine, had borne a posthumous child, but who had given her life in the process.

'Valavalisco,' Eusèbe would growl, as he spat on his fingers and coaxed the leather, 'there are things in this world that one cannot forget—the things that one does not wish to remember. Very old she became in those terrible hours, and the doctor nothing less than a crétin. And no woman—so suddenly did it occur. And then to die like any stray bitch who must have her litter of pups in the gutter. . . .'

Amazing it was to hear his tongue wag, to hear him revealing undreamed of emotions: the fear he had felt at the sight of the corpse, the resentment he had felt at the sight of the baby: 'So I sent her away to some peasants in the hills, and afterwards to the sisters at Arles. Houi, it all seems like only last week, and yet Æliana is nearly twenty.' And then he must start to excuse himself: 'What would you, Marie, my wife was dead—there was no one, and I could not dandle an infant! Moreover the sisters are excellent souls, even nuns may sometimes have practical uses. Then again, I paid well, I have always paid well, even nuns are not averse from good money. I said: "You may do as you please with this bundle, you may teach it to play with beads if you wish, or to bob up and down like a Jack-in-the-box; it is really all one, I care nothing," I said, "only do not expect me to come here again; I am not an expert in colic or croup, and moreover I am terribly frightened of measles." Santouno, but the Reverend Mother looked shocked! However, I promptly opened my purse for I knew that its contents would soothe her feelings.'

In this vein Eusèbe would ramble on while Marie busied herself with her cooking. Half indignant, half sorry for him she would feel as he rubbed his eye with a grimy hand that could certainly not improve its condition.

'Tell me, what does Æliana look like?' she once asked, for she knew that he had been to Arles to see her.

'She resembles Ceres,' Eusèbe replied, so that naturally Marie was none the wiser.

Then one evening he said: 'She has been learning to dress-make, and next week she will take a situation that the sisters have found her; she goes as lady's maid to a château that is only twelve kilometres from here. I am glad, for now that the girl is grown up I sometimes desire to have her near me.' . . . . . .

Marie thought: 'A fine pig-sty she will find if she comes! But she will not endure it very long, I imagine.' Aloud she said: 'Then you must clean up your house; if you wish I can find you some woman to help.'

'Thank you,' he replied to her great surprise; 'I would like the house to be neat for Æliana.'

The thought of her seemed to haunt him these days. When Marie had driven him out of the kitchen because she was waiting to scrub the tiles, he would hobble away in search of Christophe; and if Christophe was too busy just then to attend, he would hobble upstairs and sit with Jóusè.

'Diéu,' Jóusè would mumble, 'for twenty years you have left her completely ignored and uncared for, yet now you can talk of no one else—I begin to think that the girl has bewitched you! However, I am glad that you went to Arles; I consider that you have been very neglectful.' And unless he was feeling his rheumatism, Eusèbe would accept such rebukes quite mildly.

But once back in his home his mood might change, whereupon he would make an outlandish commotion; whacking his bedding, or banging his floors with a broom

that was losing most of its bristles; and then he would
suddenly empty his slops and his filthy water out of the
window.

'Be off! Do not get in my way!' he would bawl at some
splashed and highly indignant pedestrian.

And Jóusè, hearing the hubbub must smile: 'Now he
grows very angry with me,' he would think; 'ah well there
are compensations it seems—I am glad I escaped the contents of that bucket!'

CHAPTER THIRTY-FIVE

I

ITT was not many months before Eusèbe obtained his
desire in regard to Æliana. One evening during the
following May she arrived, having left her situation:
'You will now have to keep me for a while,' she
announced; 'I am going to look for work in Toulon. I
think I shall try to find work at some shop; I have had quite
enough of domestic service.' And she plumped her small
valise down on a stool. 'Ah, mais oui, I have had quite
enough,' she repeated.

Eusèbe was certainly taken aback by this sudden visit,
and yet he was flattered: 'You can stay just as long as you
please,' he declared; 'to-morrow I will see about cleaning
your bedroom—it is not very grand but that you must forgive.' And he peered rather anxiously at the girl, subjugated
by her unusual beauty.

Tall and deep-bosomed she stood before him, making
the shop seem even more squalid, making her own humble
clothes look strange in conjunction with so superb a body.
The curves of her breasts were generous and firm as though
fashioned to soothe and sustain creation, the long lines of
her limbs were supple yet strong, her head small and well
poised, her lips full and ardent, her dark eyes flecked with
elusive lights that at times made the eyes themselves appear
golden. For the rest her glossy black hair waved low on a
wide and unusually placid brow—the brow and the mouth
were a contradiction. But Eusèbe saw the girl as a whole,
saw only a creature who seemed to belong to an age when
men carved the lovely immortals, and the blood throbbed
with pride through his agèd veins, since was he not in part
her begetter?

'My seed she has sprung from, my seed!' he thought,
continuing to peer at Æliana.

And so he believed the improbable story of ill treatment and hardship which she presently told him; believed that the staff had been meanly fed, overworked, and the prey of their mistress's temper. Believed Æliana's graphic account of the terrible scene that Madame had made because her nightgown had shrunk in the washing:

'It was common and therefore it would not wash; all her things were like that, she is rich but a screw. However, when she threatened to box my ears. . . .'

'You came running to grandpère,' he said fatuously, 'and quite right to come running home to your grandpère.'

'Yes, as you say . . . I came home,' she answered.

But when Eusèbe, now thoroughly roused, declared that he would visit her mistress and demand an immediate redress for these wrongs, Æliana turned on him, speaking sharply: 'You will not. You will kindly leave her alone!'

'Bien, bien, that must be as you wish,' he acquiesced; 'it was only for your sake, but if you say no. . . .'

'Most emphatically I do,' she retorted.

Just for a moment he felt suspicious. Was there something that she was hiding from him? Some matter that she did not wish him to sift? Then he shrugged the unwelcome suspicion away: 'Come, I will show you your room,' he said quickly.

Thus it happened that Æliana arrived at Saint Loup in the month of plentiful cherries, in the month when green almonds swell on their boughs, in the month when the sea is perhaps at its bluest, in the month when the mingled scents of the maquis on the hills most strangely disturb the senses. In this month of our Lady, Æliana arrived, more akin to the pagan things of the earth than she was to the gentle-faced Christian Virgin.

2

Many people were curious about Æliana's arrival, but this only very mildly. In peace-time they would probably have been all agog, but by now their minds were growing war-weary. She had come to look after Eusèbe, they supposed, and they pitied her for having so thankless a task; then they read the latest news from the front, discussed it, and promptly forgot about her. However, perhaps it was only natural that Jan and Christophe should prove the exceptions; they were frankly interested in this girl whose existence had become a kind of legend.

'Let us call and pay our respects,' suggested Jan; and since Christophe agreed, they called upon her.

They found her alone, Eusèbe having taken himself off for his usual drink at la Tarasque, and after surveying them critically she invited them into the seldom-used parlour.

'Here all is filth as you observe,' she remarked, 'but sit down, that is if you can find two whole chairs! My grand-father grows incredibly helpless; I must get a woman to clean up this mess.' And somehow it did not strike them as odd that she herself had not done the cleaning.

They were awkward and shy, finding little to say, for neither of them was accustomed to women; moreover Æliana seemed a creature apart—they had never, until now, seen anyone like her. But Æliana was quite at her ease as she let her eyes dwell thoughtfully upon Christophe.

She said: 'My grandfather talks much about you, he is always talking about your great strength. Are your muscles as fine as he would have one believe?' Christophe went scarlet, not knowing what to answer. 'I have always admired great strength,' smiled Æliana.

He found this intensely embarrassing, and was suddenly conscious that his nails were dirty. He had tried very hard to remove the stains of furniture polish but had not succeeded, so that now he looked unhappily down at his nails.

'But yes, he is strong like a bullock!' bragged Jan.

'You are strong, you also,' said Christophe quickly.

How unusual they were, so virginal, so simple, and then so fiercely loyal to each other. She had quickly divined this loyalty of theirs and she found it rather absurd yet intriguing; moreover life was none too gay at the moment, so she said:

'Tell me, what can one do in the evenings?'

They looked at her, feeling rather nonplussed: 'One can walk on the hills if one wishes,' Christophe told her; 'it is cool when one walks on the hills after work.'

'Ah, but I am so timid,' sighed Æliana, 'and yet there is much that I long to see; many places round here must be of great interest . . . my poor grandfather finds himself terribly lame.'

'If you wish we will accompany you,' Jan said politely.

'That would be entirely charming,' she answered.

Then Christophe remembered Goundran's small boat—Goundran had given him permission to use it: 'Perhaps, Mademoiselle, you would care for a row? Jan rows well, he rows much better than I do; however, we both of us make quite good speed. There are several nice places along this coast . . .' For he did not wish to fail in politeness.

And so it fell out that before they left they had planned quite a number of little excursions: they would walk up to Eusèbe's vineyards, they would show her the old citadel by moonlight, they would take her to a certain olive grove where Saint Loup was reputed to have slain many pagans; these and several other excursions they had planned before leaving—somewhat to their own amazement.

'Do we like her, Christophe?' Jan enquired later.

'I am not quite sure . . .' Christophe said doubtfully.

'Is she beautiful, do you think?' questioned Jan.

'She is very beautiful,' answered Christophe.

3

After all it was pleasant to befriend Æliana who complained that her life was intolerably lonely; pleasant also to feel that she liked them so much, that indeed she was growing dependent upon them—this dependence of hers had a charm all its own, for it flattered their timid, self-conscious manhood.

'I had meant to find work at once,' she told Jan, 'but I cannot desert my half-blind grandfather. Ah, no, I must stay with him till the end.'

And this remark Jan passed on to the Curé: 'Is it not noble of her, mon père!'

The Curé did not answer immediately, then he said: 'We all have our duties, my son,' and his prominent eyes glanced sharply at his pupil. He was thinking: 'It is foolish to interfere, if I do he may take the bit between his teeth. Better wait and watch—so far all seems well.' Then he sighed, feeling youth to be a terrible problem.

Madame Roustan, however, was not so tactful and must nag until Jan flew into a temper: 'Is it her fault that Eusèbe gets drunk? You are very unjust to judge her by him—I consider it a great lack of charity! Moreover, I am no longer a child, therefore kindly permit me to know my own business.'

Marie said to Jóusè: 'This Æliana; of course I do all that I can to befriend her for I really pity her, the poor girl—imagine living with that dirty old drunkard! But sometimes I am a little afraid. I ask myself sometimes: is she good?'

Jóusè looked tenderly at his wife: 'I do not know if Æliana is good, but I fear she is inevitable, my Marioun.'

'Why?' she faltered.

But he had not the heart to explain. Ai! las, these poor mothers who having bred sons were so apt to forget that they grew into men. 'Do not worry, we can trust our son. . . .' he consoled her.

Anfos frankly detested Æliana and whenever they met he made faces at her: 'Go away! Go away! Go away!' he would squeal; 'Do not touch me!' And then he would start grimacing. At such times even Christophe could not control him, for Anfos refused to listen to reason.

Kahn thought her appearance distinctly attractive but his mind was engrossed by affairs of business; moreover he was earning the requisite price of a visit now and again to Saint Raphaël.

Only the impudent tout petit Loup expressed a supreme and disdainful indifference: 'Pòu! what is she? Just a girl like the rest. I have never found much to choose between them. As for me, I cannot be bothered these days.' Whereupon he would roll a small cigarette with the air of one who had seduced many virgins.

Meanwhile the spring drifted into the summer, and the sun became always more insistent, and the nights more fervent from the heat of the days, while the moon came up red and preposterously large, making a red-gold path on the water. Idle and ripe for love were these nights, and idle and ripe for love was Æliana, a creature of rich blood and urgent desires, untamed, unregenerate and unabashed, despite those chastening years at the convent; moreover she had now certain memories which served to strengthen the urge that was in her. Looking at Christophe as he bent to his oars or strode beside her on the hills of an evening, his luminous eyes seeming strangely aloof, Æliana would greatly desire and yet hate him.

'He cannot be human,' she would think bitterly when he failed to respond to the touch of her hand, to the nearness of her provocative body.

And then he must constantly have Jan at his heels like a watch-dog; it was childish and irritating. Seldom could she manage to get them apart; together they had found her and now they shared her, blissfully unconscious, or so it appeared, of the fact that this filled her with deep resentment. And yet Æliana sometimes thought that Jan would have been a less arduous conquest, this despite his grave talk about entering the Church.

'I could have him if I so wished,' she would think, 'but I do not want him—I want the other.' Then those full, ardent lips and that placid brow would seem more than ever a contradiction.

One evening she remarked: 'I am tired of the hills; let us drink a small glass of wine at the café.' For as Æliana knew, wine can go to the heart as well as the head if the gods be propitious.

They hesitated, greatly abashed. Had they got the price of the wine in their pockets? No matter, Mère Mélanie knew them both and would doubtless allow them to pay the next morning. Surreptitiously they examined their cash and found that they could muster five francs between them.

At la Tarasque they came on Eusèbe dead drunk but sleeping the blissful sleep of the unrighteous: 'Do not let us sit near him, when he drinks he perspires, and when he perspires he stinks,' said Æliana.

The rest of the tables were mostly taken by youngsters on leave and bent upon frolic. One observed Æliana and promptly made eyes: 'Bon-vèspre, ma bello fadeto!' he shouted.

She smiled at him, not ill-pleased it appeared.

'It were better to ignore them,' cautioned Jan.

'And you, Christophe, what do you say?' she asked.

Christophe glanced at his sun-tanned, muscular arms: 'That I do not think they will molest you,' he answered.

She was thinking: 'He is only seventeen, yet so tall, so strong—why *will* he not love me!' And suddenly her eyes filled with angry tears.

'Moun tout, ma bello!' cried the youngster on leave, lifting his glass with mock gallantry. Æliana shrugged her shoulders and ignored him.

They sat down and Christophe ordered wine, but when it arrived he drank it coupé. Jan did not, preferring to drink his neat, which however he did with a certain precaution. Neither of them could dance it appeared, though the little violinist was in excellent fettle. A nice couple of boobies to take a girl out.

'But what can you do?' she enquired peevishly.

'The Germans will very soon know!' Jan informed her.

Æliana looked bored: 'I am tired of the war. Why discuss the war when we came here for pleasure?' Her cheeks were now faintly flushed, her eyes brilliant, and taking the bottle she refilled her glass, 'Since no one has the good manners . . .' she said frowning. Presently she groped for Christophe's hand and held it in hers but not for long; she dared not risk holding his hand too long, feeling certain that if she did so she would scare him. Yet she could not force back the words that now rose to her lips in their own soft Provençal language: 'Tu lou soulèu de ma jouvènço.' Very gently Æliana murmured those words, while she thought: 'I am calling him the sun of my youth, that is what I am calling him—how will he answer?'

He answered quite simply: 'Migo—my friend.' But Jan, who had heard her, grew curiously silent.

Alone at a table just across the room sat a person very elegantly apparelled. He was wearing an open-necked white silk shirt, a green cummerbund and tussore silk trousers. By his side stood a heavy ebony cane whose jade handle matched his jade cigarette-case. And this person had been staring for quite a long time while he smoked, drinking glass after glass of cognac which apparently left him as sober as a judge and as coldly critical—it was Beauvais. Oh, yes, it was Beauvais come back from the wars with a lung that a swallow of gas had injured, with a leg so shattered and badly repaired that never again would France need his service, with a mind half outraged and half amused by the yarns with which nations must dope their victims, but with hands that could still hold a palette and brush to some purpose, and with eyes that could still judge a woman.

Beauvais had said to himself: 'Why not? And this time I think I will stay at la Tarasque. After all I may build that sacré mas with the garden running down to the sea and a pergola on which to grow grape-vines. Quite a good proposition for a wounded hero who has certainly earned his place in the sun! Anyhow, I will take a look at my land.' And so here he was, breathing none too well while he smoked and drank and stared at Æliana.

After awhile he got to his feet, helping himself with the edge of the table upon which he must lean while he grabbed for his cane. The leg that was badly repaired hung crooked, nor could he put that heel to the ground. The surgeon had been nervous for Beauvais had screamed, only once but that once had been more than enough for the surgeon—they had run out of anæsthetics.

Limping grotesquely but quite unperturbed he made his way through the dancers to Christophe: 'Pardon, Monsieur, my name is Jacques Beauvais. Am I not addressing Monsieur Bénédit? Surely I saw you some years ago when your father erected a fence round my land? But permit me to say that you have grown somewhat.' And he laughed his pleasant and youthful laugh. 'Monsieur, you make me feel like a pygmy.'

Christophe had stood up and was offering him a chair which Beauvais accepted; then he ordered more brandy. Four brandies he ordered as a matter of course:' Unless Mademoiselle would prefer something else?'

'Mais non, this will do, I thank you,' she smiled, looking into his bloodshot amorous eyes.

'Then permit me to drink to our meeting,' he answered.

After this he must try to put the youths at their ease by talking to them about local matters. He had heard that that fellow Khan had failed; what a villain with his Galeries of abortions! So now he was working for the Bénédits; amazing that he could work with those hands—every finger had bulged like a fat white sausage: 'Your father has had a stroke? What a disaster! I remember him so clearly with his bright curly beard. I used to think that he looked like Saint Paul—or was it someone else who had such a beard? In any case he looked like an apostle. And your mother, is she well in spite of her troubles? That is good; she must be a courageous woman. I saw her the morning I called at your workshop; kindly give my compliments to your mother. By the way, if I do build that villa of mine I shall ask you to make me some strong oak cupboards. So your cousin is about to enter the Church?'

'But first I will enter the army!' exclaimed Jan, 'I will serve my God by serving my country!' His voice sounded truculent and thick, he was unused to spirits and was feeling the brandy.

Beauvais nodded: 'We all know how much God loves the French, but then he apparently also loves the Germans. One becomes a little bewildered at times; however. . . .'

'Do I understand you to mean. . . .' began Jan.

'Monsieur, you do not,' Beauvais smiled.

'Ah, bon, I am glad of that!' said Jan loudly.

And meanwhile Beauvais' bloodshot, amorous eyes must keep dwelling on Æliana's face and bosom. He addressed her seldom except with his eyes, having quickly divined that she understood him. And seeing those all but articulate glances, those long ardent looks, Jan was suddenly seized by a feeling of uncontrollable fury, so that the blood pounded in his head, so that he must dig his nails into his palms to stop himself from striking Beauvais' pale face, while his own eyes turned hungrily to the girl, perceiving the fullness and meaning of her beauty. And so great was the shock of this sexual uprush, this abrupt desire to possess a woman, tha this entrails seemed to be gripped in a vice; for a moment he felt giddy and wanted to vomit. Nor could here member the simplest prayer, but must just sit staring at Æliana.

She noticed it of course, what woman would not? But her thoughts were concentrated on Christophe. Ah, now he could see how much she was desired . . . Beauvais, the wealthy, the celebrated artist. . . . What a scarecrow he was with his twisted leg, all the same he might very well serve her purpose.

She glanced at Christophe, expectant, delighted, half whore and half child in her obvious elation: 'Christophe, tu es tellement beau—tellement beau avec ton clair regard,' she whispered 'Christophe . . .'

But he seemed to be very far away. His face looked puzzled and rather anxious as though he were trying to recapture the thread of something that he only imperfectly remembered.

Beauvais took his leave, and when he had gone they also got up and left the café. Between them the cousins paid for the wine.

'Let us walk a little way out of the town; it is hot to lie in our beds,' said Æliana, 'and besides I am feeling very wide awake.' She was thinking: 'I will tell him now about Louis; not quite all, ça non, but enough, just enough.' Aloud she said: 'I have something to confess; a long time I have wished to make this confession.'

But Æliana delayed her confession until they had left the houses behind them and were sitting upon a low wayside bank. They could see the black masterful curves of the Maures rising superbly towards a sky that was pale and opalescent with moonlight.

Then she said: 'You shall be my father confessors, you shall listen and give me your absolution. Christophe—Jan— I have told a very big falsehood in order to spare your Eusèbe. I did not tell him the truth when I came here; I lied about leaving my situation. I did not leave, Madame turned me out. Her dear son Louis had come back from the front and was staying at the château with his wife—she was pretty, his wife; they had not long been married. Ma foi, she was pretty enough to content him, but no, he must take a fancy to me, must always be wanting to kiss me behind doors, to pursue me when I went into the garden to pick flowers for his mother's dressing-table. Ah, bon Dieu, what a man! Half crazy he was because I would not accept his advances. No, but never had I conceived of such passion as his. . . .'

'Why must you tell us these things?' Jan muttered.

She glanced sideways: 'Be patient, they are part of my confession—when you are a priest you will hear many others. No, never had I conceived of such passion. His wife suspected, but what could I do? I could not reveal his perfidy to her. Alas, the poor thing, I would find her in tears

325

and many a time I would long to comfort. Mais oui, he was handsome, I will not deny it, but so brutal, a beast, he would look like a beast. Do you think that perhaps all men are beasts when women deny them?'

They did not answer.

Æliana paused, then went on more quickly: 'The end came when he followed me into her bedroom. I had gone there to put away her clothes, and quite suddenly I turned round and saw him—he could walk very quietly when he wished. I wanted to scream but I felt too frightened. Ah, mes amis, he pushed me down on the bed, his wife's bed, but I fought like a tiger, I bit him! Then a fearful thing happened: his wife came in and found us . . . like that. Eh bien, I was dismissed: they refused to believe my explanation. But I feared to tell my grandfather the truth because he is old and half blind, yet so violent. He would surely have wanted to kill that man. Ah, well, now you know and I am relieved that you should; I have always hated the deception.'

Jan was white to the lips; white and trembling he sat not daring to look at Æliana, not daring to trust himself to speak. Then he suddenly turned his face away, fearful lest Christophe should read its expression. But Christophe had stooped and was moving his finger on the path as though he were writing in the dust—very thoughtfully he was moving his finger.

Æliana stared: 'Christophe, stop!' she exclaimed, 'Why are you so strange? I find you most strange. . . .'

He sprang up: 'No, no! Do not say that, Æliana! It was nothing at all . . . but just for a moment . . . never mind, it has passed.' His voice shook with the fear that since her coming he had almost forgotten.

She frowned angrily: 'Let us return,' she said, 'I am sick of you both; you behave like children.'

CHAPTER THIRTY-SIX

I

JAN stood in front of the Curé. He was saying:
'Mon père, I beg of you, let me enlist. I am over
seventeen, and if I enlist I shall get right away from
here and find peace.'

But the Curé shook his head: 'No, my son, it is
not by such means that you will find peace. Peace comes
only to those who have conquered themselves; if you go now
you will not have conquered yourself and the thing that you
fear will still be a torment. You must face it and wrench it
out of your heart. You must trust to the efficacy of prayer.'
He paused, remembering his own bitter youth. Did Jan
know the completeness of his understanding? Of course
not; how should he? And these platitudes. . . . 'You have
courage,' he went on rather desperately; 'Our Lord always
needs the brave in His service.' Then his voice shook a
little: 'Ah, my child—my dear child. . . .' For the father in
him was deeply distressed, was deeply moved by com-
miseration; 'Jan, listen to me, I do understand, and when
you are eighteen you will go like the rest; it is surely not
long to wait, have patience, and meanwhile stay here and
fight the good fight—there are so many ways of being
courageous!'

Jan bowed his head: 'As you will, mon père.'

But his fierce black eyes looked hot and resentful, and
observing this the Curé must sigh: 'It is not as I will but as
God wills,' he told him. 'Let us go into the Church; we will
pray there awhile.' And he laid a thin hand on his pupil's arm.

Jan nodded, but his eyes were still resentful.

*   *   *

That night the Curé sat huddled in his chair; he was
feeling old and unusually tired: 'I am nearly seventy now,'

he thought; 'it is therefore quite natural that I should feel old.' But he knew that it was not the passing of the years that caused him to sit huddled up in his chair; rather was it a doubt that harassed his soul. 'And yet I have acted wisely'; he argued, 'I cannot allow him to go until I must. It is surely my duty to keep the boy near me at this the most critical juncture of his life. Who will guard him from spiritual harm if he goes while these fleshly longings are so heavy upon him?'

Yet he dared not look into his aching heart, dared not face the real fear that lay in that heart together with the wellnigh hopeless hope that when Jan was eighteen the war would be over. Madame de Bêrac's only son had been killed. It was strange how this happening had brought things home. A young man whom the Curé had never seen had been killed, God knew how, in some distant battle, and all of a sudden that man had been Jan, and the battlefield the Curé's own study.

On the following Sunday he had preached very badly: 'He was dull this morning,' people had grumbled, missing the violence he had taught them to expect, 'mais oui, that sermon was more like the old days.' They had felt defrauded, almost resentful, for the Curé's war-sermons were now quite well known: there were those who would come several miles to hear them.

The Curé got up and stood lost in thought, rubbing his chin and puckering his forehead. What had he done with the silver rood—the Bona-Mors rood that had been his mother's? He had put it away quite safely, of course, but he could not remember precisely where. How strange to forget so important a thing; and he needed it now against Jan's going. In the past he had always worn it himself, but as time went on he had found it a burden. It had been so inconveniently large—just over six inches the cross had measured—and heavy, its weight had irked his neck; but now he must find that old silver rood blessed for a holy death by some saint—a saint whose name he had also forgotten.

The Curé began to ransack his cupboards, growing always more careless with agitation as he ploughed his way through the rubbish of years that his indolence had unwittingly hoarded. With trembling hands he thrust things aside or flung them down on his study floor: 'I cannot have lost my mother's rood. Ah, but no, I cannot!' he kept repeating.

In the end he found it at the bottom of a chest under three or four pairs of moth-eaten socks, a tobacco pouch, and a worn-out biretta; there it lay in its faded Morocco case; opening the case the Curé gazed at it. The silver was wonderfully bright and untarnished, but the face of the Christ had been worn smooth by time like that of the patron warrior-bishop, and because of this the eyes appeared blemished. Was there something rather dreadful about those eyes— something that suggested wounds? He looked closer. Then all in a moment he seemed to envisage those who groped in a helpless, agonized blindness, their eyes torn away by the bursting shells, their hands outstretched in vain supplication. 'Not Jan, oh, not Jan! Do not let it be Jan!' And yet they were Jan, all those groping men; their moans were his moans for their pain was his pain, and the blood that oozed from their wounds was his also.

Sweating with anguish the Curé prayed: 'Lord Christ, do not let them take my son's eyes! Lord, Lord, do not let them deprive him of sight . . . those who have eyes to see let them see. . . . You who healed. . . . Son of God, Son of Mary, have mercy so that he may see You with the eyes of his flesh, Christ crucified . . . Christ who rose from the dead . . . Christ glorified . . . it is my son, it is Jan . . . the child that for Your sake I did not beget. . . .' With a mighty effort he checked himself, conscious that his mind was beyond his control and terrified lest it should plunge into madness.

2

The frequent meetings with Æliana terminated somewhat abruptly. Jan excused himself on the plea of hard work: 'I must work in the evenings,' he said to Christophe, 'the Curé insists, and of course he is right; just lately I have been growing slack.' And Christophe did not question this statement, did not for a moment suspect the truth—Jan had never permitted interference with his studies.

As for Æliana who had so much desired to find Christophe alone, she now seemed indifferent or else distinctly hostile towards him: 'I have told you that I cannot go for long walks. You know perfectly well that I am sitting to Beauvais which is very fatiguing. Do stop pestering me!' And greatly bewildered, Christophe would leave her.

But one thing inevitably resulted from Æliana's swift change of tactics: he could not get the girl out of his thoughts and would find himself constantly brooding upon her, and the more he brooded the lonelier he grew, incredible how much he missed those walks, how dreary the evenings had become without her. And suddenly he felt an immense sense of loss that encompassed far more than Æliana: something had brushed against his life, something sweet and disturbing like those scents from the hills; had he stretched forth his hand he might surely have grasped it, but instead he had driven this thing away by his failure to recognize its presence. He had failed to recognize the presence of love, of the warm and comforting physical love in which all the world's creatures demanded their share, and in which there was neither fear nor strangeness.

Oh, but never in the past had there been such a moment for youth to rise up assertive, triumphant; and perceiving that its moment had come his youth rose to assert the right of its claim to fulfilment. Behind it stood all those men of the south, strong, virile and simple, from whom Christophe had sprung; men whose vigorous bodies had brooked no denial, whose sins had seldom been the sins of the spirit. A mighty army they stood behind youth, eager to live again in their seed, in the strength that they had bequeathed to their descendant. Thus while Jan sat bending over his books in a desperate effort at concentration, or indulged in such endless self-imposed fasts and penances that the Curé protested, Christophe found himself unable even to pray, so great was the indiscipline of his mind which could now hold no image save Æliana's.

Rather terrible days, for the more she confused him the more clumsily he began to pursue her, so that all that he did was unwisely done, as is only too often the way with lovers. Every moment that he could snatch from his bench would be passed in hanging about Eusèbe on some childish pretext that failed to deceive, and Eusèbe would look none too friendly in spite of his erstwhile affection for Christophe. Gramaci! a half-fledged, penniless boy to come mooning around like a love-sick calf. . . . Ah, but no, Eusèbe had quite other plans in his drink-fuddled brain—there was Beauvais for instance. Beauvais would be an excellent match; with her beauty and wits Æliana could catch him if she wished. Thus was added yet one more dream to the dreams that lurked in Mère Mélanie's bottles.

However, despite Eusèbe's annoyance, Christophe would arrive with flowers for Æliana—humble flowers that the old sandal-maker called weeds and that shared the slopes of the hills with the maquis: 'Look,' Christophe would stammer, 'I have brought you these, they are wild . . . not precisely what I could desire. . . .'

She would thank him coldly then lay them aside, not even troubling to put them in water.

The day came when he actually offered her the plaque that Anfos had carved for his First Communion: 'This is something I very much value,' he said, 'that is why I am anxious that you should have it.'

Æliana stared at the Chalice and Host surrounded by a choir of birds and much glory: 'Not so bad for the work of a half-wit,' she remarked in a voice that she meant to be irritating.

Christophe snatched it away: 'You are cruel!' he said sharply, 'Anfos gives of his best—he carved this with great love.'

'Then why do you not keep the thing?' she enquired.

'Assuredly I will keep it,' scowled Christophe.

But he could not remain angry with her for long, and his anger once spent he became very humble, begging her to come out in Goundran's boat, or to climb to the old citadel by moonlight, or to walk to the vineyards beyond the town: 'Just this once, Æliana . . .' he would plead, 'just this once.'

She would smile as she looked at him furtively, then turning her head aside, would refuse him.

And now even while he worked he must brood; there was neither beginning nor end to his brooding. Why had she left her situation like that? Something warned him that she had lied about it. It was horrible to love and yet to mistrust, the more so when in spite of mistrust love persisted.

'She lied—I am certain she lied,' he would think, growing fiercely and retrospectively jealous as he visualized scene after scene from her past. Then his thoughts would leap forward to the present and Beauvais.

At this time he much longed for someone to talk to, someone to whom he could tell his troubles. But youth finds it hard to confide in age and Christophe felt suddenly shy of his parents, dreading his mother's anxious face and his father's eyes with their unspoken question. He would go and see Jan, but having found him would become almost equally shy with his cousin. Moreover, Jan had grown very aloof and seemed disinclined to discuss Æliana. Then again each would secretly be feeling abashed because of the thing which both had learned yet which neither could find the courage to mention, so that presently Christophe would get up and leave with the words he had intended to say still unspoken.

Half reluctant, half eager and wholly obsessed he would hurry along to the Café de la Tarasque. Æliana would be in her usual place with Beauvais at a table not far from the entrance. Then Christophe would loiter beside the door in order to spy on them as they sat there. Very shameful indeed he would find what he did, yet in spite of its shamefulness must continue, for his eyes would seem irresistibly drawn towards those two, now always together. Every gesture, every expression he would watch with the fearful intentness of one who observes the instruments prepared for his torture. Sometimes he would walk quickly into the room, conscious that he was attracting attention; then seating himself he would call for wine, speaking familiarly to the waiter, trying to appear very much at his ease as though well acquainted with the life of the café.

Mère Mélanie would nod and smile at him kindly: 'Bon soir, mon enfant. Have you given your order? That is excellent!' For she liked his bronzed face and the poise of his youthful, muscular shoulders; moreover she observed the way the wind blew and was noting the whole affair with deep interest.

But if Beauvais saw him he would tell his companion, amused at her innocent look of indifference and at Christophe's hot flush as he got to his feet and bowed rather stiffly to Æliana.

Then one evening Beauvais insisted that he join them: 'It is always bad to drink lonely,' said Beauvais; 'come and drink with us. Allons, what will you have, some cognac? No? Very well, let us see what Mère Mélanie hides away in her cellar!'

His experienced eyes were dwelling on Christophe with the thoughtful, speculative gaze of the artist. He was thinking that the young male form at its best was undoubtedly nature's greatest achievement; small wonder if Æliana were enamoured of those finely restrained yet masterful lines. He glanced at her, shrugging indifferent shoulders. Cynical, ailing and infinitely tired, Beauvais took life these days as he found it. He accepted Æliana for the thing that she was, a creature conducive to moments of pleasure; a creature who could sometimes make him forget the ugliness that was scarring the world, the infirmities of his own shattered body. Just this much she meant and he found it enough; nor did her fidelity greatly concern him, if he lost her to Christophe it would not break his heart—she was beautiful, yes, but incredibly stupid. So now he watched Æliana as she played with the boy's tormented, resentful manhood, as she smiled and encouraged, as she frowned and rebuffed, and the game seemed to Beauvais puerile and disgusting. Quite suddenly he grew bored with them both; his leg ached and he longed to be in his bed:

'Waiter!' he called irritably, 'More brandy.'

The room was stifling, and the little violinist was making a truly infernal racket in an effort to please Mère Mélanie who insisted that he should appear light-hearted. Round and round went the lumbering, perspiring dancers, butting into each other, butting into the tables; men who three years ago had been lank, beardless cubs but whose chins were now rough and dark by the evening; girls who six months ago had been going to school but who now had the air of experienced women. Forced products, the over-ripe fruits of war, already tinged with an early decay because grown in the steaming dung of disruption. And since death was seldom far from their thoughts they clasped and kissed and danced rather grimly, not pausing to laugh when they upset a chair, or even to jest while the music continued. Kissing and clasping they danced against time, body straining to body, desire to desire, for who dared count upon time as a friend? Every woman possessed might well be the last, every lover refused might not live to be accepted. Even the youngsters at home on first leave quite failed to dispel this atmosphere of grimness, failed to make of la Tarasque the place it had been on those hot summer nights before the war when tempers were short while knives could be long, when the little violinist with the hump on his back stirred more than the air by his shrill, teasing music. For one thing they had not known the place then, with its gay and inconsequent melodrama which had frequently led to nothing more grave than a broken nose or a prick in the shoulder; for another the little violinist was sad, so that when he played he stirred only himself and that to regret—no use boxing his ears, just about as much use as smashing his fiddle! La Tarasque remained but its spirit had fled, perhaps to some limbo expressly reserved for the unregenerate spirits of places.

Beauvais leaned back and closed his eyes; the pain of his leg had grown more insistent, while the smoke of the endless cigarettes had filtered into his injured lung; at that moment he was thinking that he would not much care if a bomb were to drop and complete his destruction. In any case he was tired of Saint Loup, it was now September, he had been here for weeks, better make up his mind to return to Paris.

And seeing that they were unobserved, Æliana moved quietly nearer to Christophe: 'To-morrow,' she whispered, 'to-morrow night at the old citadel; meet me there after supper. Do not fail me, you who mean all the world. . . .'

The breath caught in his throat as her face brushed his, as he heard the ardour of those last words: 'You must know that I shall not fail you,' he muttered.

CHAPTER THIRTY-SEVEN

I

THAT night Christophe lay very wide awake marvelling because of this thing that had happened. All the world he meant to her, she had said; and indeed this did seem marvellous to him, so that he trembled lest he break the spell of the joy that flooded over his heart, lest his mind slip back again into a past that had held so many strange apprehensions.

And now he must grasp at those gentle illusions whereby a poor, troubled humanity will strive, at such times, to link body with spirit, must perforce see Æliana as one cruelly traduced, as one who had suffered a grievous injustice; must blush to remember his own bitter thoughts and those doubts which he felt to have been so unworthy, and in consequence must long to console, to humble himself, to implore forgiveness.

Oh, but he would strive hard to make amends, her beauty should be very sacred to him; he would teach her that love could be strong yet gentle, he would strive to efface what had gone before—that stark hideousness of which she had spoken. They would wait for each other. She would gladly wait until he was earning enough to marry; and one day they would have a home of their own—a little house down at the port like Goundran's. Æliana would then make a friend of Elise—they must certainly look for a house near Goundran's. Yes, but the war. His thoughts paused a moment, yet even the war now appeared less fearful for now he would have Æliana to defend, and somehow this seemed to make all the difference. She might even marry him before he went—these days there were many such hasty unions—he would ask her, as the time of his training was so near, and of course she would answer: 'I will marry you at once—I love you.' That was how Æliana would answer.

Illusions, they began to gather more swiftly, and now they were shining like clouds of glory whose very brightness rendered him blind to his youth, his poverty, his mean situation. He saw himself as one possessed of the earth in possessing the love of the creature he loved, and suddenly he wanted to shout for triumph; to shout till the moon fell out of the sky, till the stars came tumbling down through the roof, till the peaks of the Maures bowed their heads and trembled.

'She loves me! She loves me!' he wanted to shout to the moon, to the stars, to the trembling mountains.

But in spite of all this he began to feel shy and intensely self-conscious as he dressed the next morning; and his shyness increased as the morning wore on, so that he dared not look at Æliana when she passed the open door of the shop and gave him a nod and a smile in passing. Scarlet to the ears he bent over his work, pretending to be very deeply engrossed and snapping his newest chisel in the process. Indeed he would gladly have hidden himself, so painful had become his confusion; would gladly have hidden himself from Anfos who seemed to be watching his every movement, from his mother who begged him to eat his meal, from Anatole Kahn who made well-meaning jokes, from Loup whose smirk was unbearably sly, from his father whose patient eyes urged him to speak by the depth of their kindness and understanding—he greatly longed to lay down his tools and take refuge in the solitude of the hills, there to pass those interminable hours of waiting. For now in addition to everything else he was haunted by a nebulous feeling of sadness—the sadness that comes when the blossom must fall to give place to the graver claims of fruition. Inarticulate, shy and sad he felt, despite those erstwhile moments of triumph.

Then at last the day drifted into the evening, and the moon was rising over the harbour which in spite of the war still reeked of wine and the dregs of wine—the same ancient reek that engendered such monstrous imaginings, such hot thoughts of the godless god that was Bacchus. At la Tarasque the little violinist made music, and Eusèbe lolled in his corner, and Beauvais sat sipping his third petit verre while the couples clasped and danced rather grimly. Outside on the quay a quarrel flared up, burnt awhile, and died down amid boisterous laughter; some sailors swung by singing snatches of song; a stray mongrel lugubriously bayed the moon, then yelped when one of the sailor-men kicked it; from the water came the rattle of blocks and chain as a boat was prepared for a night of fishing. But Christophe had passed through the grey stone archway that had been bequeathed to Saint Loup by the Romans, and now as he climbed the quiet hillside beyond, it seemed to him that that arch was a portal whose door had for ever silently closed upon all that was strange, obscure and unreal—for nothing seemed real except Æliana.

*   *   *

She was standing with her back against the ruins, but she came towards him out of their shadows and passed into the full, soft light of the moon, so that his heart must beat thickly to see her. The moonlight fell on her ardent lips, on her brow that was serenely placid, on the curves of her breasts that were generous and firm as though fashioned to soothe and sustain creation. And he thought that never before had she looked so wonderful as she looked on this night when they two, for the first time, were meeting as lovers.

He said, as he raised her hand to his lips: 'I cannot believe I am awake, Æliana, although everything else in the world seems like a dream.'

She smiled at his courtly, old-fashioned gesture; smiled and wondered when he would kiss her mouth, when he would take her into his arms: 'And yet I am very much in love,' she told him, 'from the first time we met . . . it came like that . . . all of a sudden I knew that we must. . . .' She paused, something warned her to be on her guard, to tread warily with this unusual creature for whom she had conceived so clamorous a need, 'that we two were meant for each other,' she finished.

'Yes,' he answered gravely, 'I am sure that I also was in love from the very first moment I saw you.' He was thinking: 'I must not make her afraid; I must handle her gently . . . not like that other. Doubtless she remembers and is feeling afraid.' And at this thought a great tenderness surged up in

337

him, a great wave of chivalry, so that he gazed with deep love in his eyes yet forbore to touch her. Then he said: 'When we two are married, mon amour, I will show you how a man can care for a woman—how strong but how kind a thing love can be.'

'When we two are married?' she queried in amazement.

'Yes,' he smiled, not hearing that incredulous tone, 'and I think that we ought to marry quite soon, before I leave for my military training. I would have it quite soon, for I want you so much ... I dare not let you know how much, Æliana.

Then he told her about the plans he had made, being sure of obtaining his parents' consent. Just at first he would wish her to live in their home; but afterwards, when he came back from the war, he would work day and night, he would slave if need be, and perhaps they could then have a home of their own, a little house down at the port like Goundran's—there would be Elise with whom she could make friends, so that while he was working she need never feel lonely. And all that he said seemed incredibly foolish, incredibly lacking in worldly wisdom, to this girl who had very soon gauged the world despite those chastening years at the convent. No money, no prospects, and he not yet eighteen, a fine match! She could almost have laughed in his face had it not been that she was afraid she might lose him. Bon Dieu, the boy must be out of his wits:

'But we cannot possibly marry, my Christophe.'

'Not marry? You will not marry me?' he stammered, 'But I thought that you loved me, Æliana. . . .' And his face whitened painfully under its tan, 'Æliana, do not say I have misunderstood. . . .'

Then Æliana looked into his eyes: 'Ah, Christophe, it is surely time you grew up—do not be such a child in your understanding. We are young and we love—is that not enough? Life is sweet because so uncertain these days. Are we to lose all its sweetness, we two, because we are poor and can therefore not marry? Because my grandfather would not consent to help us by even so much as a centime? And because I myself would never be willing to live as a constant drag on your parents? Are we to torment ourselves, must we starve? You will go to the front . . . if you should not return. . . .' Her voice shook: 'But I tell you you shall not go until I have had my joy of you, Christophe—until you have had your joy of me. . . .'

And now she no longer knew what she was saying, could no longer pause to consider her words for the lash of the primitive impulse that drove her—a creature of rich blood and urgent desires, untamed, unregenerate, and crudely insistent. At that moment something died in his heart. His love for her died, but into its place leapt an impulse as primitive as her own, and he kissed her lips roughly, despairingly.

'Hold me closer . . . closer, Christophe,' she whispered.

He flung out his arms with a queer wide gesture, and even as he did so he cried aloud, for his hands seemed transfixed by shafts of pain, so that his extended arms remained rigid: 'I cannot,' he said wildly; 'Æliana, I cannot!'

She stared at him aghast. He was standing quite still, a dark, motionless figure, powerful yet helpless; nor did he speak after those first words. There was something awful about his stillness and about the bewildered expression of his eyes. Turning, she fled away down the path, leaving him there alone in the moonlight.

His arms dropped to his sides. He looked at his hands: the flesh of the palms was whole and unblemished, no wounds to account for that searing pain, no traces of blood on the work-hardened skin, and no pain any more. But fear—the old fear—only ten-fold more poignant than in the past. Covering his face he fell to sobbing.

2

Early the next morning came Eusèbe, and he apparently all but demented: 'She has gone! Æliana has gone!' he wailed as he hobbled into the Bénédit's kitchen. 'Only this moment am I come from the station where the porter assisted them to catch the train—Æliana and that lecherous cripple, Beauvais. I slept soundly—I was tired—I am always tired—and she must have sneaked out of the house and met him. Ai! las, when I went to find her in her room her things were not there and the room was empty. Blind and lame though I am I immediately rushed off . . . but too late, already a good hour too late. . . . Ai, it is finished, she has

339

broken my heart, her ingratitude has undoubtedly killed me!' Then he started to curse and upbraid the sisters for idle, loose-living, impious women who had taken his money while neglecting the child: 'Was it for this that I paid them,' he raged, 'that I fed that pot-bellied Reverend Mother, that I emptied my purse—yes, year after year—so that they might teach the child to be virtuous! Ah, the vipers, the vile, hypocritical strumpets, the usurers! I shall write to the bishop.'

Marie said: 'I am grieved for you, Eusèbe—I am naturally grieved at what you have told me. There is one thing, however, that I cannot permit: you shall not insult those good nuns in my presence; moreover if you yourself attended Mass. . . .' But at that Eusèbe lurched from the house and went hobbling quickly towards la Tarasque.

Arrived at the café he burst out afresh: 'Is this place of yours a bordel?' he shouted, 'It is here that my grand-daughter met that swine with whom she has gone off this morning to Paris. I shall make it my business to inform the police!'

Mère Mélanie adjusted a curling-pin, then she said: 'I am not yet deaf, Eusèbe.'

He stamped, groaned loudly and clutched at his back—ten thousand devils! it was stiffening again, in a moment he might not be able to move: 'Tell me all that you know of this business,' he babbled.

'What should I know?' asked Mère Mélanie blandly, 'They would often retire to his rooms together, and the waiter now tells me that they bolted the doors, but of course they had the excuse of the portrait, though why they must bolt the doors for that. . . . However, it was really none of my business.'

'But when did you last see the girl?' roared Eusèbe, by this time all but slobbering with fury.

'Yesterday evening—you had only just gone, and exceedingly drunk you were, I remember. She came in and sat with Beauvais for awhile. She seemed agitated but Beauvais was laughing. Presently she left, I supposed for her home, but I did not enquire, it was no affair of mine—you yourself have seen them here many evenings. This morning Beauvais paid his bill and departed; his tips, I am told, were extremely generous. To me his conduct was above reproach, though what may have happened upstairs in the bedroom. . . . However, I really cannot bore little holes in the walls in order to spy on my clients!'

'They might retaliate in kind!' he retorted.

Then Mère Mélanie's composure abruptly left her: 'Enough of your insults, you drunken old liar. You have called my respectable café a bordel, yes, and now you make dirty insinuations! Bien, this I tell you: not one litre of wine from your vineyards shall enter my doors next season. As for you, you can go and you need not return; you can take yourself farther along the quay. I am sick of your filth and your filthy ways; when you are drunk you pollute the floor —the waiter has made me representations. Get out! Did you hear me? I said get out!' And she laid a ruthless hand on his collar.

But habit is the only real solace of old age and Eusèbe peered at his table, at the table where he had tippled for years, dreaming those frequently scandalous dreams that lurked for him in Mère Mélanie's bottles; and Eusèbe peered at his chair, the one chair in the room with arms and a cushion; then he peered at Mère Mélanie's beetle-brows, and then at the hump on her little violinist.

'Mémère, do not be so hard-hearted,' he coaxed, squirming feebly in her masterful grip; 'mémère, listen, I am naturally much perturbed, and when one is perturbed one will speak with rashness. Let me go to my table and try to forget. Believe me, I have the deepest respect. . . .'

Mère Mélanie shook him and promptly forgave: 'Gusas!' she scolded, but not too unkindly.

So the little violinist with the hump on his back fetched a bottle of the most potent wine in the cellar, and this he uncorked with a flourish and a grin, setting the wine before Eusèbe. And presently Eusèbe forgot, as he slept to the sound of his own loud snores; for habit is the only real solace of old age, and the habit of la Tarasque was very consoling.

CHAPTER THIRTY-EIGHT

I

IN the days that followed Æliana's going, it seemed
to Christophe as though some firm hand had been
placed on the helm of his existence, while the will
that lay hidden behind that hand was trying to
capture and then to bind him until he had served its
inscrutable ends. And there came the conviction that
Æliana, she also, had been compelled to serve, that no
creature could ever exist in vain or completely escape from
this law of service.

Very ruthlessly she had shattered his love, very crudely
torn to shreds his illusions, and now he no longer even
desired this girl—he had nothing to give her but pity. And
yet he knew that through her he had come to a wider and
deeper understanding of humanity; nay more, had glimpsed
truths that all but transcended his limited vision. It was
surely the Life itself that he had glimpsed, the very essence
and purpose of God from which flowed all seen and unseen
things; all tireless endeavour, all creative mind, all sublime
inspiration, all courage, all beauty. And greatly bewildered
he thought he perceived that evil was only the shadow of
glory, of a glory not yet completely fulfilled but whose
splendour would ultimately cast no shadow, so that sinner
and saint would become one indeed, and that one the
expression of God's fulfilment.

'Even now they are not two but one,' he mused, 'an
eternal oneness—it is always the same.'

And his thoughts slipped backwards over the years to
that curious meeting with old Mathilde. What was it that
Mathilde had said about light and things intertwined . . .
had she also known? Then he suddenly remembered his
painstricken hands, and something within him faltered and
trembled.

The scandal created by Æliana and Beauvais still raged through the town unabated; few people could talk of anything else. Santouno, a nice business! But then what could you expect in view of a grandfather like Eusèbe? A drunken old villain who had even been known to behave with lasciviousness to a cork tree! Small wonder that the girl had gone to the bad on the first propitious occasion that offered. And he wringing his hands and cursing the nuns and swearing that he would write to the bishop. The bishop indeed! Boudiéu, what next? Perhaps he would write to Saint Loup himself, or to Saint Saturnin, or the three Holy Marys! Thus they talked and looked shocked and wagged scandalized heads, deploring the looseness of girls since the war, and forbidding their daughters to visit the cafés.

But Christophe and Jan when alone together avoided all mention of Æliana, for their tongues would grow stiff at the thought of her name. And this silence of theirs it was that betrayed them more completely than any words could have done, so that each divined the other's secret, and having divined it must feel ashamed, as though he had wilfully spied on his brother.

It was Jan who spoke first—from sheer desperation. They were walking towards the vineyards one evening when he stopped abruptly and faced his friend: 'Christophe . . . it is about Æliana. I cannot help knowing about you two before she went off with Beauvais to Paris. I heard many things but I would not believe . . . I did not want to believe, because. . . .' He hesitated, flushed and went on, 'because, as I think you have long known, I also . . . but for me it was a most deadly sin. I have taken a solemn vow to our Lord that I will be pure when I enter His service. You were free and I feared—ah, but how much I feared—that her coming across our path might divide us.'

They stared at each other through the gathering dusk. Then: 'Nothing can ever divide us,' said Christophe.

'But she might have bred hatred between you and me,' Jan persisted, and this thought seemed to him so fearful that he gripped Christophe's hand as once long ago he had gripped it on those same hills in their childhood. And now, even as then, he felt vaguely afraid: 'I do not want to lose you,' he murmured.

After this they turned and walked on more slowly, each engrossed by his thoughts, and when next Jan spoke his voice sounded indifferent: 'Eh bien, she has gone. She will never come back—she has ceased to exist.'

But Christophe was not deceived by those words, divining the trouble that lay beneath them.

3

The weeks passed and autumn gave place to winter. During that November the Curé Martel appeared to recapture his old eloquence, so that people were flocking to hear his sermons. In Palestine there was a great offensive:

'A crusade! A holy crusade!' cried the Curé. 'Ah, my children, it is terrible to be old. Were I young I would not be here raising my voice, but in Palestine raising my hand against those who have so long reviled and insulted my Saviour—I bless God when I think that our brave French detachment is fighting shoulder to shoulder with the English. Before Gaza the Turkish trenches have been captured. Jaffa has fallen, by the grace of our Lord. He is leading us on to Jerusalem: "Follow Me!" He commands, as He shows us the way through devastation and death to life, "Follow Me, die for Me! Yes, if needs be die that you may be one with My resurrection".' Thus did Antoine Martel, Curé of Saint Loup, strive to ease his anguish of heart by much speaking.

But now Jan was growing hourly more restless. He could no longer study, nor eat, nor sleep, as the galling frustrations imposed on his flesh began to find for themselves a new channel. In great bitterness of spirit he passed his days, but his sleepless nights were even more bitter; filled with long-ings, and with hatreds no less intense, so that when he knelt clasping his crucifix in agonized prayer, it would seem like a weapon.

'Cleanse me even as by fire,' he would pray, the while he conjured up visions of war and the flames and the blood and the lusts of war, lest he turn to his lusting for Æliana.

344

Such nights were leaving their mark upon Jan, his face had grown thin to emaciation. A kind of keen misery burnt in his eyes and shook in his words of fierce condemnation—he could now seldom speak except to condemn, and hearing him Christophe would think of the shadow.

Every evening the cousins would spend together, for Jan sought to escape from his mother and the Curé: 'Does he want me to skulk like a coward?' he would rage. 'A fine thing in view of those sermons of his! "Go," he says to the others, but to me he says: "Stay until you must go." I think he is mad—or is it from cruelty that he keeps me?'

And once Christophe answered: 'It is surely from love.'

'Then I do not admit of such love,' scowled Jan, 'I find it cowardly, and very unworthy.'

If they happened to be in the Bénédit's kitchen, as was often the case on these winter evenings, Marie would feel the blood ebb from her heart. But le tout petit Loup would feel his heart beating, and this with such violence that it ached in his throat.

'Babble; all you do is to babble!' he would gibe, 'Dis donc, how many Turks have you killed with your tongue?'

'More than you will ever kill.' Jan might retort, with a smile that emphasized the boy's weakness.

Poor Anfos would crouch on his chair in silence, and this silence of his gave them cause for misgivings, since he now seldom spoke of his own accord and when they addressed him he answered them nothing, but turned his head away like a dog that is sick unto death. Only with his eyes did he seem to speak of unfathomable things when he let them rest broodingly upon Christophe.

And meanwhile Jan would explain at great length why Christophe and he should enlist without waiting. If they waited until they reached the full age for their military service they would probably be parted, whereas if they enlisted, as likely as not they could get themselves sent to the same regiment—such requests, declared Jan, were frequently granted. But they must not lose time, they were nearly eighteen. . . . Then the blood would go ebbing from Marie's heart as it had from the hearts of countless mothers.

One night Christophe asked his father abruptly: 'If I wish to enlist have I your consent?'

And Jóusè thought: 'Ah . . . so here it is!' as a man might think who is struck by a bullet. 'Ah . . . so here it is!' Jóusè thought, for our thoughts are seldom attuned to such moments. Aloud he said: 'Can you doubt it, my son?' And his voice was amazingly clear and courageous, 'France bred you through me, a servant of France.' Then he suddenly felt a great, sickening weakness as though Christophe were being torn from his flesh, leaving behind an unstanchable, wound. 'Good-night . . . God bless you . . . bless you,' he mumbled.

Christophe slowly mounted the stairs to his attic, and his heart was heavy because of his parents. In the neighbouring attic he heard Loup's cough—a high, irritable, protesting cough that wore on the nerves of those who must hear it. Then a pause while Loup sucked a lozenge, he supposed, or sipped his glass of lemon and water. No good undressing, why try to sleep when one's eyes would only stare into the darkness? There it was again—the lozenge had failed——cough, cough; cough, cough. Christophe frowned, then sighed, ashamed because he hated that cough, so high, so irritable, so protesting.

Sitting down he began to consider Loup, thinking uneasily over his future. They could not control him, nobody could; he would take his own line if it led to the devil! What a will, what fortitude, yes, but what rages—the way he had recently flown at the doctor who had been so kind to him all his life, and who, moreover, had spoken so gently: 'It may be, my dear child, that we always need men, but believe me your heart and your chronic asthma . . . they would never accept you, my very dear child . . .' and then the way Loup had flown at the doctor. Ah, those words. They had none of them known where to look. He had flown at the doctor and called him a fool who did not know a heart from a bladder! Christophe's lips twitched at this memory—still, it would not advantage le tout petit Loup to heap insults on those who wished to befriend him.

Loup was so small and the war so immense. He would certainly lose himself in a trench, or get trodden on, or pushed into a shellhole! His hands were so small yet they longed to kill—weak hands, sick hands that refused to heal when the skin was rubbed off their palms or their knuckles—

incredible that they should long to kill. Or was it that Loup had forgotten death in his pitiful eagerness for life, in his pitiful longing for physical well-being? Or was it the thing that he, Christophe, had felt, that he still felt, the intolerable urge of their country?

How many men had been killed in the war and how many men remained for the killing? Great armies of them, great empires of men coming on and on through those rivers of blood; themselves bleeding, agonizing and hating. One must hate, otherwise one could surely not kill. Jan hated, one could see the hate in his eyes. Yet the poilus down at la Tarasque looked kind . . . perhaps one need only hate at the moment. And all over the world there were women who wept because in the midst of hate there was love. They loved, those women, that was why they wept; yet their tears had failed to unite the world . . . that was strange for their tears were the hope of the world . . . a union of grief. He paused on this thought. Was it grief that must finally win through to joy? Was it pain that would some day compel all souls to know themselves for only one soul? Was God pain? Was pain God in His fleshly covering?

What would happen if he, Christophe, should refuse to go to the war, should refuse to listen to Jan? Would he then be denying his oneness with God? But surely God was not war but peace . . . the creator of a peace that man brought to destruction. Why had nobody thought of the misery of God, the pain of God? That was it, God's pain. God was not pain yet he could not escape it because of this terrible suffering oneness. How atrocious then to add to God's pain, to add to God's wounds—God Who could not die.

Christophe suddenly dropped his head on his arms: 'No, I cannot add to Your wounds,' he muttered.

Then someone spoke, and he knew that voice. Whose voice was it? Perhaps he himself was speaking: 'You must keep beside Jan for a little while, Christophe, until. . . .' The words blurred and drifted away, as though they were being drawn back into distance.

* * *

The next morning Jan came in search of his cousin. He said: 'This afternoon I enlist. I have told the Curé. As for my mother she has not dared to refuse her consent. Are you coming?'

'Yes, I am coming,' replied Christophe.

Two days later they found themselves in the train on their way to the infantry barracks at Toulon.

4

It was not very long after this that Loup appeared in a clean cotton shirt at breakfast, although it was only the middle of the week and his linen should not have been changed until Sunday. Moreover he was wearing his Sunday suit, and a pair of shoes that Marie had bought him second-hand—they were rather ridiculous shoes made of cheap patent leather, but Loup had admired them. His nails were well scrubbed, and his hair well pomaded with something that smelt of vanilla and lamp-oil. His flashy striped necktie was obviously new and sported an elegant bijou-fix scarfpin.

Marie glanced up from the table with dull eyes: 'Are you going to church, my son?' she asked him. Then, collecting her thoughts with an effort, 'No, no, it is Wednesday, of course, your mother dreams. But why have you dressed as though for Mass?'

'That is my affair,' snapped le tout petit Loup, noisily sipping his café au lait, 'since I earn I suppose I may dress as I please. A man's clothes are not the concern of women.'

'Houi, but you speak to me roughly,' she sighed; 'I cannot understand why you like to wound.'

He could not understand it himself, so he shrugged and went on eating his breakfast. When he had finished he left the house, banging the front door loudly behind him.

Did he mean to sweep floors for the fat Monsieur Bled? Ah, foutre! he had done with that species of offal. 'Tum, tum, dada dee,' sang le tout petit Loup as he marched towards the recruiting office, 'tum, tum, dada dee; dada dee, tum, tum.' He wished that he could remember the words; they were spicy and male, rather lewd in fact, but what would you? He sucked a cavernous tooth and spat very skilfully into the gutter.

Arrived at the Gendarmerie he went in: 'Bonjour, Monsieur,' he began with great aplomb.

A couple of poilus lounging near-by nudged each other and grinned; then they looked at his shoes, nudged each other again and grinned more broadly.

The sous-officier, who stood by his desk, gazed down at le tout petit Loup with amazement: 'Eh bien, what is this? have you lost yourself? Be good enough, please, to explain your business.'

'Assuredly,' bowed le tout petit Loup, 'I am here, Monsieur, to enter the army.'

The tall sous-officier scratched his ear: 'Mais, bon Dieu, how old are you then, my infant?'

'I am nearly eighteen,' lied le tout petit Loup, 'I wish to enlist before I am taken.' Then he spoke with great earnestness, 'Listen, Monsieur, I assure you that although I may appear small I am quite remarkably strong in the arms. And when it comes to fighting, ah ça! when it comes to that they will find me a devil!' He wheezed and hastily cleared his throat; 'I am more than a devil when roused,' he finished.

But this was too much altogether for the poilus and they suddenly guffawed.

Loup swung round on them glaring: 'I have said that I am a devil, Messieurs, and I cannot do better, it seems, than repeat it.'

'And your parents, have you obtained their permission to enlist?' enquired the sous-officier politely, as he stroked his moustache to conceal a smile and turned a reproving back on the poilus.

Le tout petit Loup replied haughtily: 'Monsieur, my parents were bred here in Provence. In Provence we love our country, I trust. No need to derange yourself for my parents.'

The sous-officier remained doubtful, however: 'There is also the matter of health to consider. Come this way, if you please.' And he opened a door. 'Pardon, Monsieur le Docteur, a new recruit.'

'Enter, my friend,' said Monsieur le Docteur.

Ai! las, ai! las, le pauvre tout petit Loup; he was in, he was out, in less than ten minutes. And there were those poilus still full of their grins and their nudgings—a stupid couple of fellows. Not unkind at bottom but somewhat obtuse, that was all, so that the look they saw on Loup's face as he made his abrupt reappearance, meant nothing.

But the sous-officier was that very rare thing, a person possessed of imagination, and he gravely saluted le tout petit Loup: 'Monsieur, in the name of France we thank you.'

And hearing those words le tout petit Loup could have sworn that he shot up a foot as he stood there, at all events he felt suddenly tall as he also raised his hand to the salute: 'Vive la France!' cried le tout petit Loup in a voice that he managed to keep from trembling.

Le tout petit Loup went back to the Bazaar, and as good luck would have it Monsieur Bled did not scold him: 'You are late,' he remarked, but quite affably, for smart boys were increasingly hard to come by. Then he said: 'I shall want you to clean some windows this morning, but first you must sweep the shop. Look, I have bought you a brand-new broom. "He is worth a new broom," I thought to myself as I bought it. Allons, mon brave, en avant!'

So le tout petit Loup took off his best coat and turned up his trousers and put on an apron. And he went into action with a broom in his hand, killing nothing more fierce than a wily old cockroach. And he swept and he swept with the dust in his lungs, but with something less dry than dust in his eyes. After which he put away his new broom, fetched a bucket and proceeded to clean the windows.

*　　*　　*

That evening Loup said to his father and mother: 'I have an announcement to make, my parents,' and it must be admitted that he spoke pompously. 'I desire to announce my plans for the future. Having given the matter my careful attention I have come to the conclusion that with my fine brains I cannot do better than become a teacher. I shall therefore see Monsieur Roland at once and inform him that I will accept his suggestion. When the war is over there is not the least doubt that my studies will be completed in Paris.'

'Now blessèd be God and His Golden Saints!' exclaimed Marie; and she kissed le tout petit Loup, quite forgetting how much he disliked being kissed, which to him always seemed an undignified business.

Jóusè struggled against his thickness of speech, his facial distortion more apparent than usual, but at last he managed to blurt out some words: 'Hòu, I rejoice . . . yes, yes, I rejoice. . . .'

This then was how le tout petit Loup accepted defeat and won his first victory.

CHAPTER THIRTY-NINE

I

IT was not until his arrival at Toulon that Christophe realized to the full what it meant to become the slave of war; to submit his body and mind to be trained in the endless duties exacted by war, in the skill and resource that were needful in war, in the ruthlessness that was a part of war, as he and those like him were housed and fed, well clothed, well cared for in matters of health and hygiene, well drilled, and above all well armed, lest they fail to sustain the rigours of war or prove themselves badly equipped for killing. He would tell himself that these things had to be, that he could not escape from the need of his country, that he also would have to go out and kill. But such thoughts would neither sustain nor convince him, for his mind was now filled with its conception of God—that agonizing yet merciful God Who endured all wrongs at the hands of creation.

This conception of God was becoming more insistent, drawing sustenance from the life of the barracks. He would fancy that God heard the crude blasphemies, the bestial words, the lascivious jesting, that God heard Himself coupled with acts of shame; with the hideous details of bayonet practice; and his soul would turn sick at the thought of God's wounds, no longer glimpsing an ultimate glory in which sinner and saint would become one indeed, and that one the expression of God's fulfilment.

At times his vision must fling itself forward to the years when the guns would have ceased to thunder, when the war would be a thing of the past. But then he would see a more terrible army than any that had taken the field fully armed, for its heart would be cankered by disillusion. Great angers would rise up to shake the earth—angers sown on the once reeking fields of battle; great hatreds long fostered in those who must slay—hatreds that would leap forth to rend their masters. The lust of blood laid on the unborn child from the moment of its wanton begetting. Poverty grown in the soil of greed by those who despised the fruits of forgiveness. Misery masquerading as joy to bemuse the minds of those who were joyless. Immense and unreasoning discontents that sprang from the weariness of the flesh; despair that sprang from the ills of the spirit. And wandering through this vast desolation as a beggar who must plead for the means of subsistence, would be many an one who had grandly endured, who had sought to illumine the darkness with courage. In his worn and threadbare livery of death such an one would very terribly point to himself: 'Look well, all you who pass by, look well! I am he who lives on for the world's indictment.'

Appalled, and at moments helplessly bewildered, Christophe would crave the solace of friendship. He would try to speak of these things to Jan, but in the end would have said very little. 'There must be something . . . the gospel of Christ . . . war could not exist if it were accepted, if they realized its magnificence. It is splendid yet fearful, the gospel of Christ, because like God Himself it is gentle . . . no, no, not quite that . . . I cannot explain. But if, having faith, a man should rise up and show the love of God to the world. . . .'

Jan would shake his head: 'We would still be at war. If there is good there is also evil. The evil must be crushed that the good may live—this has been proved by the warrior-saints many times.' And Christophe would find no answer.

But one day as they sat in the Public Garden, he heard himself speaking with a sudden violence that sprang from the misery in his heart: 'Jan, why are they making murderers of us? Why are they driving us out to kill?'

Jan frowned: 'I do not understand your meaning—to me it seems that you speak very strangely. I am going to fight of my own accord, as every man should when his cause is righteous.'

'War can never be righteous,' said Christophe. And now his face was white, his voice shaken. 'God is wounded, every hour He endures fresh torments. Because of our war He is

353

covered with wounds. Were it possible I would refuse to serve, I would tear this uniform off my back, I would break my bayonet over my knee. . . .'

'You mean,' and Jan's voice came quiet and stern; 'you mean that you would refuse to serve France.'

'Before all things I would serve God,' Christophe answered.

Their eyes met, Christophe's pale and bright and tormented, Jan's dark and disturbed by his rising anger. Then a fearful thought struck like a lash on Jan's mind—ah, but no, not Christophe, the man he loved. . . .

'Come,' he said gruffly, 'our time is up, And listen; be careful of what you say—these are days when the very stones have ears.'

In spite of his misery Christophe smiled: 'I am not afraid of dying in battle,' he told him.

2

The weeks dragged on. They were always the same for Christophe, methodical, active, hopeless. His relations with Jan seemed unhappy and strained, since he dared not reveal the thoughts that obsessed him—what Æliana had failed to achieve, he would sometimes imagine that the war was achieving. But Jan was finding himself again, and for this, at least, there was cause to be thankful; yet Jan was less his than ever before in their lives—or so it appeared to Christophe.

A great sadness began to take hold upon him, together with a curious sense of detachment. He moved like a stranger among the men who, in their turn, regarded him as a stranger. They did not dislike him, but rather it was that they found themselves ill at ease in his presence.

'C'est un original,' they would say, and shrugging their shoulders would leave it at that, for they felt little interest and no resentment.

He grew homesick and longed for the things he knew: the cuckoo clock that Anfos had broken; the workshop with its scarred, familiar bench; the Virgin's picture that hung in his attic. And faces: the preoccupied face of his mother as she bent to some everyday household duty; the face of Anfos with its anxious brown eyes that reminded him of the eyes of Mirèio; the face of his father, quiet, resigned; yes, and even the wizened old face of Eusèbe. And clothes: he would want to take off his tunic and return to his sleeveless, striped cotton jersey, to his patched linen trousers grown limp with age; above all he would want to return to his sandals, for the army boots frequently tired his feet—he would find their weight unendurably irksome. Yet when he received a letter from home in his mother's laborious, childish handwriting, he would read it dully, since all that she wrote would but emphasize his sense of detachment.

Marie would send every item of news that she thought could be of the slightest interest: his father was neither better nor worse. Loup had made up his mind to become a teacher. Guillaume's widow had decided to return to Marseille; Marie did not think that the Simons would miss her. Eusèbe had been laid up with his back, and she, Marie, had hurried across to rub him. Kahn had engaged a new apprentice, a young fellow who lived in a neighbouring village, a consumptive with one lung already half gone, but he managed to bicycle in every morning. Anfos was still refusing to speak. There had been a really bad fight at la Tarasque—that great, hulking Ravous had turned up again and when drunk had seen fit to insult the Army: 'Vive la Marine!' Ravous had bawled; 'A bas les sales poilus, et vive les Marsouins!' Elise had called in the other day and had talked for an hour and a half about Goundran.

Christophe would lay such letters aside with a sigh— words, just so many words that meant nothing. They were part of a life that had ceased to exist for him, a life that had once been familiar and to which he longed fiercely to return: 'Lord, I want to get back,' he would pray, and would know that his prayer held a note of resentment, that the old inexplicable impulse to escape from something intangible was heavy upon him. Then shaking his head: 'But one cannot get back—perhaps that is the tragedy of this world, or the hope of this world, one must always go forward.'

3

When, at length, he was detailed to the regimental pioneers, the clouds of despondency lifted a little, for now

Christophe was working at his own trade, yet even this brought him no lasting comfort. As all that he did must be done to one end, the simplest tasks would often seem hateful. But thanks to the change he was quartered with the Transport and could thus wander in and out of the stables, and could stroke the warm, rough necks of the beasts, who feeling the deep friendliness of his touch would nuzzle his shoulder, themselves become friendly. And one day there suddenly came upon Christophe an urgent desire to care for these creatures, to minister to their poor, simple needs: to sponge them and groom them, and change their bedding; to see that their water was clean and sweet, their food free from dust and of generous measure; since who could foretell what might lie ahead of hunger and thirst, of terror and wounds? And they not able to comprehend the reason for so much unmerited affliction.

The Transport men were a rough lot of fellows, coarse-mouthed, coarse-fibred and none too patient. They would grin to hear Christophe telling their mules to be docile and cease from biting the mangers, to hear him addressing some trace-galled horse as gravely as though he spoke with a general. All the same they would let him help with their jobs, standing by and chewing straws while he worked, but watching to see that he did no mischief.

The Transport sergeant watched also, it seemed, and the Transport sergeant was very attentive. He had been short-handed in the stables for some time, whereas there were pioneers and to spare, an odd carpenter would never be missed; and besides, many men could be found to hack wood while how few had a real understanding of horses. This queer fellow, for all his ridiculous ways with the zebras, knew how to avoid cracked heels—most painstaking he would be over drying. He knew also, it seemed, how to cope with a mule that had learned to aim kicks with baleful precision—Gaby would let him do anything with her, even to grooming her ticklish stomach. Oh, well, he was welcome to the rancid old cow, no one else would vie with him for her favours!

The Transport sergeant was a man of action, and thus he remarked to Christophe one evening: 'Bon soir, mon Jean-Jean. What about a small transfer from the bench to the

356

stables? How does it strike you? But no matter, for I have already arranged it. To-morrow you shall come and read psalms to the mules—unless you think they would prefer a concert?' Then he chuckled, and turning, strutted away before Christophe had even had time to thank him.

So now Christophe might serve the creatures that served, and this he did right well because he loved them. And of him it was very soon being said that if he so wished he could ride the devil, or drive him in double harness with Saint Michael—for the creatures he loved grew in courtesy, as though they possessed their fair portion of reason. If the men must sometimes call him: 'Graine d'oie,' they respected his excellent seat on a horse and his light, efficient hands on the bridle; but in any case he could find in the beasts the comradeship that his fellows denied him.

And because he seemed more content when they met, Jan rejoiced that Christophe should work in the stables. He thought: 'That was only a passing mood—no doubt the life seemed a bit strange just at first.' Then he thought: 'He has always loved animals; I shall never forget how foolish he was about that old verminous bitch, Mirèio—in heaven he would have had her, nothing less!' And Jan smiled the large, pitying smile of the young who are frequently wise in all things save wisdom.

CHAPTER FORTY

I

IN April, not long after Jan and Christophe's first
leave, Colonel Prévost arrived at the barracks. He
had come upon special duty, it seemed, in connection
with the training of officers, and the Colonel in
command was none too well pleased, or so it was
judged from his fierce expression. The Colonel in command
was stout and ageing, he had long been politely shelved by
his country and beneath his aggressively military air of
importance lay a crop of sensitive feelings. However, there it
was, à la guerre comme à la guerre. The Colonel in command
puffed out his red cheeks, berated the Adjutant, cursed the
cook for a lazy lout who made poisonous coffee, chewed the
ends off a number of cheap cigars, drank a small apéritif and
subsided.

Emile Prévost on the other hand was still quite youthful,
yet his tunic was already blazing with ribbons. He had seen
bitter fighting on the French front to which he had gone with
his Colonial regiment, and there it was that he had won his
spurs, receiving unusually quick promotion. But then had
occurred one of those monstrous blunders—or so it still
appeared to its victim—that are apt to hatch out well behind
the front lines: he had suddenly been transferred to the
Staff, becoming liaison officer with the 422nd Infantry, and
now here he was at their depot in Toulon. For barely had he
entered upon that new role when along had come skimming
a young German airman with pink cheeks, yellow hair, and
an accurate eye—it should have been death, but instead had
been wounds and quite a number of small odds and ends not
too uncomfortably lodged in the body; all the same it had
knocked him out for a time.

'Mais oui, you will fight again,' the doctors declared,
'that is if you are patient and behave with precaution.'

Yes, and mark you, not even so much as a scratch until they had given him that cursèd soft job: 'Without doubt,' he would often think to himself rather grimly, 'without doubt every bomb has its billet!'

In appearance Colonel Prévost was neat to a fault; his minute moustache was a model of trimming, while his straight black hair lay so shiny and sleek that it gave the impression of being painted. For the rest he was sallow, of medium height, with intelligent eyes and a resolute mouth. When he spoke his voice was surprisingly soft, and when he was crossed it became like satin. But perhaps his most salient characteristics were his passion for fighting and his passion for comfort. He loved piping hot baths into which he would fling quite a generous fistful of expensive bath salts; he loved deep, cushioned chairs; luxurious beds; warm rooms and warm-hearted solicitous women. But he also loved the crude harshness of war, the rough life of the camp, the violence of combat. Two Prévosts there were, the one who would lead his men with the reckless dash of a tiger, and the one who would fondle a woman's cheek and be able to tell you what scent she used, what rouge, and what special brand of face-powder.

He was not much impressed by the look of the recruits when he scanned them with an eye to his personal servants, yet he fully intended to be well served, and this he was at pains to point out to the Colonel, though so sweetly that the Colonel could not well take offence and must perforce send for the Adjutant:

'Colonel Prévost requires a batman and groom—I wish them to be the best men you can find.' God! it was damnable to know oneself old, to have to be civil to these impudent upstarts and pander to all their new-fangled whims. . . . 'I repeat, the best men you can find,' scowled the Colonel. Then he offered the upstart a cigarette.

Prévost thanked him, lit it, and turned away smiling.

2

That evening Colonel Prévost sat at his desk—a large kitchen table littered with papers: 'You are cousins,' he was saying, 'is not that so?'

'That is so, mon Colonel,' Christophe answered.

'And you come from Provence?'

'Oui, mon Colonel.'

'Ah, bon; I also was born in Provence.' Then to Jan: 'You get on well together, I trust? I cannot tolerate quarrelsome servants.'

Jan's lips twitched as he struggled to hide a smile; 'We do not often quarrel these days, mon Colonel.'

'You may smile if you wish,' Prévost told him quite gravely. 'And now listen to me with attention,' he went on, 'I expect my boots to be groomed like my horses and my horses to be groomed like my boots, and both horses and boots to be groomed to perfection. I expect my own clothes to be faultlessly kept and my horses' clothing to be quite as well cared for—they must have their comforts and I must have mine just so long as we are both able to get them. At the moment I find myself in extreme discomfort; par exemple, I greatly dislike this table. It will be for my batman to use his wits; if a less preposterous table does not exist in the barracks, then to-morrow he must go out and buy one, and a pair of heavy serge curtains as well—a draught down the neck is very unpleasant. I am busy, I cannot attend to such things, they are part of the duties that devolve on my batman. Now about my two horses: it will be for my groom to watch over them in his officer's interest; the least sign of a cough due to dust in the corn, or a poor appetite due to stale, musty hay, and my groom must report to me on the instant. I shall also want you to have your own buckets and to keep them locked up in your stable cupboard; colds are frequently very infectious things, there is also the danger of influenza. No beasts are to drink from those buckets but my own.'

'Entendu, mon Colonel,' replied Christophe.

Prévost stared at the pair with speculative eyes. He was thinking: 'Quite tidy, quite clean and well shaved. Their nails not too terrible, all things considered. I incline to believe that they both brush their teeth. The one educated, the other a peasant. The one very handsome, the other . . .' his thoughts paused in search of an adjective, 'the other impressive; peculiar eyes though, decidedly queer, might do almost any damn thing with those eyes—my demented aunt

Violette would probably say: "psychic." But the Adjutant tells me good hands on a horse—trouble is that he looks to me pretty heavy.' Aloud he said: 'Eh bien, I think that is all.' Then he suddenly smiled: 'I have an idea that we three will become very excellent friends.'

And this was a way that he had with the men, he would treat them as though they were equals, at times, but God help anyone who presumed—no one ever presumed more than once with Colonel Prévost.

3

Jan found his new duties exacting yet easy, for the Colonel knew precisely what he wanted, and precisely how to explain those wants in as few words as possible to his batman. He knew also when a blunder must be sharply rebuked, and when, in justice, it must be forgiven. However, there were not many blunders to forgive, for Jan soon became quite an expert valet. The years of study had trained his quick mind to respect the enormous importance of details, a training that stood him in excellent stead, since all tasks to which we whole-heartedly give of our best have a very marked family likeness.

With great diligence then, Jan brushed, and folded, and polished, and shopped, and brewed Turkish coffee, and saw to it that the bed was neatly made in the manner strictly prescribed by the Colonel—Colonel Prévost liked his bed-clothes tucked in at the sides, but left loose at the foot for some strange reason, while the top sheet must be folded over with care lest his chin should contact itself with the blankets. On the table by the bed he expected to find cigarettes, a lighter, a commodious ash tray, the latest novel, a paper knife, and an old, much-battered copy of *Candide* without which he always refused to move; it had been in his pocket in many an action.

Yet the Colonel was so pleasant a person to serve that he frequently seemed more a friend than a master, as for instance, when he would encourage Jan to talk of Saint Loup and his hopes for the future, though he secretly thought it a pity that Jan should choose to make a career in the Church when instead he might remain in the Army. But although he himself was libre penseur, Prévost's outlook was too broad to ignore religion; like everything else it was grist to his mill for he found the world teeming with interesting people, and to all of these he would grant their ideals since to him the poorest ideal was of interest. And thus he would want to hear more about Kahn, and the old Eusèbe, and Monsieur le Curé, while his batman moved quietly round the room putting this and that ready for the morning toilet, or this and that in its place for the night.

'Yes . . . and then. . . ?' Colonel Prévost would urge with a smile as he stretched out a hand for his silk pyjamas.

With Christophe he naturally came less in contact, and this he would find himself regretting. The big, silent peasant with the curious eyes had managed to stir his imagination: 'Now tell me about your cousin,' he would say, and if Jan hesitated would grow more insistent.

All the same there was much that he would not be told; he would never be told of those visions, for instance, nor of the weal upon Christophe's back that day when Jan had struck at the couleuvre. Jan lacked the courage to mention these things: 'If I did so my Colonel might laugh,' he would think, 'and moreover they were only imagination.'

But this reticence had not prevented Prévost from discovering their great mutual affection: 'So you both enlisted,' he remarked one evening; 'you did not want to be parted, am I right?'

'Oui, mon Colonel—you are right,' Jan admitted.

Colonel Prévost said kindly: 'That I well understand, and fine friendships will frequently make fine soldiers. But have you two never been apart in your lives?'

'Never in our lives, mon Colonel,' Jan told him. 'Christophe believes that we cannot part, he says that nothing can come between us.'

'Now why?' enquired the Colonel, whose interest was roused.

But Jan shook his head: 'I have no idea, yet something tells me that Christophe speaks the truth.' Then, fearing that his words had sounded absurd, 'Will mon Colonel wear his new boots to-morrow? If so I think I will soften the backs.'

'He has quietly closed the door in my face,' thought

Prévost. Aloud he said: 'Yes, the new boots. By the way, your cousin is a very good groom.'

'I am glad that he contents you, mon Colonel; we both very much wish to content you,' Jan answered.

<h1 style="text-align:center">4</h1>

There was only one drawback to Colonel Prévost's service: it did not seem to be leading to the Front. Jan would think: 'We might as well be in Saint Loup, time is going on yet here we remain—dare I ask him about it?' And suddenly he dared: 'Mon Colonel, forgive me, but is there no chance of our getting out? I thought, I had hoped. . . .'

Colonel Prévost looked up from his desk: 'This is June and you two are now due for leave. Well, your leave has been stopped—think that over, Roustan.'

'It means . . . ah, mon Colonel, it means. . . ?'

'That I am not quite done for yet,' smiled the Colonel. Then he bundled some papers into a heap, rose briskly, fondled his tiny moustache, and after a minute dismissed his batman.

*　　*　　*

It was in July that the orders arrived. Colonel Prévost sent for his servants one morning and he said: 'I am ordered to Palestine; it has been arranged that you two shall come with me. Roustan, you must see to my kit at once, please; and I want you to get back to the stables, Bénédit, and make out a list of my saddlery. I shall not be taking the horses, of course, we must trust to what we can get out there, but I think that I may as well take my saddles. About leave; I can give you both forty-eight hours starting from to-night, terminating on Wednesday.' He spoke softly as always, not raising his voice, but under its gentle monotony there vibrated a note of intense excitement.

Christophe thought: 'Judea. . . .' And even as he did so there came upon him the curious feeling that this name, like the name Galilee, meant home; meant a place very far away from Provence yet towards which his footsteps had long been turned. But the Colonel's eyes were now fixed on his face:

'You have understood me?'

'Oui, mon Colonel, I have understood.' And Christophe saluted.

Jan was thinking: 'Palestine, our Lord's own country, the Holy Land of the old Crusaders. To fight there; if need be to die there for Christ, to lay down one's life on that blessèd soil. Oh, my God, I do indeed thank Thee for this. . . .' Aloud he said: 'If mon Colonel will tell me what baggage he is proposing to take?'

'I was just going to speak of my kit,' replied Prévost.

5

That night they travelled back to Saint Loup, getting there in the dusk of early morning while the windows of the town were still shuttered in sleep. Then they parted and went to their separate homes. No one had been on the station platform to meet them, for no one had known of their coming.

Yet Marie stood at her open doorway: 'You have come, you are here, all night I have waited . . . this means?'

Christophe gathered her into his arms: 'It means what such leave always means in wartime . . . it was good of my Colonel to grant these few hours, he need not have done so.'

'Oh, my son,' she whispered.

Then they looked at each other very intently as though each would remember the other's face, every line, every curve, every fleeting expression. And as they did this there dropped from Christophe that wellnigh intolerable sense of detachment, so that now he could stoop down and rest his cheek for a moment against her protective breast as though he were once more a little child; and she dragged off his cap and fondled his hair, twisting it gently over her finger while she murmured the simple and foolish words that are often a great consolation to children. Thus they stood in the quiet, deserted street with no one to see and no one to hear them. And it seemed to Christophe that never before had he been so completely bone of her bone, and flesh of her flesh, and heart of her heart. And it seemed to Marie that never before—no, not even when he had lain in her womb—had she held him so amazingly close, so protected and wrapped about by her body.

'Blessèd be the Mother of God,' she breathed.

And he answered: 'Blessèd be the Mother of God. Come, it is time that we went to my father.'

* * *

Jóusè gazed at his son with heavy blue eyes in which there still lingered the shadows of his dreaming: 'Is it late— am I going to be late for work? Have I overslept?' And then he remembered. 'Christophe . . . you here?'

Christophe took his hand: 'We are ordered to Palestine,' he told him.

Jóusè said nothing, for what could he say? He could only smile his crooked smile—there was little left to Jóusè these days save that crooked smile wherewith to show courage. And as Marie watched him, her mind must slip back to the evening when she had cried out in her travail on that bed that had witnessed the coming of death many times, but also the coming of life—her life, Jóusè's life, made one in Christophe.

Turning abruptly she moved to the door: 'I will go and prepare some coffee,' she told them.

Loup hurried in. He was wearing his nightshirt and his monkeyish face was blotched and angry: 'Boudiéu, I thought that the house was on fire! What hour is this to arrive?' he began. Then he realized how it was and fell silent.

And now down the stairs came a soft, quick padding, and suddenly Anfos was standing among them, and Anfos was wringing his great red hands: 'Master!' he cried out, 'Where are you, my master?'

Christophe went to him: 'I am here . . . always here.'

But Anfos clung with great strength to his arm: 'Master, poor Anfos cannot fly any more—farther and farther and up . . . up . . . up! And, master, Anfos cannot see any more . . . all is darkness . . . poor Anfos no longer sees the light. Lay your hands on his eyes and tell him to see.'

'Surely I will tell him to see,' consoled Christophe, and he laid a hand over the tightly closed lids.

'Ai! ai! there is still no light . . .' wailed Anfos.

At that moment Marie re-entered the room: 'He sees very well,' she whispered to Christophe, 'I cannot comprehend what he means—however, it is good that at last he has spoken.'

The hours alternately raced and stood still. Nothing seemed so important in life as time; nothing seemed less important, with time non-existent. In the carpenter's shop worked the new apprentice; he was very consumptive, shy and respectful. Christophe helped the poor devil to shift a plank.

Kahn looked round from his bench: 'There is no need to help him, he is not so weak as he appears—eh, my friend?'

'Decidedly not,' agreed the apprentice.

Kahn talked of the business, all was going quite well, the apprentice had the makings of a first class joiner: 'And you find the work easy, is that not so, my friend?'

'Decidedly easy,' agreed the apprentice.

Before dinner Kahn drew Christophe aside: 'Just one little word—I will do what I can, all I can. You believe me?'

Christophe held out his hand and Kahn grasped it a moment. Then they lit cigarettes and spoke of the weather: it was sultry, they said. Whereupon the Recording Angel lost interest.

Dinner over, the new apprentice washed up: 'Permit me, Madame,' he suggested, blushing deeply, 'perhaps Madame would like to go out for a little; it is somewhat hot to-day in this kitchen.'

Marie turned to Christophe: 'And you, will you come?'

'Yes,' he answered, and must smile at so foolish a question.

They walked towards Eusèbe's vineyards. It was she who had chosen this direction and when they were come to the edge of the vines she said quietly: 'Show me Mirèio's grave.'

He glanced at her, unable to hide his surprise, and she thought: 'He cannot believe that I care. Ai! las, ai! las, and now I do care, for surely Mirèio also loved him.'

Together they went and stood by the spot where Mirèio had lain for nearly ten years at peace in the merciful earth of Provence: 'She is happy—why are you weeping?' he asked.

And Marie answered: 'Because of the ointment, and because I did not quite understand. . . .'

Then Christophe knew that his mother must weep for a sorrow which she had failed to share with him. Very gently he stroked her tired, wet face: 'It is never too late to understand,' he told her.

CHAPTER FORTY-ONE

I

THE next morning Christophe knelt by his mother in the ancient church with its open belfry, and the Curé offered to each the Host: 'Corpus Domini nostri Jesu Christi . . .' And Christophe no longer felt dread for himself at the moment when he received his Lord, but instead must feel a great fear for his mother.

Her shoulder touched his; he was suddenly conscious of that poorly clad, patient and ageing shoulder. He thought: 'There is something which she must endure—it is something from which I cannot protect her.' And his heart beat wildly against his side as though it would break with her load of grief. Then they rose and together they left the altar.

After Mass they stood looking out at the sea that lay placid and vast in the July sunshine: 'I love it,' he said, 'it has been like a friend, though sometimes I have not asked for its friendship, I have just let it take me and do what it would.' For now he wished them to share the sea so that she might look at it when he was gone, and because it had comforted him, take comfort.

Presently they went to call on Elise who would be unable to go to the station. Goundran was with her, he was back on leave, very stalwart but very white at the temples. Two children there were now for Goundran to play with; Aurano had acquired a small, turbulent brother who could do all manner of delectable things by crawling and wobbling himself into mischief, and—God willing—she might have a second quite soon, for Goundran's leaves were not proving unfruitful. Yes, indeed, his Elise was once more great with child; that was why she was unable to go to the station.

'I cannot permit it,' Goundran had said, 'at the sight of a troop train you weep so much that the tears you swallow will pickle the baby! Paure pichounet, he does not like salt even though his sire is a son of the ocean.'

Christophe looked round the room. The walls were still rosy from that brush that had dripped so much pink distemper, and away in the corner was old Mathilde's chair, while on the table—would you believe it—on the table was a large dish of heart-shaped cakes!

'You used to like them,' said Elise with a smile.

'Pecaire, but he certainly did,' laughed Goundran. Then he glanced at his wife: 'They are marvellous cakes, magic cakes for the man who has learned their secret.' And at this reminder she must actually blush and pretend to busy herself with the coffee.

They stayed for an hour. Goundran seemed very sanguine, very pleased with the world as he talked of the future. The war was practically over, he said, the Allies had cracked the damned spine of the Germans. And after the war, Santo bèlli Mariniero, the world would then be a fit place to live in. Peace and plenty they would have after the war, the bill being settled with fat German money. He, Goundran, had ordered his boats to be painted in preparation for less arduous fishing.

But when Elise came to kiss Christophe good-bye, there she was splashing tears all over his tunic, and sobbing, and reminding them of the days when Goundran had allowed him to paint the green shutters: 'Never, never shall I forget it . . .' she sobbed.

'Houi, why did I mention paint!' muttered Goundran.

Eusèbe was waiting when they finally reached home. He had wandered into the house uninvited, bringing with him a bottle of vintage wine: 'The most perfect ever born of my grapes,' he informed them, 'as warm and soft as the flesh of a girl. No, no, I alone will remove the cork, I alone will violate this exquisite virgin!'

Marie got out the glasses, shaking her head, the more senile he grew the more lecherous his fancies.

Eusèbe lifted his brimming glass: 'May the gods protect you, my superb young hero. And do not forget that I christened you with wine long ago when you were a squealing infant, that I made the little red mark on your brow.'

'Enough of such talk!' exclaimed Marie, turning pale, for she was a peasant and superstitious.

Why, oh, why had he come, the old sinner of a man? And now that he had come why would he not leave them. But no, he must plump himself down on a chair, without doubt intending to finish the bottle. And the kitchen to sweep and the dinner to cook—queer to be thinking of such everyday things—and those ruthless, pointing hands of the clock, never still, always moving and always pointing.

'A long time have I known you,' babbled Eusèbe, his eye growing somewhat watery and tender, 'tell me, do you remember the wonderful day when I took you to feast on grapes in my vineyards? Yes, and do you remember the more wonderful day when I made you a present of your first pair of sandals? And do you. . . .'

Marie suddenly cut him short: 'Eusèbe, you must go, there is work to be done.'

'Ah, well,' he sighed, 'I am old, blind and lame. The old are seldom welcome it seems, very seldom.' And with this reproach he left them.

The hands of the clock, would they never be still? She must put on her apron and sweep out the kitchen. The hands of the clock, would they never be still? She must go to the sink and peel the potatoes. But the hands of the clock, would they never be still? She must cut the potatoes into neat little squares and set them to stew with the meat on the stove, then a pinch of herbs and a couple of onions.

'Christophe, bring me that bowl of milk, will you, my son?' How large he looked carrying the small bowl of milk, large and anxious; and now he was spilling the milk: 'Never mind, do not trouble to wipe it up.'

And his answer: 'One moment, I will get a damp cloth, otherwise it may leave a stain on the mat.'

A stain on the mat! She wanted to laugh—only then perhaps she would never stop laughing—the milk might leave a stain on the mat! He was wiping it up rather clumsily with a kind of slow, laborious patience. The milk might leave a stain on the mat . . . yes, and once that would surely have seemed a disaster.

Cry out like the primitive creature she was? Cry out with the terrible voice of all mothers, even as Mirèio had cried out for her young long ago in her hour of immense desolation? Cry out until the world shook with her cries: 'You shall not take him, I care nothing for honour. I care only for the child that my womb has held, that my pain has brought forth, that my breasts have nourished. I care nothing for your wars. He was born of love; shall the blossom of love be destroyed by your hatreds? I care nothing. . . .' Marie pressed her hands to her head.

'Are you ill?' Christophe asked her anxiously.

'No, my son, no, it is not that. I was trying to remember . . . did I put in those herbs?'

'Yes,' he smiled.

And she went on cooking the dinner.

2

Everything was arranged with that abnormal composure that will frequently come to us at such moments. Christophe would bid his father farewell then meet Jan and walk to the Presbytery, there to say good-bye to Monsieur le Curé. Marie and Loup, and Anatole Kahn, and perhaps the apprentice, would wait at the station. Anfos had better remain at home—they would tell him that he must take care of Jóusè.

And now Christophe was standing by Jóusè's bedside, and he noticed that his father was wearing his medals. Two large tears trickled slowly towards his beard: 'Wipe them away, my son,' he said thickly, 'my eyes are cowards but my heart is brave and . . . proud. I cannot quite raise my right hand.' So Christophe wiped the tears from his face. Then they kissed: 'God be with you, my very dear son . . . always . . . always.'

Christophe answered huskily: 'My father, it is difficult to find words. . . .'

'We have no need of words any more,' said Jóusè.

3

In the kitchen Christophe found Anfos, alone. He was sitting with his head on his folded arms, but he sprang up the moment he heard Christophe's footstep: 'Anfos, I have come to say good-bye. Anfos . . . what is it? Will you not speak?' For the madman was gazing at him very strangely; there was love in his eyes, and amazement and awe, there was joy, yet also something like horror. 'I am going, I must. Anfos, give me your hand . . . this is our farewell.'

Anfos did not answer.

4

The Curé opened the front door himself: Jan and Christophe followed him into the study. He motioned them to chairs then sat down at his desk—the shabby old mahogany desk upon which his pen had so often lain idle. The orange tree in the little garden had lost most of its blossoms for now it was fruiting; it had many green leaves, and between the leaves glimmered polished green globes that were turning golden. The garish Madonna still stood in her place not far from the Curé's threadbare elbow, while above the tubular iron stove hung the fine wooden crucifix carved by Anfos.

The Curé said, almost humbly: 'It is good of you both to come here, my children.' And his prominent eyes turned and rested on Jan. 'I know only too well the feelings of parents. Up to the last they must cling to their sons, and their sons to them at a time like this; therefore I say it is good of you to spare a few minutes for your spiritual father who is no longer quite so young as he was.' And indeed he did look a very old man; the white locks on his brow were receding and sparse, his temples were heavily veined and hollow.

Christophe stammered: 'But we could not have gone to the front without asking you to give us your blessing.' For he felt the great burden of sorrow and love that lay like a cross on the Curé's shoulders.

And as though Jan had felt it also, he broke in: 'To have gone away without saying good-bye? Ah, mais non, that could never have happened, mon père. Do I not owe you everything? Think of all you have done for my education.' Then he grew very red and stared down at his boots: 'My real father died before I was born . . . Eh bien, what I am trying to tell you is this . . . because of mon Curé I have not missed him.'

'Thank you, my son, for those words,' said the Curé.

They talked for a little while of the church, and of how the Curé would make restorations some day when the workmen returned from the war and the congregation could better spend money. Saint Loup's altar was letting the rain in, he told them, the last storm had wetted the saint quite badly. And the Curé now ventured a very small joke: 'It is possible even that he may catch cold, for he cannot well put up an umbrella!'

Presently Jan glanced at his wrist-watch: 'We must leave you, mon père.' So the Curé rose, while they knelt to receive his benediction.

Then the Curé opened a drawer in his desk, and he took from its case the old silver rood blessed for a holy death by some saint—a saint whose name he could not remember: 'This rood belonged to my mother,' he said gravely; 'Long ago it was blessed for Bona Mors. See, it has a very strong chain and can therefore be safely worn round the neck. I myself have had it a great many years, and now I am going to give it . . .' His voice faltered, 'to give it to . . .' He had stretched out his hand and had given the old silver rood to Christophe. He thought that he cried out: 'No, no, it is Jan's!' Yet he knew the next moment that he could not have spoken, for Christophe had slipped the chain over his head and was thrusting the crucifix into his tunic.

'How can I thank you for this, mon père—how can I thank you?' Christophe was saying; and Jan's eyes were brimming with gratitude because the gift had been offered to Christophe.

The Curé stared at them; then he found his composure and spoke calmly as befitted his office: 'I shall not forget to pray for you both. To-morrow I shall offer my Mass for you both, begging our Lord to preserve you in safety. And I hope you will sometimes pray for me, and for all who are charged with the care of souls, that we may not fail before heaven in our duty.'

* * *

After they had left him he stood very still; and erect he stood, in spite of his years, as a man might stand who faced death with courage. And he strove to lift up his heart to God, to lift it beyond the love of the creature, so that it might serve none other than God. But his heart would rise only a very little and must always return to the place whence it came—perhaps because it was wiser than he, knowing better where it would find its Creator.

5

Christophe stood with his mother on the platform. The train was late, trains were always late these days and when they arrived, overcrowded.

Loup was there, and Madame Roustan was there with her arm through Jan's, and Eusèbe who had hobbled along by the aid of a stick and immediately joined the family group, and he reeking of drink every time he exhaled, to the great indignation of Madame Roustan. But for all his foul breath the old pagan was sober, and because he was sober was melancholy, so that his eye kept filling with tears which he smudged away with a dirty forefinger; then he wiped his nose on the cuff of his shirt with his usual splendid disdain of convention.

Oh, but quite a number of people had come: Goundran together with his pretty Aurano; the Simons, in memory of Guillaume their son; the Hermittes, because they were Marie's neighbours; Mère Mélanie, gladly preparing to weep, and with her the little hump-backed violinist. The fat Monsieur Bled had also arrived, and the Doctor who never pressed for his payments, and Monsieur Roland who had hurried so much that he felt himself bound to unfasten his collar, and Kahn's new apprentice, very humble and shy, and wishful that they should ignore his existence. And last but not least, the kind-hearted woman who had used to give Jan of her choicest peaches for the sake of that boy of hers who had died, but who now for his sake gave Jan cigarettes, since the boy had he lived would have been a man also.

Marie thought: 'It is odd to feel so much alone, here are many good friends yet they seem like strangers.' For she had not yet learned that the bitterest thing about grief is its sense of complete isolation.

But Christophe divined her thought and he said, taking care that his voice should reach her only: 'Distance does not exist, it is all here and now; there is neither time, separation

374

nor distance. Where you are I am; where I go you shall come. . . .' What was he saying? Whose words were these? And to whom had he spoken such words before . . . where you are I am . . . had it been to Anfos?

She looked at him with her good faithful eyes in which there was love but no understanding.

Far away down the line a white curling cloud; then a dull, thudding sound that came nearer and nearer; then shouts and a huddle of grinning masks as the poilus crowded up to to the windows, struggling like cattle for a breath of fresh air, but still ribald, light-hearted, good-tempered and long-suffering. Jan kissing his mother. Everyone pressing forward to shake the extended hands of the poilus, to shake Jan's and Christophe's hands in farewell.

'Ah, the dear brave fellows, so handsome, so young!' Mère Mélanie choking with emotion by now, and repulsing her anxious little violinist.

Eusèbe peering up into Christophe's face and harking back to his thoughts of the morning: 'Many years have I known you, mais oui, many years. I remember the day when you were baptized. . . .' But the train will not wait for old Eusèbe, and others have just as much right to a word:

'Bonne chance! Bonne chance!'

'Take care of yourself and come back soon!'

Then Goundran's gruff voice: 'But naturally he will be coming back soon. Diéu! have I not said that the war is over?'

Le tout petit Loup as red as a beetroot: 'Christophe!'

And suddenly he is blubbering. One tear for Christophe and ten for himself; yes, but actually blubbering, le tout petit Loup, and in public, for all his fine scholarly brains that are destined to get him quite soon to Paris. Ai! las, Ai! las, le pauvre tout petit Loup—ten tears for himself but at least one for Christophe.

Marie dry-eyed and dazed in the arms of her son; his lips on her cheek, and his arms so strong that they hurt her. But how has this come to pass? A short time ago and her son was a baby. His arms are not there any more. He is gone. She can see his face close to Jan's for a moment, then those unknown faces are crowding between.

'Bonne chance! Bonne chance!'

'Do not stay away long!'

The train has begun to move out of the station.

* * *

Over the waste land that led to the line beyond the platform, someone was running—a man with rough hair and a thin, unkempt beard: 'Stop! Stop! it is God you kill!' he screamed wildly.

No one saw or heard the man but a peasant who was driving an ox-cart near-by on the roadway—he was stupid, he stared. 'Stop! Stop! it is God! It is God you kill ... it is God! It is God!' The peasant left his team, but too late, for the man had already reached the line. Was he crazed? He was standing with outstretched arms. 'Stop! Stop! it is God. . . .' Then the engine struck him.

A great sickening jolt as they flung on the brakes: 'What has happened? What is it?' 'Some poor devil is done for!' 'But who? Let me see—move that carcase of yours!' 'Stop kicking my corn, fils de noble vache!' 'But who is it?' 'Ah, bon, already a corpse, a fine omen!' Then a laugh: 'Only one among many. Le voila! they have dragged what is left of him out . . . Merde, it makes me feel quite homesick for Flanders!'

Jan had been pushed back by the jostling poilus: 'Is it anyone from our own town?' he kept asking. 'Tell me, is it anyone from our own town?'

Christophe managed to shoulder his way to the window, and he saw the poor remnant of human flesh, so torn, so fearful to look on in death. The face had been all but obliterated, yet he knew that indescribable blur.

Returning to Jan, he said quietly: 'A little child has died ... it is Anfos.'

CHAPTER FORTY-TWO

I

ON either side of the French Detachment stretched the far-flung, powerful forces of Britain, mile upon mile they stretched east and west, the arms of a giant on the trunk of a pigmy—a political pigmy, or so it was said by some, but for all that efficient enough, since most of its members had seen hard service.

The September night was bountiful and moonlit, having about it the quality of stillness that engenders a deep and refreshing sleep in those whom the toils of the day have wearied, having about it the quality of peace that engenders a mood of prayer in the religious, having about it the quality of mystery that engenders romance in the hearts of lovers. But the night could bestow none of these gentle things, for its spirit must submit to the violence of war, to the thunder of the Turkish artillery whose barrage dropped now upon No Man's Land and now upon flesh and blood in the trenches.

The men of the Légion d'Orient crouched, waiting; they had something to wait for, those Armenians; and the Syrians, they also had their memories and could therefore wait with comparative patience, cursing softly and often in Arabic while doing quite a lot of hard thinking.

Colonel Prévost had said, and no doubt with some truth, when an officer of the Tirailleurs had spoken disparagingly of this mixture, Colonel Prévost had said: 'A weak brew? Well, perhaps, but a good dash of hate gingers up the worst cocktail; moreover if they trust their leader they will fight. The worm that is baited too long may turn and surprise its tormentors by becoming a scorpion.' And then he had whistled a bright little tune, which meant that the brief conversation was ended.

A queer medley the Légion d'Orient; the Syrians fine-looking fellows for the most part, with the dignity of the Arab race and the eyes of those who look out on wide spaces. The Armenians as different from each other in type as a carrion crow from a mountain eagle; some tall, finely featured, agile and brave; some squat; some resembling Jewish pawnbrokers; a people that while struggling to find itself had been marred in the making by persecution, but a people that never lost sight of its wrongs or despaired of a possible day of vengeance.

Christophe sat with his rifle across his knees; he appeared to be staring intently at nothing. On one side of him Jan was telling his beads, his face tense with a kind of fanatical rapture; on the other a weedy Armenian crouched—Toto, he was nick-named, after the lice that revelled in his greasy and tender skin; it was all but impossible to de-louse him. Toto flinched at every burst of a shell and he talked in a rapid, hysterical whisper. His French was fluent but execrable, and while he whispered he scratched his armpits:

'My mother, I think of her,' he was saying, 'my mother lay hidden for two days in a dung-heap, and she big with child, her time almost come—that was in 1896 when my father was murdered at Constantinople. Men, women and children they bludgeoned to death, my father's brains were splashed on the pavement. I was born with the taste of dung in my mouth, oh, yes, but I was baptized a Christian. My poor people have died in their millions for Christ, and now I am going to avenge my people! My uncle and my mother they both escaped, they were saved by a family of Catholic Armenians; we had always been Gregorians up to then, but after that we also became Catholics—the Catholics were being protected by the French, so my uncle thought better get French protection. I am glad to be here; I shall fight for France, for Jesus Christ and my dear dead people—it is good to have something for which to fight, when I think of my people I feel like a lion! My uncle he saw a remarkable thing: it was outside the station at Constantinople; the railway cutting was piled with our dead and dying, they had thrown them into the cutting and because they were there the train could not pass, it was blocked by our martyred dead and dying. My uncle has told me this many times: a tall Englishman left the train, he has told me, a man very young but whose hair was quite white, and whose clothes were all white, my uncle thought drill—that was in August, 1896, when the mob was rewarded for killing my people. The Englishman carried those who were dying back into the station—they dared not refuse him: "This is terrible!" the officials exclaimed to the Englishman because he was English. And my uncle says this: "He was all white," he says, "but after a little while he was scarlet." That is why I am glad to be here in this trench fighting for France and also for England.' A shell burst a trifle too close to be pleasant and Toto ducked, then the whispering continued, 'With my bayonet I shall slit many Turks; oh yes, oh yes; "blood for blood," I shall say, "my mother ate dung, and now you, filthy dogs who kill innocent Christians, you can eat your own entrails!"'

On and on went that rapid, hysterical voice. Christophe heard it, but only with half his mind, for his mind was engrossed by thoughts of Anfos. Kahn had written telling of the madman's last words: Anfos had said they were killing God, that was why he had wanted to stop the troop-train. He, Christophe, had many times pictured God's wounds, the more agonizing because God was immortal. God's wounds ... but supposing God could, in fact, die, could be wounded to death by His merciless creatures? Even now it might well be that God was dead, that the world was abandoned to this horror of war because it had slain the one source of mercy. If that source had been slain then the world was doomed, he was doomed, Jan was doomed, and this man who whispered. And Christ ... what of Christ? He also had died; He had died on the Cross ... yes, but had He risen? Queer to harbour such doubts and yet remain sane, sane enough to be valuable to one's Colonel—but perhaps the mind could disguise its real self; or perhaps every creature possessed two minds, one acutely self-conscious, the other automatic. Back there in Lydda that letter had come. ... What had he been doing back there in Lydda? He had found an olive grove close to the town; he had walked to it all alone one evening and had suddenly felt an anguish of soul for which there had seemed no discernible reason. Round Saint Loup there were many such olive groves, but this one in Judea had struck him as different. Then Ramleh where Jan had become all on fire at the sight of that ruined church of the Crusaders—Jan had actually knelt down and kissed the stones surreptitiously, when he thought no one was looking. It was clearing now, his brain felt less dazed, he could see quite a number of clear little pictures. The Colonel's horses; they had both been abandoned, the one dead of sand fever, the other gone sick and left to die with the Veterinary Section. It had been very hard to leave that sick horse, for its filming eyes had reproached and questioned. But the time was so short, the Colonel must tramp when the railway came to an end, if need be: 'My feet are no more precious than my men's'; and this saying had gone the round of the regiment. Then: 'Bénédit, you are returned to duty; I can do with an extra orderly, and moreover, every able-bodied man will be needed.' 'Oui, mon Colonel.' He was always replying: 'Oui, mon Colonel,' in a steady, brisk voice—that was why, no doubt, they considered him useful. Yes, and so he was useful with the part of himself that appeared to be purely automatic. . . . The camouflaged country, a kind of grim game, a gigantic and very ingenious deception—to what purpose the rank and file were not told. Then the great Concentration Camp of the English. The English were friendly, good-tempered men; they would grin and want to exchange tea for wine. Jan thought them like schoolboys, as indeed they appeared—one was always expecting them to play marbles. Their own French Detachment, absurdly small yet comprising a bewildering assortment of colours, from white to black and from black to white with every intermediate gradation. Colonel Prévost treated with marked respect because of his record on the French front . . . and now Colonel Prévost was waiting in a hole that they had dug for him, he and Jan together, just before they themselves had taken up their positions.

* * *

'Christophe.'
'Yes, Jan?'
Jan had put away his beads and was looking at Christophe rather shyly: 'Christophe, there is something I want to say— All our lives I have felt as though we two were brothers,

380

very close to each other, as it were one flesh in spite of our quarrels. . . . I wanted you to know.'

'I think we have both always known,' replied Christophe. Then he said: 'Listen, Jan, if anything should happen, promise me that you will take care of my mother. . . . I feel that I want to give her to you.'

'Where is the old silver rood?' Jan asked him, 'Let me lay my hand on the old silver rood before answering.' So Christophe unfastened his tunic and Jan laid his hand on the silver rood: 'In the name of our crucified Lord, I promise.'

The chaplain passed with bent head, walking quickly. He looked strange in his soutane and battered steel helmet. Someone had been hit farther down the line, they could hear him trying to scream and choking.

'Our chaplain is brave, very brave,' murmured Jan. 'They say he fears nothing in war but one thing: that a man should die without Holy Communion.'

After this they fell silent. A Syrian groaned as he loosened a putrid sock that was sticking. Toto was beginning to eat and drink; rough wine, hard-tack, and meat from a tin—all he had, the field kitchens having been forbidden. The men shuffled, and sighed, and swore under their breath, and examined their equipment for the hundredth time, while the shadows grew darker along the whole front. Christophe glanced up at the changing sky—it could not be long now, the moon was waning.

2

Darkness; but a darkness that was falling to pieces, that was splintering into millions of atoms, that was racked and disintegrated by sound. The earth was being disintegrated and the darkness was hailing down on the earth, those millions of atoms that had been the night hailing down and piercing like sharp, black darts. . . . The earth rocked and gave, the earth held up its arms in supplication and its arms were struck off. There was no earth any more, no sky and no air . . . those who moved must be souls in some undreamed of hell, a hell of sound . . . nothing was left but sound . . . the whole universe was writhing and dissolving in sound, the sound of that terrific bombardment.

Guns were answering guns, the Turks were replying, shells crossed and recrossed, they were bombarding heaven. Through a pall of dense smoke and choking dust the men of the Légion were leaping forward. He, Christophe, was leaping forward with the rest . . . his mouth was wide open, he could feel himself yelling, he could feel the great strength of his muscular thighs, the great strength of his work-hardened muscular hands. Jan was near him, vaguely discerned through the smoke, they two were close on the Colonel's heels . . . the Colonel was waving an arm as he ran; he was leading his men, he had sworn to do it. He was glancing round . . . his face was quite changed . . . but perhaps every face now looked like the Colonel's.

They were pouring into the enemy trenches, touching bodies that felt like their own—human bodies. Some creature was trying to defend itself by shooting at close quarters, it must be mad . . . it had failed . . . it was dead, with a gaping belly. This detestable vigour that possessed the limbs, that surged up to the brain and set it ablaze; it was like a heady and poisonous wine, one wanted to sing, one wanted to sob . . . one was doing all manner of things at once, loving and hating, pitying and killing. Was this Christophe who had so often pictured God's pain? His lunges were ruthless and accurate, but now he was using the butt of his rifle . . . what was it that had gushed out over his hands? Jan's foot was on a man's chest, he must wrench . . . the Sergeant had warned them against such thrusts, bones were awkward things, the Sergeant had warned them. Toto was vomiting while he killed, the vomit was red, he had drunk too much wine, it had soured in his stomach because of his terror. He was retching but he dared not stop to be sick . . . was the smoke less dense? one could see things so clearly . . . blood was trickling onto Toto's hand from a long, shallow gash across his wrist. . . . And the guns, were they suddenly making less noise? one could hear other sounds. . . . O God, O God, the groans of the dying, the shrieks of the wounded, the angers that thundered deep in men's hearts. . . . A mule had broken loose, no, two mules, over there on the right—they were dragging their traces. But how could one see them so far away? As they galloped they were leaving great splashes of crimson. Shoot them, someone! Have pity on them, God; are You dead? Shoot them! Shoot them! They do not understand . . . they suffer and do not understand. . . . There was no God, men had killed their God; that was why, being dead, He could not feel pity. Jan was leaning forward the better to lunge . . . he had lunged and blood spurted into his face . . . a baptism of blood . . . he was coughing and spitting. He had stumbled. A-a-h, would you? A mighty thrust, then a sickening weight at the end of one's rifle.

A pause for the second wave to come up. The Turks were leaving their wounded behind them . . . that boy with the delicate, clutching hands and the soft white skin—he looked like a woman. On again. Jan, for Christ's sake, do not crush out his life! For Christ's sake . . . Jan was mad, he must be mad, he was killing in the name of the Trinity: 'In nomine Patris, et Filii, et Spiritus Sancti. . . .'

* * *

Hours had passed . . . were they hours or years that had passed? He and Jan were still fighting side by side . . . amazing how close they managed to keep to each other, they had seldom been separated. The Colonel's automatic had jammed; Jan was thrusting his own weapon into his hand, then snatching a rifle from a dying Armenian. Stop! Stop! it is God you kill . . . it is God. . . . Anfos also was mad for there was no God—if there had been He must surely have pitied those beasts, and that wounded boy with the face of a woman.

A battery had opened fire on their flank, they were being forced back to the slopes of a wadi; they were trying to find cover among the rocks. The Colonel was waiting for reinforcements . . . the Colonel had lighted a cigarette . . . it was bad, this cross-fire, very bad indeed. Now Toto was down. He squealed like a pig, rolled over and over and squealed like a pig, clutching at his guts. Do not make so much noise, stop that squealing, it opens the wound, you fool! Toto made one feel angry, squealing like a pig, one felt angry as one dragged him to comparative safety.

* * *

They were reinforced. Was it morning or evening? What blue eyes he had that young German gunner standing there in the middle of five dead men . . . his blue eyes looked vague, he appeared very stupid, for he would not use that big mauser of his. And now he was resting his hand on the gun; when he withdrew it a part remained behind on the muzzle . . . he was stupid indeed, staring down at his palm that was burnt to the bone. He was dead like the rest . . . yes, but who had killed him?

Bells . . . how strange to hear bells in battle. And so faint they sounded, as though far away—faint yet clear. They were playing a Provençal hymn: 'Jesus Christ, the Shepherd, the Lamb, and the Victim.'

Blood everywhere; the soil watered with blood. Christian and infidel made one in their wounds, no difference at all, and made one in death—lying side by side, united in death.

'Jesus Christ, the Shepherd, the Lamb, and the Victim.'

The Armenians had fought well, they were still fighting well, intent on avenging the wrongs of their people, but the Turks appeared to be in full flight. Here and there a stand made by exhausted men who were ready to die and thus asked for no quarter. They went gallantly, those who had stayed to die. . . . Christian and infidel united in death . . . it was always the same, an eternal oneness. But was it the same now that God was dead? Who was ringing those bells so persistently? They had come very close, very close to one's ears . . . they seemed outside oneself and yet inside one's brain. Could the Colonel hear them? Did Jan hear those bells? Jan knew the tune well—an old Provençal hymn: 'Jesus Christ, the Shepherd, the Lamb, and the Victim.'

CHAPTER FORTY-THREE

I

THAT night came the order to halt on their objective. In the morning they would go forward again, but meanwhile—sleep. The men flung themselves down, some too heavy with weariness to eat until rest had brought ease to their aching bodies. Those whose duties would take them to the Listening Posts damned their luck and looked at the others with envy.

Christophe found himself detailed for a special patrol, together with five Syrians and two Armenians. The French Lieutenant in command rubbed his eyes, for his youth was making him feel extra sleepy. He was dreaming of a certain immense feather bed into which he had used to creep with his parents; it still stood in the corner of a spacious room with blue brocade walls and a painted ceiling:

'Bon Dieu,' he murmured disconsolately, 'how little one imagines at five years old what is going to happen to one at twenty!'

The Sergeant was rumbling with soft, rich oaths. He was dreaming of a world that was guiltless of vermin and Turks alike, above all of patrols undertaken after a hard day's fighting. A passing Armenian dropped an open tin of sardines, and they as precious as ortolans on toast. The oil splashed over the Sergeant's boots:

'Sacrée face de ver!' growled the outraged Sergeant.

The Corporal was more patient, he took things as they came—lice, bugs, Turks, patrols, and even Armenians. What would you? Life was made up of such trials, they were doubtless the stones on the path to heaven. However, the Corporal also had dreams, not the least of which was a brothel in Paris.

Christophe stood and gazed down at Jan; he was peacefully sleeping with his head on his arm. Sweat had mingled with the grime and blood on his face, and the sleeve upon which his cheek rested was bloody. One hand was clutching his rosary; he must have been telling his heads again, for his thumb still marked the place in a decade. And while he gazed at him Christophe was conscious of a curious feeling of desolation, as though Jan had failed him by falling asleep:

'Could you not have kept awake for an hour, just until I had gone?' he heard himself saying, 'Surely you might have kept awake for an hour . . .' Then he frowned, 'I am being unjust,' he thought, 'Jan is utterly spent, that is why he sleeps.' Yet he felt a sudden impulse to wake him.

'Jan!'

But Jan only stirred slightly and sighed, so Christophe passed on and left him sleeping.

2

The Patrol was well beyond the Listening Posts. It was creeping forward, each man for himself, each man all eyes, all ears, and all nerves. Every sense concentrated in eyes and ears, every nerve responding to the least sound or movement. A few thin clouds drifted across the moon from time to time; they were unexpected, clouds were seldom seen before the month of October. The light was shifting and treacherous, the ground difficult and bristling with pitfalls.

No one spoke, it was not a moment for speaking. The Armenians and Syrians gripped their rifles. What was lying in wait for them just ahead? The silence was uncanny after the day, but no one could tell when it might be broken. They kept together as best they could, though each man was expected to use his own wits and particularly his own observation. A Syrian slipped and fell with a thud, it sounded like a cavalry charge; the men held their breath and stood motionless. Then the Sergeant hiked the Syrian on to his feet with a whispered oath, and once more they moved forward.

It was while they were climbing the side of a slope that Christophe found himself dropping behind them, found himself treading with infinite care, scarcely breathing lest someone should turn and observe him, and he wondered why he was doing these things. His brain seemed confused:

'I shall get lost,' he thought. Then quite suddenly: 'I am already lost, there is noting left of me any more—there is nothing left of Christophe but pity.'

Pity. All his life he had known it, but never until now had he known it completely, for now it was clutching him by the soul; his soul was shaken and rent with pity. Gentle yet terrible it clutched his soul. There was no escape, for it would not let go. It had sprung upon him from the grief of the night, from the torn and bleeding heart of the earth, from the pain of those helpless and bleeding bodies; it was hurling itself against his will, overcoming his will and possessing his reason. Gentle yet terrible with gentleness it wounded; his soul was a deep and gaping wound, every wound that he had inflicted was there, the many made one and as one beheld, and as one endured, and as one repented; 'Forgive . . . forgive,' he prayed desperately, 'you whom I have caused to suffer, forgive me.'

*   *   *

He was crouching in a shell hole—how had it happened? No matter, he must crane up and see if they had missed him. Apparently not, for they were moving to the right; that meant that they were working round the hill. It would be fairly dark on the far side of the hill; all the better, his absence would go unnoticed.

Climb free of the shell hole and creep down the slope—how easy it was when one's body obeyed one. His body had detached itself from him all day; his body had been unspeakably cruel; and cowardly too, it had saved itself, killing others in order that it might live—Oh, most hateful yet pitiful life of the body. But how peaceful it was on this wide, quiet plain; the air smelt sweet like the air in Provence. Perhaps wild lavender grew near this plain, perhaps the hillsides were covered with maquis.

Dead men . . . it was better to die than to kill. Two dead men lying stiffly side by side with their arms and legs sprawled out in the moonlight. Never mind, it is over now, it is past, you are dead—it is better to die than to kill. There is only one fear, if God also is dead. . . . Do you think that perhaps it was you who killed God? Or was it a Provençal peasant called Christophe? Never mind, it is over for you now, it is past. Christophe lives and his soul is one terrible wound . . . do you think that it may have been he who killed you?

But could God be dead when the night was so blessèd and filled with an inexpressible peace—with a peace that seemed to pass all understanding? What if a soldier should die for the world, for the sake of the gospel of peace, would they mourn him? Would they turn from their wars? 'We have slain a just man. . . .' But someone had already preached the gospel of peace and been slain . . . a man who was born in Judea. . . . In Judea, it was, that they had crucified Him. Jesus, who had been born in Bethlehem; yes, and Anfos had carved Him a lamb for Christmas, then had wanted to play with the lamb himself. Christmas, the birthday of Jesus Christ . . . Jesus Christ, the Shepherd, the Lamb, and the Victim.

Something was pressing against his flesh, it was something that he had almost forgotten; the rood was pressing against his flesh. He drew it out and stared at it gravely; then he let it hang loosely around his neck: 'If I pass any more dead soldiers,' he thought, 'they will see it like this and it may console them, but I think all the dead are left miles behind . . . Lord, I did not kill them, it was my body.'

And now those bells were beginning again: 'Jesus Christ, the Shepherd, the Lamb, and the Victim.' Remote and yet near, beyond yet within, they a part of himself, he a part of their ringing. Ancient bells that rang out for the youth of the world, for those who would presently find their Lord concealed in the fragile disc of the Host. Bells of peace that had sounded above the groans and the fearful detonations of war. Bells that swung from a belfry in far away Provence yet were here on this moonlit Palestine plain . . . distance did not exist, it was all here and now, there was neither time, separation nor distance. Palestine and Provence —names, names, only names. There was neither Palestine nor Provence, neither friend nor foe, neither infidel nor Christian, but only those ringing, singing bells: 'Jesus Christ, the Shepherd, the Lamb, and the Victim.'

Yet surely his body was once more detached and no longer the instrument of his being? His body was doing such curious things; it was moving with a stealthy precaution; it

388

was creeping on all fours where the moon lit its path, then rising warily inch by inch when it found itself protected by shadows. It was crawling behind thick patches of scrub, behind rocks, and when it did this it listened for the sound of the patrol, for the sound of a shot that would cut like a knife through the silent night. Silent? but the night was quivering with bells: 'Jesus Christ, the Shepherd, the Lamb, and the Victim.'

Metal clinked against metal; the silver rood was clinking against a button of his tunic. Too much noise, too much noise! A large, muscular hand moved upward and closed itself over the rood, firmly holding the cross in position. Then the body paused in a patch of blue darkness to take off its boots and its blood-stiffened socks which it carefully hid in some neighbouring bushes; then it started to move its toes this way and that with a sigh of relief. There were stones on the plain yet the naked feet did not feel the stones —it was good to be once more wearing sandals.

On and on. But how long had that body been walking? A very long time for the body felt tired, and it seemed to have lost all sense of direction. The hill that the patrol had been skirting was gone, it had suddenly vanished from off the earth—but then perhaps it had never existed. And the bells were fainter; so faint they had grown that their tune was incomplete, notes were missing: 'Jesus . . . Shepherd, the Lamb . . .' breathed the bells; a soft blur of indistinct, somnolent sound before that last all but deafening peal: 'Jesus Christ, the Shepherd, the Lamb, and the Victim.'

Rest—the body must rest. It must sit with its aching head and shoulders supported. It must sit or drop down on this spot where it stood. But if it failed now who would speak the words? Someone called Anfos had known of the words a long time ago, a lifetime ago: 'The words! the words! Master, where are the words?' 'What words? I tell you they do not exist!' A most cowardly lie, a most damnable lie—the words were the Life, which alone existed.

He groped his way forward and sank to the ground with his back against a tall, sheltering boulder. It was dark just here, dark and quiet and immense—yes, and something else, too which he could not fathom. Where was he? Perhaps he also was dead like those men who had lain so amazingly still with their arms and legs sprawled out in the moonlight.

'Master, the words!'

'Hush, Anfos, speak softly. It is time that you slept, it is growing late. Sleep, Anfos, for sleep is a comforting thing.'

'Master, oh, master—the words! the words!'

'But are not you also a dead man, Anfos? I seem to remember that Anfos is dead, that he died to prevent us killing our God. Have we killed our God? Can God be killed, Anfos?'

Then it came; the illimitable Presence that yet appeared so strangely familiar. The Kingdom, the Power, the Shadowless Glory that yet stooped beneath the burdens of those who were spent, that yet toiled with the patience of those who toiled, that yet humbled Itself to the needs of the humble. The Timeless, the All-Wisdom; the Judge yet the judged; the Consoler who yet desired consolation.

Christophe dragged himself stiffly on to his knees. His body was shaken and torn by fear, but his spirit gazed up into pale, bright eyes that it seemed to have seen before, to remember.

'Who are you?' he gasped. And even as he questioned he envisaged the pitiful limitations of the mind, for ever struggling with doubt, for ever seeking to chain faith to reason—the timid, self-conscious, mistrustful mind. . . .

'I am the Indestructible Compassion.'

Then suddenly all the travail of creation, all the anguish and doubt, all the fear and blindness being drawn into one vast, courageous heart: 'I am the Indestructible Compassion.'

And now there was passing a mighty concourse of beings who sought that haven of refuge: those broken and crushed on the wheel of war—the boy with the smooth skinned, womanish face; the blue-eyed, bewildered young German gunner; the man who had baptized Jan with his blood: the blundering, sorrowful, kindly Guillaume. Yes, and countless others ruthlessly slain—most horrible they were because of their wounds, yet forgiving even as they sought forgiveness. And with them came Anfos, the faithful madman who had died in an effort to save his Creator, together with those who still suffered the flesh but whose needs had lent wings to their captive spirits: Jóusè Bénédit and Marie his wife, and the ailing child that had sprung from their mating; the Curé who must carry his cross of love; the parents whom Guillaume had left behind, and who grieved with the dreary grief of the ageing.

Oh, but they were endless. And now to that throng were added the inarticulate creatures who groaned in bondage yet not without hope—who waited in earnest expectation. The beasts who had laid down their lives in battle, who had patiently suffered for the sins of their masters; Mirèo, her gaunt flanks covered with sores, yet with God in the eyes that she turned upon Christophe; the starving mongrels that Christophe had fed. Aye, and even the battered and bleeding couleuvres whose stripes he had once been privileged to endure in union with One who Himself had been scourged for teaching the blessèd gospel of mercy.

And kneeling before this supreme revelation, the past became clearly illumined for Christophe. It was this that he had been asked to share, it was this that he had divined with his spirit, it was this from which he had sought to escape, it was this that his quaking flesh had rejected.

Christophe signed himself with the cross of his Lord, then he struck his breast with the strokes of contrition: 'My God, I have turned You away many times because I feared, and once I denied You. And my hands are guilty . . . do not look at them, Lord. Have pity and do not look at my hands, only show me how I may make reparation. Lord, I am not any more afraid. . . .' And even as he spoke the Presence moved nearer.

And now It seemed to engulf him entirely, the while It was being Itself engulfed and drawn into the fleshly form of Its creature. At that moment Christophe knew all the sorrows of the world, all the sorrow of God, but also the joy of God's selfless and all-embracing love, in that terrible, that triumphant communion.

*   *   *

He had thrown away his rifle and was walking through the moonlight on a track that led over the plain to the northward. He was taking no heed where his feet should tread, yet he knew that somewhere beyond lay a well, and that once long ago he had drunk of its water. He was holding the silver rood in his hands, He had slipped the chain of it from his neck and was holding the cross up before his face, a small cross and yet it seemed strangely heavy. He had borne such a burden as this once before, but then it had rested upon his scourged shoulder.

The moon had dropped behind the low hills; it was dark yet he neither faltered nor stumbled. He remembered this darkness that came prior to the dawn; it was chilly and always intensely silent. But where were they, those whom he had come forth to seek bearing the silver rood in his hands? Surely they could not have fled away in fear before this emblem of peace? Follow . . . he must follow until he found them.

The darkness was lifting; a faint, nebulous colour was spreading quietly over the landscape, a faint breeze was stirring the hair on his brow. Listen . . . what was that sound to the left? He stood motionless staring towards the sound. And surely that was a low white wall with a few poor, straggling buildings behind it, and beyond those again a close huddle of roofs? More sounds . . . the sudden wail of a child over there among that huddle of roofs; then wheels and a short, sharp word of command. Were they evacuating the village? Did it actually lie in the line of the troops? It must lie in the line of these oncoming troops; and with them . . . who was it that mattered so much, that had always mattered because greatly loved and greatly loving? Jan, it was Jan . . . love alone could unveil the eyes of the Spirit. A small point of light that flashed out through the gloom for a moment—someone was lighting a lantern.

He had turned from the track and was walking swiftly towards that dim but incautious glimmer. His arms were thrust forward and his hands clasped the rood as though they were clasping a most precious gift, a priceless gift, 'We are coming,' he whispered.

And now he had reached the dejected outskirts of the place and was conscious that he was speaking. He could hear his own stumbling, choking words; they amazed him, they sounded very like madness, but a madness so sublime that his soul leapt and sang:

'I am Christophe. I have come to ask your forgiveness,

With these hands of mine I have killed our brothers, and yet with these hands I now bring you God's peace—the peace that passes all understanding. I have come first to you whom I have most wronged, but presently I will go out into the world so that the world may be healed by my message. In the name of Jesus Christ lay down your arms. He is here, and He tells us to love one another, for our wounds are His wounds. . . . Look, I am unarmed because I am you and you are me, we are one and the same and that one is Christ, and Christ is the Indestructible Compassion. God so loves the world that He gives Himself. . . .'

They had torn the silver rood from his grasp. There were five of them, ragged and starving men demented by blood and appalled by defeat. And no word of it all had they understood—he had spoken to them in his Provençal language. They surrounded him, dragging him to the ground, then they spat in his face and one of them struck him. And they stripped off his shabby and war-stained clothes, wrenching them roughly away from his body; and all the while they spat in his face, and one after another they cursed him and struck him. For a moment he tightened his splendid muscles, flinging off the foremost of his tormentors; then he suddenly lay quiet under their hands and they heard him speaking as though to himself: 'I am the Indestructible Compassion.'

Someone had opened a door quite near him; he could smell the familiar fragrance of timber, and the pungent odour of planks newly planed. He thought: 'I am home again in Saint Loup; I am glad to be back with my mother and father. Soon I shall see that very old woman: I am going to be taken to see her by Goundran.' And he closed his eyes, smiling contentedly; so happy it was to be once more a child, so happy and guiltless and safe it was to be waiting there for the coming of Goundran.

A man had passed in through that open door and had come out again, having found what he needed. They had locked the door; Christophe lay wondering why—his father so seldom locked his workshop. They were lifting him up. He was heavy to move. They were forcing his body against the door and straining the fingers back from his palms, so that the palms lay exposed and helpless. An unendurable pain in his hands, in his feet—an unendurable pain.

'Lord, if You are with me still do not stay . . . do not suffer. . . .' But the words sank down and were lost in a bottomless pit of physical anguish.

His head moved quickly from side to side as though he were trying to see those hands, to comprehend the cause of such suffering. Then it drooped as though he would see his feet and look on the rood they had nailed beneath them. But presently he became very still and his dying eyes gazed out to the east—to the east where the flaming, majestic dawn rose over the world like a resurrection.